Advance Praise for *The Mercy*

The Mercy, Volume One of the 'Jessica LaFave Mysteries' series, provides . . . a mystery that includes . . . a series of psychologically gripping encounters that appear to lead in one direction, then twist to take an opposite path.

It's difficult to claim that a genre mystery is truly original: with so many reads permeating this market and so much of them predictable, the presence of something truly remarkable and different is a breath of fresh air.

The Mercy is this breath, lacing and entwining its readers with a complex spider web of events that ultimately questions who is the real victim, and centers around a journey that takes the protagonist over the border and into other worlds, entirely.

So go ahead: imbibe of *The Mercy* for what it is: a beacon of originality in a genre replete with predictability - and one that adds a heavy dose of psychological insight to its story of friendships, murder, and choices gone awry.

Does madness always show? *The Mercy* answers this with exquisite precision in a fast-paced read recommended for genre fans and those who usually prefer the thriller format (the latter will find its psychological depth and self-analysis the perfect touches, here.)

Diane Donovan, Senior Editor and Reviewer, *MIDWEST REVIEW OF BOOKS.*

An Austin, Texas–based psychologist looks into a childhood friend's murder and uncovers secrets that could prove fatal in DeShong's thriller. An often riveting tale in which solving a murder helps the protagonist learn more about herself.

Anna Cooper, *KIRKUS REVIEWS*

The Mercy

BARBARA DESHONG

For Hal, of course.

PREFACE

I wrote The Mercy because I had to. What I believed only happened in other families—bad families with serious problems—happened in our family. I didn't want to write a professional article or another non-fiction book. I wanted to share what really happens. What it feels like. Maybe one person will find a little peace in the horror. That will be enough.

CHAPTER 1

A police black and white screamed past the warm-up ring and the horse under me exploded in a copper-sheened bolt of lightning. *Oh, Lord, let me live.*

My gloved fingers scrabbled for a chunk of braided mane. Too little, too late. Still, maybe if I could—

I risked a downward glance. Tried to reset my boot in the stirrup.

Mistake. The sandy ground soared up and slammed into my face.

Ow—ow! Shit in a shoebox.

Torrents of sweat plastered my shirt to my back and I was blind. The annual August horse show wasn't called the "Texas Hotter than Hell Classic" for nothing. I rolled up on one hip. My attempt at sophistication already shot, I gave into the urge and rubbed sand, saltwater, and Maybelline deeper into my eye sockets.

Why did the Pot Police have to pick today for one of their swirly lights and shiny badges melodramas? The sweeps, intended to intimidate the junior equestrians who tended the knee-high marijuana hedge behind the hay barn, were a waste of taxpayer funds anyway. The fathers of the

Flower Mound Country Club farmers, among the highest profile attorneys in Texas, flicked away pot charges like too much sugar on cinnamon toast.

Not to mention that I'd established a new personal best for shortest time in the saddle. I needed deliverance and fast. Translation: I needed Camilla Cervantes. Camilla had saved me from horses out to kill me since we were five and, in the months since the suicide, she'd snatched the back of my collar each time I leaned too far over the abyss.

Good ole self-centered me. My rear in the sand, my hand out for help when Camilla had troubles of her own. I'd seen an odd glint in those straight-shooter green eyes of hers last night. A shine that, were she anyone else, I'd have read as fear.

Riders, trainers, and barn workers--including the groom who'd rescued my runaway bad boy--trekked between the barns and the warm-up ring. I patted myself down. My exhibitor number was miraculously still pinned to my back. Most of most of my equestrian togs had survived the crash. Only one vicious smear of horse lather on my hunt coat.

Yes, a coat. In August. In Texas. Which shows how your life can twist off once your priorities are out of whack.

Now to escape the warm-up ring alive. Think NASCAR with a figure-eight track. Then require half of the drivers to race in a clockwise pattern while the rest cannonball in the opposite and head-on direction. To keep things interesting add a hearty sprinkle of confused drivers cutting back and forth across the track.

Take away the safety gear and erect walls, fences, and water hazards randomly on the raceway and you have this morning's horse show warm-up ring. It was amidst such delusional gaiety that I sat in the hot sand surrounded by hyped riders smartly turned out in tawny breeches, dark hunt coats, and French-cuffed white shirts with gold cufflinks. Trainers thwacked whips against their boots and bellowed commands. Terrified assistants scurried about adjusting heights and switching out fences with no regard for the safety of themselves or others.

Each rider, dead set on besting every other rider in the ring, was absorbed in a relentless self-centered agenda. There is only one rule in the warm-up ring: Absolutely no spirit of cooperation will be tolerated.

Camilla was on the horse show grounds, I knew that much. I'd seen her white Jaguar parked near where she'd parked yesterday. By now she'd have sensed I was in trouble. Camilla has powers. She says she can see the woman I used to be still inside me. I'd have to take her word on that.

Hoof beats closing in rattled the fillings in my teeth. I dug my fingers in the sand and spun out of the way.

"Heads up!" Diana Sloan, the self-appointed supreme monarch of the Flower Mound, screamed, as she galloped by so close to my face I caught the tang of her custom-blended Neiman Marcus fragrance. Her mare, as tranquil as Diana was aggravated, floated past and sailed effortlessly over the four-foot Ferrari Wall, a silver barrier emblazoned with a crimson trio of Ferrari rearing horses.

The Ferrari Wall was the sinister obstacle my horse, NoMoneyNoMoneyNoMoney, had refused to jump three times yesterday in spectacular fashion. And was the original reason Camilla agreed to meet here before my first class. So where was she?

Yep, my horse's registered name is NoMoneyNoMoneyNoMoney. I know. Perfect.

Diana cantered loose and easy toward a white picket scoop gate, not bothering to hide a smile. Hey, I'd just made her day.

She'd shrieked "Heads up," but what Diana really meant was: *Just because you can't afford a decent horse, doesn't mean the rest of us should have to risk our lives!* While I trusted the other riders to give me a break, Diana had reason to be less than careful. Or, she believed she did. If I'd been Camilla, Diana would have done her 'accidental' best to trample the manicured hooves of her half-million dollar Austrian mare all over my friend's tiny half-Mexican body.

As for me and NoMoney, Diana's distain had a point. What kind of nutcase not only drags herself out of a comfortable bed to blister in the sun, but also shells out a fortune she does not have for the privilege of jumping a fresh-off-the-track racehorse--whose prior training consisted of "turn left and go fast"—over tiers of potted plants?

It would mean a lot to me if, just once, Diana was the rider who pranced in front of the judges with smudges on her coat and skid marks on her face. Of course, with the perfectly coifed golden curls, long legs, and classic features—earning her the nickname Lady Di--the judges wouldn't even notice.

I, too, have the blonde hair, but that's where any likeness to the ladies of the Flower Mound drops off. Old money breeding shows in the bones, in the hands. Wrists and fingers are slender and delicate, suitable for diamond tennis bracelets and heirloom nuggets. One look and you knew these ladies did not pay for riding lessons by working the Taco Bell window after school.

I am a trespasser, a stowaway on the Queen Mary of elite sports.

As for the long legs, every jumper course atop NoMoney is a battle to keep one less-than-dainty boot on either side of the horse.

Camilla is an inch shorter than I am, but she possesses what I do not—coordination and poise in any situation. And great hair. She's the only woman I know, other than lusty wenches on romance novel covers, whose plentiful black hair deserved the label "raven," which is how I spotted her in the drug test tent. A swirl of black hair caught a breeze and peeked from behind the show veterinarian cradling the hoof of a horse who clearly wanted to be somewhere else.

"Pay attention, Jessica!" one of the celebrity trainers shouted. His rider, a fine-boned woman I didn't recognize, bore down on me. My survival was not a priority on her relentless personal agenda.

I scrambled to the rail, backed up to the fence, and closed my eyes. I'd wait here for Camilla. I'd calm my nerves soaking up the aromas of saddle-soaped leather and expensive perfume and listening to the familiar rhythmic thud of hooves in deep sand.

Really. Why *was* I out in this heat, my body served up like a banana split for orthopedic surgeons? I could be home asleep with the dogs, the air-conditioner cranked down to freezing to the fourth power.

The woman in the veterinarian tent turned. Not Camilla.

I know there are women out there making better choices. Women who spend their time and money on Pilates, home decor, foreign language courses, European vacations, a decent wardrobe, pool parties, creative writing seminars, charity balls, and beach houses. Women who have undamaged skin and bones without lumps from healed fractures. They aren't required to work sixty hours a week to pay horse expenses, nor do they jolt awake in the middle of the night picturing themselves splattered all over a colossal silver wall, their blood mingled with the crimson silhouettes of the Ferrari stallion.

I hope they choke.

"Eleven minutes until the first horse *must* enter the ring," boomed the show steward's amplified baritone. "The one minute rule *will* be enforced," he said, in a tone usually reserved for a Declaration of War or the Super Bowl kickoff.

Camilla, where are you? More than my trivial, though painful, horse misadventures goaded my rising concern. Last night, after a message that a patient of mine had smashed up the lobby of Shoalbrook Hospital, I'd hopped in my car and was about to scoot when Camilla rapped hard on my window.

"Jess, can you hang around a few minutes?" she'd asked. "I'm making a big change in my life and I need to talk to you."

"I wish I could," I said. "But I have an emergency admission over at Shoalbrook."

"Sure. Okay."

"Believe me, I'd much rather stay, but the front office staff is dodging clipboards and furniture."

"Tomorrow, then." Camilla stepped back from the window. "Tomorrow will be soon enough."

"You sure?"

"Of course. I'll meet you in the warm-up ring before your first class, hop in the saddle, and convince NoMoney that the Ferrari horses aren't fire-breathing dragons. We'll talk after."

Her words were assurance enough to send me on my way, but her cadence was off. Still, I'd hummed up the window and driven away, my thoughts already on the best way to handle the out-of-control patient.

Ouch. A clod of damp sand thunked my cheek and shocked me back to the moment. No time left for a practice run. I'd best collect NoMoney, pray, and close my eyes on approach to the Ferrari Wall. Should I be spared fatal injury, Camilla and I would have time later to correct my mistakes.

Two more patrol cars and four understated Crown Victorias streamed past and parked in front of the main barn in that mish-mash way only police cars are allowed to park.

I grabbed the top rail and hauled myself up on my boot heels. A few rows of pot did not merit unmarked cars.

Officers, their faces hidden behind black stretch masks and with automatic rifles in full view, swarmed out of vehicles like streams of pissed Texas fire ants. I wasn't the only one who'd noticed. The mood in the warm-up ring had imploded. Trainers hushed, riders steadied stutter-stepping horses, and green-card-challenged grooms scattered out of view.

Police cars? Assault rifles? Not here. Not at the Flower Mound Country Club. I'd wake up any second now.

An ambulance rolled up to join the police vehicles. No lights. No siren. I knew what that meant. No hope.

An agonizing possibility cracked to the surface in a primal corner of my brain.

No. Not possible. Still, the impact walloped my gut and doubled me over for a full minute. *Keep your head down, you're going to be sick. Keep your head up, you can't breathe.*

Denial kicked in hard. I straightened my spine and reshuffled my thoughts. Expecting the worst was one of my most dependable and least attractive Rose family traits. Camilla would stroll out into the sunlight any moment. "Goooood morning my brave friend!" she'd sing-song, the way she had since we were kids. She'd make a joke about my trademark disheveled condition, climb aboard NoMoney, and save the day.

Saving people was Camilla's specialty. Her gift.

Don Wilder, the APD Chief of Detectives, stepped out of his Crown Vic and made for the main barn. I'd worked psychological profiles alongside him on enough cases to read his stride and the set of his shoulders. Any wisp of hope flittered from my heart.

My brain couldn't find a slot for the images that did not belong. *No. . . No, no, no.* The air whooshed out of my lungs. I gripped the rail and locked my knees. The stable was our haven, our safe place when life stumbled in other departments. So what were men in suits, automatic rifles, and more plain, dread-bearing sedans doing in our sacred harbor?

How could the world change so fast? One minute, today was about my foolish lack of horse show talent and now it was all horror and nausea.

I'd been wrong. Camilla's car wasn't parked close to where she'd parked it yesterday.

Her Jaguar was parked *exactly* where she'd parked it yesterday.

CHAPTER 2

Silver stars on sparkled wire ribbons cascaded from Camilla's parted lips. First the galaxy arched upward, then, like loose diamonds caught in flight, descended and scattered stars over her small breasts.

What horror was in your life, Camilla? What did you need to talk to me about?

Before I left Shoalbrook Hospital last night, I'd made certain my patient was snug between cool sheets, a call button at her side. And Camilla? Who had taken care of her?

The Chief of Detectives and I stood behind the waist-high chain draped across the door of the murder stall. I'd talked my way into the crime scene, which was a major surprise. The last time the Chief and I had crossed paths was in front of an aggravated judge and Don Wilder had been on the judge's side of the matter.

The usual comforting barn aromas—fresh-cut alfalfa, metal polish, and the tangy molasses of sweetened oats--were tinged with a nose burn of black powder this morning. Only a hint though, only a little cold death in the midst of so much animal heat and so many passionate riders. A fresh wave of anguish curdled in my stomach then sent up devil snakes to coil around and crush my chest and throat.

"I've never known anyone like her," I said. Silent tears burned rivulets down my face. "I am a better person because she was my friend."

Camilla's petite body sat braced against the back wall, her legs straight out in front of her on the straw-covered floor, her calves and small feet in glossy high-top New York Dehners, her sterling spurs at the proper angle, the choke collar of her formal white riding shirt neatly fastened. Her hands were in her lap, her arms arcing three towers of what looked like hundred dollar bills.

"The stacks of money make me sick." I said and turned away. "Whoever made this altar either didn't know Camilla or hated her."

Camilla's always vibrant emerald eyes were unpolished malachite, flat and staring. A magenta-edged black hole marked the center of her forehead.

As beautiful as Camilla was, even in death, she wasn't the siren who'd lured local and federal authorities to the Flower Mound Country Club. That honor went to the grand dame on guard at Camilla's side, a three-foot ceramic skeleton lady who managed to be both elegant and grotesque at the same time. The first time I'd seen an altar to Our Lady of Holy Death, we were ten years old and Camilla's father had just been murdered. Camilla was afraid he wasn't in Heaven yet.

"So, Doc, what's your take on the skeleton babe?" the Chief asked.

Don Wilder, the hometown kid who'd spurned alcohol, drugs, and parties to graduate first in his class at the police academy, ruffled his fingers through plentiful, but tamed, sandy hair. His eyes were honed on my face, ready to catch any give-away that I was too personally involved to profile the scene.

Since I was, on more levels than he could imagine, I'd have to watch myself. No flinches. No meltdowns like happened in front of the judge.

The Chief, a few years older than I, still wore a dark suit through Texas summers while the other detectives had jumped on the approved untucked *Guayabera* option. Sunglasses hooked in his breast pocket were Don's only concession to the sweltry sauna of Texas in August.

"Doc?"

I shook him off. A scream crept into the back of my throat and stabbed for release. I grabbed a groomer's finishing towel and bit down. This was too much. Life was too much without Camilla. Selfish me again.

"This bony chick is *Santa Muerte*, right?"

I nodded and sank my teeth into the towel so hard my teeth met through the cloth. I ground them back and forth.

"What do you know about her?" he asked.

What did I know about Our Lady of Holy Death?

Chief, I could blow your ears off.

"Well, I know this much for damn sure," he said, anxious to get started on the evidence. "When you see Santa Muerte, you best check over your shoulder because hell isn't far behind."

"Something like that," I managed.

Santa Muerte stood majestic in a lush purple gown tiered like a monstrous birthday cake. Pillows of white icing lace flared under each ruffle. The bodice and skirt were tucked with ribbons of rhinestones and tiny gold birds. An overwhelming violet hat of tufted velvet adorned her skull, a peacock feather in the hatband swirled to the floor, its tip lodged under one of Camilla's boots.

I removed the towel and from my mouth and allowed a test exhale. Don was one of those men who did whatever he had to do to quiet a woman's tears. Sob out-of-control now and he'd kick me off the case convinced he was doing me a favor.

"An altar like this--" I paused to gulp twice. "A blood sacrifice like this is an offering. Our Lady of Holy Death, usually called the Angel of

Death, is being asked to guide a recently deceased loved one, someone important--"

"A drug lord." The Chief tapped 'record' on the device clipped to his belt.

". . . A *loved* one . . . through the Land of the Dead to Heaven."

Don took a step back. The "Land of the Dead" wasn't what he'd expected or what the police department wanted to hear in the first hour after the discovery of a high profile murder at the ritzy country club.

"Looks to me," he said, "like Mrs. de la Cruz was in a high risk commercial enterprise and got herself crosswise with the board of directors."

Something in my heart detonated. Fragments broke loose and ripped fire through my veins.

"How dare you?" I stepped back, killer glare in attack mode. "How *dare* you assume Camilla was involved with drug trafficking without knowing anything about her?"

The creek of perspiration rolling down my spine went to ice.

"She's your friend. I get that you want to protect her."

"Protect?" I switched my attention to the empty cement bathing racks beyond the rear doors of the barn. "If my goal was to protect Camilla, I'm a little late, wouldn't you agree?"

He looked away, doing his best to counter my cold shoulder inattention to the scene.

"Would you like to know about the *cartel* Camilla commands?" I asked.

"Shoot."

"Camilla rescues--rescued little girls forced to work as prostitutes in Mexico City's *La Merced*. The Mercy. You've probably heard of the place. The side streets around the market are famous for supplying men who like them sweet and flat chested."

"Doc--"

"But don't let my news slow down your investigation." I should have stopped there. I didn't. "You'll find plenty of champions for your 'bad seed Camilla' theory when you interview Flower Mound friends and neighbors. If horse show acquaintances can pass for friends and if a country club can pass for a neighborhood."

Thirty seconds of silence. Then Don pointed toward the inlaid globe cradled in the bony fingers of the Angel of Death's raised left hand. "I'm not the one doing the talking."

Across the pearlescent pink shell of North America, thick block letters spelled out, *"¡LOS INSURGENTES ESTÁN AQUÍ!"* (The Insurgentes, the Rebels, are here!).

"My Spanish could use some work," Don said, "but I'm relatively certain *'Los Insurgentes están aquí!'* is Mexican cartel for 'kiss your Texas ass good-bye'!"

That did it. I wanted to know who killed my friend. The Chief wanted to gear-up for a cartel invasion.

"Camilla," I said, teeth threatening breakage, "would never be involved in anything that made the lives of Mexican children worse."

"Look, I don't want to fight with you. But, one thing's for sure, Doc . . ."

I used the towel to wipe saltwater and rage off my face. Time to re-group. I took three long breaths then offered him an opening. "Okay, person-who-doesn't-know-Camilla Cervantes, tell me, what's this 'one thing' you are so precious sure of?"

"I'm sure that whether Mrs. de la Cruz was a drug trafficker or an angel, she's the first bullet in an all-out war."

"The first bullet?" I struggled to swallow. "Camilla is a *bullet?*"

He straightened his spine into official mode--police business is business--and turned back to Camilla. "Given your relationship with the victim, I'm ignoring protocol here. I'm taking this risk, not because you are a friend, but because you know more about this freak show than anyone in the department."

"Yes, I certainly do."

And a few minutes from now, on my drive out of the Flower Mound Country Club, I'd tell Mr. Sure of Himself exactly what I thought about his bullet theory. How my heart froze and my mind slammed shut when he called Camilla's murder scene a freak show.

"I also know more about Camilla Cervantes," I said, "more than you or anyone with the police can find out or comprehend."

He winced then let my retort slide, bigger fish and all. Behind him, scene recorders popped photos at two per second, ran video, and daubed and taped surfaces with an eerie urgency. The free press on both sides of the border had been killed and buried long ago, but these officers knew the truth. For them, this altar signaled the arrival of something bigger and more horrific than anything Austin, Texas, had ever known.

The murder stall was adjacent to the rear barn entrance so that sunlight slanted across scene. The amethyst rose on Santa Muerte's breastbone twinkled in the gold morning rays like an obscene beacon. The Chief pointed toward the mini recorder on his belt.

"Tell me what I'm looking at," he said. His insistence was a test of nerves.

Fine. I was willing to pay the cost of admission. I launched a methodical description of Santa Muerte's apparel and accessories top to bottom. I rambled facts and slipped in a few multicultural chunks for the detectives to chew on. All was steady until my eyes slid to the postcard propped against the skeleton lady's dainty satin slippers.

Oh man, oh man. My heart stuttered and my voice caught. I shot my attention up and away from the postcard, grabbed my towel, and waved Don back a few inches. His face went from attack mode to concern.

"Need a little space here," I said. "Need a minute."

On the postcard, the nude Saint Mary Magdalene flaunted her bountiful breasts and plump thighs without shame in front of an unfurled scarlet drape. Not the serene Mary Magdalene with downcast eyes who traveled alongside Jesus. No, this was Saint Mary Magdalene the prostitute. The Chief didn't know anything about Camilla's work in La Merced, but the creators of this altar did.

"Look, Doc, even if you're the expert on the Mexican and Catholic parts, maybe those aren't important right now."

I glared blades of fire. "What did you just say?"

"I *said* Eric Townsend or Dr. Davis can be here in twenty or less. You don't need more emotional damage in your life right now."

"Thank you, but *I'll* decide how much emotional damage I can manage and still function as a professional."

"It's time for you to reel it in. It hasn't been that long--" He hooked his fingers around my elbow and steered the two of us toward the front of the barn.

I jerked free of his gentleman-officer-manly grip and reversed to face Camilla. Her green eyes lasered a beam straight into my brain and heart. *I'll lead the way*, she said.

"I'm bringing in another psychologist to do the scene," the gentleman-officer-man said. "We're done."

My lips rock-hard, I paused long enough to feign serious consideration of his plan. The *Jaws of Life* couldn't pry me off this case.

CHAPTER 3

"Really, Doc," the Chief said. He'd backed off the aggression for a softer attempt to dislodge me from the profile of the murder stall. "If you're not up to this . . ." the Chief said.

I wasn't. But whether you are "up to" the sudden and permanent ripping away of someone you love does not matter. When what's done is done, the only choice left to you is to breathe before you pass out, then breathe again. Get on a plane, land in Tucson, order flowers, make arrangements. Fly home. Act normal. You are a psychologist. You cannot do anything else. You cannot undo dead.

Breathe. Then breathe again. "I am the *only* right person for this profile."

Don tapped off his recorder and edged in as close as he could without actually putting his arm around my shoulders, which would have undercut both of us with the hive of officers working the scene. I'd known Don longer than the stepbrother and the psychiatrist I married. We'd been a couple once. Twice actually, before we'd accepted that his unbending dedication to the l-a-w and my more relaxed interpretation of l-e-g-a-l meant the best we could do was to be excellent friends and colleagues.

We focused on Camilla. The killer or killers had gone to considerable trouble to build the altar, but hadn't decorated with vicious symbols or defiled Camilla's body. As *livor mortis* settled, instead of going blue or black, the blood drained from Camilla's skin left her luminescent. She was a porcelain angel.

"If your choice is to stick, Doc, I need more than descriptions to justify your participation. I need expert interpretations. Let's start with the stars."

I managed a semi-professional tone. "The *Narco-trafficantes,* wisely, do not trust their village padres to pray for their safety and success. The stars are a statement that the powers of Santa Muerte extend beyond this planet, that their so-called religion of death will one day destroy Christianity along with other Earthbound religions."

"That's a big statement."

"Blood sacrifices in Mexican culture go back centuries before Europeans came ashore. When a chieftain was murdered, Aztec priests butchered tens of thousands and flung their still beating hearts on twitching heaps to prepay the Chief's trip to Heaven. The streets were turned into rivers of blood."

The Chief pinched his forehead and squinted, as if to remind me that I was speaking in a professional capacity and should keep *National Geographic* and *History Channel* references to a minimum. Lest I be judged a nutcase by certain officers who considered my status as a psychologist meant I was already halfway down the road to squirrely.

"Of course," I said, "the soulless *narcos* have turned Our Lady of Holy Death into a corporate whore. Now she's supposed to do everything from bless automatic weapons to brainwash governors, mayors, and the police." Cut the rage. Deep breath. Quick pause. Charge ahead. "One cartel hotshot died because he trusted Santa Muerte to make him bullet-proof!"

"I don't think we have to scroll back to the pyramids to make sense of what looking at here." He paused, gave me a moment to absorb his second 'cut the history crap' warning.

"I thought you wanted expert interpretations. I agree the money, the body, the Santa Muerte . . ." My jaw was so tight I could barely squeak out the words.

"Forget the stars. What we're looking at is Los Insurgentes' laying claim to the Interstate 35 corridor straight through Austin. If we don't answer with all the resources we have, we're talking your Aztec rivers of blood from the Capitol building to the border. Corpses stacked up like cordwood."

Cordwood? "Right now, what we are talking about is one woman whose life has been taken. Not a war."

"I have a responsibility here."

I could practically see the wheels behind the Chief's forehead on 'fast forward'. Road blocks, reinforcements, assault gear, press skirmishes, and prison riots. He signaled an okay for evidence gatherers in head-to-toe paper clothes to move in.

"Wait." I grasped his bicep and forced him to look into my face. "Stop now. Please! You're talking 'cordwood' while I am doing my best to describe a woman--no the *body* of a woman who's been a critical part of my life practically since we were born--into to a court admissible record. Yes, the *victim* is my friend but, Don, you are, too. Can't you, for a few lousy minutes, talk with me about Camilla as my friend instead of Camilla as a faceless pawn in the drug war?"

He waved off the techs.

I gazed on Camilla's girl-like chest scattered with stars. A light breeze, a blessing, swept over her and the heavenly bodies shimmered. Little pretties in a world of ugly.

Don matched my focus and dropped a hand on my shoulder. "I can. I can do that."

"Everything fell apart for Camilla when her father was murdered."

"I should give you credit for knowing Mrs. De la Cruz," he said, his expression softer. "And I hope you're right about her cartel involvement."

"She has no one around the Flower Mound to speak up for her but her mother and me."

"I understand."

"No, you don't understand." *But you will.*

"Don't worry, Doc, this case is special for the police, too. Mrs. De la Cruz is just a little girl in the family picture on the Citizens Honor Wall at the station."

We had our differences, but I trusted Don Wilder. The very Boy Scout quality that drove me crazy also guaranteed that every word he spoke was the truth.

"She was only ten," I said. "Eileen did her best. It's just that her father was so special to Camilla."

The Chief overrode protocol again and tucked me into a squeeze, an affection interrupted by a shoulder tap from his lieutenant. Don turned away to speak with him. I eavesdropped enough to catch that the man who'd called 911 had been located.

"I need to sign off on an arrest at the front of the barn," Don said, then hesitated. "I didn't mean to interrupt your direction—about Camilla's family."

"I can wait. Thank God, Camilla's daughter has her grandmother."

"What about the child's father?" Don asked, with a 'be right with you' nod to the lieutenant.

"Ana Teresa's father?" Cool move, LeFave. Old Faithful. The inane and obvious junior high repeat-the-question stall.

"The victim is married, right?"

"Not anymore. I mean, I don't think she is." My words came out raspy and startled.

"Well, no matter what this looks like, we have to clear the ex."

Don pivoted toward the clutch of waiting officers. Over his shoulder he said, "When I get back, I want to hear what you know about the husband."

Well, for starters, Chief, I slept with him on his wedding night.

CHAPTER 4

Sounds pretty bad, I know. But it wasn't like that. I have made some spectacular bad calls where passion was concerned, but I would never have hurt Camilla. Ever.

Don conferred with his troops at the barn entrance though he could have been on another planet from where I stood. Without his stake in the solid and logical truth of the moment, the protective barrier between the Land of the Living and the Land of the Dead thinned to slippery over-stretched cellophane. How could I stand here in the barn aisle, in the world we'd shared, and Camilla be gone? Her body to be detailed on numbered pages in my report?

What should I do with my eyes?

To stare at Camilla when she couldn't look back or look away, struck me as a loathsome invasion of privacy. To turn my back, mean and rude. I chose a spot in front of her boots and concentrated on the cork floor under the straw.

George. I needed my friend, George Griffis Ramsdale III. And I needed him now.

I bummed a phone and punched in the most forbidden of George Ramsdale's private numbers and held on for eight rings to his message. I exhaled heavy, measured breaths through the three minute blank space after the tone. No words. He would not hear about Camilla in a message. Then I hung up and hit re-call. Eventually, he'd figure it was me and give in.

"All owners, riders, and spectators, all persons not involved in securing the animals," an official voice announced over the public address system, "must vacate the premises immediately. Contact information will be collected at the gate."

Good luck with that, buddy. The men responsible for the horses had evaporated and the equestrians of the Flower Mound County Club were not accustomed to taking orders from anyone.

Eleven revolutions through the eight rings, three minutes of heavy breathing, and redial routine, George picked up.

"I thought . . . we had . . . an understanding," he said, through the wounded wildebeest howl he called a yawn.

"George---"

"My dear, as you are keenly aware--"

"Bad news, George."

". . . I would gladly choose a buck-naked public flogging over a horse show."

"Really bad."

"What's with the sketchy breathing? You crash again? Your unplanned dismounts occur with far too much regularity for you to feel a need to keep me updated, Miss Rose," George said, referring to me by my maiden name as he had since my long ago unsuccessful job interview in the Ramsdale Law Offices.

"Also," George said, through a smug wheeze, "there's a whole wide universe beyond the gates of the Flower Mound Country Club that does not give a frog burp about horses leaping over furniture. I proudly count myself among them."

After a brief and pathetic post-high school marriage, I'd claimed my spot in the lecture halls of the University of Texas and applied for a part-time secretarial position. Unconvinced that my extensive fast food and horse grooming experience qualified me for office work, George had turned me down for the job. Equally convinced teenage divorcees were easy, he'd volunteered to handle my divorce with all costs to go to my stepbrother and soon-to-be ex-husband.

On the three hour limo return trip from the courthouse in Houston, where I was still officially a resident, George changed his mind about teenage divorcees and I concluded that all lawyers weren't blood-sucking beasts. We opened several frosty bottles of Moët Ice Imperial Champagne and a window of pure honesty that forged a once-in-a-lifetime friendship few people ever know. Since then we'd held each other up through marriages, divorces, and the worst kinds of deaths.

"Really bad news." Don would be back any second. No time to tippy-toe George to the deep end.

News helicopters hovered above in crisscross patterns. Studio-to-chopper radio flak and whaps of huge propellers added an apocalyptic touch to the pastoral morning gone horribly wrong.

"Wait. Miss Rose, are you in some kind of war zone?"

"Camilla is gone, she's dead."

"I can't hear you!" His voice swooped up and down with the loop used by children playing hide-in-seek.

"Camilla is dead, George! She was murdered out here at the horse show!"

In one of those hideous moments of awkward timing, the helicopter whaps hit a dramatic lull just as I shrieked my announcement. Technicians on either side of me suspended activities to assess my stability.

There was a vacant pause on George's end. Then: *"Our Camilla?"*

"Yes."

"Mexico City Camilla?" The Ivy League slick had vanished.

"I'm with her right now." I gulped tears for all I was worth. How could I say this? "She has a bullet hole in her forehead."

"I'm there, twenty minutes, tops."

"There's no way you'd get through the gate." Sobs I'd held in check stuttered out like erratic gunfire.

"I'm not without a few smarmy lawyer tricks."

I pictured his thick black eyebrows arching with every word. George was near forty, with dark eyes and a full mustache, kept immaculate by *Les Salon de Messieurs,* fifty-one floors beneath his Petroleum Tower living quarters. He was Mafia-looking, in a 'good family' sort of way. And, if the situation required, George could indeed unleash an impressive variety of smarmy lawyer tricks.

"You'd need a tank this morning." I rubbed my sweaty-teary face on the arm of my stained hunt coat. "Don Wilder is calling the murder a drug association hit."

"A drug 'association', Miss Rose? Is 'association' your sissy word for *demented homicidal cartel?"*

I filled him in on the scene. Midway through my description, his phone beeped as he landed in Google.

"That's 'L-O-S-space-I-N-S . . .'" he said. "How do you spell 'In-sir-gen-tiles'?"

I corrected his word carnage.

". . . Oh holy mother of pearl! I'm seeing torsos, mass graves . . ." He sucked in a breath. "You get out of there—now!"

"Not yet."

"Drugs, prostitution, kidnapping . . . I'm looking at eight severed heads parked on oil drums in Tijuana. Eight severed *people* heads."

"Camilla's not involved with any of that business."

"Ex-*cuuse* me? Camilla not involved with prostitution? If you can recall—which I seriously doubt, given your perpetual state of intoxication—on the day before her wedding, Mrs. de la Cruz marched us right through the Mexico City valley of the whores. Hookers to the left of us . . . hookers to the right of us . . ."

George met Camilla on the Freedom Celebration Trip eleven years ago. Camilla's marriage to the gorgeous Diego De la Cruz happened to be scheduled on the weekend after the gavel came down on my ill-conceived teenage attempt at playing house, which happened to be the same weekend my friend Nancy Margaret Scarletti turned in her final "Thanks, but no thanks" to the Sisters of the One Holy Cross.

Our goal had been to celebrate Camilla's happiness and drink enough tequila to blot out the disasters we'd made of our first attempts at adulthood. At least that was my goal. The key to happiness? Set achievable goals.

"La Merced is a market," I said. "Not a valley and Camilla was showing us where she did her charity work. She took prostitutes *off* the streets."

"What about that girl you brought back with us?"

It figures he'd bring up Adriana. She'd ridden fourteen hours in the backseat of my Mustang with George. If she breathed throughout the trip, we didn't hear her. We'd dropped her off at a safe house in San Antonio. Which might seem odd to anyone who hadn't grown up near the border, but it wasn't for us.

"Don't mention your little hospitality smuggling favor to the police," George said.

"If Camilla had a connection with Los Insurgentes, and that's a big 'if', it was probably only to pay for protection."

"How much is it?"

"What?"

"The 'protection'. I want to sign up."

If only George was kidding. More beeps, chimes, and gasps.

"Meet me at El Cristobal in an hour?" I asked.

"Sure, of course. I'll be way-ay-ting . . ." Tap, tap. "Hang on a sec, wait, wait . . ." Tap, tap, tap. "Here you go. . . . I ran Mrs. De la Cruz with her maiden name. You never told me her father was a hero."

"That was over twenty years ago. Nothing to do with the cartel world we live in now."

"Probably not, but this article doesn't say anything about a trial. Did they ever get the guy who did it?"

"I don't know. Are you thinking there could be a connection?"

"I have no opinion one way or the other."

"Then why are you asking?"

"Because of the important life lesson to be appreciated."

"Which is?"

"Just this, Missy. When amateurs like you and me--like Camilla's father--go up against thugs, we lose. We get ourselves killed."

"Why are you telling me this?"

"Call it a pre-emptive strike, Miss Rose."

George knew I'd dig for every detail. I'd be obsessed. He also knew I was ridiculously in over my head.

Which didn't matter. I owed Camilla. I owed Camilla's mother, too. Oh, God. Eileen. An ice pick lodged in my chest. Camilla was more than a daughter to her mother. She was everything. With what she'd endured already, how could Eileen ever live past this loss?

I knew from experience that a chunk of who Camilla's mother was would die with the news that the future she'd looked forward to, that she'd depended on, was gone forever. The straw and cork floor blurred beyond my tears.

Today would be a marker day for Eileen Cervantes. As was the day Mr. Cervantes was murdered. As the day a patient of David's killed him to hide a slimy secret, was a marker day for me.

A marker day is a day when something unexpected and irreversible happens all at once, and every event in your life is re-sorted into what came 'before' and what happened 'after'. A marker day is a scar in the tapestry of your life, a streak of gristle that runs from top to bottom. All moments after are woven with less innocence. A marker day leaves you with permanent regret and an ache that doesn't go away even though you stop talking about what happened and fake that you've moved on.

A gentle wind air-brushed the decorations in the stall and sparked the stars into another silver shimmer. The tip of Santa Muerte's peacock plume broke free of Camilla's boot and floated toward me. Along with the feather tip, a white rose petal caught the breeze and came to rest near my toe. Then several more. Another white and two pink ones. Too delicate to be from common bushes. These were tea rose petals.

Rose petals on an altar of death? In the world I knew, pink roses were for innocence and white roses were for peace.

Were the petals part of the altar? Not likely. More probably they were strays from yesterday's regal mantles, thousands of woven roses placed over the withers of championship winners. Or errant bits of plant life freed from corsages worn by evening-gowned trophy presenters as they wobbled through deep sand in satin heels, their gold and diamond accessories catching the coliseum lights.

But, for me, for now, the petals were blessings. When I recalled the murder stall, I'd think of the petals as tender touches where tender touches did not belong.

Then boom.

Chief Wilder exploded from his car ripping pages out of his dashboard printer like a starved grizzly slapping up salmon.

CHAPTER 5

"You have not been honest with me, Doc!" Chief Wilder came at me in giant, determined strides.

I jumped back, slammed my shoulder into a steel cross-tie post set in the barn aisle and whipped to attention. The clip chains whirled and clanged around the post in a decelerating series of gongs. What the hell was up with him?

He stopped six inches from my face, eyes ablaze. He had a thick clump of computer readouts gripped in his fist and a whole new attitude toward his profiler.

Video cameramen, fingerprint dusters, and the masked man vacuuming one stall over, stopped dead.

"What are you officers looking at?" the Chief said, to no one and everyone. Cameras clicked, vacuums resumed.

Don Wilder had just called me a liar. Fine. I wasn't as pumped to help the police as I was twenty minutes ago anyway. I concentrated on the brushwork of the print specialist powdering the stall across the aisle.

Plaster dust, alcohol astringents, and solvent fumes, now dominated the usually sweet atmosphere. Exhibitors were paired with detectives on benches in low-voiced interviews. Riding crops at their sides, velvet hard hats in their laps. With each hot blast of air, crumpled exhibitor numbers skittered over the asphalt, now nothing more than very expensive tumbleweeds.

Only the horses hadn't acclimated to strangers that smacked of gunpowder. Their cries and anxious steel-plated kicks against stall slats kept the heartbeat of the morning in crisis mode.

Not that my heart needed any juice. Don's alpha lion attitude was plenty.

"Your *friend,* Mrs. De la Cruz," he said, his eyes lasered on my reaction, "has sallied back and forth through border customs twenty-six times since the first of the year!"

He shook the Global Entry read-outs over my head, as if I'd purposely not mentioned Camilla's split life. And he was all over it.

"I know. But hang on. There's a good reason--"

"Fifty-three trips if you count one way." He slapped the pages against his thigh, then looked away and hung his tirade on an abrupt hold. "Also, one of the perimeter guys said your right rear tire is low."

"Okay. . . . *What?*"

What was it with men? Jump on your case with all fours one minute, then go tender whenever a female, super model or ax-murderer, has a vehicle emergency? I'd bought a fresh set of tires a few months ago. That one was low was a surprise, but way down on my priority list.

"A woman with Mrs. De la Cruz's habitual itinerary," Don said, again studying my face for a flinch, "would be particularly valuable to Los Insurgentes."

With established *narco-trafficante* routes concentrated along the coasts, Los Insurgentes had set up headquarters in Mexico City and revitalized the ancient *Camino Real.* Now a pipeline for Colombian agricultural products, the Royal Road was once the footpath of Spanish conquistadors and priests in search of gold to steal and souls to save in what was now Texas and New Mexico.

Even before George's mention of Adriana, I'd had no intention of sharing everything I knew about Camilla with the police. But Don's sleazy insinuations made my decision to withhold information easier to live with.

"Point taken, Detective Wilder. My friend is half Mexican. Enough said. Should I dig around in the tack room for paper and pen? Scratch out a toe tag for Camilla?"

"Don't do this, Doc."

"That way you can assign Camilla's 'cordwood corpse' a number and get on with more important people."

"Just so you know . . ." He waited until he had full eye contact. "I'm not recording."

"And, why not?" My teeth ached from the pressure. "Do you think I'm going to burst into flames over some border records?"

"No. I'm not recording because I've known you to say and do things you've regretted later."

"Fine."

"Judges don't make good enemies, Doc."

"Message received, loud and clear. . . . Anyway, that judge was ignorant and a racist."

Two weeks ago, I'd intemperately attempted to halt the deportation of three barn workers. When the judge refused to let me speak, I'd puffed up and tailgated the immigration bus—with thin louvered windows like those on cattle cars used by the Nazis--all the way to the Rio Grande International Bridge.

I was fortunate not to be arrested for harassment, and I'd blown my whole day for nothing.

"The thing is, border records . . ." He whacked the readout on his thigh again, harder this time, ". . . are just the beginning, and I think you know it."

"Camilla flew back and forth frequently because she has a close relationship with her mother." I whirled and fired my eyes straight at him, but held my thoughts in check. I reminded myself that Meltdown Jessica was a luxury I couldn't afford this morning. "Also, Eileen is a devoted grandmother."

"If Mrs. De la Cruz was so close to her mother, and Mexico is a slaughterhouse, why didn't she live here?"

"She lived part-time in her father's Mexico City house to feel close to him." Oh, the half-truths rolled out so easily. He'd learn the real reason Camilla chose to stay away from Austin soon enough. "And, as a matter of fact, Camilla was in the process of moving here full-time so that Ana Teresa could go to better schools."

"Fifty-three border crossings worth of better?" Whatever surprise Don was building up to was serious. And not good news for my team.

"Again, you don't know Camilla." I barely moved my lips. "You don't know her mother."

"Make the smart choice. Back out now, Doc."

"Not happening."

"Okay, then. Your happy family story gets you past the border records." He thumbed through his stack for the pages he wanted. ". . . But doesn't explain why Mrs. De la Cruz is a frequent flyer on Mexico City criminal radar."

"I don't know what you're talking about." On the outside, I allowed an expression of mild surprise. On the inside, my ribs caved and stabbed leaks in my lungs.

"I think you do."

"There. You did it again. You called me a liar."

"You're too close to this one, Doc."

"I would never sandbag you like that."

He flapped his bloody printouts again. "And to make the victim bio complete, the arrest records pair Mrs. De la Cruz and Los Insurgentes over and over. Going back years!"

The ground rocked under my feet. Camilla was the kindest person I'd ever known. Given her bold project in La Merced, the arrest record wasn't a complete shocker. But Camilla teamed up with a hideous mass-murdering cartel?

I fixed my eyes on the white rose petal on the stall floor in front of me. White petals for peace. I slowed my breathing and glanced into Camilla's spark-less eyes. *Peace be with you.*

"If you two were as close as you say you were," the Chief said, riveted on my expression. "You had to know something about what Mrs. De la Cruz was into."

My heart banged against my sternum. *I'm making a big change in my life and I need to talk to you about it.*

Don stepped in close again. "Bail, Doc. Your priorities are upside down on this one."

I kept all doubt out of my expression. "So, that's it? You're running this investigation as a straight up cartel hit?"

His eyes didn't meet mine. Instead he checked out the activity at the front of the barn.

"Look," he said, "I'm not saying Mrs. De la Cruz threw in by choice. But what happens if one of these little girls she's bent on saving takes a chain of bullets to the face right in front of her? What does she do if she wakes up to find a row of tiny heads on her doorstep?"

There was truth in his argument. Tens of thousands of good people had been co-opted in the last few years. If the target refused the 'invitation', he came home to a houseful of dead people. Bodies if he was lucky, pieces if he was not. Seventy thousand murders, maybe ninety thousand, maybe a hundred and fifty thousand. Who knew? No one bothered to flip the bodies face up anymore to identify the dead, much less attempt to figure out who killed whom.

"You still want in on this, Doc?"

"Every step of the way."

He sighed and turned back into the man I knew.

"I cut you off earlier," he said. "I don't want to stop you from bringing in history or psychology or anything else that helps make sense of this crime. Forensics will be a bust, surveillance cameras were covered." An apology, Don Wilder style.

"Thanks."

"I will personally review every detail, every artifact of your report. But, right now--"

"I know. You have a responsibility."

"Be prepared for your friend's reputation to take a serious hit."

"She never wasted time protecting her reputation. And even if she'd been inclined to care what other people thought of her, Camilla lost that war when was ten years old."

"Did you ever visit Mrs. De la Cruz in Mexico City?"

"Once."

"Notice anything not on the up and up?"

"That was over a decade ago." *If you can recall--which I seriously doubt, given your constant state of intoxication—Mrs. De la Cruz marched us right through the Mexico City valley of the whores. Hookers to the left of us. . .*

And there had been that weird cockroach digging through my luggage. The tuxedoed three-foot man with a helmet of coal-black finger-waves parted in the middle above his wrinkled powder-white face.

CHAPTER 6

The Chief slanted his shoulders toward the entrance to the barn, his ammunition stuffed in his armpit. Time to go.

Fine. I could work better with digital photos, high density video, and without two dozen techs and the medical examiner breathing down my neck. Also, at my own laptop I could switch back and forth between crime scene material and the sort of culture and history sites that would send action-driven detectives into orbit.

Don could throw file cabinets of evidence at me, but the "big change" on Camilla's mind last night had nothing to do with cartel business or business of any kind. We didn't have a business-discussing relationship. I knew from the tone of her voice that she'd wanted to share a deeply personal issue. But that sort of 'knowing' clearly didn't interest Don Wilder.

I was on my own. Fine with me. In the United States, we still identify the dead and search for killers.

"I'm sorry for your loss, Doc."

Don turned his attention to Camilla's body, as he had each time we'd hit a wall. He hesitated. "Mrs. De la Cruz was a lovely woman."

"Yes, she was one of those fortunate children who landed the best genes of each parent. Her eyes are her mother's. The full black hair and high cheek bones, are her father's Mexican Indian heritage. Camilla was beautiful on the inside, too. I've lost a piece of my heart."

Don pivoted us away from the murder stall. Back to business.

"About the ex-husband . . ." he said, as if he knew precisely what to say to edge me toward the door. "I'd rather hold off on the interview with Mrs. Cervantes. You said you know the ex?"

Oh God. There was no way out of this discussion.

"Knew him, I guess. In a way."

"He is the father of the victim's daughter, right?"

"He hasn't been a part of Ana Teresa's life. If he ever even saw the baby, I didn't hear about it."

"Was there a divorce?"

Only Don's remark about allowing Eileen Cervantes some private time kept me from breaking for my car.

"I've seen dozens of pictures of Ana Teresa and the family. Birthday parties, holidays, vacations. Diego wasn't in any of them."

Nor were there many other guests at Camilla's celebrations. A fresh bolt of grief rippled through the cells of my body. Eileen was the only child of older parents long since deceased. The only family she had left was her granddaughter. A girl whose smile, long dark lashes, and big green eyes were just like her mother's.

"So, the husband or ex-husband's name is Diego de la Cruz?"

"I think."

I also thought: Black hair brushing wide shoulders, revolutionary style. Tall with dark eyes and Aztec iron cheekbones. Diego's electricity for life had pulsed through my veins with such force on the weekend after my teenage divorce, I could barely remember two months earlier in Houston when I'd roamed the aisles of Target studying ingredients in food products and assembly instructions for furniture, to keep from going home. When all I could feel was numb and all I could see was failure.

With Diego, I wasn't the kind of woman who roamed Target. I was the kind of woman who bet the house every night. A thrill made easier by the fact I had no house.

"Do you know how to locate Mr. De la Cruz?"

"No. I'm not sure it's even possible to find him. Back then, Diego was a freedom fighter for poor farmers in Southern Mexico."

He took a step back. "A *what?*"

I skipped past his bewildered stare.

"Chief, when you run Camilla's courthouse records you will discover that Camilla was pregnant before the wedding. She and Diego were good friends who over-indulged at a fund-raising campout and Ana Teresa was the welcome bonus. What you will not find in the records is that Camilla and her mother were both delighted. On short notice the two of them put together the wedding they'd been planning since Camilla was a toddler. By the evening of her wedding, Camilla was fairly serious about the handsome Argentine banker-polo player she invited to the party."

"Mrs. de la Cruz brought a *date* to her own wedding?" Don's hand went to his hair, which was his 'tell'. When an answer didn't fit with the world he understood, he smoothed his part.

"Sounds crazy, I know. But it was a crazy time, free love and all that. Of course Diego couldn't participate as a regular father because of his work--"

"As a—now how did you put it? A *freedom* fighter?"

"That's what I understood. I was nineteen, Chief. And naïve and hammered most of the time." *What the hell was a freedom fighter?*

"This de la Cruz, did he seem like the kind of guy who'd hook up with Los Insurgentes?"

"Absolutely not."

Because a man leading an army of farmers against wealthy land owners loaded with private security would definitely not be in the market for guns. And, speaking of violence, there was the matter of the bloody clothes on the floorboard behind the driver's seat in Diego's car. I hadn't even asked.

The off-the-grid worlds of Camilla and Diego were so far beyond my life experience, I hadn't questioned anything. Add my alcohol-fueled determination to escape the angst of my mother's sudden death and my father's equally sudden remarriage, followed closely by my ridiculous marriage and divorce, and who knows what sorts of sketchy reality I'd chosen to ignore?

"Doc, I wasn't fair asking you about the ex and drug trafficking. Everyone in Mexico ends up in the cartel business. I don't care how honest or fine-intentioned a person starts out."

His pronouncement conveyed an authority that shook my foundation.

"About the wedding . . ." I said, once I'd shoved Don's pronouncement under an avalanche of denial. "Camilla and her mother considered themselves plenty of family for Ana Teresa. Still, Camilla wanted her daughter to know she had a father, if only in wedding pictures and stories of his noble profession." I squinted--*dared* him to make another 'freedom fighter' crack.

God, I didn't even know if Diego could read and write.

"Camilla has—had a boyfriend," I said, with more intensity than the announcement deserved. "Scott Maris. He produces her mother's show."

The Eileen Cee Show, the most popular talk show of its type in the Southwest, had blossomed from Eileen's efforts to find help for other families torn apart by violence.

"Serious relationship?" Don asked.

"I don't know."

"I thought you being best friends and all--"

"I've seen Scott driving Camilla around in his yellow Lamborghini. He whizzed past me on his way into the Flower Mound as I was leaving last night around seven."

"Seven?" He repeated for the recording.

Why *didn't* I know how important Scott Maris was to Camilla? My struggle to fit the scene in the murder stall with what I knew about Camilla, the pretense that I knew what was going on, had taken its toll. I had no idea what was going on. The barn walls spun, slowly at first then the planks whirled, and my stomach lurched. I grabbed a rail.

"Come on, Doc. You've overdone it here."

Don took my arm and led me to a bench in front of the next stall over.

"Seven o'clock was the last time you saw Mrs. De la Cruz alive?"

"Yes." I tightened my grip on his arm. "I wonder when Eileen last saw her daughter alive? What time was it when Ana Teresa saw her mother for the last time?"

He settled me on the bench.

"Don, I can't help thinking their lives might be different if I'd stayed last night."

"No, I suppose you can't. Still, I'm glad you're here for Mrs. Cervantes."

Which is when I thought of something I could do for Camilla's mother. Something only I could do.

"Let me do the preliminary," I said. "Give Eileen a few hours or even a day."

The Chief texted his request for identification forms. Then he and I were quiet together while we waited for his lieutenant.

I signed the lieutenant's clipboard forms three times on two pages. The two of them witnessed. Now I could go.

There are some things a mother, even a stepmother, shouldn't have to do. Removing a blanket, soaked with your dead child's urine, from the hatch of her car and carrying it out to the dumpster after the ambulance leaves, is one of those things.

CHAPTER 7

Jorge's cheap Chinese bell and chain tinked against the smudged glass door. I paused in the alcove while my pupils dilated from the pinpoints required to drive in fire-ball sun to pupils wide enough to spot George in our usual back corner booth.

"Unspeakable horror strikes at the most exclusive address in Texas . . ." boomed out of the television above the Cristobal bar.

He waved me over and pointed, in sequence, to a tall glass of ice, a bottle of Carmel Valley fumé blanc, a steaming mug of coffee, and an icy bottle of Topo Chico, lined up on the table in front of him. My sophisticated buddy considered provision of the desired beverage to accompany one's dining experience an essential part of a righteous life. Today he wasn't taking any chances.

His sweeping beverage invitations were accomplished without his eyes veering from the broadcast, a bone-chilling seriousness in his expression. I could forgive George's submission to the media hype since his only experience with Camilla had been the weekend of her wedding. He would do anything for me, but her death had not knocked him off his lofty stilts.

Jorge's lighting system, eight flat screens sized modest to movie house, bounced fractured rainbows around the hot pink walls. Beyond the radiant media, Jorge's décor was limited to sepia and white photos of Mexican Revolutionaries Pancho Villa and Emiliano Zapata.

The East Austin restaurant, once a tortilla factory, consisted of a six-stool bar across the front and black vinyl booths along the walls. No windows. Smoky square stains on the mesquite plank floor left by black cast iron corn grinders a century ago.

"*. . . The horsey set was traumatized this morning when the daughter of television personality Eileen Cervantes was discovered murdered in her horse's stall. Her body was covered in stunning diamonds and sapphires. She was wearing riding clothes and a purple velvet hat. Along with the body, the altar included hundreds of thousands in cash, and the skeletal remains of an unidentified second woman.*"

"Ridiculous. That chick needs to fact check her rumors." I gave the television a dismissive scowl and slid into the booth across from George. It was a good thing I was still numb. Otherwise, I would have screamed until I couldn't breathe anymore.

"Just hang on, Miss Rose, before you pass judgment on the modern American media experience." George's attention skipped from the screen to me and back. "It gets better."

"Of course it does."

Eyes fixed over the bar, he pushed a plate of cheddar-drenched tortilla chips across the table, in case my desired dining experience called for orange. As if I could eat. But he was a guy and he was trying.

We were the lone customers and practically family, so Jorge left us on our own while he stood two feet in front of the murder story. Jorge, who modeled his dress and facial hair after the Revolutionaries, shook his head and twisted the ends of a cloth napkin that matched the walls.

"As we speak," George said, "Foxx Headline News is taking a poll on whether or not to air shots of the body."

"Are you *insane?*"

"With a warning, of course."

"Has everyone gone insane?"

"So, Miss Rose, what's your vote? Yes? No? Show the body? Don't show the body?"

If I'd had any strength in my shaking hands, I'd have reached across the table and choked the man. George was the only person I have ever known who truly didn't care what other people thought. Not even me. Not even now.

I took a long, throat clearing drag of the frosty Topo Chico, a carbonated water imported from Northern Mexico. I know. Most people do everything they can to avoid the water in Mexico and I pay two and a half a bottle for it. Sort of gives you a blueprint of the way my brain works.

"Well, fine, Miss Rose, don't vote." George tapped his phone twice. "How-ev-varre, in keeping with my impeccable trash television standards, I am vo-o-ting 'Nuuuuuuu'." He tapped once.

I wagged my head without acknowledgment. George didn't care what I thought, but he cared too much how I felt. My devastation had soaked his brain and left him clueless.

One of the first things you do on marker days is gather up the pieces of your life that are the same and cling to them. The cozy, black vinyl booth with its familiar rips, jalapeño stains, and tortilla fragrance, was the same. Also the same were the counter-balances in my friendship with George.

We were a tight fit, not because we were similar, but because we were opposite cut pieces of a jigsaw puzzle. Here I sat, sweaty, streaked with dirt, and my shirttail half out, while George was so fresh I caught a whiff of manly orchids. My call might've woken him, but he'd arrived decked out in full-cut French linen togs and buttery Italian accessories. The sort of attire worn by everyone but me, during the weeks I packed up my cargo shorts and cashed in my obsessively collected Hilton points at the resort in Los Cabos, Mexico.

"Don't blame me, miss too-dainty-for-reality-television," George said. "It's your buddies sending in pics of this morning's *nar-kiddo* handiwork, which further confirms my belief that people who jump horses over garden gnomes are batty."

"The who?"

"The nar-kiddos."

"Fine."

Now the screen over the bar showcased the Flower Mound burgundy and pink granite entrance, built like the rest of the club to precisely replicate the Firenza Ricché resort in San Remo, Italy. In Texas, mega wealth is conveyed by surrounding yourself with everything Italian--preferably Tuscan----and nothing Mexican. Or Spanish, just in case. From atop the walls, gold-footed Roman winged-goddesses watched over dozens of floral condolence sprays already lined along either side of the ornate brass gates. Not Princess Di level yet, but working on it.

Outside the country club gates, cherry-picker buckets sprouted out of news vans and weaved like mutant grasshoppers set to devour everything in their path. Sprinkled among the media trucks were private security guards in place to maintain the sanctity of Flower Mound residents and to protect the health of the imported Hilton Head turf on the golf course.

"I didn't see your land yacht in the parking lot," I said, to pull George's eyes away from the broadcast. "How'd you get here?"

George has driven a new model Lincoln sedan every year since he was sixteen. Sad, but true.

"Tell me you did *not* park out in the open, Miss Rose?"

To avoid my "you're being an idiot" expression, he shifted his glance to a short man who'd entered the restaurant and now stood in the alcove. Jorge motioned the man to wait.

"I parked in the lot out front," I said.

"Tell me you covered your license plate, for God's sake?"

"No, Chicken Little, I did not. I don't mean to destroy your self-esteem, but we aren't important enough--"

George threw up his hands in his "Miss Rose, you are hopeless, goal post" stance. "At least I had the good sense to switch my plates out with the guy's boat next door."

"George, you live in a penthouse."

His financial statements left most Flower Mound residents in the Texas dust, but the thought of neighborly neighbors or an estate with a yard, gave George the willies.

"So, the valet found a boat in the garage. Also, being of sound mind, I parked my car in a resident's garage one street over."

"You just happen to know someone who lives . . . Never mind." I was too close to collapse to hear George's smarmy lawyer explanation.

His mention of my car reminded me of the low tire. The leak must be pretty bad because the car had a little shimmy fit on every turn between the Flower Mound and El Cristobal. I'd watch my speed on the way home and take my chances.

When the news went to commercial, Jorge led his customer to a booth on the opposite wall. Before the man opened his menu, Jorge was back in position. A customer-ignoring, napkin twisting drama, no doubt, playing in restaurants around the world.

"Check this out, Miss Rose." George rotated his phone to show me a dozen headless men hanging off a bridge tied by their ankles.

My throat closed off. "Stop it!"

"I just want you to know what kind of animals you're dealing with."

"I know what they are like!" I flipped his phone over. "I just left a murder scene with Los Insurgentes horseshit all over the place! I don't need more horror stories. Camilla is dead! I need a friend!"

At that moment, George knew what to do and dove at the opportunity. He swept over to my side of the booth and held me until I stopped crying and promising vengeance. After I'd calmed down, George reclaimed his spot across the table.

"See," he said, "looking at those headless guys helped you get all those nasty pent-up emotions out in the open. I tell you, Doc-*tor* Miss Rose, I could totally do your job."

"I do feel better."

His gaze whipped back to the screen over the bar.

"Good. You are going to need all your strength when the police discover we are drug mules."

I reached across the table, shaped my fingers around his chin, and swiveled his face in my direction. The seven other screens blared the various sports and sports interview programs George usually kept on an intravenous drip. He could choose from those.

"Time to flip over your pool raft, George."

"Pretend Mrs. De la Cruz wasn't cartel connected if you must, Miss Rose. Play make-believe all day, but we are in some very deep shit. All your fault, of course."

"Of course."

He leaned forward and locked in on my eyes. "You see . . ." He ticked sugar off the rim of his glass into his lemon drop martini, made with orange juice in deference to the hour. "I have this whole Mrs. De la Cruz situation figured out."

"Well, the FBI will be delighted."

"The Foxx weatherman showed how these nar-kiddos sew false linings inside the luggage of innocent travelers. Takes four minutes, tops. Not to mention how easy it is to stuff packages in wheel wells and gas tanks."

"You want to tell me you know what a 'wheel well' is?"

"You are the one who staggered into breakfast going on and on about some dwarf stuffing product in your luggage."

"Product?"

"Call 'em like I see 'em, Miss Rose." He dragged a tostado triangle a full circle in the bowl of queso.

"I said there was a guy going through my things and that he was weird. And you said . . . I think the exact quote goes something like, 'Gee, a small person in a country of small people, how utterly shocking!' You told me I was crazy."

"No, I said you were too inebriated to know the difference between a dwarf and a purple people eater."

"What you never understood is, the guy was scary because of the *way* he was tiny."

"Like you remember."

"I do." I did. Sort of. Maybe. "You know how people with genetic 'dwarfism' often look out of proportion? How their head is larger than normal and their arms and legs are really short?"

He didn't answer. No sense encouraging me.

"The thing is, my tiny man wasn't like that. He was a perfect two-and-a-half foot dandy in a black suit. He had gold rings set with big, fat gems on every finger and each thumb."

"Right. Diamonds and rubies on all his wee fingers and toes. He offered you three wishes, then flapped his stubby arms, and flew out your window into the night."

"He had this chalky white face and dyed black hair in crimp waves like a creepy character out of a silent movie."

"Forgive me, Miss Rose, but on the same trip, you also claimed a giant iguana chased you down the hall and that a family of squirrels slept under your bed."

He returned his allegiance to the television.

"Okay, so I had a lot to drink."

"My point is, you need to be careful, Miss Rose. You have lost a wonderful friend and I will do whatever I can to help you through this. That said, you need to accept that this same, recently deceased, dear friend--*used* the two of us and Nancy Margaret Scarletti, a virginal almost-nun, as drug mules."

First the Chief blasts me with criminal records and now George claims Camilla took advantage of me? The Chief was wrong. George was wrong. They were all wrong and I would prove it. The need to find out what happened at the horse show grounds last night crawled up my back and set up camp at the base of my brain.

As for the freak going through my luggage? When he realized I was awake, he'd wheeled and skittered out of sight like a Houston cockroach splits for under the fridge when you flip on the light. Or that's the way I remembered him. Now that I grasped the emotional catastrophe I'd been all those years ago, I could accept that the tiny man was more likely a character in a dream or one of those monsters running around in your head after three days with little sleep and lots of tequila.

Besides, I'd asked myself back then, what possible interest could some weird little man in Mexico City have in a tourist boob like me?

CHAPTER 8

George's scare tactics sent me to the neon tangerine door of the ladies' room. An art project of Jorge's grandson, in the center was a two-foot purple rose dusted with glitter. Nothing generic at the Cristobal.

I splashed cool water on my face and used a wad of paper towels to swipe off the top layer of grit, make-up, and tears. I didn't bother with the debris around my swollen eyes.

"You want to see this, Miss Rose!" George hollered as I closed the tangerine door.

George directed my attention to the broadcast above the Cristobal bar where a square-faced brunette with stick arms posed in front of a random convenience store and told the story of Mr. Cervantes' murder twenty years ago. At least George had his answer. In a successful attempt to save the life of the clerk, Camilla's father was shot twice in the chest by a white man in a cowboy hat who has never been identified.

Citizens south of the border would be shocked that a channel would pre-empt regular programming to follow the investigation of a single murdered person, even the daughter of a celebrity. The notion that time would be allotted to detail the victim's family would be beyond imagination.

In Mexico, even an infamous murder brought only brief surprise, then nothing. When the Lear jet of a high-ranking Mexican official-- comparable to the U.S. Attorney General--crashed in downtown Mexico City, the follow-up press conference opened with statement close to: "Be careful to not make too much of this incident. Planes fall out of the sky all the time in Guatemala and Mexico."

George leaned across the table. "Now, as I was saying earlier . . . about Mrs. De la Cruz . . ."

"Hey!" I slapped the table so hard the basket of chips jumped.

"What?" George bolted up straight.

"Would you stop with the Mrs. De la Cruz shit? What happened to *our* Camilla? Back in Mexico City, you would have proposed to her if Camilla hadn't had a husband and a boyfriend."

I poured a glass of Carmel Valley over ice. "Give me a break here, George. Less than an hour ago, I saw the murdered body of Camilla on an altar to Our Lady of Holy Death. Now, here I am, safe and sound at El Cristobal with you, Camilla's life and death hijacked by the media. How is my brain, much less my heart, supposed to catch up and make sense of the sense of the morning? You weren't close, I get that. But you knew her once and you've kept up with her through me."

"Which is not the same as actually knowing a person."

"What are you trying to tell me, George?"

"The truth is, I don't feel as close to the woman as I did before this morning's disturbing events. Keep it in your multi-concussioned skull that when these cartels make a point, they don't take out just one person and allow her friends and relatives to go on piling up retirement accounts. These devils cut a prit-tee wide swath."

I was suddenly aware of the air-conditioning vent blasting frigid air straight into my face.

"My story is," he said, "that I haven't seen Mrs.—Camilla--in over ten years and that was mostly from a distance. I certainly could not pick her out of a lineup or tell some short guy pistol-whipping me where the coke is stashed."

"You've lost it."

"And . . ." George said, his eyes locked on his phone. "If Camilla's midget cocaine stuffer isn't enough proof we were drug mules, her bodyguard had a rocking tattoo of your Santa Maria nar-kiddo saint."

I held up a palm. Not that a S.W.A.T. team could have slowed George's paranoid landslide.

"Joaquin was Camilla's *driver,*" I said.

He handed me the phone. The screen showed a row of prisoners with their forearms thrust through cell bars. "Check out the tat, second guy from the left."

He scooped a glop of cheese onto a chip, squeezed a jalapeño over it, and slid the entire concoction in his mouth the glow of satisfaction on his face.

"That's the death saint, right?" he asked.

"Could be."

"The same bony babe was all up and down the forearm of Camilla's bodyguard."

"I didn't see any tattoo on her driver."

George made a fist with a thumb spout and aped pouring booze into his mouth.

What I remembered was how small Joaquin looked when six-foot-one George slid in to ride shotgun and pressure for a Cuban cigar detour. I'd expected the typical American black-suited ex-con limo driver type, a big slick driver for a big slick car.

"The police want to interview Diego," I said, going for nonchalant without a chance in hell.

George cocked an eyebrow. "Diego?"

". . . de la Cruz. Use your powers for good, George. See if you can find something about him on your almighty phone."

"You, Miss Rose," George said, "are like the smoker who says she doesn't smoke, then bums cigarettes all day."

The constant contact lifestyle hadn't worked out for me long before cell phones. In high school, I'd hidden my phone phobia by painting myself as the victim of cult-strict parents who monitored my every word and forbid calls before noon or after nine. Once cells phones became as common as underwear, I'd tried to conform a dozen times without success. Turns out, I am constitutionally incapable of walking and talking. Also, where would I carry the little bastard? I'd opted out of the purse-carrying fad after the sixth grade. Thus I carry pens, money, identification, credit cards, pills, snacks, keys, and occasional glasses in the pockets of my black stretch jeans in winter and cargo shorts in summer. My feigned concern with fashion was a lame, but handy, excuse for my lack of tech availability. The truth is, I'd rather be out-of-step than interrupted. And I lose things a lot.

My heart quickened as George searched for a hit on Diego. What was that about? George's phone was state of the art, but it wasn't a time machine. There was no way I could go back to the weekend I spent with Diego and make any sense of what had gone on. Not that I had any reason to return mentally or physically to the Mexico City of Camilla's wedding. Dredging up those three days would be the dumbest and most dangerous move I could make.

George shook his head. "Nope. Nothing on a 'Diego de la Cruz'."

I closed my eyes. "Oh well."

"Let me restate that. There are several billion Diego de la Cruzes in Mexico, but when I factor in a reasonable birthdate range, city, and cross-reference with Camilla--no individual stands the test."

"Keep trying."

"Yes, dear. . . . Not even a blip. Nada. Nil." He sighed. "This is nuts."

Then he darkened his phone. He took a gulp of his coffee and a swig of orange juice martini, then heaved forward in the booth. He steadied his elbows on the table and beamed his eyeballs straight into mine.

"I have a question for you," he said.

"Go for it. But, keep in mind, I'm fragile here."

"My point exactly. You need to slow down, take some time to grieve. You do not need to go poking around in the criminal element of Mexico City."

"I thought you had a question."

"You know I'm right," he said.

"I haven't poked around in any element anywhere."

"Not yet. But you will. And God only knows what's going to come flying out."

"I'm not brave enough to do anything stupid."

"Interesting defense. Here's my question—we are talking a cartel here, and, with the locals, the feds, and investigative reporters around the world, devoted to this case, what on *Woo Woo Planet Psychologist* makes you think you can add anything to the search?"

"That's just it. Maybe Los Insurgentes is the whole story and maybe Los Insurgentes is not."

"'Maybe' is close enough for me to find other hobbies."

"What if the police and the feds are wrong?"

"Sorry, Miss Rose." He wagged his head and scooped sugar into his coffee. "I'm going to have to go with science and skill over intuition and wishful thinking on this one."

"I believe the motive was more personal. If I can find one little piece that points away from a straight cartel hit, it could change the direction of the investigation."

"The truth is, you don't want to accept that Camilla was involved in drug trafficking."

"I want justice."

"I want to end world hunger."

I related my take on the altar and the rose petals. "So there. I want to know, 'why' the postcard, 'why' the petals, and what did Camilla want to talk to me about last night?"

"May I suggest that you ask the bad guys those questions in the ten seconds before they shoot you?"

"Maybe Los Insurgentes wasn't working alone."

"There's that 'maybe' word again."

"All I intend to do is dance lightly around the edges of Camilla's private life."

"Ah, yes. *Dance.*" He clasped his hands on the table and twiddled his thumbs. "So, Miss Rose, why doesn't your 'lightly around the edges' plan make me feel all safe and warm inside?"

"Cold heart. Also, I don't believe you looked all that hard for something on Diego."

"Fine." George heaved a sigh and air-tugged through more sites on his phone. His expression slipped from that of a man who adored the web to that of a man in a dentist's chair waiting for the Novocain to kick in.

"Still can't find anything," he said. "I've even paired with every synonym I can come up with for 'freedom fighter', farmer, soldier, and communist."

"Communist?"

"Freedom fighter, communist, same thing. . . . And no one escapes the mighty eye of the Google. By the way, you have cheese all over your elbow."

"Keep trying." I picked off congealed chunks and set them in a pile.

Diego hooked up with Communism actually made sense, given the photograph he'd shown me of his parents. The details of which I'd best keep to myself if I wanted George's continued cooperation.

His focus drifted. "You might as well face reality, Miss Rose. Diego ran with a rough crowd."

"And?"

"Your lover boy is dead."

Thud.

"Okay. Two more minutes of this jumping bean haystack search and that's it," George said. Then he jerked to attention, his eyebrows in full salute. "Well, hot tamale rainbow!"

George grinned, eyes and teeth all a-twinkle. Which meant he'd discovered something I didn't know, and that 'something' was more evidence to support his jaded view of mankind and refute my kinder opinion.

He slid the phone my direction. "Check this out."

"I don't want to see Diego dead."

"This shot is from back before he was killed."

In the photo, Diego rode point for a ragtag army mounted on the wiry horses descended from the Arabian and Spanish breeds of Hernán Cortés and other conquistadors who trampled the Aztec Empire. The black bandana mask highlighted his sharp Indian and Castilian features, his almost black eyes that crinkled slightly at the edges. Gentle, yet with the promise he would not back down from violence.

Whoosh. That fast, I was forty stories above Mexico City in the Angel Sky Bar across the table from Diego. Across the universe from my dismembered life in Texas.

"Forget finding anything else on Zorro there," George said. "The most likely scenario is that he died violently at the hands of very bad people not long after he impregnated then sort of married Camilla."

"You don't know." Somehow on that fuzzy weekend long ago, I'd had the good sense to not mention the peculiar pile of blood stained clothes on the backseat floorboard of Diego's car. Not that George would have believed me back then.

"Your boy looks a little more sinister without the shower, shave, and the rented tux, doesn't he?"

"Yeah." *Better.* "George?"

"Yes, dear?"

"Say the police are right and the obvious answer is the right answer."

"Score one for reality."

"Still, I think Diego would want to know that the mother of his daughter has been murdered."

"I'm going to pretend you didn't say that."

"Diego grew up an orphan. He should be made aware of his daughter's situation. Camilla would want him to know."

"And you know that, how?"

"One phone call. That's all I want. That's all I'm going for here."

"You are such a bad liar."

"Of course, I'll listen if Diego knows someone with a personal reason to want Camilla dead."

George ordered another orange juice martini.

I handed back his cell. "This photo is time-stamped before the wedding. Can't you find anything more recent?"

"No . . ." He blazed through screens. Nothing." Then the phone went face down on the table. George arranged his lawyer all-business face. "Look, Miss Rose, before--when I said you should let the police handle this--"

"I heard you."

"Yes, but you didn't listen. You need to face something, psychologist buddy of mine. You do not deal well with death. In fact, you go kind of crazy. And now, with the way you want to dive--"

"The eyes of Texas are upon you!" warned the facedown phone.

George grabbed it. Grinned. "Another photo tag . . . . Whoa!" He hooted. George is not given to hooting. "This is definitely not your best moment, Miss Rose."

There we were, the Freedom Celebration Trippers in all our glory. Camilla, arm-in-arm with her Argentine banker-polo player, Nancy Margaret, George, and, on the far right, yours truly, arm-in-arm with

Diego, father of Camilla's child. We toasted with champagne flutes and toothpaste commercial smiles, none of us that long out of braces. The whole world was before us. We'd "Saluded!" and pledged that after the libertine Freedom Celebration Trip, we would go forth to live amazing and righteous lives.

That was the plan.

It took me two weeks back in Texas to mess that up.

CHAPTER 9

In the wedding photograph, Camilla's face radiated an innocent joy I hadn't seen since before her father was murdered. And now Ana Teresa at almost the same age had lost her mother to violence. The wretched coincidence, if that's what it was, had me inches from a semi-public breakdown.

"I should get home," I said.

"Wait." George caught my forearm before I had my feet under me to exit the booth. "We're not done here. I saw that unhinged stubborn look in your eye when you connected with that photograph."

"You made your point, George. I'm lousy when it comes to losing people, and you don't believe I can add anything to the search for Camilla's killer. Mission accomplished."

"What I'm saying is --cartel people aren't normal."

I knee pumped to stand. He held my wrist captive on the table.

"I admire your loyalty, but, Miss Rose, you need to distance yourself from Camilla Cervantes."

We went eye-to-eye. No flinch on either side.

"Distance myself? Oh, I think I've done plenty of that. When we were kids and Camilla needed me the most, I was afraid of her. Oh, and I did a pretty good job of distancing myself last night, if anyone's counting. George, I have a commitment to Camilla."

"Camilla is dead."

"Dead doesn't mean the same thing to everyone."

"Use your commitment to support Camilla's mother and daughter."

"Because Camilla is dead, doesn't mean my relationship with her is over."

George looked at me as if my head had just exploded.

He could see I'd slipped off into mysterious territory George knew existed, but he'd never traveled. He'd dropped me off to burn a candle at St. Mary's Cathedral plenty of times since the suicide. When he asked why I went in, I told him that in the candlelight I could see hummingbirds.

He never came inside. But he didn't comment. With friends, acceptance tops understanding.

"I'm not backing off, George." I stood to go.

"Wide swath, Miss Rose, wide swath."

He pointed toward the television.

"Camilla's house!"

The broadcast had switched to a Google Earth camera that first panned Mexico City, then zoomed in on the suburb of Cayoacan and *Las Palomas* (the Place of the Doves), the hacienda where we three first-time losers from Texas had spent our Freedom Celebration Trip. No way could I walk out now.

"The picture of the Celebration Howdy Doodies was taken in that courtyard!" George said, and eased up on my arm.

Already out of fresh information, news channels had widened coverage to seductive sidebars. The narrator swirled thick red circles around the homes of Cayoacan's most famous residents— Russian Revolutionist Leon Trotsky, and artists, Diego Rivera, Mexico's world renowned muralist, and

Frida Kahlo. Frida Kahlo was Mr. Cervantes' favorite which meant Frida became Camilla's favorite, too, even stronger after the convenience store shoot out. Which is saying something since Kahlo's bloody and raw scenes evoke the viewer's most primitive aches and fears and are often too gory and downright scary for delicate adults.

While in *Las Palomas* readying the bride, I'd been shocked by the surreal Frida Kahlo scenes on the wall above Camilla's bed. A deer pierced with arrows and with the head of a woman, vines growing out of Frida's buried body, her babies that had not survived to birth, pyramids and skulls, and self-portraits with Diego Rivera, the man who tormented her with his lack of devotion, painted as a cameo in the center of her forehead.

When Camilla had caught my wide eyes, I'd sputtered one of those over-enthusiastic compliments that pop out when you are startled by a friend's hideous haircut. Something stupid and artificial like, "Oh, I can see why you like Frida. She's amazing!" Camilla believed my enthusiasm and rewarded me with a Frida print of my own--three generations of women. All dead. Her gift was quickly hidden away in my luggage, and was now obscured under papers on a desk in a little used storage room-office.

Camilla adored the artist because of her father, but she had a second connection. Camilla and Frida were both daughters of an Anglo--Frida's father was German--and an Indian from Mexico City. In many photographs of Camilla, even as a teenager, the stuffed Frida doll her father had given her, complete with black braids and the famous uni-brow, was at her side. As kids, she and I always chose horses over dolls, so that I didn't meet the stuffed Frida until she was tucked into the Paris hospital bed with the barely alive Camilla.

Had I really flown to Paris all by myself when I was twelve? Camilla was the brave child, not me. I don't believe most thirteen-year-olds could have survived the rape and beating Camilla had somehow lived beyond. I hadn't distanced then. I wouldn't distance now.

Then symbol crashes interrupted my silent vow. The eighty inches of flat screen torment over the Cristobal bar filled with a blazing orange and blue expanding and shrinking "BREAKING NEWS" banner.

Scott Maris was posted on the entry steps to Lone Star Studios surrounded by a mob of local reporters hungry to make their marks before national teams arrived and pushed them to the back of the crowd. The expression on Scott's face suggested he'd been selected to sacrifice his body for the good of the tribe.

"Please, ladies and gentlemen," Scott said. "Please give me some room."

I kicked George's shin.

"Ow!"

"That guy is Camilla's boyfriend!"

Scott Maris wore an electric blue sport coat, dark half-moons at his armpits. Perspiration dripped from his jaw and soaked a tie that must have once resembled red and blue wrapping paper. The crisp detail of his mottled cheeks, garish red eyes, and quivering chin, made me question whether high density television was always the best choice. His thick dark hair had a cowlick in front, giving him a schoolboy look while the rest of him reeked adult tragedy.

"Mr. Maris," the reporter nearest his face said, "you know how dearly Eileen's fans hold her in their hearts . . ."

"One question, that's it," Scott said, and let her finish her sentence.

". . . What can Eileen's many friends and fans do to help?"

"The best way to help Eileen Cervantes is to respect her privacy."

His point made, he pivoted and bolted through the double doors. Two Lone Star Studio security guards closed ranks to block reporters. Frustrated journalists pelted the robot duo with questions.

"Is it true that Camilla Cervantes is known as the Madam of Mexico City?"

"Is Eileen in danger?"

"What about Eileen's granddaughter?"

"Is it true that Camilla Cervantes was a drug cartel witch?"

"What about the governor's daughter and the other riders at the Flower Mound Country Club? Are they safe?"

"What about the poor Mexican children Camilla sold as prostitutes?"

"What the bloody hell?" The stab went all the way through my heart.

With the disappearance of Scott Maris, the news feed went live to another, more familiar location. Two women, one in wedge heels the other in riding boots, stood practically arm-in-arm in front of the Flower Mound Country Club's Gold Room Restaurant as if welcoming guests to a very private party.

"I think I'm going to throw up," I said.

I wasn't kidding. I seized George's fingers with one hand and used the other to press the iced wine to my forehead. Then the broadcast descended from sickening to vile. The ice pick in my heart twisted.

The long-legged woman next to Jane Bailey modeled full-tilt equestrian finery—tailored black hunt coat, kid gloves, a crisp white ascot with a gold horsehead pen, and a velvet hard hat in the hundred degree weather. What were the odds? What were the *freek*-king odds?

Diana Sloan. The woman who had never forgiven me for persisting on the club equestrian team where I clearly did not belong. The woman who downright hated me for standing by Camilla when the number one topic around the Flower Mound pool and tennis courts was Camilla Cervantes's alleged wanton seduction of Stephen Sloan.

"Can you believe it, George? Diana managed to wheedle Bailey through security with a Gold Room reservation! Diana talked her way into a sealed crime scene. For *lunch*!" I was burning up from the inside out.

George scooted to the edge of his seat and gripped my hands. "You need to breathe here, Miss Rose. Your face, I'm worried here."

"And here's the kicker. Jane Bailey just *happens* to be the woman out to steal Eileen's audience with a show in the same time slot."

"Miss Rose, remember you've had a shock. Like you said, you're fragile."

"Why is Diana Sloan allowed to utter one *word* about my friend? Why? You want to tell me *why?*"

Ms. Bailey, microphone in hand, auditioned a wide smile into the camera, then caught herself, and went somber.

"Mrs. Sloan, thank you for taking time out of a day that has to be very difficult for you."

I cracked. "Gag. Gag. Gag! George, I can't take this! Eileen can't take this!"

"The public is left with so many questions," Bailey said, with enough heartfelt concern to melt the polar ice cap. "As a long-time friend of Camilla Cervantes, what can you tell us about her?"

I crushed George's fingers. *"Friend?"*

"Well, she does have on the same Princess Anne outfit," George said.

"Diana detests Camilla!"

He leaned away from me. "That's harsh."

"Harsh? I'll tell you harsh. A few years ago—in that very same Gold Room—*Mr.* Diana Sloan invited Camilla and Ana Teresa to an evening pool party for his seven-year-old daughter. Camilla shows up, and surprise, surprise! She and Ana Teresa are the only guests, if you don't count the babysitter hired so that Stephen and Camilla could be alone."

A disconnected blink from George.

I aimed a finger Smith and Wesson at the enemy.

"It gets worse. Stephen confessed his desperate love to Diana, packed his bags, and landed on Camilla's doorstep in Mexico City. This is interview sick. Sick!"

"I didn't know--"

"No one knows the truth because no one ever listened. No one has ever been on Camilla's side. Did I tell you Don called Camilla a *bullet?* A bullet in a drug war? What's a bullet cost? Eighty cents?"

George tightened his grip on my hands. "Hold on. Listen. We have to listen to know what we're up against."

I forced my lips together to keep my ears open.

"Camilla has always been, well, different from the rest of us," Diana said, her artfully deep blue and silver shaded eyes gazing straight into the camera with the sincerity of a deceased ox. "Still, I was as stunned as her other friends when I found out she was involved with prostitution. You just never think of someone who's educated and well-off selling her body like that."

My heart threatened to crack my breastbone.

Jane Bailey moistened her lips. She looked tired. "Mrs. Sloan, could you explain what you mean by 'different'?"

I shoved back from the table, flipping over the basket of chips, and sending the salt shaker on a roll. The slick leather soles of my boots skittered for traction.

"I'm thinking you shouldn't drive, Miss Rose!"

"I'm thinking I don't give a shit."

Diana stepped toward the camera and arranged her shoulders in an exquisite three-quarter pose I recognized from when she played the lead in *Swan Lake.*

"Well, Jane, when we were little kids, Camilla started a voodoo cult with two other girls. Also, she used to run away a lot."

"I see . . ."

"Still, most of us accepted her until she tortured and murdered Major. Then Camilla burned down her family's barn to cover it up. That's when she was sent away to the mental hospital."

CHAPTER 10

TWENTY TWO YEARS AGO, The *Dorados*

"Now we sacrifice our blood to Our Lady of Holy Death," Camilla says.

Everyone dies. We are old enough to know that. What we don't know is how a little girl's daddy can leave for the store on the night before her tenth birthday and never come home.

Invisible fingers clutch my throat. *I can't do this.* I cough, twice. *I have to do this.*

Camilla Cervantes, Nancy Margaret Scarletti, and I sit cross-legged on the straw-sprinkled cork floor of the darkened stall. The other riders, trainers, and parents, at the Flower Mound Country Club Horse show can't see or hear us in this abandoned barn. Our knee bones touch above our high-top black riding boots.

"If she is pleased," Camilla says, "the Our Lady will guide my father to Heaven."

Our Lady of Holy Death is our queen. She stands in the center of our circle. She is as tall as a Barbie Doll, but nothing like a Barbie.

I can hardly breathe. The Angel of Death is so glamorous and so horrible at the same time. I can't stop looking at her.

She is a statue in an evening gown the color of midnight. Her extra-long skirt has diamond sparkles and dribbles behind her like dresses movie stars wear to the Academy Awards. The Angel doesn't look anything like a stupid plastic toy. She's more like one of those elegant, smoky-ivory ladies in long slinky sleeves, with every wrinkle smooth and perfect. The kind that rich people buy in Europe and set on white grand pianos.

Also, Our Lady of Holy Death is a skeleton.

Two weeks ago, a robber shot Camilla's father dead at the Sac and Pac, where he'd gone after the housekeeper tripped over the dog and dropped an egg she needed for Camilla's birthday cake.

Specks dance and float in the lone sunset beam that filters through a gap in the barn doors. Muffled announcements from the world we left behind leak in, *"Next in the ring is Number 146, Candlewood . . . ridden by. . ."* along with distant flinty clops and scrapes of steel horseshoes on cement. Even the medicine smells of liniment and Absorbine have faded in this place.

"We're a secret club now," Camilla says.

A club. Of course, a club. We're already dressed alike in canary riding breeches and fancy white shirts with silk ascots. Girls in a club have codes and secret handshakes.

Camilla said "sacrifice our blood," but she means pretend sacrifice. We aren't going to slice each other up like the Mexico City Indians in her father's books. In those pictures, men in spotted animal skins stand on pyramids and cut the hearts out of people who are still alive and screaming bloody murder.

Camilla is sort of like those Indians, the ones her father called 'the People'. She has lots of the same kind of hair that's so black it's almost blue and a squarer face than Nancy and I have. Also, Camilla is small like the Indians. What if she's too much like the People?

I'm being stupid. Camilla is a little girl like us. There won't be real blood. No knives, for sure.

"We are the *Dorados,*" Camilla says. "The golden ones."

"Of course, the golden ones," I say, all monkey-see, monkey-do. *I want to be just like you.* I am also small for my age, but in a stubby, pale hair stuck to my big head sort of way.

Nancy Margaret doesn't so much as twitch. The spidery silk net her mother slipped over her dark curls must have stretched out to web her entire body. Did she forget to breathe?

"To Our Lady of Holy Death," Camilla says, and grasps our hands.

Nancy Margaret and I close the circle. A current shocks my fingertips, runs up my arm, passes through my body, then shoots down my other arm. First ice, then fire.

There's something new and scary in Camilla's eyes. *Please, don't let there be real knives.*

I lock my attention on the skull-faced Angel in the movie star dress.

"Jessica? Nancy Margaret? You are both going to help me, right?"

I'd eat a bale of hay if Camilla asked, and Nancy Margaret would do whatever I did.

"Just because my Daddy's dead, doesn't mean he's not my Daddy anymore. His spirit is here with us now."

What does she mean? Ghosts?

Nancy Margaret cracks. She swallows hard and flicks her wide eyes over her shoulder in the direction of the adults.

"There's nothing to be afraid of," Camilla says. "Spirits are always around us, my father told me. We can't see them, the way we can't see hummingbirds unless we know where to look."

Nancy Margaret shifts her eyes back to Camilla and the Angel of Death skeleton lady.

Then out comes the knife.

A hideous give-away tear collects in the outside corner of my left eye. I blink; I will the tear to suck back into my eye.

The blade looks like black glass. I know it's marble because the edges are chipped out like the chest-slicers in the hands of the murderer priests on the pyramids.

Camilla doesn't have a daddy anymore. You cannot fail Camilla. Still my chest shakes and my breath spurts out in little puffs.

Camilla raises the knife over her head, her fingertips on each end. The ray of dying sunlight pings the glinty marble surface and shoots a golden streak that blinds me for a second.

Nancy Margaret crushes my hand. I squeeze back harder.

Camilla closes her eyes. She hums. Then chants something she must have memorized from one of her father's books on the People because her words are not like Sunday school songs or even English.

I do my best to keep up with Camilla's chant. Nancy Margaret mumbles.

Camilla lowers the stone blade and rests it on her thigh. She drops her gold "CC" cufflink in the straw and folds back the stiff French cuff of her shirt, then the sleeve. One, two, three. She poses her wrist over Our Lady of Holy Death.

"I'll go first," she says.

CHAPTER 11

We were ten years old. Ten. Camilla's father had just been murdered!

I punched the gas pedal, jerked the wheel into a right hand turn on the haunches that would have impressed the most persnickety of horse show judges, and roared out of the Cristobal parking lot in a gravel tornado. Good thing I wasn't still paranoid prissy about the car the way I was in the first years after David bought it for me. When I'd flinched at the luxury, he said he'd chosen a Lexus because it was a reliable car. I hoped he was right because I'd drive it the rest of my life.

The glass towers of downtown Austin, the billowing clouds, even the strangers on the sidewalks, were rimmed with blood red crusts. The world had turned on Camilla again.

Camilla had suffered and survived more than any other woman at the club or in most of the world. She'd worked her heart out to accept fate and make a life. Camilla had won that battle. So screw Diana Sloan. Screw the whole damn Flower Mound Country Club.

Two days after the only meeting of the Dorados, Camilla slipped out of her house, saddled her pony, and rode eleven miles to the cemetery. The police found her the next afternoon stretched out asleep on her father's grave. That night, Camilla set fire to the Cervantes' barn, but only after she'd made sure no animals were inside. Major, the riding team's German shepherd mascot ran back in after the flames started. No one knew why.

I threaded into traffic on Interstate 35 with a surprise low-tire swerve toward the mid-line. The guy on the inside lane, in absolutely no danger, leaned on his horn until I looked, then shot me the bird. Life goes on. All I asked was to make it through downtown and into the hills of west Austin before I crashed or shattered.

The stories had flown back then. Wild accounts, launched with the midnight barrage of fire trucks, police cruisers, and ambulances, that lit up the Flower Mound like an apocalyptic movie set. The favorite rumors were the animal torture story and the version in which Major re-entered the barn to save an abducted child. The kidnapping story stayed around the longest, even though no missing children were ever reported.

Camilla, Camilla, the Flower Mound Killa.

Exactly what kind of Pollyanna world did I think we lived in? Yes, juvenile records were sealed, but there is no law against gossip. I banged my fist on the steering wheel until it throbbed and bit my lip until I tasted the bloody tang of copper and salt.

The story would play out like this:

Camilla was "different."

Camilla was mentally ill.

Camilla tortured and killed small animals, and maybe babies.

Camilla burned down her family's barn.

Camilla was attracted to violent people, the sort of criminals who, as children, also killed small animals and burned down barns.

Camilla put herself in dangerous situations.

Camilla was responsible for her own bloody murder.

Drug trafficking was not the only profession that took no prisoners and left no witnesses.

A beat up blue Subaru pulled up along the curb in front of the Mt. Laurel house as I turned into the cove. Perfect. First Diana Sloan and now Zack Harvey, Boy Reporter and Scientologist Pain in the Ass.

To ease tire repair, I parked in the driveway of my miniature version of the sleepy Guadalajara plaza hotel where my family stayed the last summer the Roses were a family. There were two other houses in Mt. Laurel Cove, one Tuscan and one Provence French Country.

While I'd been going for a home ambience to match the tranquility I loved, George and others, after a few margaritas, were known to make free with Taco Bell analogies. Still, the house was close enough to the converted haciendas of my childhood that, sometimes, I could close my eyes and drift south to a hideaway far away from the fears and complications that come with the American Dream.

Sometimes. Not today.

Zack Harvey, natty in a dark suit, hopped out of the Subaru and air-mailed a smile more offensive than the bird flashed on the freeway. Then he stuck his hand in the air and performed a full arc wave. Somewhere a used car dealership was missing its welcome manikin.

Zack's stiff appearance was most likely required to restrain his happy dance. He'd been waiting a year. As lead writer for an online Scientology column, if he could connect my name to Camilla's murder, or better still, to Los Insurgentes, a big fat revenge opportunity was within his grasp.

"Hope you brought your lunch and a pillow," I shouted, as the garage door cranked up. "I have nothing to say that you can print!"

I darted inside. The rumble of the garage door closing provided a few moments of peace before that sound was replaced by newsreader voices emanating from the kitchen. There was no escape. Concepción, my longtime housekeeper and friend, had her own reasons to be heartbroken and anxious about Camilla's murder.

Concepción crash-landed in my arms before I'd breached the doorframe. I embraced her thin shoulders, my chin on the top of her head. The babes circled my ankles in full-out "Thank God, you're home at last! We could not have survived another second!" hysteria. The boy dog's vocal chords were stuck on his level five ecstasy wail, a sound similar to the sustained shriek of lottery winners.

When Concepción squeezed her okay, I stepped back to welcome Suzi Wong the Queen, a white Pekingese with one brown ear, and Sammie Davis, Jr. the Affectionate, the eight pound black and silver mottled shelter product of a Shi Tzu and a traveling man.

"Horrible," Concepción said, her eyes on the floor. *"Muy, triste. Droigas* (drugs). Everywhere, Jessie." For her, the misery wrought by drug traffickers reflected shame on all Mexicans. "My girl, my Ana Teresa, I am so sad for her."

Camilla's daughter was family to Concepción. Without siblings, or even aunts and uncles from Camilla's father's side, Ana Teresa saw Concepción as her extended Mexican family, and Concepción, whose large family had been scattered and decimated by the cartel wars, heartily welcomed the role.

I collapsed in a chair at the kitchen table. Home. Safe from the outside world.

Concepción slipped her aluminum crutch in her armpit and occupied her shaking hands with the Keurig machine, her twisted right shin and doll-sized foot slinging outward eight inches off the floor. An ornate silver crucifix swung from the rosary of garnet beads tucked in the waistband of her white cotton dress.

A millisecond before the doorbell chimed, Sammie abandoned his appreciation dance and charged for the front door. Once in position to save the household, he reared back and threw his body against the door over and over as if the house was on fire.

Zack, with true Scientologist recruiter doggedness, wouldn't give up until chased off the property at gunpoint. Fine. At least for now there was only one reporter to dodge. Maybe I could persuade him to pass the word that I was not available to speak with the press. Right. Like Zack Harvey would do me, or any other "demon psychologist," a favor.

I tucked Sammie to my chest and opened the four-by-four inch brass-framed peeping hatch in the carved door.

"Go away!" I said, before he could part his lips. I closed the hatch.

He leaned on the doorbell. "Not this time, Dr. LeFave. This time I win!"

"For you to win, I'd have to play, and I'm not."

"You'll play."

Play what? I reopened the hatch.

"For once in my life," he said, as if he was ninety instead of twenty, "I have an edge on the big story. For once I have a personal contact." His precisely parted blond coif didn't move in the breeze and his grin took up most of his face. "I know you are one of those horse show people."

"I can't imagine why you consider me a personal contact after I had your little brochure-toting 'counselors' barred from the university campus."

"Our breakthrough religion offers assistance to unhappy students brainwashed into attending college."

"No. What you *sell* to young people away from home for the first time and struggling with classes--is a few re-packaged New Age sayings along with the promise of unending prosperity and the ability to heal the body of any disease or injury without medical assistance."

"You're afraid our religion will cut into your income."

"Oh, that's it. The 'For Sale' sign goes on the lawn in the morning."

"Look, Dr. LeFave, all I want is a few lines to run as an exclusive, and I leave you alone. Also, you need me."

"Go away." I closed the hatch and turned for the kitchen.

Zack whacked a sheaf of papers against the door. What? Another man threatening me with a wad of papers? I took a peek.

"I heard you talking with your friend at that old Mexican food place across the tracks."

"You followed me?"

"You are desperate for info on Miss Cervantes and her husband and I am the person who is going to help you get what you need." He scrolled his papers into a tight roll.

Zack's offer to assist the enemy was beyond ridiculous. *So, close the hatch.* One more time, the mention of Diego overrode good sense.

"Okay, Zack. I'm listening."

A pop, then a white pipe shot me in the face.

"Ow!" I jumped back and grabbed my nose.

A blast off the palm of Zack's hand had fired a tube through one of the tiny squares.

"I'm not asking for a handout," Zack said. "That photo is a mere sample." The grin was apparently a permanent feature. "Scientology is big in Mexico City."

"I will not bother to look at your *sample* before I drop it in the trash." A two-year-old could see through that bluff. It was all I could do to not roll my eyeballs toward the floor.

"Zack you can't--"

I was blinded by a flash. Zack was proving to be quite lax when it came to taking orders from me.

"Oh, nice one!" he said. "The crime networks are throwing cash for photographs. This one of you scowling behind bars ought to pay for my week in Tahiti. Love the jailhouse effect."

"This is private property!" I rubbed my eyes, still seeing spots.

"Maybe you should take a handful of your happy-happy pills, Dr. LeFave."

The obnoxious little guy was giddy with power.

In retaliation for national and state licensing boards blocking Scientologists from presenting themselves as trained professional counselors, Scientology 'trainers' had pumped millions into a campaign to defame mental health professionals. According to the propaganda passed off as 'research' Scientologists claimed that pharmaceuticals for depression were mind control and proof that psychologists and psychiatrists were instruments of the devil. Insulin and aspirin? More poison pushed by "the evil medical-industrial complex." CPR was likely okay, as long as you did it to yourself.

I snapped the hatch closed. "Why am I still standing here?" I asked Sammie, who ignored me. He was already in my arms, why would he care where my feet were?

"You decide, Dr. LeFave," Zack hollered, his voice fading as he trotted for the Subaru.

He knew I was still behind the door, ears wide open.

"I'm thinking a photo montage with the caption, 'Psychologist Jessica LeFave, longtime friend of Camilla Cervantes and the victim's celebrity mother, has a secret criminal past! Dr. LeFave is now in seclusion, hiding out from the press and the police'."

I snuggled Sammie in closer and unrolled Zack's teaser gift.

Sheesh. What a nutcase. The woman in the fuzzy black and white photo was an angry mess. Her clenched fists slammed the steering wheel of an older Lexus stopped at a kiosk on the International Bridge between Nuevo Laredo and Laredo. Her expression would scare scorpions into witness protection.

Uniformed federal police from two countries and locals committed to 'protect and serve' stood guard around the Lexus. Border Patrol aplenty. Standard accessories included weapons for poking, in case I didn't tuck my tail under my outrage, and limp back to Austin empty-handed. Which I did.

How did he come up with this photograph in less than two hours?

Zack Harvey could be a problem.

CHAPTER 12

I chucked Zack's border surveillance glamour shot in the wastebasket and continued down the hall to the closet where connections for the elaborate security system David had insisted on were buried under random horse gear and dog crates. The service contract lapsed long ago, but they'd left the impressive little battery operated control panel. *Adios doorbell.*

Today wasn't about me or Zack Harvey. Today was about Camilla.

If Zack used his privileged, and likely illegal, access to information and happened onto something juicy, I'd listen. Unless it was more rumor mongering. Or a prelude to an extortion attempt. No, I'd probably listen anyway. There wasn't exactly a line of people at the front door pleading to locate information for me.

Back in the kitchen-office, I lowered the volume on the counter television and took my usual place at the rough-hewn *rancho* table I'd discovered in an abandoned bunkhouse on a grapefruit orchard in the Rio Grande Valley. The hacienda style kitchen was walled with my favorite Talavera pattern—white tiles mixed with cobalt blue diamonds and bluebird accents. The window over the sink looked onto the back courtyard. When I'd left for the horse show, the sun barely up, Concepción stood at the window sipping coffee. Now the shade was drawn tight.

"He was a bad man at the door?" Concepción asked. She'd witnessed more than one patient in a tough spot, thus Zack's antics hadn't thrown her.

"No, he's a Scientologist."

"Dios mio! Tom Cruise!" Concepción crossed her arms on her chest. She was a good Catholic, but certain men in in Marine dress whites can turn a woman's head and the fact that Tom was barely five foot seven suited her fine.

She brought coffee to the table and sat beside me to watch news on what was now internationally branded the "Flower Mound Country Club Murder." Concepción would be important in Ana Teresa's life in the months ahead. Suzi and Sammie would be, too.

I know most adults don't choose to wake up every morning with a little warm dog or two snuggling along their ribs, but I do not know why. I'd taken too many microbiology courses to deny potential sanitary issues and half of my psychology professors would claim mental concerns, but along with the horses, the babes had helped me stay afloat for so long, I couldn't image going solo.

Not when I had a choice.

The furry pals picked up on my despair, hopped into my lap, and licked my face with the fervor of a first and last kiss. Unlike her 'brother', Suzi Wong was of noble birth. At least that's the reason the little boy down the street with the "Free Puppies" sign gave me when he asked for a ten dollar handling fee. Sammie's trademark was his fierce, unflappable friendliness while Suzi was quite the snob, so the kid must have been telling the truth.

Brain science was on my side. Touching, watching, even thinking about dogs—assuming you are a fan--raises brain endorphins, creating the hormone-high runners experience after the first ten miles. So, there you are. Run ten miles or enjoy a few dog hugs? Not a tough decision.

Sammie's other remarkable trait was his unique communication style. Since every dog I'd ever owned was known as the rudest barker in Mt. Laurel Cove, I'd crowned Sammie as the canine to turn my reputation around. Thus, he became the behavior project of the Mad Scientist. Every time the tiny six-week-old lovable black puff tightened his throat to bark, I'd launched myself across the room with my yellow and red Pool Warrior water blaster. I never had to squeeze the trigger. All I had to do was point the plastic gun in his direction and he froze mid-bark.

After a few weeks, all I had to do was say, "Don't make me get my gun, Sammie Davis," and he quieted.

I cuddled the babes, sipped coffee, and let my brain drift, mesmerized by the increasingly fictitious media account of the murder and the murder victim. Then I settled Suzi on the floor and reached for my laptop. Best to make notes while the feel of the scene was fresh. Before the rumors piped into the homes and phones of the world became 'facts'.

Not that anyone at police headquarters was holding his breath. The Chief had hyped my input, but my descriptions and interpretations wouldn't add up to 'probable cause' while forensics and Los Insurgentes 'static' coming over the border might. In the real world, detectives stop for lunch and spend days, weeks, months, and years, collecting evidence before an arrest is made. Which worked in my favor. Not only could I allow my senses to guide me, a friend does not have to prove 'probable cause' before dancing lightly around the edges of her friend's personal life.

"You have her picture."

Concepción pointed to the aerial view of Frida Kahlo's blue house now featured on the broadcast. She hopped to standing, leaned her crutch against the table, and tagged the wall for balance as she made her way down the hall to a seldom entered office.

The house was loaded with unused rooms with white adobe walls sparsely decorated with Mexican paintings, ironwork, and a collection of wooden crucifixes from the Southwest. Just the sort of lovely rooms that would have purpose for a woman who knew what to do with them. Sadly, I wouldn't know *feng shui* from *egg foo yung.* My decorating mantra was pretty much: "You can never have too much Mexican shit in your house."

Thus, Concepción and I ended up at the kitchen table, no matter the task. We could have shared a small apartment easily, and would have, if David had not built and paid for the house on Mt. Laurel Cove.

She returned and handed me the framed print with a headshake of disapproval, the reaction most people had to Frida Kahlo's paintings, especially this one. Desperate to catch every word of the broadcast and satisfied that I was stable enough to be alone, Concepción retreated to watch story updates at a higher volume in her bedroom toward the back of the house.

I used the coffee mug to prop up Frida's painting next to my laptop. With every passing minute, I realized I knew less about Camilla's life than I'd assumed. There was nothing in the Frida painting I could connect with the horrors of the morning, but, there was a baby in it and Camilla was pregnant with Diego's child when she gave me the picture. Wasn't that enough of a connection for me to track down Ana Teresa's father? Camilla would want the father of her only child to know what happened to her. Right?

One phone number. Ten or twelve taps. That's all I needed. To start.

The odds weren't looking good. George had netted zip on his genius phone and the notion that Zack Harvey could turn up anything on a peasant revolutionary or a 'freedom fighter', if there even was such a thing, was the silliest sort of wishful thinking. Maybe the Chief could track down Diego, but not anytime soon. Never, if the case closed without a dip into Mexico.

With no other pad to launch my rocket, I Googled the Angel Sky Bar, a glass-walled paradise at the top of a Mexico City hotel, and the only club Diego and I patronized that hadn't been erased by tequila and embarrassment. The online photograph didn't do the club justice. The address and phone number were listed below a gold-flecked marble bar topped with twenty brands of Mexican tequila.

Another whoosh rippled through my body.

What if?

To tamp down the ridiculous "what if" rumbles, I focused on the television while I punched in the number. The broadcast now featured flash interviews with celebrities plugging their latest projects and tossing out clichés to claim similarities between their childhood emotional breakdowns and those of the Flower Mound Country Club Murder victim. At least the media hadn't cashed in on the grisly mass gravesites along the roads and in the jungles between Mexico City and the border. Yet.

Four rings, then a message at the Angel Sky Bar, in scatter-fire Spanish. I closed the call. I didn't want to leave this sort of news on a recording, especially on the machine of a bar Diego may not have frequented in years. If 'frequented' was ever the right way to describe Diego's relationship with the Angel Sky Bar.

Come to think of it, why would a man in Diego's line of work take a woman for over-priced drinks at the most cosmopolitan bar in Mexico City, spectacular view or not?

Okay, LeFave, put the phone down. Disengage fantasy life and focus, before you say or do something dangerous you can't take back.

The little black dog squealed and zoomed off of my lap. Yikes! Zack was back at the front door, now battering with his fists. This had to stop for Sammie's sake.

As the project of the Mad Scientist, Sammie proved I could implement the behavior management tools expected of even the most mediocre psychologist. However, there was one tiny downside. When you block one reflex, another behavior jumps in to fill the void. Now, when a situation arose that called for barking, Sammie registered the stimulus, choked the forbidden response deep in his throat, and spurted air through his windpipe as best he could. The result was an agonized whine which varied with the occasion.

Most of the time he howled as if he'd been abandoned and left for the buzzards. But he was quite an artist in several vocal ranges. He'd perfected an endless repertoire including a staccato yip-wail indicative of being stabbed with an orange-hot poker and a weeping wail that mimicked an Italian wife at her husband's open-casket funeral. Most of the time, he stuck with his staples, the 'hello,' 'let me have a bite,' and the tortured 'intruder at the door' all-out-panic wail.

I could have trained him out of wailing, but even the Mad Scientist could not hold a gun on a crying puppy. By the time Sammie was six months old, my dog owner reputation in the Cove had reached a low usually reserved for death row criminals.

I held Sammie to my chest, cooed comforts, and peered through the barred hatch.

"Can it, Zack! You're going to give my dog a heart attack!"

I was too late. Zack had canned it, and split. When I opened the door, his business card fell at my feet. His personal cell number was circled in thick red ink. On the back, he'd printed: "Your cell? Your fax number? Medical hit in Mexico City. Time matters."

A medical hit? What was a medical hit? Bomb in a hospital? Camilla's extensive psychiatric history?

Sure. I'd keep his little card right next to my heart.

Camilla didn't need more rumors circulating through the Flower Mound, America, and just possibly, the Universe. To Eileen's friends, Camilla was still the frightened and frightening girl she was after her father's murder. If they had any idea what troubles Camilla had overcome, starting with Timbercreek Hospital in Dallas, if they knew about the assault she'd survived, I'd like to think they'd go at her personal life with less vengeance. Maybe if they knew that during my visit after the rape, Camilla had used her little writing pad—she couldn't talk with the ventilator her mouth between the wires holding her jaw steady—to ask me questions about every girl and mom at the Flower Mound just like she did in her letters. Not one negative word about anyone, but of course, the monster who'd done this to her. Barely alive, she was still the kind Camilla I'd known since I was five, the little girl marked as an outsider long before her father was murdered and the barn burned down.

Camilla's emotional problems and even the story of Camilla's supposed seduction of Steven Sloan were more colorful and "expected" because of the true reason the dark under-sized little girl with all that wild blue-black hair never had a chance.

Camilla was half-Mexican.

Eileen had called my parents from Paris back then. "Can Jessica come to France? Camilla wants to see her so badly, and her doctors think a visit from a friend could help her find hope."

France? *France!* The Paris adventure, no matter the reason for going, would not have been remarkable for my country club riding buddies. But, for me, the trip was the biggest thing that had ever happened in my life. I hadn't closed my eyes on the night before or on the flight over. Instead of reading the six books I'd insisted were barely sufficient, I'd worked my way through two rolls of film with shots of every flight attendant, each tiny plastic plated meal, the in-case-of-crash card, the Coke mini-cans, and each of the six cute little bathrooms.

That week spent with Camilla deepened our relationship in a way that would last a lifetime. We weren't little girls anymore. Camilla had been raped. Childhood was over.

Every night in Paris, I knelt on the floor beside Camilla and lit a candle. The first night a pair of hysterical nurses jumped on me and yelled a list of rules in French. After that, I used tiny birthday candles nicked from inside birthday cards in the gift shop and kept our little altar under the edge of Camilla's sheet. Once we were in the "light" I said prayers, mostly a re-mix of Sunday school verses and I sang bits of popular songs, though anyone who wasn't immobilized and heavily sedated would have claimed my tuneless screeching was harmful to the patient.

But that was then. The report I'd promised the police department was now. Sammie Davis settled between my feet and moaned the "wha-aa, wha-aa" of a siren winding down as he dozed off. Suzi claimed a strategic position between the refrigerator and me, just in case.

Back to my laptop. The photograph folder automatically downloaded from the station showed a hundred and six files and more to come. The first was a wide angle of the murder stall. I'd start with the traditions and mythology behind each piece of the altar, give my insides a little rest before I moved to psychological interpretations of the scene. Not that the spiritual worlds of the Aztecs and early Spanish Catholics weren't loaded with deep psychological meaning.

I straightened the painting propped against my coffee. Only Camilla would see beauty in this most gut-wrenching of Frida's works. Then I noticed two elements in *My Birth* that did not fit with the malicious theme, the way the pink and white petals, mere dots in the murder scene photograph, did not belong on an altar to Our Lady of Holy Death.

In the painting, the blood was dark. Not fresh, though the bodies were still in action. The already rotting blood flowed onto pristine, perfectly tucked sheets, which made no sense in a depiction of the worst kind of death. Even more puzzling, the wide edges of the pillowcase under the dead, but still birthing, mother were embroidered with lacy pink and white tendrils.

Why would an artist bother with a touch of beauty in a room of horror?

To provide a little hope to go up against death?

A little love in a manifesto of hate?

Camilla had been that little bit of hope and love for the girls of La Merced.

CHAPTER 13

The reality of La Merced knocked me over the afternoon Camilla escorted the Freedom Celebration tour through the city's magnificent market. She took her time though only a few hours remained before her wedding.

The smells hit me first. Scents of lime, wafts of guava, vanilla, peeled mangos, sizzling tacos al carbon, and the luscious fragrance of softening cinnamon-laced chocolate. The fragrances of La Merced bloomed, burst, and faded with each corner.

The colors were a new world, a vibrancy in nature I'd never known existed. The oranges glowed. Apples were stacked in scarlet pyramids, the bite of cider in the air. Tomatoes were deep red, ten varieties, turgid with flavor. Around the edges of the fruit market were rainbows of halved melons. The aisles were endless and stacked to the ceiling.

Next the meats. Like most *Norte Americanos*--accustomed to politely packaged chunks of deboned red flesh and skinned white flesh in thoroughly bleached snack packs—I was blown away. Beef, poultry, seafood, pork, and lamb, each had its own domed gymnasium where meat was separated and stacked high on tables with no refrigeration. Mounds of livers, tongues, ribs, steaks, and fish, all sold by cut and day of catch or slaughter.

Today's meat was the most expensive, yesterday's a bit less, three-day-old meat was a bargain. The oldest cuts were ground into a paste and sold by the scoop. For the cook who's a stickler for freshness, there was a section with animals penned and pooled where sellers slaughtered and dressed the purchase as the chef looked on. Most vendors operated low hibachis in the aisles and grilled for buyers in a hurry or hungry.

The full body emersion into the colors and flavors of La Merced was nothing like a trip to Costco or Walmart. Walmart and Costco shoppers are dwarfed by soaring walls of merchandise encased in room-size cellophane-sheeted chunks, off-loaded from semis and arranged by forklifts in the middle of the night. Shoppers are insulated from each other and products by vast spaces of gray painted concrete floor. Plenty of room to steer the family around in a molded plastic racecar the size of a small apartment.

Not so for shoppers in La Merced. Over-filled booths burgeoned into impossibly narrow aisles. Shoppers twisted and turned to skirt jutting items, often body to body with other shoppers and soft-spoken children offering samples from the family garden or kitchen. Or holding up a 'please adopt' warm ball of soft love from a basket of tight-eyed kittens.

Another difference was La Merced's awe-inspiring section devoted to supplies for witches, dream sellers, and regular people who heard the call to cast a spell, perform magic, contact the dead, or improve their financial future. Kiosks were crowded with flowers, incense, candles, gleaming crucifixes, ceramic saints, and rosaries--blessed and unblessed. Beyond the traditional icons were shelves of animal skulls, jars of spider legs, a variety of placentas, dehydrated mice, rats, stone and candy skulls, all sorts of herbs, and ceramic bastardized skeleton saints.

Giant warehouse stores in the States are frigid, efficient, and require an entry pass. La Merced was alive with the heat of people in a constant party mood. No invitation needed and class distinctions disappeared. Since our visit was on Saturday, there were many families, from the elite to the desperate. Beaus and husbands buying flowers for their sweethearts. Parents treating children to fresh made candies and *cascarones,* eggshells filled with confetti, to crack on each other's heads. Little girls wore crowns decorated with bright ribbons that trailed down their backs.

Every corner of La Merced was more than crowded, people on the move--hawking, cooking, toting, playing. Busy people, but not people in a hurry.

"Payso—oo, un pay-sooo, un pay-aa-so-o!"

Angel-faced children tapped our legs, tiny palms upturned. I'd even spotted a chimpanzee walking on his palms and flat feet, his back a twisted hump. My stomach fell. Oh, God. The low galloping creature was a human.

After our tour of the market, Camilla led Nancy Margaret, George, and me, out onto the main boulevard fronting La Merced. Up to that moment, I'd been the consummate tourist, careful to guard my separateness. On my face was pasted the generic tourist brochure smile that said, "Ah, yes, it's quite enlightening to see how some people have to live. But really, I have nothing in common with these people. I should have worn a hat. I hope we don't have fish again for dinner."

The vapid freedom of those thoughts, the exemption from caring, was something I'd lose a few minutes later. No, that's not what happened. What slipped away on Camilla's afternoon tour, only for a breath or two, was the tequila guzzling, man-chasing, carefree façade holding me together.

The Freedom Celebration trio, absorbed in our own struggles to stay tethered to the Earth, had only a vague sense of Camilla's work in the barrio. We didn't ask questions because the notion that a Flower Mound Country Club playmate, a girl who'd achieved high marks at the finest European schools, a girl who showed expensive horses—devoted time and money to the girls we saw along the avenue in front of La Merced--didn't match up with any reality we understood.

We simply didn't get it. Perhaps one day I'd mention these girls in a travel anecdote over a glass of expensive wine. More likely their images would simply fade away.

Then, it happened.

I was touched to my soul by a stranger. To her, I was no one. One more gawking, foolish passerby. But the beautiful girl whore with the double-layered yellow hibiscus behind her ear would never fade completely out of my mind.

The girls of La Merced.

Alluring and composed they waited, twenty feet apart, their backs bowed against storefront walls. Not the burned out, boxy matrons who dominated the border trade. These were the shy children who sit behind the card table in front of your neighborhood Walgreens selling Girl Scout Cookies. A few could have been over twenty, many could have been eleven. Mostly they dressed competitively in black, red, or white spandex tube skirts and netted hose with matching see-through blouses over training bras. Plastic jewelry. Sandwich-sized plastic purses slung from their shoulders by long, thin straps.

She stood in a doorway--twelve, thirteen, maybe. Her girl body concealed in a modest dark skirt and white blouse, no doubt, outgrown and donated by one of the rich girls going to the convent school. She had light brown skin and full black hair tucked into a barrette on the base of her neck. She was soft. Unafraid. She smiled, her dusky eyes gazed straight into my well buried heart. Her message clear.

Could you spare some of what you have? Surely, a gringa on this dirty street as one more sightseeing lark has a dollar she doesn't need?

Of course I could spare a dollar. But I didn't reach for one.

Two days after my stroll through La Merced, I would be back at the University of Texas to pin down the kind of future the girl with the yellow flower could not imagine. I'd curse how tough I had it while I sucked black coffee and jotted down chemistry formulas at the Longhorn Efficiency Apartments.

The beautiful girl whore would be right here. Waiting. Two weeks after that, when my larky, sightseeing gaze landed on the married professor-doctor who would offer me the world, the beautiful girl with the double-layered hibiscus behind her ear would still be here. Alone. In the shadows of La Merced.

With nothing.

The girls of La Merced brought back the image of Camilla's daughter at the horse show yesterday. Oblivious to the chaos, Ana Teresa had set up a chair and a small table in the aisle in the main barn. She'd taped a sign on the front: Office of the Texas Secret Express.

Somewhere in the brain of every girl there must be a time when a cell lights up and commands: Go forth, child, and form a club.

"To Houston! And hurry! Special message from the president!" hollered Ana Teresa, stationmaster of the Texas Secret Express Club though she was the smallest child. Ana Teresa handed a folded sheet of lavender paper to the girl waiting on a black pony.

"To Houston!" The rider shouted back. She'd saluted, spun with Paul Revere urgency, and galloped for the barn area designated as Houston.

Ana Teresa, stood on her tip-toes handing off messages for Dallas, El Paso, or San Antonio between her classes throughout the day.

One thing was for sure. Ana Teresa wasn't a girl with nothing. She had a good life with a grandmother who loved her. She also had a father. A father I intended to locate and inform of Camilla's death even if my announcement resulted in nothing more than fulfillment of my personal commitment.

Ana Teresa also had quiet times, downcast eyes that reminded me of Camilla after her father's murder. But she was different from her mother in that she had many friends and sometimes giggled and shrieked like the other girls.

Camilla had always kept to herself. Her request to talk to me last night was out of character and should have startled me out of my routine.

CHAPTER 14

I settled at the kitchen table, a blank document on the laptop screen, fingertips over the keys. Don Wilder wasn't as excited about my scene profile as he'd indicated in his apology, but I needed a paragraph or two completed today. At least an outline.

Date: click. Time: click. Police Department Consultant Secure Identity: Click, click, click. Victim's Name: 'smart spelling' finished her name after the first three letters.

The rest of the page was blank. Maybe I should pull a form out of the list and use those questions as a guide. I updated the time stamp. Seemed like I should put in a title. Something like "Camilla Cervantes de la Cruz, One Woman Crusade." A title was not only a dumb idea but would give away that I wasn't even taking a stab at objectivity. I updated the time stamp.

With Suzi and Sammie dozed out, the only action in the room was the cursor. Wink. Wink. I nudged Sammie with my toe which he pretended not to notice. I updated the time stamp. Wink. Wink. So that's why they called the blinking little stich a 'curser'.

I didn't need a few paragraphs or an outline. What I needed was a step-wise plan to find justice for Camilla. Distance myself? I don't think so.

I picked up the phone and punched in the number for the Angel Sky Bar. Hung up before the tone. A call back would make me feel like I was getting somewhere. I'd leave a message. Leave my phone number at a Mexico City bar? Not a good plan. Then again, what if someone at the bar knew how I could reach Diego?

Sammie tapped my shin and laid on one of his tiny teeth grins. *"Hey, lady, I need a warm spot."* I understood that feeling.

"Okay, Sam, but only if you promise to whack me up the side of the head if I drift off task."

He hopped up on my lap and stuck his nose under his paw.

I entered the number for the Angel Sky Bar. This time maybe someone would be walking past the phone and answer. I'd hang up if the call took off in a scary slant. Before I had to make the choice, my eyes were wrenched to the screen on the counter television.

The broadcast had jumped from a pretty face behind a desk in a shiny studio, to a barren field of lumped black dirt surrounded by a square fence of soldiers at attention, legs spread, boot-to-boot. Inside the square, Federales shoveled body parts from shallow graves. The field was dotted with tiny yellow plastic flags on metal stems, the kind we use here to designate spigots for automatic sprinkler systems. Skulls were lined in rows on the flat bed of a truck. Between the soldiers, the outstretched arms of wailing parents, spouses, and children, undulated like alien tentacles.

Competition for news on the Flower Mound Country Club Murder had accomplished an over-the-border freedom of information highway that had defeated CNN and the BBC. Secret agreements, death threats, and airtight international pacts of silence, in place for decades, were out the window once the gossip channel lawyers went to work. Reality sucks.

My fingers again tingled over the laptop keys. George would have a good laugh when I told him about my attempt to contact someone at the

Angel Sky Bar all these years after I'd staggered out of the club. Now, if I could report to George that I'd spoken with the manager . . . . Was the manager's name mentioned in the club's message? I punched in the number again. No mention of the manager.

If I left my number, someone would call back and even if he or she had never heard of Diego. I'd have a definite contact in Mexico City. Once I'd set the sequence of calls in motion, my brain would be freed from obsession and I could concentrate on the Chief's report.

Rationalization is a muscle. Use it or lose it.

I ignored my earlier paranoia or good sense and left my number. *Maybe I should have left George's cell number, too.*

Sheesh. My best hope to resist punching in the number for El Angel Sky Bar like a phone-seeking pigeon on crack was to focus on my computer screen and concentrate on scene evidence piece by piece.

"Come on, Sammie, you promised to help." He cocked his face sideways in an impossibly cute apology.

The phone chimed. I jumped, cracked my knee on the underside beam of the heavy table. Whoa. The Angel Sky Bar that fast?

"Dr. LeFave?"

A woman. American accent.

"Jane Bailey here."

Talk about emotional whiplash. "Okay . . ."

"Several sources have informed me--" she said.

"Ms. Bailey, did your sources also 'inform' you that dozens, maybe hundreds or thousands, of journalists have been beheaded in Mexico for calling a lot less attention to cartel activities than you have?"

"Those of us with the task of informing the public must have courage."

"Right. That's what this conversation is about. Courage."

"It's just that I thought you, as a longtime friend of Eileen Cervantes' daughter--"

"Her name is *Camilla* Cervantes de la Cruz. I have nothing to say about Camilla, but I can give you a hot lead on an unhinged Scientologist harassing a local psychologist."

"What?" In my silence, she regrouped. "Now, Dr. LeFave, about Ms. de la Cruz, I thought with all the stories, you--"

"Ms. Bailey, you made a mistake with Diana Sloan. A big mistake with me."

Dead air.

"I want to avoid any more mistakes. Which is why I called."

"This isn't a good time."

"I can call back. When's a good time for you?"

"My Birthday's in late January. I'll have some time then."

"I wouldn't have called, but I believe you and Mrs. Hypatia Scarletti's daughter--"

"Nancy Margaret."

What?"

"It's Miss Scarletti and her name is Nancy Margaret."

The current that had seared through the clasped hands of our little circle in the darkened stall long ago shot from my ear to my heart. First ice, then fire. I hung up.

She knew.

If the one meeting of the "Golden Ones" had not heralded the beginning of Camilla's decent into a list of psychiatric disorders, maybe Nancy Margaret and I could have seen the our little club as precious or even a somewhat normal childhood rite of passage. We might have shared the extraordinary happening with others.

But we didn't.

After Camilla was sent away, Nancy Margaret and I closed off the afternoon in that darkened stall with one dying beam of sunlight. We never spoke of it, even to each other. I was the only person, other than

Nancy Margaret, still seeking a spiritual path and secreted away in a Tibetan ashram for over two years now, who would recognize the crossover between the Santa Muerte murder scene and the blood ceremony of the short-lived Dorados.

How could Jane Bailey know?

She didn't. She probably didn't.

Then again, who knew what kind of fantastic story could be in the works? With Facebook and Twitter aglow without a nano-glimmer of fact-checking, with Diana Sloan in Jane Bailey's pocket, and with Zack Harvey threatening blackmail, I could be declared insane and dangerous within minutes.

Well, fine. Let'em rip. Camilla never let gossip slow her down. Jane Bailey's incredulous interruption gave me just the boot in the rear I needed.

"The victim's name," I typed into the record, "is Camilla Maria Cervantes, married name, de la Cruz." From there I proceeded on automatic. ". . . Our Lady of Holy Death, as worshiped by drug cartels, is a bastardized combination of the Aztec Queen of the Dead, *Mictecacihuatl,* and *Señora de las Sombras* (Lady of the Shadows)."

I split the screen with the murder stall photo on the left. ". . . When represented with an outline of blue flares, Santa Muerte is sometimes mistaken for Our Lady of Guadalupe, a particularly ironic misidentification since worshippers of the patron saint of Mexico, ask for the spiritual strength and courage to do what is right by family, friends, and God. Devotees of Santa Muerte pray for the power to kill and the guile to go unpunished. Santa Muerte was first popularized in Mexico and Latin America as part of the Catholic Day of the Dead."

The Day of the Dead.

Steel fingers crushed my heart, followed by the now familiar struggle for air, and the plummet into catastrophic darkness. Which was the opposite of what was supposed to happen with celebration of this holiday. The Day of the Dead is set aside each year as a celebration of life, not death.

Joy, not sadness. When we were little, Camilla told the amazed Nancy Margaret and me about the day-long party at the cemetery when you got to sing and dance with those who have already been taken. The one day in a year when you can look square into the smirking face death and shout: *"Hey, Death, is that the best you got? A little fear? Eh. So what? Yes, you'll take me, too, one day. But not today! Not today!"*

Which makes it odd that the murderous narcos adopted Santa Muerte as their patroness and that my brilliant and beautiful stepdaughter, Kelly, a non-Catholic Anglo girl, set to graduate as the youngest valedictorian at the University of Arizona, would choose that day to die. With her decision, a shroud had dropped around the person I was before, the person I would never be again.

Stop it, LeFave. Today is about Camilla. Maybe this time, maybe for Camilla, you can do something right.

Sammie squealed and wrenched out of my lap before I heard the knock on the door. He smacked the floor, four paws skittering. He spun a full three-sixty on the slick tile then shot for the front of the house.

Suzi staggered up to join Sammie and me. I peeped through the hatch. The man looked as if he'd taken a trip through the McDonald's deep fryer on his way to my house. Before I had the door fully opened, Sammie's intruder wedged his foot across the threshold.

"Have you told anyone?"

CHAPTER 15

The sweaty half-moons on Scott Maris's not so electric blue sport coat streaked to his waist. Any man in his right mind would have shucked the jacket hours ago.

"Of course not." My stomach flipped. "I haven't told anyone."

"Thank God." Scott let out a sigh he'd been holding a while and wiped is forehead with his sleeve.

Okay LeFave, your response was quick, gave nothing away, but what are you going to do for a follow-up? Most important was maintaining a peaceful, unsurprised expression. Camilla, of course, told him she intended to speak with me last night. If Scott could see the blank page in my head, he'd be gone and I would have missed my second chance to discover the life change Camilla had in the works.

A pathetic deceiver, I directed my attention to Concepción's Our Lady of Guadalupe shrine in the corner of the courtyard. I eked out a "Hmmm . . ." as if I noticed a surprise among the photographs, silver *milagros* (miracle charms), candles, flowers, and tiny gold crowns.

Sammie saved me as he so often did in awkward conversations. Haunches down between Scott's feet, he stared upward, his misguided vocal cords locked into a wail best described as the screech of an off-key national anthem crooner stuck on the "land of the free-ee-ee-eee!"

"Would you like to come in?"

Scott peered over my head and took in as much of the house as he could. "Are you alone?"

"Concepción's in the back of the house. Please, come in."

"We're the only ones who know. And I'm being followed."

Scott hauled in a deep breath and strode through the house without a glance left or right. He landed in the chair next to where I'd sat, his eyeballs straight to my laptop screen.

"I wish I had half the courage Camilla had," he said.

Ditto.

Suzi, who knew a stranger in the house loosened the rules, took up a spot with her determined face flattened on the glass of the French doors to the back courtyard. I let her out while I fought to settle my expression. Ten seconds later we heard a splash.

Scott turned toward the sound. "Oh my God, your dog just fell into the pool!"

The panic in his words had nothing to do with Suzi.

"She'll be okay."

I pointed to Sammie. "And the little black dog here on his deathbed? He'll live."

Scott flicked his eyes back to my screen. I should watch my step. He was terrified. He was also high.

I closed the computer, turned Frida's *My Birth* face down, and offered coffee. A shared cup of coffee would equal conversation and the mug would give me something to hide behind.

He pondered. "Do you have a beer?"

Even better. Without turning my back on him completely, I retrieved a Tecate from the refrigerator and joined him at the table.

Scott threw his head back and drained half the bottle. A bodacious Rolex with a diamond bezel twinkled from under his shirt cuff.

"Camilla and I were in love," he said. "I'd do anything for her."

"I didn't know." Love, won or lost, requited or unrequited, certainly qualified as a personal motive. Tell me more. I fought back the volley of questions that would blow my cover for sure.

"There's a lot you don't know about Camilla's life," he said.

"I'm sure you're right. As of this morning, my number one goal is to correct that situation."

He gripped his bottle and leaned toward me. "Dr. LeFave, what they said about Camilla burning down a barn, killing a dog, and maybe . . . was that true?"

"I have no idea." So this was how it was going to be from now on. Even with someone who claimed he loved Camilla. "I wouldn't think the answer would matter to a man who'd 'do anything' for Camilla."

"I would--and did--anything she asked. I loved her so much it made me a crazy person. Coming here was crazy, but that's what I mean. Anything she wanted, I'd do. I couldn't stop myself. She wanted me to protect you."

My heart jumped, premature questions ticker-taping across my brain. Lucky for me, Suzi growled, her face mashed into the outer glass of the closed door *next* to the door I'd left open, and gave me a reason to look away. I sat down, my best active-listening expression in place.

"Camilla and I had an argument out at the stable," Scott said, "a loud one. I was being an idiot, like always. I threw a halter or some horse thing in her direction--not at her. Just in her direction . . . . You want me to let your dog in?"

"Suzi's fine. You were arguing about her plan?"

A veil of skepticism rippled over Scott's face and his expression hardened.

"Her *plan?* Which plan?"

Scott was in the talk show business. Even high, he'd recognized my question as a blind stab for information. He stood and pivoted toward the front door.

"Please stay. Like you said, Camilla wanted you to help me."

"What Camilla and I argued about is not important."

"Everything that happened last night is important."

"I'm going to be arrested, aren't I?" He sat back down.

"Because I'll mention to the police that you and Camilla argued?"

"No. There were other riders still at the barn who heard plenty."

"If you're worried about how the argument looks, you should go to the police before you receive an invitation."

"I wanted to talk to you first. Camilla said when it came to important situations, you always knew what to do."

A flash of Camilla's forehead with its perfectly placed hole flared up, in case I might fall for Scott Maris's flattering claim that I knew what to do in important situations.

"Okay, then," I said. "My advice is that you should tell me and the police why you and Camilla were arguing."

He scratched at the gold "T" on the red label. "She said you even went to see her in France."

Scott wanted to confide in someone close to Camilla and wanted to be that someone.

"Oh, yeah," I said. "I was a great friend. Eileen offered over and over to make arrangements for me to visit Camilla in Dallas or Phoenix. I was too chicken to go into a mental hospital, but I told Eileen my parents wouldn't let me go. Then, when the offer was Paris--I was on the next plane."

"That's not how Eileen and Camilla thought about it."

"Camilla was more than raped. That bastard knocked out her front teeth, broke her jaw in multiple places, and crushed her larynx, before he started in on her body. When I saw her, I didn't think she'd live until the next morning. And now this. How is Eileen doing?"

"Really bad. I can't imagine anyone taking it worse. She blames me for not keeping Camilla safe. But she blames herself even more."

He glanced toward the front room again, scooted to the edge of his chair, and held up his bottle.

I switched the empty out for a fresh one.

"I failed Camilla and now I'm next on the list. I know I am." Fear lent his words a thin boyish tone. "I was the one who met Camilla at the airport, the one who knew what was going on. Party's over for me." He studied my face up through his lashes.

"Maybe we can help each other."

"I know what you're thinking, Dr. LeFave. 'If I was so worried about Camilla, why did I leave her alone at the show grounds?'"

"Good question." Camilla might have his heart, but Los Insurgentes had his *cajones.*

"I didn't kill her. I couldn't hurt Camilla. I loved her. All I wanted was to know what was going on. She was moving here full-time, you know, for Ana Teresa to be near her grandmother and for the schools. I'm already living in the house at the Flower Mound Camilla picked out for us."

His devotion rang true, but the details of his relationship with Camilla did not land straight up.

"I don't know how I can help you or myself," I said, "unless we share what we know."

"About last night?"

"What do you know about Camilla's work in La Merced?"

"No more than you probably."

"What about Diego de la Cruz, Camilla's ex-husband?"

"That he is Ana Teresa's father and that he's not around."

"What about an address? A phone number for someone who might know how to reach him?"

"No. Why is de la Cruz important?"

"Because he is Ana Teresa's father. And because I want justice for Camilla. I assume you want the same."

"Of course." His eyes darted around the kitchen without seeing anything. "Doesn't matter if I do get arrested. If I go to jail, at least I'll be alive."

"Talk to me."

"Okay. But you have to listen. You are in danger."

"I was Camilla's friend. That's it."

"That's enough." Sweat popped out anew on his forehead.

"Scott, you're paranoid. That's what happens with long-term cocaine addiction. I don't believe a Mexico City drug cartel cares if I live, die, or play chess with pogo sticks."

My heartbeat throbbed in my ears. Forget putzzing with the Angel Sky Bar, I took another beer from the fridge. No human should ingest three dark Tecates in ten minutes, but I was confident his liver was accustomed to the onslaught. And I had to keep him with me.

I held the bottle out for him.

"Help me out here, Scott."

"Okay." He sat back. "Actually, I'm relieved."

Down the hall, Concepción screamed. "Celestino! Jessie, they've arrested my brother!"

Scott leapt to his feet. I grabbed for his arm. Missed.

The green glass bottle slipped through my fingers and shattered on the tile.

CHAPTER 16

When I returned to the kitchen, Suzi scowled, her defiant mug still pressed into the glass pane of the door next to the open door. A member of the LeFave family before the mad scientist project, she intended to bark until I opened the door she preferred. Which I did. Suzi Wong is a taker.

I switched the television to a British news channel for the soothing narration, popped the top off a Topo Chico, and held it up for a long fizzy swig. Then I started in on the green glass shards and beer with a broom and a roll of paper towels. Concepción felt a little better with my assurance that the police had only arrested Celestino because he reported the crime and because he didn't take off like the others, and that George would make sure her brother was safe at the jail. She'd stayed in her room to call family scattered throughout Mexico.

Suzi made time lapping up as much Tecate as she could. The boy dog curled into a ball and moaned softly under the table. Sammie knew his world had changed, but he didn't know how or what was next. We made a good team.

Task accomplished, a babe on each shoulder, I dragged my body down the hall to my bedroom. My breeches and once white choke-collared shirt were so sandy and stiff, I couldn't stand myself. My boots were bowling balls of fire. I settled the dogs on the bed and went to start the shower. Over my shoulder, the giant cool bed and warm babes beckoned my body which was weary from the inside out. After my shower, I'd lie down for a few minutes. Or maybe now . . . just for a few . . . I closed my eyes, let my mind drift.

Today was the first day after Camilla died. No need to rush. Hurrying doesn't mean you can skip a single teardrop. Camilla was gone. 'Gone' hits a truer chord than 'dead' or 'deceased,' or the God-awful 'expired.' Gone marks the end of something good. The end. Underneath the pain and exhaustion, a scrabbling ache fluttered in my chest. *Gone.*

Time separates you from the universe when you suddenly lose a person you believed would always be in your life. At first, when the news hits you—no, not right then, but a few minutes later, when you are convinced the news is true--time stands absolutely still. When time starts up again, the clock creeps along for a few unbearable hours. You would give anything to have the day over.

Then, all at once, time is gone. The day she died is over. And you'd give anything to have it back.

Next you live through 'the first Monday since' and 'the first Tuesday since' and so on, for a week. Somehow you exist through 'the first interminable Christmas' and 'the first birthday'. After the holiday markers, time takes off. Runs away, out of reach. Now time is no longer a measure of hours or days. Time becomes a unit of distance. The longer you live, the further away you are from the day the unthinkable happened.

The further you are from yourself.

"Bong, bong." Pause. *"Bong, bong."*
What?

The chimes emanated from my nightstand phone, the unlisted phone known only to George and the medical exchange. My brain came to life in that confused place where dreams and reality overlap and it seems you can choose to go either way, but you can't.

My knees ached and sand gritted into my cheek.

I checked phone ID. How did he . . .

"Ready to play, Dr. LeFave?"

I jerked to sitting. The light outside had slipped from blazing orange to lavender. Dusk already. How could I have let that happen?

"Probably not. You said 'medical hit'. I have access to U.S. criminal and hospital records. If you're talking Mexico, international permissions are impossible right now."

"Once again, you underestimate the information gathering skills of my religion."

"I think that's called 'marketing'."

"Give me an hour. Check your fax for a photo of your friend. Four days ago. Passed out in an emergency room. Looks like a drug overdose."

"Wait--"

Click.

Zack knew exactly how to play the game. Most likely Zack Harvey's information mounted to no more than a boy with time on his hands and the skills to make creative use of records hacking and Photoshop. Maybe I wouldn't even bother with Zack's fax.

Yeah, and maybe I'd never clip my toenails again, either.

Because I'd check out Zack's information didn't mean I'd accept what he had to say at face value. Yesterday, I would not have answered his call. If by some freak of nature I had answered accidentally, I would have dismissed his emergency room claim outright. But things had changed.

Yesterday I was sure Camilla would have told me about an emergency hospital visit, no matter the reason.

I'd promised to take Concepción to the jail to see her brother and still hadn't peeled off my show clothes or initiated combat with the boot remover. For that battle, a belt of caffeine was an absolute necessity. Suzi and Sammie trotted behind me to the kitchen, then parked their butts on either side of my ankles while I rumbled through the drawer of single brew coffee canisters.

"What do you think guys?" I asked my assistants. "Doughnut House? Or Paul Newman's Special Blend?"

Tails wagged evenly with each option. I was on my own. Paul Newman's Special Blend was a bit harsh on an empty stomach. But Doughnut House made me think of the police. No way I wanted to examine my relationship with law enforcement at the moment, so Paul New—

The scream of a man spattered with buckshot burst from Sammie's lungs.

Oh, God.

A streak of black fluff shot through the kitchen, rounded the corner, and, unable to establish traction, smashed full speed into the wall. He re-grouped and made a right to the front door. What was that about? No one had knocked.

By the time I arrived, Sammie bounded in hysterical circles two feet above the tile, his agonized wail louder and more desperate with each circle. If the person outside my door had a soul, he had an index finger on the number for the Society for Prevention of Cruelty to Animals.

My first guess was Zack Harvey with dubious information and a stack of glossy brochures. My second was that whoever was following Scott Maris wanted to know more about the occupants of the house. Then again, could be George's make believe paparazzi. If my streak of really bad luck was still on course, I'd open the door to a messenger from Los Insurgentes who wouldn't have the courtesy to wait through the questions George suggested I ask the shooter before he blew my head off.

Still. Why not knock?

I peeked through the monk's window. Hmm. No one in sight. No one in the courtyard, no vehicles in the cove. I did notice that my tire was now completely flat.

Sammie was close to exploding an internal organ.

"So, what now, Sammie?" The boy dog was a bit deranged, but he did not make things up.

Someone or something was out there. Or had been. UPS or FedEx would try the doorbell and leave a package. I opened the brass-framed window again, stretched up on my tip-toes, and locked my eyeballs downward. No package.

I picked up Sammie. "Little buddy, there's no one out there. Not even a bug."

Wham! Sammie pushed his back legs off my chest with such force I stumbled backward. He hit the floor scraping for a hold on the tile. Three enormous bounds and he now stood on his hind feet between the long leather couch and the windows across the front room. He dropped the needle back down on his squall of torment.

"What is it, Sam?"

I crossed to where he paddled air, picked him up, and carried him back to the alcove in a baby-bundle hug. Which always calmed him. Except it didn't. His legs churned in washing machine mode. Then his paws hit freeze.

"Thwack!" came from the front of the house.

Get down! Flashed across my brain.

Sammie squirted out again, and I landed on my stomach beside him. He returned to his paddling ballerina pose at the front windows. What was that sound? A revolver with a silencer?

"Wait for me, Sam-sam, please wait," I whispered.

I crawled Marine-under-the-wire-style, boots dragging, to where Sammie quivered, his nose puffing a circle of fog on the glass, his eyes locked on a target beyond the courtyard.

Chin on the window ledge, I scanned left to right. Nothing moved. No one. Squint-eyed, I swept the yard and the street. Nothing.

"Hang on, little buddy." I rubbed Sammie's head and clamored up on my knees. Checked left and right again.

There! I caught something. A flash of black the size of the neighbor's Labrador retriever. The evil Lab who loved to jump his fence and torture Sammie.

Then, no. Something glittered in the darkness. The neighbor's dog did not glitter.

A dutifully repressed memory sparked in the back of my brain, flooded my nervous system, then exploded into a shriek that ripped the lining out of my throat and rattled the windows. Sammie bounced into my arms to rescue me. He was perfectly quiet, his round black eyes wild. His little heart thumping.

Golden rings with gigantic stones—those glitter.

Chapter 17

Oh, God. The 'gunfire' was the snap of a miniature dandy in a prim black suit shutting my curbside mailbox. The peculiar tiny man was not a dream character or one of those monsters running around in your head after three days with little sleep and lots of tequila.

This was not happening. Not happening. Not happening.

With my scream, the tuxedoed roach had scuttled across the cove and disappeared in the dense cedar and oaks of the cul-de-sac. Sammie's bizarre abrupt silence had been a wiser response than my scream, which ended any doubt that I was in the house. And not particularly brave.

What a liar. Not even a bug, I'd promised Sammie.

If the police were right, Camilla was murdered to send a message from one hideous, faceless, drug cartel to another hideous, faceless drug cartel. If she was killed to settle a score in her personal life, it was a life I realized, more with every moment, I knew little about. Thus, her murder had nothing to do with my simple world. Nothing to do with me.

Back in the kitchen, I grabbed the phone and stabbed in George's number. No way I could make it through the ring and hang up routine five times without damaging an internal organ myself. Each time I hit the message, I screamed for the full three minutes allowed.

George picked up on my third attempt.

"George! The roach! The cockroach!"

"What?"

"The cockroach! He's here! The cockroach is at my house!"

"Time to slow down on the Carmel Valley, Miss Rose."

Nothing to do with me.

"He was here! At my mailbox. The dwarf, George, the dwarf!"

He sucked in his breath and kept it. "What is going on?"

"Exactly. What the hell *is* going on? I'm scared, I'm really scared."

No more minimizing the odd ambience in Camilla's Mexico City house, no matter how soused and crazy I was. No more pretense that our excursion through La Merced had been a cultural treat equivalent to parading non-Texan visitors through the Alamo.

A pause on George's end. Then, "Whatever you do, Miss Rose do *not* go out to your mailbox." His tone was a couple of octaves toward soprano from his usual voice. "He probably planted a bomb that can blow up the whole cove."

"George?" Air. I needed air.

"What?"

"Why is it every time I reach out to you to calm myself down, you always find a way to make things worse?"

"I just think you should take precautions." His breathing told me he was on the move, the phone tucked between his chin and his shoulder.

"He knows where I live, George. Why does he care where I live?"

"I--"

"I need you here now!"

"Still no paparazzi at your place?"

"No! Just criminals and freaks. Hurry!"

George was right about one thing. When narco-trafficantes send a message, the more dead bodies, the merrier.

I called into the Chief of Detective's private voice mail and left a near hysterical report of the cockroach sighting, which meant nothing to him since the only mention I'd made of the Freedom Celebration Trip was the wedding. I hit redial: "While your officers scan data bases, find out what you can about Scott Maris. He knows more about Los Insurgentes and Camilla's murder than he's telling."

With guard dog Sammie snuggled into my chest, a piteous groan bubbling in his throat, I double-checked all door locks then settled the dogs on the bed. With Herculean effort I liberated my feet from my high-tops, tossed aside my sandy riding clothes, and bolted through a health department recommended shower.

The night had just begun and riding boots are not made for running.

Minutes later, garbed in Longhorn burnt orange sweats, flip-flops, and Sammie, I took up the boy dog's earlier position at the front windows. I had a panoramic view of the cove. No lights inside or outside and no moon. I'd spot the Town Car's mega beams the millisecond George turned in. Too bad about the security system. Wonder how much would cost to have it back in service in, say, fifteen minutes?

But no worries. George could make it from the downtown Petroleum Tower to Mt. Laurel in ten minutes. Any second now he'd park his big Lincoln next to my disabled vehicle and join the babes and me. Where was he? He'd better not be holding out for a clever parking spot.

He should be here by now. He'd heard my panic. Why wasn't he here?

Oh, no. Of course. George had been intercepted by the police or Los Insurgentes. Maybe both.

By now my phone was tapped, if Scott Maris knew what he was talking about, and he certainly knew more than I did. Scott had 'dropped by' to feel me out, to check out if Camilla had spoken with me last night and to determine if I'd retrieved the letter or bomb out at the curb.

Scott was now aware that I knew nothing about Camilla's plans, but Los Insurgentes did not know I was harmless. What had that bejeweled man, no doubt a miniature ambassador for Los Insurgentes, put in my mailbox?

If Los Insurgentes thought I knew too much, they'd assume George did too. What had I done? Had I just lured my best guy friend to his death? Whoa. Slow down.

I closed my eyes. *Please, Camilla, please. Tell me what's going on?*

Okay, okay. Get a grip, LeFave. Put your degrees and expensive training to the test. This was the perfect moment to initiate self-hypnosis. Cool air in. Warm air out. With the proper breathing and concentration, I could transport my mind. I could replace the image of the cockroach with the image of something lovely. Pleasant. Soothing. Bambi's forest would be nice.

You are in a misty forest . . .

I pictured Bambi crying for his dead mother. So forget the misty forest. A cool body of water would be an excellent choice.

Before you is a peaceful lake . . .

Forget the peaceful lake. Self-hypnosis transported me to a body of water all right--the swimming pool at the Las Vegas Flamingo Hotel circa 1947. A lake with bullet-ridden bodies floating in it. My gray matter had seized on the similarities between my cockroach dilemma and the final hours of Las Vegas gangster, Bugsy Siegel, and dropped me into his world.

Bugsy had been too cocky. Like me, he'd under-estimated the ruthlessness of powerful people several rungs up the gangster food chain. Bugsy, aware he'd fatally messed up, had, like me, cut the outside lights to better spot headlights on approach. Then he'd sat down across from the wall of windows in the front room of his girlfriend's Beverly Hills house. And he'd waited. I took my place on the long sofa beside Bugsy.

First cones of golden illumination highlighted his pretty face. Then a hurricane of shattered glass blasted into the room. Bugsy, a bizarre grin on his face, bounced up and down and side-to-side next to me as he soaked up fifty bullets from rapid-fire machine guns.

Or, at least that's the way I remember Warren Beatty played him in the final scene of the movie.

Oh yeah, this self-hypnosis stuff is magic.

CHAPTER 18

The phone in my hand chimed.

I jumped, Sammie slipped through my elbow hold, and splattered onto the tile his tiny feet scrambling for traction. I bent to rescue him. The phone slid free and took an impressive double bounce on the tile. It took three bangs on the wall to re-establish a dial tone. My eyes had adjusted to the darkness in the Mt. Laurel house, but my heart rate and shaky hands hadn't adjusted to cockroach claws in my mailbox.

If I insisted on tile floors and couldn't adapt to a cell phone, maybe I should at least get a headset or an implant of some sort. Something about imminent death had me less particular about people invading my personal space.

The phone call was George closing in. Had to be. I propped Sammie on my shoulder and tapped callback.

"Dr. LeFave. Thanks for returning my call."

"Oh, shit. I mean, *what?*" I scanned the cove. No lights.

"Jane Bailey here, I just called . . ."

"Oh."

"Do you have a minute?"

"Yes."

I would have spilled my guts to a taped political survey if it would chase Bugsy's bouncing and bloody ghost out of my living room.

First I heard a soft gasp of surprise. "I—never mind. Thank you for talking to me. About Mrs. de la Cruz, I have a daughter myself. Frankly, I'm disturbed by the ugly rumors on the day a mother's only child has been murdered."

"Haven't those rumors boosted your ratings?"

Jane Bailey was quiet. She had no way to know that on the back screen of my brain, machine gunners in limos and narco-trafficantes without faces were headed for Mt. Laurel.

"Ms. Bailey, I'm going through a crisis at the moment. Forgive me if I'm a tad rude. But it has crossed my mind that your career will benefit with Eileen off her game, even for a few months."

"Dr. LeFave--."

"It's been done before. Remember the "Texas Cheerleader Mom?" *Please, George. Turn into the cove. I'm going into full-out idiot mode here.*

"Who? I moved to Texas from Missouri two years ago."

"Oh, the Cheerleader Mom went national." I should stop. Back it up. Change the subject. Reporters record their calls. "Surely you heard about the Houston mom who put out a contract on the mother of her child's friend to improve her own child's chances for a spot on the cheerleading squad?"

"The way the Cheerleader Mom figured it, her daughter's pom-pom rival would be too distracted to make a good showing at tryouts."

"That's horrible."

"It *was* horrible, and I don't know you well enough to dump that dreadful story on you." *George, please hurry.* "It's just that I'm in a situation here, Ms. Bailey."

"I won't take much of your time. First, I wanted to apologize for the interview at the Flower Mound Country Club. Mrs. Sloan presented herself to me as a concerned friend."

"Okay . . ." After I'd compared her to the Texas Cheerleader Mom, Bailey deserved a minute.

"Also, I'd like to provide our audience with another view of Camilla Cervantes, a perspective from someone who is both a psychologist and a longtime friend. Someone who can provide a clinical perspective on bipolar illness."

"Bipolar *disorder.*"

The idea of a live interview held a certain appeal if I could trust Bailey to stick to pre-approved questions. That I even had that thought was evidence enough that my mind was tanking at an astonishing rate.

Headlights flitted across the front windows. George.

A big car circled Mt. Laurel Cove and drove slowly back out of the cul-de-sac. Had to be George. He'd survey the paparazzi situation before he made a commitment.

Seconds later the car, an APD black and white, parked under the street light on the opposite side of the cove. Could be the Chief ordered surveillance to prevent intruders. Could be the officer was here to make sure I stayed in my house. Either way, the police presence would discourage Los Insurgentes. Maybe even Zack Harvey.

I tuned back in to Ms. Bailey.

". . . A viewpoint, Dr. LeFave, that no one, other than her mother--"

"Ms. Bailey, Eileen will be destroyed by this crime."

"Jane, please, just Jane. I know. That's part of why I wanted your input . . ."

Sammie Davis shrieked, kick-bounced off my chest, and lit out for the French doors to the back courtyard. Something huge crashed on the flagstone beyond, taking plant life and terracotta down and with it.

Not possible. The wrought iron fence was a deer fence, ten feet high. The gate had a padlock.

Another crash. More aftershocks. I had to get the patrol officer's attention. With less than a minute to establish surveillance, he wouldn't key on a back door invasion.

I wheeled toward the living room and the front door.

No save Sammie and Suzi first!

Whip reverse to the kitchen.

"Hello? Are you there, Dr. LeFave? Hello?"

Oh, yeah. The phone under my chin. "Ms. Bailey? Jane? Jane?" I rasped.

The siege at the rear of the house accelerated. More crashing. Now shouting. Someone screamed. I scooped up the babes.

"There's someone breaking into my house!" I held Sammie to my chest and our hearts throbbed in spastic rhythm.

"Pardon? I can't hear you . . ." Bailey's voice broke. "Dr. LeFave, are you okay? Should I call 911?"

The other line blinked. I checked the ID, dropped Jane Bailey's call, and punched the flashing green button next to George's name.

"George! You're too late! They're breaking in through the back courtyard!"

I couldn't make out his words. Only sputters. I heard hollers and whistles from the crowd in the background. He was calling from a club or a sports event. Great. More sputters from George, clipped curses, threats. In the foreground I heard what sounded like gigantic cymbals slamming together or metal boxes smashing to smithereens on the street.

Four seconds later, Lady Gaga fell face-first into my kitchen.

Chapter 19

"Run, you ignorant bastards! Run for your lives!"

George yelled over his shoulder at his entourage armed with cameras, light poles, and reflector screens. The gang skirting the small pool suspended their attack on the Mt. Laurel house and faded into the darkness.

I slammed the doors behind him, so stunned and relieved I wasn't spurting blood in twenty places, I barely managed a squeak. Sammie filled the silence with rat-ta-tat gunfire and bounced his little front paws back and forth from the Saltillo to George's shins. Suzi ambled over and rubbed his ankles like a hungry cat.

"I thought I was going to have to kill me a photographer!"

This was my White Knight?

George ripped off his platinum locks and death white rubber face.

"What? What?" One syllable sentences were all I could manage.

He popped the mask back and forth across his thighs as if knocking off rainwater.

"Lady Gaga, George?"

"Only mask in my closet."

"I'm not asking."

"Those blood-suckers out there are your fault, Miss Rose."

"Oh, for sure they are. I must have ordered the wrong Welcome Wagon service."

"You promised the paparazzi weren't here."

He scruffed Suzi behind her ears, pushed out the sides of the mask to make a rubber boat, and settled Sammie on the floor in Lady Gaga's head. The boy dog cooed appreciation. He'd wanted a rubber mask boat his whole life.

"The paparazzi weren't here, George, until you managed to turn my house into a bad lounge show."

He brushed me out of his way, grabbed the newspaper off the kitchen counter, and lunged for the front room constructing a megaphone on the hoof. The swirl of crusaders from the back courtyard now panned the front of the house with spotlights on small cranes. The patrol car presence held them at the curb.

George flung open the front door and stomped through the courtyard. He breached the wrought iron gate, swung it extra wide, and let it slam-jangle behind him. With the clang of the iron hinge, reporters on the front line ducked.

"Hey!" George said. "I said *hey!*"

His followers whipped to attention and froze. I half-expected them to salute.

"Your attention, everyone! Your attention! *Now!*"

All hope faded that my neighbors would ever consider me normal.

"Ladies and gentlemen of the press, in case you are not aware of the law, in Texas it is not a crime to *shoot* a person who comes onto your private property without an invitation! And shoot to kill!"

George's hollered presentation must have alerted the officer to the potential for a lethal dustup, because he brushed away the hungry mob with his siren and a blitz of yellow, blue, and red sweeping lights.

Task accomplished, George used his key to relock the back gate and joined me in the kitchen. Once he was out of the mask, the fashion balance in our relationship had righted itself. George in French linen slacks, blousy white shirt, Bally belt and shoes. Me in well-faded University of Texas burnt orange sweats and one flip-flop.

"What about Celestino?" I asked.

"Taken care of. He will be provided a menu in English and Spanish thirty minutes prior to each meal."

"Thank you. Concepción is panic-stricken and I don't blame her."

"Okay, let's see what we're dealing with."

George swooped the television remote off the counter, switched the mellow British broadcast to his source for news beyond sports, the Jane Bailey channel, and plopped down at the *rancho* table. Sammie Davis and Suzi Wong were still into their "Thank God you're back, George!" leaps and yips. He pulled them into his lap, along with Lady Gaga's face now clutched tight in Sammie's tiny front teeth.

The television newsreader announced that the Hotter than Hell Horseshow Classic had been cancelled due to security concerns.

"Hope the world doesn't stop turning," George said. "Has a horse show ever been cancelled before?"

"Once."

Wow, he must be worried. George had never asked a horse question before. "The show was at the polo grounds in Midland, Texas. It rained, a flood actually, but we kept going. With all the water, the jumper hooves were making sinkholes in the turf. So, the polo club made us close down the show . . ."

George wagged his head. For a moment, I thought he regretted the flood and my missed weekend of jumping horses over things. Then I realized his frown reflected disapproval of the counter television. He unplugged the screen, set it on the floor, and headed back into the front room.

". . . Because," I continued, a bit louder so he wouldn't miss a word, ". . . because the *crown prince* of Saudi Arabia was playing at the Midland Polo Club the next weekend . . ."

George staggered back into the kitchen, shoved aside the coffee maker, hoisted the sixty-inch flat panel onto the counter, and plugged it in.

"The real crown prince, George! Anyway, the polo hotsie-totsies claimed we were ruining their precious polo field, which was true. The take-off and landing spots were deep bogs by then. And forget the grass, that was long gone . . ."

George tidied up the angle of the screen, then whirled to face me as if I'd suddenly materialized out of a puff of smoke.

"What in God's green *earth* are you talking about, Miss Rose?"

"Horses . . . . Sorry, I forgot."

Once he had his smut channel up on the giant screen, he repositioned himself at the table.

"Now, about this short guy at your mailbox, Miss Rose, you're sure it was the same dwarf?"

"He is not a dwarf, George. He's a perfectly proportioned mannequin off a wedding cake. There's something seriously wrong with him."

"Okay, then. Are you sure it was the same perfectly proportioned wedding cake toy?"

"No, I'm not sure at all. How could I possibly be sure with the hordes of tuxedoed tiny men dripping rubies and diamonds roaming the neighborhood?"

"Good point."

"Why was he at my house, George?"

"Wide swath, Miss Rose. Wide swath."

I pushed down the returned urge to choke the man.

George hopped up and dumped Sammie gently out of Lady Gaga's face. In case a photographer lurked outside, he crowned his head with the tube mask and tugged Lady Gaga's cheeks left and right until he was a rock star again. I followed two paces behind him.

"Stay away from the door!" he said, with the terse pitch of a firefighter who'd made a tough decision about who to save and who to let die. He pointed to the front door in case I didn't comprehend which door he meant. "I'm going in."

"But you said--"

He trotted through the courtyard, yard, and into the now quiet street. I flipped on the exterior lights and surveyed the scene through the eerie front windows with the babes. I checked for Bugsy's perforated body before I sat down.

George-Lady Gaga waved at the cop who jolted to attention and blurted something I couldn't make out. Then George jerked open the metal mailbox flap and shoved his hand and arm inside the cylinder the way a veterinarian palpates a mare to check for pregnancy. He swiveled his blonde woodpecker head left and right as if he expected blind side attackers. Then he waved to the officer again and shrugged, as if disappointed that the mail hadn't arrived.

Back in the kitchen, George brewed a one minute cup of the Ethiopian dark roast he had shipped regularly to my house. Then, he plunked into a chair across from me, his forehead in a snit.

"What?" I asked.

"The little freak slashed your tire."

"No, the leak started this morning. Probably drove over a braiding needle or a tail comb out at the horse show."

"Not unless someone out there takes out tangles with a machete."

Nothing to do with me.

"Okay, more likely your usual knife, but there's a definite slit," George said. "A slash."

"Oh, God."

"Wide swath--"

"Stop it!"

"No worries on the tire anyway, Miss Rose. If some nar-kiddo wanted you dead, he wouldn't stop at tire damage."

George's presence had relaxed me when he'd arrived, and now Ole Reliable had kicked me back to running horror scenarios in my brain.

"You piss off anyone in the horse show crowd lately?" he asked.

"Not that I noticed."

"A slashed tire is usually someone with a personal grudge and too chicken-shit to go face-to-face. Or, who knows, maybe some husband or father who couldn't afford a new set of golf clubs went berserk. Just had more expensive horse manure than he could take, and cut up a whole row of cars. In any case, we have a more immediate situation bubbling on the front burner."

The idea of a random slashing made the flat tire notion bearable. Even the theory that 'if Los Insurgentes wanted me dead I'd be dead, so don't worry about it', calmed me. Denial is a beautiful thing.

"Okay," George said, rocking onto the back legs of his chair. "If the dwarf wasn't here to put something in your mailbox, he must have been here to take something out."

"Like what?"

"That giant stucco eyesore can hold a couple of kilos, easy."

"Ridiculous."

"If I remember correctly, the last time you saw this creep, he was stuffing cocaine into your luggage."

"That's your fantasy, not mine."

"Just living in drug-crazed reality, Miss Rose. It's not my fault that many citizens in our land of opportunity require a snort to survive the American Dream."

The slashed tire had distracted me from the obvious. I crossed to the counter and collected the mail. "Concepción brought this in earlier."

"Where is Concepción?"

"In her bedroom. Calling all over Mexico. Informing the few relatives she has left about the murder and her brother's arrest."

"Why? Don't her relatives watch Univision?"

"Mexican news outlets fired crime reporters who weren't already dead a long time ago. Something about body parts showing up as parking lot decorations."

"Now that doesn't sound very fair."

"Yeah, well, here 'bombshells' get ratings. In Mexico, 'breaking news' gets you inside an oil drum."

Today's delivery included four credit card offers, two packets addressed to 'current resident', a *Texas Monthly*, a letter telling me I'd won either a blow-up houseboat or eight million dollars, and one hand-addressed envelope. No return address and Mexican stamps. I waved it in front of George's eyes.

Resigned to his fate, he staked his elbows on the table and rested his chin on his fists. "Well, let's hear it. I can't believe I ever let you drag me into this whole sordid Mexico City underworld drama."

George had had his own marital struggles that summer. His wife of less than a year had been on a trek around the world "to find herself," which she claimed to have lost by marrying into the wealthy Ramsdale family. Ramsdale American Express statements from Rome, Cairo, and Dubai, convinced George that, while she might not find her 'self', she was looking in all the right places. George's marital dilemma was just the sort of pathetic tale that had qualified him for the Freedom Celebration Trip.

"Okay, George, why *would* a well-placed, handsome, and temporarily married, lawyer such as yourself throw in with two nineteen-year-olds bent on self-destruction?"

George sighed. "Ah, yes, Miss Rose. This is the question I have asked myself a thousand times."

I took a sip of coffee to clear an opening in my clenched throat and slow my heart. I read out loud.

"'Dear Jessica,

I'm writing this letter from Las Palomas, in case we do not have a chance to speak privately before word is out about my plans. I have been warned that if I do not change my mind, I will be in grave danger, but I am determined. You should be aware that anyone who sides with me will be at risk. I am confident I am making the right decision for Ana Teresa and for myself.'"

I peeked up at George. "Oh, God, George. She did have a chance to speak to me. But I took off. I wasn't there for her."

"Keep reading, Mother Teresa."

"'I am confiding in you because you have been with me since the beginning and you have always accepted me. When you came to France, I was so afraid and lonely. Then when you showed up for my wedding! I hope you still have the print I bought for you in the market. Maybe you were just being nice, but when you said you understood why I love Frida's paintings, I believed you and loved sharing her stories with you the way my father shared them with me. The one I gave you is my favorite. If you do not understand the choice I'm making, look again at Frida's picture.

Remember that death and life are not separate, and pray for me.'"

I looked up again. "This part about life and death not being separate? She's talking about this club we had when we were kids. The Dorados."

George was instantly distraught. "That voodoo business? I thought that was a joke."

I gave him a one minute version and he was more distraught than ever.

"'Most important, I trust you completely in judgment and in heart. I know that should anything happen to me, you and Concepción will watch out for Ana Teresa. In Texas and in Mexico City my little girl has people who love her. Still I worry.'"

"She's talking about Diego," I said. "I know she is."

"Miss Rose, your child-like, thinly disguised, and hormonally driven judgment is painful to watch. Los Insurgentes and your wedding cake mannequin are Mexico City people, too."

"That's insane."

"Did you ever get around to asking Camilla about the creep going through your luggage?" he asked.

"No, she'd showed us such a great time, I didn't want to seem ungrateful."

"How delightfully psychologist woo-woo of you."

I slammed home a killer glare and started back in.

"'You understand, Jessica, that it is sometimes necessary to avoid the police. Tell no one of this letter. It is not always good news to be the chosen one for a person such as me. I hope, when the time comes, you will not think I have asked too much.

This is not a gentle warning.

Your Friend Always,

Camilla Maria Cervantes'"

"George, you know what this means, don't you?"

"Something deep I'm sure."

I dropped the letter, picked up Frida's painting, and studied the women. How could this be anyone's favorite?

"George?"

"Present."

"You realize that had I stayed at the show grounds last night__"

"Not going there."

"If I'd stayed I would know why Camilla was murdered."

CHAPTER 20

There's something terribly wrong with the baby.

She's not a baby, for starters. And she's dead. You can see that much, if you have the courage to linger. The vista of *My Birth* is straight-on between the mother's legs as she gives birth.

Frida wanted her audience to feel what she felt, to experience the pain of the childhood polio that left her with an uneven and disfigured leg, and to absorb the shock she felt when her young teen body was pierced by a steel rail in a horrible bus collision. The accident that almost ended her life, left her with constant pain and internal scars that later killed every baby she struggled to bring into the world.

My Birth, painted in 1932, was the first in a series the Mexican artist used to document major events in her life. The project was her husband Diego Rivera's suggestion as a way to dispel her ever-present physical pain and depression.

In *My Birth*, the deceased baby, half in and half out of her mother, has the head of the adult Frida Kahlo and droops into a pool of blood. The face of the mother, also dead, is covered by a sheet to honor Frida's recently deceased mother. The weeping Virgin of Sorrows, her head pierced with daggers, observes the grim process. She weeps the Virgin of Sorrows weeps she can see the future and can do nothing to change it. The Virgin of Sorrows knows that the baby girl is stamped for sadness, that her birth is not joyful, but rather the entryway to a terrible nightmare she will not be able to escape.

It wasn't hard to see why Camilla identified with Frida beyond the similar ethnic heritage. The Virgin of Sorrows had wept at her birth, too. The murder of Camilla's father was the 'polio' that left her crippled, her torrential emotional disorder, coupled with the Paris rape and beating that left her barely alive, was the 'steel rail' that pierced her young body and destroyed her dreams.

Frida considered *My Birth* her most joyous work. The images she painted represented her resolution to give new birth to herself, to accept the scars of fate and concentrate on the abilities she still possessed. Of course, Camilla, who remembered every Frida story her father told her, would choose *My Birth* as her favorite. By sharing the pain of her personal destruction, Frida had found the courage to live with horrible physical pain and a way to accept that she would never have what she most wanted in life—a child. Camilla had found the courage to live beyond the rape and beating and to accept the impossibility of having what she wanted most in life—her father.

That both women had discovered a way to live beyond their pain was a fact that both amazed me and left me with a secret, selfish ache for what could have been if Kelly had found a way to survive.

And now some sonofabitch had ripped away the life Camilla worked so hard to make for herself. Frida's canvases featured dismembered body parts, bloody splashes, skeletons, and cutaways of corpses underground. But she'd also gave her viewers hope. Sprinkled here and there among the gore, she painted symbols of life and love—lush plants rooting out of corpses, calla lilies sprouting from rot, fruits mixed with skulls, the delicate lace under the head of a dead woman.

Had Frida Kahlo painted the murder stall this morning, she'd have included the joyful, naked Saint Mary Magdalene and the tea rose petals. An observation that told me absolutely nothing about Camilla in the murder stall or what I was supposed to realize from the painting.

I settled *My Birth* on the kitchen table facing away from George, who sat who sat with a Tecate in one hand the remote in the other.

Even with the patrol car out front, the separation between houses and insulating woods meant that beyond the windows all was quiet and black. The television screen, ridiculously over-sized for the room, dominated with color flashes and sporadic garish commercials. The effect was right out of Star Wars.

"George?"

"Guilty."

Sammie, curled in his Lady Gaga boat in my lap, wailed a reminder that his tummy needed scratching. I obliged.

"I won't let Camilla down," I said. "Whatever that means."

"What if 'what that means is' that some drug lord adds you to the daily list of contract kills?"

"I'm not crazy enough to think I can go up against a cartel. Camilla's letter is not about drug trafficking."

"Right. I'm starting to worry about your mental state."

"Camilla's writing about something personal or she wouldn't have written me at all. Here's the painting she mentioned."

I held the print up between George's eyes and the television.

"*My Birth*, my ass!" He scooched backward and flapped his hands as if the picture was on fire. "More like my *after*birth!"

"Camilla bought a Frida Kahlo print for you, too, George. Where's yours?"

"The first trash receptacle we passed on our lovely afternoon prostitute cruise."

"We were idiots."

"I won't deny that," he said. "Why couldn't she give you one of those Kah-loco prints with piles of fruit and monkeys on the uni-brow's head? Didn't you think her choice was a little weird?"

He squeezed honey into his already sugared coffee. Suzi appreciated his whooshy efforts and ooched closer.

"Not exactly. This was her favorite. She was getting married, having a baby. Somehow her gift of *My Birth* made sense."

"That is so much bullshit."

"Okay, I pretended it made sense. The truth is, when I looked at this picture then and when I study it now, all I see is a dead mother giving birth to a dead baby watched over by a stabbed Virgin of Sorrows."

"Not to be crass, Miss Rose, but what Camilla has is common with the women in this picture is that she, too, is a corpse."

"Maybe Camilla expected me to remember what we were talking about when she gave it to me."

George mimed pouring liquid into his mouth from a two-handed canteen. "Good luck with that. While you're channeling that weekend, you might want to revisit the tattoo on Camilla's bodyguard."

"Her driver."

The shiver of doubt I'd held at bay since the Chief waved his Mexico City crime reports in my face took an icy trip through my nervous system.

"What if I'm wrong, George?"

"About Camilla's bodyguard being her driver? You are wrong."

"No. About everything. Life is different in Mexico. I know I've denied this all along, but there's some truth in what the Chief said about how gangs force people into cooperation. What if Camilla really was in trouble with Los Insurgentes and wanted out?"

"Then, I guess we can safely say that pulling the plug on a drug cartel isn't like canceling your cable service."

CHAPTER 21

"There it is, Miss Rose, the church!" George aimed the remote at the Google Earth zoom on the historical section of Mexico City.

"What church?"

"*Your* church!"

"What?"

I peeked from behind my laptop where I'd spent the last half hour researching Mexico City websites and altars to Our Lady of Holy Death while George kept up with Google Earth sweeps and side stories on the Flower Mound Country Club Murder. My hope was to locate another connection to Diego beyond the Angel Sky Bar, not that leaving a message constituted connection.

"The church where you and David got married!" George sat forward and tapped the enormous Cathedral.

"Hardly."

"Too bad. I was about to be very impressed."

"That's the *Catedral Metropolitana de la Asunción de María* (the Metropolitan Cathedral of the Assumption of Mary). It holds thousands, George, thousands."

"So, I wasn't the only one of your friends and relatives who did not receive an invitation?"

I scooched my chair from behind the table and toward the screen. "What I told you was that David and I were married in a *Registro Civil*—a government office the size of a closet—located around the corner from that Cathedral. We had our rings made at the gold market right . . . here." I took the remote out of his hand and tapped the western edge of the *Zócalo*.

"We had one guest, the taxi driver witness. The little jeweler delivered the gold bands to our hotel room on the most romantic night of my life."

"Oh." George sat back. Through all our time together, I'd never shared the story.

Ours was the kind of wedding, I'd believed, best accomplished as invisibly as possible. Later I wished I'd brought a little courage to the situation and made sure his daughters were part of the ceremony. On an afternoon a couple of years later, the two of them asked to see my wedding dress. When I said I didn't have one, both little girls were sad for me. Until one of them asked why she wasn't invited, I'd assumed they wouldn't have wanted to attend.

One more wrong assumption where David's girls were concerned.

With the Google Earth survey of Mexico City's El Centro, from the Zócalo to La Merced, all sorts of disconnected details from Camilla's wedding weekend zapped around my brain. But the zaps were pins of fire that soared, burst, then, one by one, floated down and out without fleshing into images I could link with people and places.

Then a rush. One of the tiny points of light hesitated, turned course, and settled into a corner of the Google shot. I tapped the screen. "There! See this street behind the Cathedral?"

"That's where you were married?"

"No, Diego stopped twice at a store on this block."

"So? It's a store. My guess is a liquor store."

"No, it's an antique and religious items store. Diego didn't buy anything. He stopped there to talk with several men. I think they were waiting for him when we arrived."

"We call that a mob planning meeting here. In Mexico I think the term is a mass murder strategy conference."

"I don't know what was going on, but whatever they talked about, they were intense. Maybe you're right. Maybe the expensive tequila sours and noble stories were a façade, but those stops were real and important in Diego's life. Something important to Diego might have been important to Camilla. They met through her work in La Merced. Now I'm getting somewhere."

"Slow down with the 'getting somewhere.' May I refer you to my earlier statement regarding your way of dealing with loss?"

"I heard you and agree with you completely. I don't deal with death straight on. Maybe I can't. Maybe hiding from the pain by running after something else is the best I can do for now."

George's expression softened. "Just keep in mind there are people who care about you and don't want anything bad to happen to you."

"My commitment to Camilla is deeper than my own issues. I believe Camilla would want Ana Teresa's father to know that his little girl has lost her mother and I already have some leads on how I can find a phone number, maybe even an email address."

"Right."

"The manager of the Angel Sky Bar is practically in my pocket." I grabbed the portable phone and slid the laptop off the table and into my lap. "He should call any minute now."

George broke his devotion to the screen to stare at the phone. "You left your number at a bar in Mexico City?"

"Yes. Maybe the bar manager won't call, but storeowner was definitely a friend of Diego's. If I can just remember the name of the store . . ."

Focus, LeFave. Just a name. Think. Think. I hit redial for the Angel Sky Bar. After six rings, the receiver was answered then cut off before I'd said two words. The next attempt went to the message after two rings.

Who was I trying to fool? I only remembered the Angel Sky Bar because I'd helped myself to an etched souvenir goblet. Sammie had a better chance of coming up the name of the religious antiques and icons store. Then boom, my problem-solving brain hopped into the twenty-first century. Memory doesn't matter anymore. Three taps and I had the Google Earth Zócalo frame. I focused the shot on the street behind the church. I clicked another Google tool and captured the phone number of *San Luis Fernando Artes.*

"Got the number," I said, as if I could impress George.

"It's not like some random shopkeeper is going to know Zorro."

"Buenas tardes," I said, smiling as if the man in *San Luis Fernando Artes* could see my face and appreciate my friendliness. I tore a sheet out of my notepad, crushed it into a ball, mouthed "smart-ass" and bounced the paper bomb off George's shoulder.

--

"Yes. English is great. I'm looking for a friend of mine."

--

"Diego de la Cru--"

Click. Dead.

"Dang!"

George retrieved the wad of paper I'd airmailed and banked it off my forehead. "Told ja."

He returned his focus to the screen.

"So, he didn't talk to me. The store could be more of a lead than you realize."

"Or more of a delusion than you realize."

"The first time I saw Our Lady of Holy Death was when Nancy Margaret and I helped Camilla's father get to Heaven."

George wheeled to face me. "*What?*"

"The first time--"

He wagged his head as if denying any part in a very bad crime. "No, no, no, no. Back up on the stream of consciousness, Miss Rose. I'm your friend, so I know where to file what you just said, but I'm thinking you shouldn't spill your whimsical history with the police or these media whackos."

"Of course not. All I care about is the truth behind Camilla's murder. Anyway, the next time I saw Our Lady of Holy Death was when Diego took me to San Luis Fernando Artes."

George reversed to stare at the television.

"Interesting, right?" I said.

"How about terrifying? Does it occur to you that an antique store in the heart of the city would be a perfect front for a cartel? Think of the import-export opportunities."

"Santa Muertes are easy to find in that part of the city. In fact, all the shops on the block behind the church are loaded with Catholic artwork and Day of the Dead ceramics."

"Sigh. And me with all my Christmas shopping done."

"I can't believe the Fernando Artes guy won't talk to me."

"Oh, well. It's a good thing you have that bar manager in your pocket."

"Yeah, well whoever is in charge at the Angel Sky Bar must be new on the job. He's stopped taking my calls."

I hit redial for San Luis Fernando Artes.

"Buenas tardes, Señor."

Click. Phone dead. George stared, ready to pounce on the hopelessness of my quest.

"Yes," I said, to my imaginary pleasant storekeeper. "I'm the woman who called before."

Silence.

"Sure, sure," I said. "Thanks. Yes, a phone number would be lovely. Let me get a pen."

Silence.

"Oh. You can't find it? Okay. Great. You can call back and leave Diego's number on this phone and thank you so much."

I attempted a satisfied grin and checked George's expression. He hadn't bought one syllable.

Still somehow I felt closer to my goal. More images from San Luis Fernando Artes oozed into consciousness. The high ceiling, the narrow, plaster-walled room, the lovely-scary Santa Muertes, the dusty angels. The dusty emotions from a time when I had no fear of freedom or passion. A time when I had nowhere to go, nothing to lose.

"George," I said, my hand on his shoulder, "I don't think we'll ever again feel as alive as we did that weekend."

Too much had happened, too many mistakes.

"I'll settle for just staying alive, Miss Rose."

"As for my call to Fernando Artes, I don't consider it a total bust. At least we know not everyone in Mexico is too busy dodging bullets to answer the phone."

"Doesn't it bother you," he said, "that every time you mention Diego's name, the phone goes dead? Doesn't it trickle across your mind that there's a reason for that?"

I carried Sammie to the counter, slipped Camilla's letter back into the envelope, and placed it on top of the up-side-down photograph under the plastic divider tray in the silverware drawer. My personal treasure chest where I kept the stack of letters I couldn't read and the flash drive with Kelly's high school valedictorian speech.

"Perfect," George said. "Your plan is to hide the information the killers are after in a kitchen drawer?"

"George?" I sat back down. "We should go Mexico City."

"No, we what we should do is go to Vegas and check into the Cosmopolitan under assumed names."

"You know I have to do this. Ana Teresa's father deserves to know that the mother of his child has been murdered."

George gazed at the ceiling. "Ah, yes. Let's worry about what good ole Diego deserves. Camilla was mixed up with drug traffickers. How can you possibly persist in the fantasy that your lover boy is some kind of noble hero of the people?"

"It's possible."

"No, it's not. Let's take a look at the evidence. First of all, the man is not on the Google-Bing wire. Which means he's dead, or that Diego de la Cruz is such a common man, uh, name, that I can't shake him loose from the horde. Either way, you aren't going to find him."

"I've thought of another angle. Diego's parents were friends with Frida Kahlo and Diego Rivera."

"If I'm not mistaken those two people are dead."

"Yes, but they have websites and people who maintain lists of all their activities including their friends. His parents knew them well."

"And you know this because? Let me guess. Because a handsome stranger bought you booze and told you his family knew rich and famous people? That's a fresh approach."

"No, because he showed me a photograph of his parents marching down the *Paseo de la Reforma* (Reform Walkway) arm-in-arm with Frida and Diego under a Communist Party banner. I didn't mention it before because I knew you'd go all whacky over the 'communist' thing." And why I wouldn't give up the bloody clothes in Diego's car without a loaded gun at my head. The hammer cocked.

George sighed. He pulled out his plastic brain, changed his mind and dropped his head into his hands, and wagged back and forth. Then he looked up and landed me one of his dreaded 'time to get serious' glares.

"Miss Rose, I cannot watch you go down this Diego-was-so-special trail any longer. You saw what you wanted to see and Diego saw what he wanted to *have*."

"He was named after Diego Rivera."

"And I was named after George Washington."

"Maybe Diego really was, and still is, a freedom fighter. Why is that so hard for anyone to believe?"

"Because a raggedy-ass farmer does not marry a rich heiress."

"Still--"

"Not to be cruel, Miss Rose, but did you hear from Camilla's husband after that weekend? A phone call? A nice bouquet, perhaps?"

"Everything about my life was different then. The weekend was more of a time out. I didn't expect him to get back in touch."

"Of course, you didn't. I don't want to burst your delusional bubble. But a picture of a couple of internationally known artists leading a parade of Communist protestors sounds like something cut out of an old magazine or stolen off Wikipedia."

The picture was a black and white on slick paper folded in Diego's wallet. Must be a copy, I'd told myself. Otherwise, he wouldn't treat it with so little care. I'd pushed questions about the photo out of my head, the same way I'd dismissed Camilla's bloody and peculiar taste in art.

No way would I admit it, but now that I was less of an emotional wreck and sober, now that I'd spent years in the study of human behavior--the whole 'freedom fighter' pose did ring more like a pickup line than a way of life.

I regrouped. "Even if Diego is a lying jackass, he's Ana Teresa's father. I want to know he is aware that the mother of his child is dead. That's it."

Maybe George was named after George Washington. His profile matched George's on the quarter. Stoic. Metal.

"Okay, George, you're right. If I found Diego, I couldn't let go without asking him if he knows who could have wanted Camilla dead." Not even a blink.

"Which," he said, "is irrelevant because to ask Diego a question you'd have to find him, and you are not going to find him."

"I know it's a long shot. Maybe he hasn't seen Camilla since the wedding, but we have to try."

"We? . . . Us?"

"Just thinking out loud."

"Oh, yes. Thinking. Weighing alternatives, considering the facts. You are simply 'thinking out loud' with only the most innocent of motives. Nothing manipulative or confusing at all, Miss Rose."

"That works."

"I'm not going to Mexico."

"I don't expect you to. My thoughts are all over the place. I confuse myself. Like you said earlier, I've had a terrible shock . . . and, like you said, you want to do whatever you can to help me through this . . ."

"I am not going to Mexico and there's not an ant's teeny-weenie *speck* of possibility that you can change my mind."

"I'm shocked you'd even suggest that I would pressure you to do anything you didn't want to do."

George's eyes were Frisbees. He threw up his hands. "Go for it then."

"Thanks. I will."

"Hide a letter-- sought by a machine-gun wielding drug lords--in your silverware drawer and take on a drug cartel all by yourself!"

I don't know what made him think I'd be by myself.

CHAPTER 22

George stayed over since the Mount Laurel house featured a patrol car out front and Concepción in the kitchen. Also he picked up my vibes that I needed him close. Tomorrow was big and even the plans were out of my comfort zone. Even further beyond what George would tolerate which is why I would play stealth travel agent.

Anyone, including George, who'd compared my house to a Taco Bell would retract their evil comments with one bite of Concepción's rolled brisket tacos and fresh Texas Gulf Coast shrimp tostadas made with homemade tortillas, crushed peppers, and ripe tomato chunks. The fragrance of fried corn, jalapeños, and limes permeated the house. Camilla was there, too, though I was the only one who saw hummingbirds when Concepción lit the table candle.

George and I, along Suzi and Sammie, had been our version of family since David was murdered. Concepción joined up on the afternoon she'd bumped my shin with a packet of cheap white washcloths as I crossed the International Bridge from Nuevo Laredo to Laredo. I'd bought half of dozen packs and suggested I could use some help carrying my load of Emiliano Zapata paraphernalia to the immigration barrier.

She'd grabbed the iron rail behind her and bounded up, her face joyful--as if I was a long lost relative bearing gifts. She quickly took my bags, no doubt out of fear that when I noticed her distorted leg I'd back out of the arrangement. As we reached the center point of the bridge I did back out of the original deal. She'd be right. I was indeed a long lost relative of some kind. I suggested I would need help unloading Emiliano in Austin, if she'd like to hire on.

She'd curled up under a rug and after a turn back at the Carrizo Springs checkpoint we made it to the land of opportunity through a hidden niche in Big Bend National Park where the water was low enough to drive across. When I'd called George with the news of my new friend, he'd charged over to the Mt. Laurel house with a threat to call immigration. Small, quiet, Concepción met him at the door with Mexican cinnamon-laced creamy sweet coffee and a tray of warm *pan dulces*. The original reason for his visit never came up.

George took his usual spot next to Concepción at the table set with over-sized Talavera bluebird plates and ice water in cobalt goblets. Salt in tiny crystal bowls with wee silver spoons similar to the shovels sophisticated people use to snort cocaine, if the movies count as a source.

Concepción murmured grace, and we ate as best we could with the Jane Bailey channel blaring layer over layer of hysteria. George and Concepción had out-voted me on the entertainment. When I'd pulled the 'this is my house' routine, they'd exchanged shrugs without breaking contact with the set.

The current broadcast featured a panel of 'therapists', a title requiring no license and broad enough to include foot-massagers, camp counselors, even Scientologists. The facilitator in New York tossed questions to experts around the nation who batted back and forth the old, reliable and unanswerable, nature-nurture controversy. "Is a person with bi-polar symptoms born that way or driven to the disorder by unfortunate circumstances, such as over-involved parents, negligent parents, growing up in poverty, or growing up in a family with too much money?"

After ten minutes of colorful opinions, the experts were asked why drug cartels took advantage of people with mental and emotional disorders and the panel veered off into stories of entertainment icons who have overdosed and those who couldn't seem to stay out of jail.

Ticker-tape Twitter updates from random viewers streamed along the bottom of the screen:

"My Aunt Gertrude had a mental disease and she killed four people."
"Women who work after they have children are ignoring the will of God."
"It's the corporations."
"Do you know your credit score?"

Under normal circumstances I would have continued to beg for a merciful channel change. But not tonight. George didn't know about Mexico City. Not for sure.

While Concepción dropped blobs of dough into the deep fryer for *sopapillas* and George had his head in the fridge, I transferred my plate and laptop to my back office to arrange our vacation in peace and concealment. Also, watching George slosh blueberry syrup over the treats Concepción had already double sugared required a tolerance only possible when life is in an easy stretch.

Tonight was not an easy stretch.

American Airlines cooperated and George and I were booked on a morning flight. That part was easy. The part about what to do once we landed? That's where my itinerary started taking on water.

When I told him I was headed for Mexico City, George, unimpressed with my earlier telephone detective work, would ask, "So, what's your plan, Miss Rose?"

"I'm going to find Diego," I'd answer, a sing-song claim that would come out way too close to *"We're off to see the Wizard, the wonderful Wizard of Oz!"*

George would feign great surprise, then ask, *"How* are you going to find Diego?"

"By checking out the places he and I went on the weekend of Camilla's wedding," I'd say.

To which, he would retort, "You've got to be kidding me, Miss Rose. Do you think a place and people freeze when you are no longer there to watch?"

"Yes," I'd say. "I think that Mexico City and the people I met there will be exactly the same. I am quite sure they held a meeting and made a pact: 'When this Jessica Rose person leaves town, we will have no reason to go on with our lives, so nobody change.'"

George would not think I was funny. The reality was, in recent years, Mexico City had changed in ways no one could have imagined. Atrocious, heart-breaking ways. Wealthy families, proud to support the opera and the symphony, have always ruled the country by paying off politicians and controlling the law-making process. But when Mexico became the main route for shipping Columbian agricultural products, the power switched to gangs who had no interest in cultural progress and who maintained their dominance through terror.

Then there was the matter of law enforcement agencies with confused loyalties. *Nine-one-one* didn't promise the same reliable assistance in Mexico. If I landed in trouble and needed police help, my chances ran forty-to-sixty that my request would lower my chances of survival.

For now, I wouldn't think past step one: find Diego. Did I really expect to locate him by quizzing current employees at two businesses he patronized over a decade ago? I needed more. But the only person I could think of who might have a lead on his whereabouts didn't need an intrusion from me. If she knew how to find Diego and wanted to, she could do that without my help. The very idea of an interfering call to Camilla's mother made me want to wash my hands. Still, I owed Camilla my best effort.

One of Eileen's staff would answer. I'd assess how things were going in the Cervantes' house and back out if I was an unwanted trespasser. When Eileen picked up, the thin rationalizations I'd leaned on to make the call fluttered away, my throat closed off, and Concepción's tostadas were a chunk of metal in my stomach.

Still, I was glad to hear her voice. I started with a rush of tears, regrets, and promises. Concepción and I would do whatever we could for her and Ana Teresa. Anything, just let us know. Then I asked about Diego.

"I'd like to help, Jessica," she said. "Ana Teresa's never met him, you know."

"No, I didn't know, not for sure."

"But I have no idea of how to find him or if finding him is even a good idea. Diego and Camilla had an understanding from the time she found out about the baby. I don't want to go back on her wishes."

"Maybe she'd feel differently if she'd known . . ."

"There are other reasons to stay away from Diego, Jessica. Dangerous reasons."

"I don't think there's much chance I can find him anyway."

"Jessica, this business with the cartel, it's not over. The police, the federal agents, think Los Insurgentes will continue making their presence felt here and across Texas." Her voice quaked. "Camilla loved you like a sister."

I held my breath. Eileen didn't need to know about my slashed tire, though maybe I should take the hint. I would have, if I could erase Diego's dark eyes from my memory. If I hadn't seen, or believed I'd seen, kindness in those eyes. If I hadn't seen, or believed I'd seen, more in Camilla's eyes than cartel business when she'd asked me to stay at the horseshow--and still I'd driven away.

"I won't do anything crazy. It's just that Diego seemed like the kind of man who would want to know that the mother of his child has been murdered." *Seemed?* Earlier, with George, I'd said that Diego *was* the kind of man who'd want to know.

"Whether you find him or not," Eileen said, fear for me and her granddaughter overriding exhaustion, "I'm sure you understand that Ana Teresa has more than enough to deal with right now."

I did. I had no intention of pressuring Eileen or Ana Teresa to allow Diego into their lives. As far as I knew, he hadn't bothered to look up his own daughter in since she was born. If Eileen didn't want him in the family, Diego would live with that.

"Of course," I said. "I'm sorry for bothering you at all. Really, I am. I didn't think you'd answer or . . . I should have waited--"

"It's okay, really. When your name came up on the ID, I was glad. I wanted to talk to you about something else. Something I don't feel I can speak about with my friends. They never knew Camilla after she grew up. They never gave her a chance. If only a few of them had come down for the wedding, not one did you know."

"I know."

"I invited almost thirty, Jessica. Thirty. Of course, they all used the 'too dangerous to travel in Mexico' excuse."

I'd been a wreck on the run the weekend of the wedding. Still, as lost as I was, I'd registered Eileen's disappointment and sadness. She didn't have any extended family, so the empty family pew wasn't a surprise. The lack of response from her Flower Mound buddies, however, came off like a boycott.

"It's Ana Teresa," she said. "I'm afraid of what this loss will do to her. When she is sad, she is inconsolable, the way Camilla was."

The way Camilla was when her father was murdered. My insides shuddered. A pin stick landed on my soft spot for unhappy little girls.

"Camilla made a life for herself, but I don't think she ever recovered, not down deep." Eileen choked up with sobs. "Jessica, Ana Teresa is more like her mother every day."

Could fate be that cruel? Bipolar disorder has a strong genetic component. Had the Virgin of Sorrows wept as Ana Teresa came into the world? Had Camilla's daughter, too, been stamped for sadness?

"I can't go through all the doctors and the hospitals again, Jessica. I won't let them take my little girl again, you, of all people, understand. What can I do if she gets worse? I'm so afraid."

"I won't let them take Ana Teresa from you. There are other ways to treat disorders now. Camilla burned down the barn, that's why her doctors over-reacted. I can help. I know the system."

"I'll always remember you as the one friend who never gave up on Camilla."

Eileen's voice cracked, a break of regret and fear that cut my heart. Next to what Eileen and Ana Teresa experienced today, my quest to find Diego came off as trivial. Was I caught up in a selfish project to assuage my guilt for failing Camilla? Worse still, what if my determination was nothing more than my need to run from the pain? Or, hormones and a desperate longing for an innocent time in my own life that could never be again?

"Jessica, please don't underestimate Los Insurgentes. I can't stand anymore loss. I couldn't take it if something happened to you."

"Diego would want to know. He has a good heart, Eileen," I said, a piteous offering.

Like I would know what Diego wanted or what kind of heart he had.

Though Eileen was too gracious to point it out, she hadn't forgotten my cloddish behavior on the weekend of the wedding. She had good reason to doubt my estimation of Diego de la Cruz and the wisdom of my campaign to find him. I had more than good reason.

"I know the two of you had a good time," she said. "But you do not know him. I don't know him either, for that matter. Diego is from a different world."

Yes, he was. And now that I'd replayed the bloody clothes in his car, the intense stopovers behind the Cathedral, and George's lecture on what men wanted, my romanticized playbacks of Diego were harder to maintain. The balloon of confidence I'd had when I first decided to find Diego was peppered with leaks.

When George, Nancy Margaret, and I had set out on the Freedom Celebration Trip, we'd made a pact. All bets were off. Anything goes. Once the weekend was over and we'd returned to real life, we would never talk about or question anything we did in Mexico City.

We would never go back.

CHAPTER 23

Back in the kitchen, I watched George drown a second plate of sopapillas in inky syrup while he caught up on world events ala ESPN. On the screen, a panel of college football coaches disclosed strategies for the upcoming season. One promised that his team intended to play the whole game every time they went out on the field. Another claimed that this year, his team would show up to play football.

I posted myself between my good buddy and the coaches' revelations. "George?"

Sammie, who'd followed me to the office and back, planted his rump next to my feet and gazed up at George. He trilled a birdsong, tail awag. My personal cheerleader.

"Yes?" George's eyes were locked on the screen.

"I want you to know, up front, that I'm perfectly okay with you riding out our vacation in the spa at the Airport Hilton, steps away from the American Airlines counter. Perfectly fine, no hidden agenda."

Which was the truth. It was one thing for me to believe I'd seen something good in Diego's eyes, and another to ask someone else to take that chance. It was also true that I needed to know I was not absolutely alone in real world Mexico City.

George refused to acknowledge my presence. I suspended his boarding pass in front of his nose. "Don't worry about paying me back. I used Advantage miles. First class. *Lots* of Advantage points." I let the paper drop.

He faked a grab for it, then let it flitter to the floor. He leaned away from me, as if I'd spent my time away from the kitchen smearing dog poop over my body.

I scooped up his ticket and waved it in the airspace between us as if drying the ink on a million dollar check.

"That would be the Hilton Resort in Los Cabos?" George said. He faked another grab.

"Close."

The ticket landed on Suzi's head. She didn't notice.

"Even if crime news is on blackout in Mexico, the story's all over the Internet," he said. "Your lover boy has to know Camilla was murdered."

"It's not only the news services that are shut down. It's everything and everybody. Last night in Cancun, the corpse of a rock star was found in the lobby of his hotel after he'd bad-mouthed Los Insurgentes between songs."

"You *do* know how to sell a vacation, Miss Rose."

He reset the television to the Jane Bailey channel in case I'd forgotten the murderous nature of Los Insurgentes.

"George, I have to go, you know I do. I keep thinking how awful it was for Camilla when she lost her father. I will not let Ana Teresa grow up without a parent, unless I know for myself that Diego doesn't want to be a father, or if Eileen chooses to keep him out of the picture now and forever."

George heaved a deep breath and sat back. *Oh, no.* I knew that look.

"Miss Rose, we've known each other a long time, right?"

Here we go.

"Earlier I tried to talk you out of this foolishness by pointing out that your Communist buddy Diego did not bother to send you as much as a thank you note."

"And I said--"

"You had some kind of comeback, but now I'm thinking this boyfriend agenda has flaws of a deeper nature."

I knew exactly where this was headed. I focused on the television.

"You must have considered that this crazy idea of yours, this quest to find Ana Teresa's father that could get you *killed*, might be about another father who wasn't around to watch his little girls grow up?"

"No." Bull's-eye. "That's crazy."

"I politely disagree. This obsession is about Camilla, but it's about Kelly, too, about the fact that David's daughters lost their live-in father when you two got together."

"A father makes a difference in a daughter's life."

"This man is not David. Diego's made no effort."

"Maybe Diego had his reasons and when he hears about Camilla, he'll change." Me and my rose tinted binoculars. "I have to find him."

He shook his head. "What if Diego already knows Camilla is dead and he simply doesn't care?"

"I care. I have to know he's made a choice. Really, all I need from you is moral support."

George swiveled his head my way, glared, and cocked an eyebrow. "Hmm."

"So you're in? You're coming with me?"

He whipped his attention back to the television. "Not a chance."

I sat down next to my buddy. Since my first mention of Diego, George knew I'd head for Mexico City. He'd also known he would do everything he could to talk me out of it, because--unlike the many times I'd talked George into crazy plans—this time, I was starting to believe he meant what he'd said. Starting to believe he was not going to Mexico. I was out of persuasive tools.

The fax machine hummed to life on the counter, a welcome break in the brittle atmosphere. A few moments booting up, then the equipment stuttered, whined, clacked, and spewed through nine gyrations. Sammie kept up the fax thump and squeal through two additional rounds.

George hopped up and retrieved the stack. He riffed the pages, shrugged, and handed them to me.

"Who's Zack Harvey?"

"Tom Cruise groupie." I brought George up to date on the Zack Harvey international web of Scientology.

The first page was time stamped four days ago. Under the stamp was Zack Harvey's personal cell phone number underlined three times, and a hospital discharge note, *"El paciente seguirá el tratamiento en los Estados Unidos."* The next four sheets were photographs of a small woman, who could have been Camilla Cervantes, on a gurney in a hospital emergency room. Standing along the wall behind the gurney, were workers in hard hats, some with paint splashed pants, others in kitchen worker garb. One held a blood soaked towel around his hand.

"Drug overdose," George said, as if announcing the sky was blue.

"That's what Zack said. What kind of world do we live in that everyone jumps to a drug overdose?"

"The real one. What's the Spanish blurb?"

"'Patient will continue treatment in the United States.'"

"Screams rehab."

George crossed the kitchen and punched the Keurig for another blast of Ethiopian aroma therapy and caffeine.

"Maybe the murderer first tried to kill Camilla in Mexico City?" I said.

"Nothing like attempted murder to get a woman thinking about making a big change in her life."

"Still, as far as this fax goes, my money's on Zack Harvey, Photoshop, and revenge. I'm not convinced Zack would choose to advance his career over an opportunity to wreck mine."

"I'm sticking with drug overdose."

The last time I'd seen Camilla, her eyes had been bright. Too bright?

"Sorry, Miss Rose." He spooned scoops of sugar into his cup from a Talavera bowl, "but we're back to Los Insurgentes and I'm back making plans to fake my own death."

The fax hadn't inspired George to pick up the airline ticket, that's for sure.

I sat down next to him and forced myself to focus on the broadcast. George wasn't going to give in this time. The narco-trafficantes had truly changed the world as I knew it. And I was alone.

The Jane Bailey channel re-ran the sky view of the Zócalo, this time overlaid with floating photographs of Camilla and posh mansions at the country club. The video montage, now the standard introduction for updated rumors on the Flower Mound Country Club Murder, even had a haunting theme song.

I pointed at the screen. "Construction of the Cathedral you are looking at began in 1573."

"I'm not looking at any cathedral."

"It's the oldest Cathedral in the Americas. Building began fifty years before the Pilgrims even landed at Plymouth Rock. I bet you didn't learn that in your seventh grade American history."

"Don't see a cathedral."

A switch had flipped in my brain and I couldn't even slow down. Now that I knew George wasn't going to change his mind, I might as well enjoy the view.

"Get this, George. You know the photograph on the wall at El Cristobal? The one of Pancho Villa and Emiliano Zapata sitting on golden thrones?" I pointed to the south end of the Zócalo.

"No."

"That picture was taken right here." I tapped the screen. "In this very palace, in 1914, when the Revolution ended."

"Miss Rose, if you are trying to get me to go home and never come back, you can just ask."

"Hang on!" I waved him off. The camera plus voiceover swept toward the excavated temple next to the church. "That's the Plaza of the Three Cultures! This guy is going to talk about the Aztecs!" My love of history, once more, renders me child-like.

". . . Only a few blocks from the colorful Zócalo, abuzz with carefree tourists, is La Merced, the largest public market in the city," the smooth talker said, over a shot of the endless aisles piled high with produce, meat, and flowers. "Here, beyond the displays of healthy foods and saintly religious decorations, La Merced is home to a darker marketplace . . . a mesh of filthy streets lined with prostitutes. The specialty in LaMerced is very young girls."

I needed oxygen. Fast.

The screen switched off the Google cam and onto to a medley of strippers and seedy hooker corners in major U.S. cities. One shot of a woman in a red bra and panties, her six-inch red spike heel balanced on the rim of a toilet, a needle jabbed in her arm. "The House of House of the Rising Sun" moaned in the background.

". . . The degrading world of prostitution is one most Americans never encounter. Yet, in Mexico City, out of sight of family and friends, Camilla Cervantes, daughter of well-known talk show host, Eileen Cervantes, was drawn to this dark haven of pedophile sex and dirty money. The question on all of our minds is, 'Why would a wealthy and beautiful Flower Mound Country Club heiress . . . who could have anything she wanted . . . who could have run in the highest circles of society . . . end up in La Merced?'"

"What's happening, George?" I clutched his arm. "How can they say this shit?"

George's expression was first startled and then unreadable. He said nothing, but gears unlocked and churned behind his dark eyes.

"I can*not* freak-*king* believe this!" I said, clutching harder. "Nothing has changed for Camilla, nothing! When I came back from Paris, the Flower Mound crowd was sympathetic to my face. Later, I overheard them say how Camilla had always been wild and crazy, and that anyone who would do something as stupid as get into the car with a stranger should expect to end up a victim. She was raped and beaten, and that was supposed to be her fault. She was thirteen years old, George, barely thirteen!"

"What's happening here is . . . is . . ." No part of his face moved with his words. "Is diabolical."

"Of course," I said, "the gossip always circled back to the barn fire. *Camilla, Camilla, the Flower Mound Killa!*"

My heart beat so fast it scared me. My skin blazed. I willed my ears to listen to the bastard narrator.

The bastard paused his 'shocked' prattle to re-run a clip from the earlier panel of therapists kicking around why a good little rich girl would go bad. A Dr. Chambers from Chicago said, "I did not meet with Miss Cervantes personally. However, the extremes of her childhood difficulties suggest--"

"Suggest," I blurted. "There's his horseshit cop out."

". . . that Miss Cervantes was suffering with bipolar disorder," the doctor continued. "Her attraction to prostitution and drugs was likely a manifestation of the manic phase. People experiencing mania crave intense stimulation and danger. This craving often plays out as insatiable and sometimes bizarre promiscuity."

"Unbridled horseshit!" I blurted and looked around for something to smash. "Royal flaming horseshit!"

"Even I am a bit taken aback." George, still impassive, touched the keypad back to ESPN.

"Not one mention of Camilla's charity work!"

"Charity work doesn't sell car insurance, Miss Rose." He bent down, rescued his boarding pass, and blew off invisible dust. "If you believe Camilla would want you to give Diego a go, I'm in."

I hugged him hard. "Thank you. Thank you."

I wanted to leave for Mexico City now. I was sick to death of the Camilla stories Austin, Texas, had to offer.

"However," George said. "I shall do my moral supporting from the Four Seasons, not the Hilton. Now, tell me again, why am I going?"

"In case of emergency."

"If I could be any value in a Mexico City emergency, I would tag along on your little scavenger hunt. What possible help can I be at the hotel?"

"In case I'm being tortured until I give up a name and phone number for the ransom demand."

"Get in line behind my ex-wives."

"I'm just kidding. Sort of."

"Kidnapping is the one thing I'm not worried about, Miss Rose. You dress like a homeless person. One look and a kidnapper will assume you could not possibly know anyone with money or taste."

Chapter 24

It was midnight when Concepción and I returned from the jail. A welcome baseball broadcast filtered into the hall from George's room. The Astros were losing, but no big deal. We Astros fans long ago stopped mourning our losses for the same reason Mexican authorities stopped identifying corpses. There were just too many.

I checked that the patrol officer--who now had camera feeds set up around the house--was in place, then stripped down for a much needed soak in the Jacuzzi.

Thank heaven for Sammie Davis, Suzi, George, Concepción, and the police officer. With what the Chief had told me about Camilla's Mexico City connections, the smart money would skip Vegas and set up permanent residence in the Alaskan outback. As it was, I left Don Wilder with the assurance that George and I were headed for Miami South Beach to escape the local media intensity. Morning was soon enough to bring George up to speed. Let him sleep in blissful ignorance of the truth about the cockroach.

The *tiny* man? Now that was irony at its best.

I eased into the warm bubbles, rested my neck on the edge, and steadied my head on the cool tile ledge. David had designed this part of the house, but he loved me and knew my ache for arches, Saltillo and bluebird tiles were my reverence for the Rose family that ended when I was seventeen. Cobalt glass sinks, stone trimmed marble counters, and a wall of glass onto the back patio and the pool made up of tiny cobalt tiles, a gift from Concepción's cousins.

Sammie Davis, Jr. sighed and stretched out on the cedar shelf next to my iced Carmel Valley. He'd had a rough day. Suzi made it as far as the furry bath mat where she snored like a cartoon lumberjack. She'd positioned her royal self where I'd most likely trip over her, feel guilty, and she'd score a Beggin' Strip.

Time to let go of the day Camilla died. There was no other choice. Get on a plane to Tucson. Make the arrangements. Breathe and breathe again. And tomorrow?

Get on a plane. Land in Mexico City. Make the arrangements. What arrangements? *Don't jump ahead of life, LeFave.* Breathe and breathe again.

Was I really poised to dive face-first into the dark backside of the largest city in the western hemisphere? The capital city of a country so deluged with violence that the free press had ceased to exist? What sort of imbecile does something like that of her own free will?

A possessed imbecile.

I have a confession.

I wanted to know everything about Camilla's life. Everything. Even when I didn't like what I found. Why?

Because I wanted to be worthy of Camilla's trust. Because while I'd stopped advertising my opinion, I still believed a personal motive had contributed to her murder and that I was the person most able to discover that personal reason. But those noble, perhaps foolhardy reasons, were not the whole story.

There was something more fueling my search. Something personal, something deeper, maybe even profane. I wanted an answer to the question--so scary I'd never said it out loud--that had haunted me long before this morning.

Both Camilla and Kelly were diagnosed as bipolar. And, as much as I hated to admit it, Camilla's behavior, like Kelly's, was sporadically typical of the manic side of the disorder. The truth was, Camilla's handing Diego off to me at her wedding wasn't funny and it wasn't normal. No matter how casually a woman takes vows, she does not, if she is her right mind, pawn her new husband off to a friend in front of everyone.

The truth was, no friend, in her right mind, goes along with the offer.

But then, I was excellent at not seeing warning signs when I didn't want to see trouble.

Whatever her difficulties, Camilla, like Frida Kahlo, had accepted fate and fought to make a life for herself. My question? What did Frida and Camilla have that Kelly didn't?

Was there a moment for Camilla when she could have gone either way?

Was there a moment recognized by a competent professional as a crisis, a psychologist who gave Camilla a treatment plan that included hope instead of platitudes? Was there a moment when someone who loved Camilla stepped in and said something or did something that convinced her to live? If yes, what was that something, and why hadn't I known what to do?

I did not continue asking myself what I could have done because I enjoyed the pursuit. I continued because I did not know how not to. Maybe the truth was in the details. There were details in Kelly's life that were different from Camilla's life and details in Kelly's suicide that set it apart from a typical check out. But that's another story, and now was not the time to tell it. Tonight was about Camilla.

My shoulders and neck were tangled knots of fiery muscle. Aches from the fall off NoMoneyNoMoneyNoMoney broke through locked muscles for the first time.

I upped the water temperature, took a sip of the iced Carmel Valley, and closed my eyes, drifting. My stint in the horse show warm-up ring waiting for Camilla seemed years and years ago. I let the bubbles roil over me. Time for the Scarlett O'Hara defense mechanism. Like Scarlett, I'd had enough torment for one day. I'd think about *El Viborito* the Snake in the morning.

Sounds brilliant, doesn't it? Very psychologist like. But if I could make the Scarlett O'Hara approach work for me, I would have slept more than three hours at a stretch since Tucson happened. I'd be able to defend myself against the accusing night creatures with the sulfur-burning yellow eyes.

With a long cold drag of Carmel Valley, I surrendered and swung wide the gate for the ghosts and lost dreams to shove each other around in my head. Diego showed up too, but the pleasant-scary stir in my stomach didn't fit with tonight. Tomorrow maybe. Tomorrow was about the unknown. In the unknown there was hope. I'd used up all my chances with Kelly, but maybe I had a one chance left to help Camilla.

Sammie inched his way along the cedar shelf and licked my eyelids. I kissed him on his cool precious nose and he was content. What would we flawed humans do without the Sammies in the world? Forced to wait innumerable times while I iced swollen knees, massaged painful fetlocks, and fed Cokes and carrots to my horses, George accused me of thinking animals were people.

George was wrong. Ask Eileen. Ask Ana Teresa.

I love my sweet Sammie Davis and the slightly arrogant Suzi, but George was off the mark. When you lose a pet, as much as it rips your heart apart, eventually, you can check the newspaper, scan the internet, or go to a shelter, and find another sweet dog who is looking just for you.

There is nothing you can do when you lose a person.

Nothing.

Salud. Thank you, my little friends.

Salud, Camilla.

Vaya con Dios, mi amiga.

CHAPTER 25

"Are you going to eat that?" George asked, as he swiped the miniature cinnamon roll off my miniature plate.

We were 36,000 feet into the blue over the Sierra Madres. I'd bumped up my usual black stretch jeans with a full sleeved Navajo shirt and a turquoise nugget and silver milagro necklace. George, in a pale blue linen shirt and Stefano Ricci slacks, brought our combo up to a reasonable level of fashion acceptability.

Cozy in the window seat, gray leather defining our world, George looked almost as relaxed as he had before the murder. The sweet roll he'd snatched was already cut into bite size bliss bombs.

George might be relaxed, but I wasn't. My nerves required Mexican Revolution level diversion.

"Did you know that Pancho Villa hid out in the very mountains we are flying over right now?"

"Nope."

Pancho, spurring his lathered steed into a canyon hideout below, beat the hell out of the image dominating my brain since my chat with the

Chief. The image of men in black masks with automatic weapons--maybe Los Insurgentes henchmen, maybe police, who knew the difference-- jabbing a short blond *tourista* into a black SUV with tinted windows.

"Yes, George. General John Pershing--the same distinguished military hero known for his gallantry in World War One--and twelve thousand American troops chased Pancho Villa into those mountains below us and still could not find him."

"I am deeply ashamed for my country." He finished off his saucer of sweets. "Now, please stop your distraction dance, Miss Rose. Get on with what you're avoiding talking to me about."

The moment I referred to the tiny man as a notorious cartel boss, George would cannonball up the aisle and set off an international incident attempting to exit at thirty-six-thousand-feet.

"The Chief agreed to extend surveillance at the Mt. Laurel House into the foreseeable future," I said.

"Excellent. Sammie and Suzi are safe. Too bad you treat your dogs better than you treat your best friend. What about Camilla's mother? Does she have plenty of security?"

He collected the sugar packs on my tray and ripped open three at once. He flocked both tray tables with sweet snow, then tapped the rest into his coffee.

"Definitely. Private and extra city police, federal, too, I'm sure. Though for Los Insurgentes, Eileen's more valuable alive and terrified. She's still in shock, I could tell that on the phone."

"And the little girl?"

"Ana Teresa is the child on the planet most likely to be kidnapped."

The flight attendant used tongs to place fresh gooey rolls on each of our plates as per my buddy's request. I used his joyful sugar anticipation to ooze into the cockroach subject.

"George, Don did some checking on my tiny man. He's known as El Viborito which means 'Little Snake'. He runs operations in La Merced."

George hesitated. He cocked an eyebrow but continued to slather whipped butter on his roll.

"I don't suppose you are saying the Little Snake-O is a surgeon?"

"He was into trafficking drugs and running prostitution--"

"And shooting people--"

"--before Los Insurgentes popped up. Years before we were in Mexico City for the wedding."

"Knowing he's a veteran crime boss isn't exactly reassuring."

"Camilla would have been forced to cooperate, to arrange protection for sure. Could be she was buying girls away from the creep."

"Girls like the silent child who rode next to me from Mexico City to Austin?"

"I don't know exactly where she fits or if it's important to know. But if Adriana was a Viborito project, it would explain why he was in my room on the weekend of the wedding."

George leaned sideways and thumped his head on the window.

"*Why?* Why, sweet Lord? Why, when this blonde first inflicted herself on me, *why* didn't I simply turn her down for the job, trot downstairs and throw myself in front of a truck on the freeway?"

"Because you love me. Love at first sight."

"Maybe medication could help me with these tragic life-destroying decisions."

"Camilla deserves the best I can do. She was a good person. I was lucky just to be her friend."

"Will . . . you . . . stop it!"

A rare intense expression pushed aside George's sweet roll delight. He rotated and sat sideways in the seat.

"What?"

"I absolutely hate it when you say shit like that."

"Like what?" I knew exactly what he meant.

"Your song and dance about how *every*one else is such a *wonderful*, good person. About how fortunate you were to be Camilla's friend. How about how lucky Camilla was to be *your* friend? I can't take watching you tear yourself up like this. Ever since Kelly's suicide, you've walked around like you are a defective person. You are not the only person on the face of the earth who has messed up and people ended up hurt. I can't really even say you messed up. You were a great stepmother and both girls loved you."

"Obviously not great enough."

George slammed his palm on the console, then aimed a finger gun at my temple. "Stop. Stop it now."

"No, George, no. You don't under--"

"*Yes, George, yes*, Miss Rose. And I *do* understand. You are the one who does not get it. You do not know if Kelly would have killed herself even if her father had stayed with the family. You will never know."

I could not breathe. I wanted to flail my hands in front of George's face and beg him to leave me alone. If anyone other than he had pushed on me, I would have. I would have committed whatever violence was necessary to bury the subject. I stared straight ahead. Fine. My expression made clear that I would never make eye contact with George again. Ever.

"What I'm saying," George continued, "is that when you are close to someone who you think is more careful with people than you have been in your life, you turn them into some kind of do-no-wrong angel. You've done that with Camilla and you did that with David. David is the one who left his family."

"He wouldn't have--"

"You don't know that either. And, whether she wanted the divorce at the time or not, his ex married someone who loves her. So give it up."

"Okay, I'm trying. I really am." I turned to face him. Fake courage all over my face.

"Good." He shook his head. "For someone who went to a lot of trouble learning how to help other people deal with their demons--"

"I know. I know. I'm just not ready to talk about it."

"*It?*"

"I'm not ready."

George shrugged acceptance, piled extra icing on a buttery bite of his sweet roll and motioned for me to open my mouth. "It doesn't have to be me, Miss Rose, but you need to talk to someone about 'it'."

"Working on it. Promise."

"And, while you're 'working on it', you have to be kinder to yourself, commencing with this little piece of heaven."

He planted the treat on my tongue. Delicious. My mind and body were so excited and so terrified about the unknown ahead, I was surprised I could still taste.

"I'm not asking you to think awful things about Camilla," George said. "I agree she was a good person, even an exceptional person. But she wasn't perfect. No one is. And right now, today, you need to face that she was involved with some black-hearted people."

"I know."

"All I ask is that you accept the fact that--as far as weaknesses and strengths are concerned--you did not know Camilla as well as you thought you did."

"Maybe."

"And you do not know yourself as well as you think you do."

"Probably."

George wasn't finished with his speech, but he could see that if I sank any further into the past, I would lose my courage and never forgive either one of us. We needed to make plans, synchronize our watches.

"By the way, Miss Rose, what's your backup plan if lover boy turns out to be this Little Snake's right hand man? What if he's shoulder deep in drug money and doesn't appreciate being found?"

"He's not like that."

"I don't even want to know what you are basing your opinion on. But, how's this for a little reality? A handsome bad boy gets Camilla pregnant on a drunken holiday, and being of sound mind, she wants to make sure her child will not be exposed to the criminal element. Thus, she forbids him to come around to play daddy, and that's why he's never been in the picture . . . . Or he's never been in the picture because he is D.E.A.D."

The flight attendant noticed how much fun George had with his icing and set a baby saucer with a white blob between us on the console. As George reached for the icing, I grabbed the plate and held it over my head.

"You are my only moral support, George, and I'm not nearly as brave as I look." My words were fierce but my eyes filled with tears. "You do not get this pile of butter and sugar until you promise to be more optimistic."

"No *problemo.*" He collected the fresh goo and stacked dishes on his crowded tray. "We're already in the crossfire, we're better off dancing than standing still."

I was lucky to have George as a friend, too. He was born knowing the message of the Day of the Dead. He was born crunching on sugar skulls.

George retrieved his cell phone from the seat pocket in front of him and plunked it on my tray.

"What's this thing for?" I asked.

"That ransom call."

"Okay."

"Why, Miss Rose, why didn't you tell me that the dwarf is rat king of the crime bosses last night?"

"Would you be on this plane?"

"Oh, sure. Why would I let a little detail like certain death at the hands of someone called Snake, get in the way of a vacation?"

"Think of it as payback. You played me when you waited until we were on the drive back from Houston to inform me that my divorce was the first time you'd ever been in court."

"And, as it turns out, the only."

George concentrated on balling up the last of the icing for his remaining chunk of pastry. Which was fine, since my head was no longer in the conversation. Mexico City loomed closer and closer. La Merced. The Mercy. Diego loomed closer and closer.

Had Ana Teresa's father played me?

CHAPTER 26

On the evening of October 2nd, 1968, a few days before opening ceremonies of the Olympics in Mexico City, a secret force of soldiers, police, and federal security agents, gunned down several hundred unarmed students, civilian protestors, and bystanders in what is known as The Night of Tlatelolco.

What would amount to billions today had been invested to showcase the host city as a successful democracy. If the cameras of the world, already gathered for the Olympics, diverted to the demonstrators protesting laws that maintained the grip a small percentage of obscenely wealthy citizens kept on the majority of Mexicans who lived in desperate poverty, the carefully scripted presentation of Mexico City would be seriously blemished.

The uprising was led by the National Strike Council made up of delegations from seventy universities and preparatory schools. The protest was initiated when the Mexican government declared that the principle of the autonomous university would no longer be respected. A move equal to abolishing the right to speak out against government policies.

If you watched every minute of the 1968 Olympics, you would have heard not a peep about the men, women, and children cut down on the cobblestones of Tlatelolco Plaza. What is known about the assault is what the few who escaped in the confusion dared to say. When the sun backlit the spires of the plaza church the next morning, not a body, a bloodstain, or the slightest evidence of struggle remained.

The official statement to the press was that six or twenty, or maybe slightly more, "armed and criminal snipers" had attacked the police and were fired on in self-defense.

Diego's mother and father, the parents of a baby boy named after the nation's best known artist and revolutionist, were two of the bodies the government "disappeared" from history.

At least that's what the gorgeous man across the marble cocktail table in the Angel Sky Bar told me.

The plane arced south, then back northeast to line up with the runway. A thrill took charge of my brain and my body, a thrill that took root long before I knew Diego. My blind love affair with this country began in the summers when my mother wrote articles on traveling in Mexico with children.

I gripped the armrest and bade hello to the snow-capped keepers of the Valley of Mexico, the still active *Popocatépetal* or Smoking Mountain and the quieter volcano, *Iztaccíhuatl* or Sleeping Woman. I spotted the gold domed Fine Arts Palace and the copper cupola of the Monument to the Revolution, favorites since those summers when the five Roses piled into the peach-colored van we'd been packing for weeks and headed south.

Each of us slipped contraband into the car. I sneaked aboard extra books and the plastic two-dollar Target bargain bucket binoculars I wasn't supposed to bring because they were worse than no lenses at all, and the camera I'd been forbidden to bring because, over and over, I would stop and arrange everyone for a picture, then say the shot wasn't perfect, because

I didn't want to spend the money to develop more than one roll of film. My older sister, of course, just *had* to have her fake white alligator make-up box with its stupid little handle on top, and my little brother hid tiny metal cars and trucks and hundreds of green plastic army soldiers all over the vehicle.

We only did what our parents modeled. My father hid cigars under the maps in the glove box and my mother wadded the netting for collecting fascinating rocks into a little ball and stuffed it in with the spare tire. Which made sense because she made her best discoveries while my father changed tires.

Mother wrote every day for the papers back home and we gave her plenty of material beyond the food, the blossom-adorned swimming pools on converted haciendas, and what it was like for children meeting others with different backgrounds and speaking a different language. We provided periodic colorful diseases, new uses for Mexican curios, and we ended up lost on mountain roads after we'd beg to see this or that village. My mother could turn a disaster—like the time the luggage rack flew off the top of the van and we spent the afternoon on the side of a mountain retrieving our clothes--into fun. She thought we were all hilarious, which was what readers liked most in her columns.

On our drives from village to village, we dopey, happy kids waved wildly out the windows to everyone we passed and they would smile and wave to us. Not until I was a few weeks into my first clinical internship did I realize that my family experience was the exception not the rule. That's how dopey happy we Roses were.

My mother died at home of a sudden asthma attack two months before I graduated from high school. Within four months, my father married a stranger with three problem children and bought a second house in South Africa to be near his new wife's family. My fourteen-year-old survival-mate brother ran away to the Guatemalan coffee *finca* of a distant relative and my older sister left town and got married. Maybe if we'd lived in the city instead of the country, the ambulance would have arrived in time. Maybe then, after high school, I'd have gone downtown to the university as planned, instead of down the aisle in some kind of make-a-family panic.

Maybe if my mother had survived, I would have said "No" to my stepbrother, "No" to Diego in Mexico City, and "No" to the married professor I met two weeks after the Freedom Celebration Trip. Maybe I'd have a Tuscan masterpiece in the suburbs and three blond cherubs by now. But I didn't and I don't, and there's no way to go back and change what happened.

The plane bounced twice on the runway. Two hard pops that jolted me upright. Had I romanticized the city and its citizens as if the Mexico of today was the Mexico of my childhood? Was I doing exactly what I taught others not to do? Letting my emotions, instead of my best thinking, make my decisions?

No question about it. The Mexico City I planned to visit was the resplendent, innocent country before Los Insurgentes and the others. Given the eighty or a hundred thousand recent murders, this approach could be a problem.

CHAPTER 27

Unlike the scorched brown landscapes of Texas in August, greenbelts between the runways of the Benito Juárez (first Indian to be President of Mexico) International Airport were bright with the year-round grass of the Tropical Zone even at two miles above sea level. Unlike the steel and glass terminals in the U.S, this airport paid tribute to the culture of the country before Hernán Cortés and his armored ilk clanked onto the soil of what they thought was India, the continent they named the "New World" because it was new to them.

Terminal buildings had high plastered walls splashed with orange, blue, scarlet, and yellow. Red and purple silhouettes of eagles, snakes, and pyramids. Clusters of black uniformed and armed soldiers were visible under jet bridges. Welcome.

To clear Immigration and Customs, George and I slapped on "just another day in the neighborhood" faces and strolled between walls of federal police, army troops, and private security officers. Could they tell I wasn't breathing? Dark eyes flicked back and forth in the narrow slits of their sweater masks. As we passed, officers nodded and tapped their shoulders in some sort of code.

We merited extra attention as the only Anglos. Which meant that we either didn't keep up with the news or that we were clearly insane.

Once beyond the baggage pick-up area where automatic rifles outnumbered backpacks, we stepped out onto a huge exit porch under cloudy skies. People shouted directions and asked questions about transportation. Airport traffic police blew whistles for reasons not apparent to the casual or foreign observer.

George didn't attempt any last minute save-the-damsel chivalry. He respected me too much. Instead he gave me a quick hug. Then he stepped back and made a picture frame with his fingers.

"What?" I asked.

"Just want to remember what you look like, in case I never see you again."

He flagged a limo and split for the Four Seasons. I waved my zone ticket for *Zona Centro* and hopped into an airport certified cab.

Ah. Freedom. Here I come.

Now I could wander the haunts from the weekend of Camilla's wedding without anyone urging me to slow down, to pay attention, or to stay off a certain street. I couldn't turn back time, but I could play my encore according to the rhythms in my heart. I wanted to find Diego, but I wanted to find Camilla, too. And who knows? It wouldn't hurt if I bumped into the woman I was before Tucson happened. Even a reflection would be nice.

My certified taxi driver was not as into the escapade as I was. He was excited, all right, just not about my journey. Instead, he was one hundred percent committed to an Australia vs. Mexico soccer match on a miniature black and white television jammed between the bucket seats of his car, a white and orange compact of unknown species.

He did not acknowledge my presence or the shoulder-to-shoulder soldiers that lined both sides of the exit ramp.

I flicked my glance to the side view mirror. What if I was wrong and Los Insurgentes considered me important enough to track? Oh well, with lane divider stripes considered experimental art in Mexico City, once in we melded into traffic, there'd be no way to tell if I was being followed. Since there was nothing I could do to change the situation. I put denial in charge.

The driver's taxi license was at eye-level on the back of his seat. I made out his name through generations of cellophane packing tape. Tomás Lopez Antonio Rodriquez Alonzo.

Australia missed a long swooping shot. The teams regrouped which gave Tomás Alonzo an opportunity to check out the stream of traffic that zoomed one inch beyond his front bumper. He reared back, threw his weight into the accelerator, and darted into a break a NASCAR driver would have turned down.

We were fish in the riptide of odd small cars and ancient black smoke-belching trucks with tattered canvas-covered beds. Once our position was established, Tomás whipped his concentration back to the soccer game.

Oh, God. The first time I'd ever seen my little brother pray outside of church was in the back seat of a Mexico City taxi. And that driver, unlike Tomás, had been mildly tuned into the road. Still, mentally dodging cars and sucking back gasps provided a reprieve from the relentless mantra now front and center in my brain. *"What do you think you are doing? What do you . . ."*

Two minutes out of the airport, the broad avenue was flanked with two and three story office buildings, interspersed with smog-stained white, turquoise, and yellow stucco apartments in various states of ruin. I knew from Camilla that behind the crumbling walls, a dozen or more people survived in each small compartment. Families who limited electric lights to late night activities and emergencies. The residences had the appearance of the Appalachian side-of-the-mountain homes of my relatives who never repaired, or repainted, or reset a faucet by replacing the appropriate part. If a tile fell off the bathroom wall, it stayed where it was, unless it made a good doorstop or fit the burn hole in the kitchen Formica. If a cabinet knob came unscrewed, the door was forever after knob-free.

Of course, the living spaces in Mexico were decomposing because there was never money to buy supplies or tools. The houses of my relatives were falling down because repairs and maintenance were not priorities. Not ever.

But Mexico City isn't about houses or office buildings. The heart of Mexico City throbs in her streets, living reefs where each person, animal, and vehicle is connected to every other by an invisible ooze and pulsates as one body. Everyone belongs—the children and old men hawking churros and pushing ice cream carts, the occasional young man in a high buttoned black business suit cutting between the street's regulars. Shawled women in dark skirts trudging for rented sinks at the public water tap, boulders of laundry on their heads.

Bikers tagged onto the taxi. Vendors of all ages popped up and grinned in the windows. Tomás had an established traffic light defensive strategy. Without it, his windshield would have been 'cleaned' at every intersection by a swarm of eight- and ten-year-old boys armed with rags and buckets of murky water.

In the roadway were brazen entrepreneurs engaged in all sorts of attention-drawing entertainment in hopes of a few pesos. One man choreographed green and blue parakeets along his arms, shoulders, and his head. Another swallowed a flaming rod during the red light. A man with a ragged mat unrolled the rug at any pause in traffic, covered it with ice, fell over on his back, and lay there until traffic encroached.

Tomás now allotted eighty percent of his attention to the soccer game and twenty percent to the other death-wish taxis, drooping power lines, and small brown people who'd rarely, if ever, been to the part of their giant city where I was headed. I closed my eyes and leaned back. I'd made it this far and I was fine. Why did everyone make traveling in Mexico City sound so scary?

Then wham!

My face smashed into the back of the driver's seat. Blood leaked into my mouth where the reopened lip cut bled a metallic taste. Oh, God, what did we hit? Tomás threw up his hands.

"Goooooooaaaaaaaaaaaaaaaaaaaaaal!"

Horns beeped, blasted, and wailed. I leapt to my feet, bonked my head on the roof, and didn't feel a thing. Maybe a little dizzy. Adrenalin took care of the pain. I reached over the seat, high-fived Tomás, and yelled, "Geronimo!" Which had to be inappropriate on several levels, but who cared?

After three minutes of honking, street dancing, and *"Viva Mexico!"* the checkered flag went down and we were off.

"Say, Tomás," I asked, still clutching the back of his seat, "I'd like to drive through La Merced on the way to the Zócalo."

Tomás squinted at me in the rearview, then shrugged, as if he'd concluded, "Mexico has a lead in the game, why not take the crazy gringa where she wants to go?"

My request was born of the giddy freedom in my chest and surprised me as much as it did Tomás. In San Luis Fernando Artes and the Angel Sky Bar, I'd sense Diego with me. I'd find Camilla in La Merced. I wanted to find Camilla first. Invite her to come with me.

The weekend of the wedding, I'd been too busy outrunning myself to appreciate Camilla's brave and generous La Merced project. This time, sober and in search of the truth, I'd have a chance to figure out which parts of our Freedom Celebration weekend were real and which parts were self-serving 'memories'.

Had I imagined the vibrancy of the market, the stark humanity, the girl with the double-layered yellow hibiscus behind her ear?

I anchored my nose on the little wing window that didn't open and squinted into the crystal-edged rays filtering into the streets of Camilla's Mexico City. I hadn't imagined everything. The seductive smells consumed my senses as they had before--guavas, papayas, mangos, pomegranates, and fresh squeezed limes and oranges. Coffee, cinnamon, chocolate, blended with the pit smells of *tacos al carbon* sizzling on low hibachis.

Tomás turned onto the broad avenue that made up the west corridor of La Merced, the market now familiar around the world as the domain where the "lovely, but disturbed," victim of the Flower Mound Country Club Murder played out her sordid "secret" life.

The people who hawked merchandise, cooked on sidewalks, and sold plastic bags for what amounted to two cents, could have been the same people from my first tour. Beyond the foods, the walls of floral arrangements, the cooking pans, ropes, electronics, and umbrellas, the incense of the witches' corner beckoned. Shelves of spider legs and calf placentas, tiers of retablos, candles, flowers, traditional and bastardized religious icons. Postcards of the saints.

Santa Muertes, Mary Magdalenes. Pink and white rose petals.

"Pay-so, peso, un pay-soooooo . . ."

Camilla and Diego met through their work here in La Merced. Had they met nearby? Maybe just inside one of the dozens of two-table cafes? What if finding Diego turned out to be as easy as rounding a corner?

Was I going over some sort of a sanity line here?

If so, Camilla was along for the ride, her rosewater breath on my neck. *"There's nothing to be afraid of . . . Spirits are always around us."* She tapped my shoulder. *"Thanks for coming."*

The girls were in their places. They waited with their plastic shoulder purses and see-through blouses, their backs against storefronts, reading romance novellas. Not hookers, not sporting girls. These barely teen girls opened their little books and lived in fantasies of passion while they waited to sell emotionless sex. For them, sex had nothing to do with love stories.

Sex wasn't 'making love'. It was a job, not a violation of humanity. Or that's what we tourists liked to think.

On the last evening of our Freedom Celebration Trip, only a few minutes before her wedding, I'd asked Camilla if she thought I was awful not giving anything to the girl who'd caught my eye. I'd only asked so she could do the polite thing and take me off the hook. So that she could insist I shouldn't worry about the girl with the double-layered yellow hibiscus. But that's not what Camilla did.

Camilla looked at me with those serious green eyes, and said, "A quarter, even a dime makes a difference when you have nothing."

Chapter 28

Tomás, apparently impressed I knew La Merced existed and convinced I shared his vision of Mexico in the World Cup Finals, rewarded me with the route with most stunning approach to the Zócalo. He backtracked out of the market, then turned northeast onto the magnificent Paseo de la Reforma, a dazzling visual feast that most in U.S. citizens don't know exists.

In my ear, Camilla pointed out figures from her father's stories of great Aztec chiefs in feathered headdresses and jeweled clothes made of gold thread. My personal soundtrack echoed his tales of blood sacrifices to the Angel of Death (with a pre-conquistador moniker) and the story about the illustrious European court of the only king and queen the Americas have ever known.

Crazy Mexico. Indians. Gods. Royalty. I heard violins.

The Paseo de la Reforma, legacy of Mexico's emperor, was constructed to connect his palace with the royal offices on the Zolcálo. His models were Vienna's Ringstrasse and the Champs-Élysées in Paris. Each traffic circle of the Paseo is crowned with a towering monuments to equal European glories, including one with a gleaming marble sculpture of the Roman goddess Diana.

Oops. Diana. Diana Sloan. What was she doing in my head? Did her parents know when they named her that the Goddess Diana was famous for her expertise as a hunter and, in some descriptions, for her hatred of men?

Directly ahead soared the colossal dark stone likeness of the Aztec chief Cuauhtémoc, the "One Who Descended like an Eagle." Camilla told us how the great chief, in charge when the Spanish arrived, surrendered to Hernán Cortés with the promise that his life would be spared. As it worked out, what Cortés meant was that the mighty Aztec would be allowed to live long enough to be tortured until he gave up, or manufactured, locations where more gold waited to be pillaged.

As for the Emperor Maximilian and his glamorous wife, the Empress Carlotta von Hapsburg (best played long ago by Bette Davis in the movie *Juarez*), after two short years of rule, Maximilian faced a firing squad and Carlotta returned to her Hapsburg home and went insane. Maximilian, a kind man duped by self-aggrandizing European royalty into believing the Mexican people wanted an emperor, offered the captain of his firing squad a pile of gold not to shoot him in the head so that his mother could see his face one last time.

Then Maximilian stunned Mexico with his last words, "I forgive everyone, and I ask everyone to forgive me. May my blood, which is about to be shed, be for the good of the country. *Viva Mexico! Viva la independencia!*"

Which seemed downright noble to me, maybe even more noble than the famous "Remember the Alamo!" cry, since those cowboys had opportunities to surrender or run, and Texans have been way short on forgiveness ever since. Of course, this being Mexico--and with the whole Cuauhtémoc debacle stamped in their minds—the captain of the firing squad accepted Maximilian's pile of gold, then ordered the entire *Juárista* firing squad to shoot him dead-on in the face.

Camilla and her stories.

Tomás eased into the historic El Centro district via Calle 5th de Mayo. The narrow streets, the width of three jousting lances in accord with the wishes of conquistador Hernán Cortés, were peppered with canvas-tented trucks loaded with soldiers, more automatic weapons at the ready. Clumps of masked military troopers conversed on corners.

My usually iron clad avoid-reality mechanism, locked into place when I'd plopped into the backseat of the taxi, was springing some serious holes. My decision to come to Mexico had to be the seminal from-the-pot-into-the-fire exhibition. I'd put a lot into my theory that I wasn't important enough to follow. A tail on the flight would have been simple. Mexico City was the home office for Los Insurgentes, which meant El Viborito definitely paid the salaries of many of the cell-phone chatting, armed police and soldiers around me. Once I hit the sidewalk, I'd be easy to pick out. Easier to follow.

Not that my search to find Ana Teresa's father would interest Los Insurgentes. *Said Pollyanna to Pooh Bear.*

Tomás pulled up to the curb along the western edge of the Zócalo. Today the vast open space teemed with what had to be over a hundred thousand rabid fans in front of a four story broadcast of Mexico vs. Australia. Supporters from toddlers to grandparents jumped up and down, yelling "Viva Mexico!" and slurping guava, coconut, and banana ice cream bars on sticks.

I paid Tomás and piled on a ridiculous tip, since I didn't know how he'd react to a kiss on his cheek, and struck a course along the back wall of the massive Cathedral. The sun warmed my shoulders though the breeze, cool at this altitude, lent a freshness to the air. The row of religious icon stores, the current inhabitants of the ancient high-ceilinged structures on *Calle de Tacuba*, had the surprising familiarity I'd experienced in La Merced. I even recognized the unique below ground entrances I'd stumbled down those moony nights, giddy and clutching Diego's arm.

Mexico City is sinking. The city was built on a string of islands in a lake. With growth, the waterways were filled and buildings constructed on barely dried ground. As a result, the structures, particularly the splendid thick-walled churches, were now as much as twelve feet below the sidewalk and accessed by stone stairways.

Perfect for a swooning gringa chick with one foot in the Land of the Living and one foot in the Land of the Dead.

The dusty window displays of San Luis Fernando Artes were crowded with Day of the Dead and Santa Muerte objects--skeletons, skulls, black robes, black candles, all sorts of grim altar pieces. I scanned for a match to the Skeleton Lady in the murder stall and several fit the bill. One even boasted a purple tufted hat with a peacock feather. Mixed in with the skeleton figures were traditional Catholic favorites—Jesus with his chest open to reveal his gold-rimmed bleeding heart, plaster Virgin Marys, cherubs, candles, a five-foot gold-leafed St. Michael the Archangel, with soaring wings and raised sword, and an even taller gold-leafed St. Francis of Assisi with delicate white marble doves in his outstretched palms and around his bare feet.

San Luis Fernando Artes was the only place Diego and I visited that hadn't been part of the party design. For the umpteenth time since I'd thrown myself into this journey, I regretted not asking a single question. Any reasonable, sober person would have asked why we'd stopped at the store multiple times, or why Diego and his buddies made an effort to speak where I couldn't hear them. I wouldn't have understood their high velocity conversation anyway, but I might have picked up the topic. Maybe if I knew something about what was important to Diego, criminal or not, I could justify my quest.

Heck, I might even find him.

With Saint Michael's wings and St. Frances's doves as cover, I strained to detect a sign of life inside the store which was several times deeper than it was wide. No movement, no sound. Only shadows in the dark interior.

Once I'd shown myself and spoken a word, I'd be sent packing, do-not-pass-go-or-collect-two-hundred-dollars. Thus my plan was to employ the sneak-up tactic honed to perfection on my older sister. I'd slink like a jungle cat until I was close enough to pounce on the storekeeper before could lock me out or escape through the rear of the store.

I tried the brass door knob. Either the door was tight due to the sinking problem or it was locked. I checked around me. I was the only person on the street who wasn't on the way to someplace else.

What if the icon stores only opened during holiday seasons like fireworks stands in Texas? My call could have been answered on a forwarded phone. The thought that my plan was a loser from the start staggered me. Could be I'd be back at the airport within two hours of landing. George wouldn't give me any grief, since his preference was to pay the freight and fly out of Mexico City as soon as possible.

Then a phone rang inside.

"Bueno." His gentle voice gave away that he was the "hot lead" who'd hung up on me yesterday. Eight times.

I turned the knob again and leaned into the door. Squeak. Screech. Creak. So much for my surprise attack. My sister would have bopped me on the head by this time.

A man shuffled his feet and stood up somewhere in the semi-darkness of the store. He saw me before I could make out his face, mostly because he had one and a half eyes on the television on the back wall. He paused, pulled his attention away from the match, and strode up to the front.

"Buenos días. ¿Cómo puedo estar de servicio?" (How can I be of service?)

I had nothing. How could I have gone to this much trouble to be where I stood and not have thought through what I would say to maximize my chance to learn anything about Diego? Then again, if I'd done a lot of thinking I would be in my kitchen with Suzi on my feet and Sammie Davis, Jr. in my lap instead of ten feet below the streets of Mexico City.

Since I hadn't rehearsed anything, I said something stupid.

CHAPTER 29

"I have a saint collection," I said, to the storekeeper in San Luis Fernando Artes. Which, given my pathetic Spanish, likely came out closer to "I have a saint fetish."

Luckily I didn't have to continue the charade. In case my hair color and silly remark hadn't screamed "irritating woman from yesterday," the soft-spoken, but determined man recognized my voice. And, since miracles never cease, I recognized his face.

"I told you," he said. "I do not know this man you are looking for."

Excellent. He spoke English. I could pester people best in my native tongue.

"Diego de la Cruz brought me to this store." I said, going for a reason to decelerate my ejection from the premises. "It's been awhile. "I don't expect you to remember me, but I got the impression you and Diego knew each other well."

He cocked his head. "What gave you that impression?"

"What you and Diego talked about sounded important."

He glared and studied my face. "What did we talk about?"

"I don't know. My Spanish isn't that good and, at the time, I'd . . . I was . . ."

A slight smile peeked through his gruff determination. *"Claro que si."* (Of course.) You, Miss. *Sí, Sí. Muy borracha* (Very drunk)."

Had George called ahead and ordered every contact in Mexico City to remind me as often as possible that I'd been none too sharp all three days of the Freedom Celebration Trip? I wanted to say something to redeem myself, but my Spanish wasn't nearly up to a spanky rebuttal.

"It's Enrique, right?" popped out of my mouth, one more instant and startling information retrieval. Could be I'd picked up his name when I'd Googled the store. More likely, the smells, the colors, and people of La Merced, had awakened links I had, for good reason, kept hidden from myself and everyone else.

Enrique's eyes searched my face. "Your name?"

"Jessica LeFave." I handed him a business card. Now or never. "I must find Diego. There's been a death in his family."

Enrique glanced at the card. "Diego has no family."

"Actually--"

"Diego has no family!" he repeated with the unnecessarily caustic tone used by every West Texas State Trooper who has asked me if I knew how fast I was going.

My confidence teetered. Enrique's refusal to admit Diego's marriage to Camilla and the very existence of Ana Teresa, punched another leak in my Mexico-City-is-a-family-destination bubble.

"Now leave, Miss."

He strode to the rear of the store, sat down in a swivel chair, and rotated so that his back was to me. His eyes on the bloody game.

So this was it? How many times did I have to be told that Diego de la Cruz wasn't the friendly good guy I wanted him to be? How many times did I have to be told I was not welcome?

What had I been thinking? That I'd find Ana Teresa's father waiting for me on a street corner? That Diego and I would catch up with amusing memories while we sipped tequila sours high over Mexico City at the Angel Sky Bar? Then what? We'd jump in a limo and end up on a beach where we'd gallop horses side by side in the surf, sea breezes furling our hair?

Well, Earth to LeFave. Denial of Diego's world on a crazy weekend as a divorced teenager bent on oblivion was one thing. But now? *This time, you've gone too far, sister.*

My little fantasy that nothing had changed in Mexico City was suddenly self-centered and foolish. What if Diego had married again? Heck, I'd been a wife, a stepmother, and a widow, since that weekend long ago. What if Diego's new wife and family didn't know about Ana Teresa? Did I think I could just stomp into Diego's reality without concern for the way he'd chosen to live? Without respect for the agreement he'd made with Camilla?

It's not like our brief relationship, if you can call it that, had crossed his mind. I couldn't expect the time we spent together to mean as much to him as it had to me. Or to mean anything at all. I flashed on the photo of Diego riding point with a straggly army of farmers. Also, he was a busy guy.

Still I had to know his situation for myself. Camilla would want the father of Ana Teresa to know she'd been murdered, on that point I was firm. If need be, Diego would be as far as the information would go.

The floor creaked with each step as I closed in on my prey. I planted myself next to the swivel chair. I'd come this far. I wasn't leaving unless I learned Diego was dead or until Diego told me, personally, to hit the road.

"Diego had family once," I said, straight and steady. "His parents were killed at Tlatelolco."

Enrique turned and checked me out, hair to Nikes. I focused on the game and managed a soft *"Ole!"* when Mexico stole a pass. Rooting for Mexico had drastically improved my relationship with Tomás Alonzo.

At least, what Diego told me about his parents was the truth. That one victory, or perceived victory, was enough to reset my bowling pins.

"Diego has no family." Enrique split his focus between me and the game. Definite progress.

"It's not true that Diego has no family. He has a daughter."

"Diego has never married."

At least Diego was not D.E.A.D.

"Yes, Enrique, Diego is married, or at least he was. He married a friend of mine on the weekend he brought me to this store."

Enrique reached for a red push button desk phone and made three quick calls. On the third call he repeated my name several times one syllable at a time from my card. I grabbed his arm.

"No, no, not LeFave. To Diego, I am Rose--Jessica Rose!"

A rush flared through my body. As if, in that moment, the sins and scars melted away and I was that wide-eyed, just-released-from-marriage-hell, nineteen-year-old. The girl who followed desire without the good sense to be afraid. Without the experience to know that some decisions born in passion can rearrange the lives of others in ways that cannot be retracted or forgiven.

Enrique hung up the phone. Without saying a word, he crossed the store, locked the front door and the cash register, and tugged the chain of the bare light bulb attached to the thirty foot ceiling by a twenty-four foot cord. Already on the go, he waved for me to follow him out the rear door.

Which I did without a blink. Because I do not have the judgment of a cognitively challenged frog.

CHAPTER 30

Apparently, I have no survival instincts at all.

Here I was, deep in Mexico City, kidnapping capital of the universe, and hometown of the kill-one-kill-all Los Insurgentes cartel. Back in Texas, my car sat with a slashed tire, and yesterday, I'd been paid a visit by the crime kingpin of this city. And what had I just done?

Without so much as an inquiry regarding our destination, I had, pretty as you please, followed a stranger into a deserted back alley.

My foolishness didn't stop there. Of my own free will, I'd sucked in my breath and gouged my stomach and rear to squeeze into the back seat of Enrique's vintage rust and celery Volkswagen Beetle.

The engine pinged, sputtered, then grabbed and held a rhythm on the fifth try, and bounced us into the rutted alley. Ouch. Iron springs popped through the patched, thin fabric seat and stabbed my derriere in three places. The passenger seat would have been my choice. Regrettably, I had not received an invitation.

Which was unfortunate. Imprisoned in the back seat, my *Escape Option Number One*--Throw open the door of the vehicle in which I am being held captive and fling my body onto the pavement—was history.

I'd made two solid decisions so far. I hadn't folded to George's insistence I carry a gun. My second good decision was to plant His Harvard Highness at the Four Seasons. Had I managed to bribe a firearm through the airport, and by some miracle, convinced George to come with me into the city, this would be the moment he shot me until he ran out of bullets. Or shot somebody.

Enrique turned out of the alley and weaved in amongst the hordes of trucks, buses, and police vans. The flaking metal bug and the confidence of his backseat prisoner were way overmatched. But I had no energy to devote to fear of a smash-up. All my strength and wit were required to prevent head and shoulder injuries as I was thrown first against one side of the car and then slammed over to the other. I fumbled for a seatbelt, but I'd have settled for a roll of duct tape. The notion I might find a seatbelt confirmed that my starry-eyed childhood fantasies were still running the show.

Enrique hadn't muttered one syllable since he'd hung up the telephone. He was not a happy man and I was clearly the source of his misery. I leaned forward and asked him where we were headed. (Yes, I'm that naïve.) Enrique said, he was so sorry, but he spoke no English. I'd understood enough of his phone conversation to know he'd disagreed with whoever asked him to take me to Diego. If indeed, in spite of my lack of skills, that's where we were headed.

Could be we were minutes away from a darkened room where I'd be tied to a chair with a sack over my head and two hours to come up with six million dollars.

Enrique continued to hunch over the wheel in a 'leave me alone' pose. Then traffic slammed to a broom-in-the-spokes freeze and Enrique threw his entire body into the horn, revealing the real reason he'd been crouched with his forehead practically pressed into the windshield.

In Mexico City, traffic lights are 'suggestions' and heeded only by the meek. Intersection management works as follows: When one direction of traffic has the most cars ramming through the intersection, that team dominates and stays on offense until a weenie driver among their lot is intimidated by the insults and blaring horns of the competing team. The alert opposing team recognizes the weak link and dives through the hole, backed up by an impressive offensive line. Rinse and repeat.

There were plenty of police officers. Most stood in horseshoe formations outside bars with televisions broadcasting the big game. I didn't blame the officers for ignoring traffic violators. The police aren't paid much and they're not stupid.

We cut from downtown onto a wide boulevard alive with push carts and eager children selling sugar-shelled gum pellets as children have since 1906 when the chewing gum, called *tziktli* by the Nahuatl speaking Aztecs and pronounced "Chicklets" by the English, was packaged for commercial profit. The median on this route featured artsy hustlers—acrobats, painters, jugglers, contortionists, and fortune tellers. And musicians if you count monkey-toting organ grinders.

The taller buildings thinned out after four or ten miles. Now streets were narrow, the pavement bumpy and buckled, unrepaired since the 1985 earthquake which killed ten thousand, or forty thousand inhabitants, according to the Mexican government's impeccable corpse counting agency.

The potholes added a new challenge to my backseat survival. When Enrique spotted a pothole, he jerked the wheel left or right with every muscle fiber in his body, which sent me flailing for a grip on whatever I could reach. Once I'd seized a metal rib on the underside of one edge of the seat, Enrique would jerk the wheel the other direction, and catapult me to the opposite side. Though the road was cursed with many dangerous obstacles, there was, apparently, no speed limit.

I can't say he was trying to kill me. But I can say, with absolute certainty, that Enrique was not overly concerned about my health.

Here, further from the city, pedestrians were smaller and darker, the women with single braids down to their hips. The low buildings had dirt or partial tile façades and looked more like unfinished products than houses in disrepair. Some white, pink, or turquoise, most cinder block gray. Roadside and sidewalk sellers offered homemade candies laid out in woven straw trays and six tacos for about a dollar. Businesses were mostly family-owned convenience stores with their entire inventories—novellas, used clothes and shoes, matches, unrefrigerated soft drinks, and huge glass vats of fruit juice--perched on window sills. Emaciated dogs peeked out of doorways followed by naked brown toddlers with mussed jet-black hair. I smiled and waved and the children waved back.

I scooted forward and asked Enrique again where we were going, this time in rehearsed and pretty damn good Spanish.

Nothing.

I dropped back into the seat, resigned to my fate. I was now stranded in a barrio distant from the city, the airport, and the Four Seasons. Oh, well. I'd be okay. I still had *Escape Option Number Two*--George's cell phone. Because this part of Mexico had to be just loaded with cell towers.

"Por favor," I added, my tone begging for mercy.

Enrique sighed. *"Usted quiere ve Señor Diego de la Cruz, No mas."* (You want to see Mr. de la Cruz, that's what you get. No more.) He hunched forward again, though there was little traffic to prod with his horn.

If Diego was the generous hero I believed him to be, why was Enrique so hostile to my request? Why wasn't he polite or even friendly?

Because Los Insurgentes is not concerned with customer service, that's why.

How could I have ignored the bloody clothes? I'd had plenty of chances to ask Camilla about Diego and I'd never broached the subject. I'd gotten a kick out of the idea of Diego as a rugged, courageous 'outlaw', just as Camilla had liked the 'idea' of a wedding announcement in the paper, the bride pictured beside a handsome 'freedom fighter'.

But, when it came to facts, what did I know about Diego—really? I knew that he was the sort of man who'd be fine with not seeing or providing for his child. I knew he was the kind of man who had no problem jumping in the sack with a woman he'd known only a few hours. I knew he had been expendable to Camilla. Oh, yes, Diego was a quite the package.

The Chief's words pulsed in my ears: "Everyone in Mexico ends up in the cartel business. I don't care how honest or fine-intentioned a person starts out."

Okay, LeFave, what are you going to do if Diego pulls a gun and repacks your luggage with tiny cellophane baggies?

I'd do what any tourist chump would do. I'd mumble and stumble my way through U.S. Immigration and Customs, positive that DRUG SMUGGLER was stamped in blinking neon on my forehead. At least I wouldn't be alone.

I flashed on George back at the Four Seasons. Oh, mama.

Nothing Enrique said or did when I mentioned Diego's family proved Diego had told me the truth about his parents or anything else. George was right. I ate that history stuff up like a trophy wife devours credit cards. Could be Diego's moving tale about the Night of Tlateloco was Mexico City's version of the guy who picks up a woman in a bar claiming he's an international man of intrigue. What kind of nut job calls himself a 'freedom fighter' anyway? In my state of emotional wreckage, I would have believed he was the reincarnation of Cuauhtémoc, the "One Who Descended like an Eagle."

Diego's eyes were what kept me in the hunt. Those shiny, almost black, eyes that crinkled at the edges. I'd seen gentleness in those eyes. Whatever else was true in his life, Diego was a good man. I was an excellent judge of a man's character.

That's why I was in Mexico back then to obliterate my brief and ridiculous marriage to my stepbrother.

Oh, yeah, Dr. LeFave. Judge of a man's character is your big-time specialty.

CHAPTER 31

Enrique parked the dingy Volkswagen in a dingier mud and gravel lot behind a white-washed two-story building with louvered glass windows cranked outward. Each opening was secured with a grate of black metal rods, the kind designed to keep people in as well as out.

Bars. Not a good sign. Maybe on Tiffany's in New York. In Mexico, not so much.

The only positive omen was a green cross painted on the back wall and not by a professional sign company. Enrique's fierce protection of Diego now made sense and George had been on the mark. The gorgeous Diego was gorgeous no more. This was some sort of sickbay so at least he wasn't dead--yet. However, I was about to discover just how soon my freedom fighter would require a blood sacrifice to Our Lady of Holy Death.

If Diego had been in this third world prison-hospital or hospital-prison for a long time, at least I had a more acceptable reason for why he'd ignored his daughter.

My trusty driver exited without a word. What now? He stood with his forearm on the lid of the VW and studied the sky. A couple of minutes or an hour dragged by, my anxiety now at a delusional level. Enrique checked his watch and made a brief phone call. Could be the cramped rear seat of Enrique's car was as far into Diego's life as Los Insurgentes intended me to venture.

Enrique kept his eyes on the rear door of the building, no doubt for the person or persons he'd rousted with the phone call. People who would take this crazy blond woman off his hands. People who would also take the hands off the crazy blond woman. Enrique knew I couldn't squeeze myself out of the back seat with any sort of speed and that if I did make it out without debilitating injury, I'd be posed in the crosshairs of whoever was watching.

My commitment suffered a severe hiccup. What now? As if to taunt me, the title of a snappy article I'd written came roaring to my rescue. "Be an Actor, Not a Reactor," I'd preached. Okay then. I would not be a victim; I would not wait for others to determine my fate. If something positive did not happen in the next thirty seconds, I would smash out the back window with my Nikes, thrust my body through the opening—the glass and bloody mess be hanged--and run like hell for Texas. Or, I would stay right where I was in this miserable German-jewel-of-perfection prison and cry like a little girl.

Turns out Enrique had a soul. His angry face crumbled—a little—with my first sniffle. He shook his head, leaned into the car, punched the release, and pulled the driver's seat forward for me. My knees and hands shook so violently on my crawl to freedom that Enrique offered to escort me to the door, which was a supreme blessing. I'm quite sure his plan had been to drive off and leave me to enter the fortress on my own. Destined to fumble from cell to cell asking for Diego in timid, jerky Spanish.

If indeed I was where I thought I was.

I tagged behind Enrique over the mud on a ragged walkway of dismantled plywood crates stamped "Panama Banana Company" in red-ink block letters. He rapped on an unpainted back door with chunks cut out of the frame from numerous break-ins. The door was also fitted with black iron bars. A petite woman in a light blue uniform with a stiff white collar, who could have been a nun or a nurse, answered. She and Enrique exchanged glances but no words. I was expected, but not anticipated.

The woman stepped aside to reveal a yawning linoleum hallway lined on both sides with young men, their arms, hands, and heads wrapped in blood-soaked rags, their faces turned away from me. Along with the men were mothers holding crying children, coughing older people, and fever-shuddering patients if all ages. Stoic expressions gave away that these citizens expected pain in life and that they'd been waiting far longer than we'd endure in the States without a winnable lawsuit. The wall was smudged black with oil from previous columns of the sick and injured. Midway down the hall a girl sat at a card table in a uniform similar to the woman who'd let me in. She looked eleven or twelve at the most. In front of her were packs of gauze and tape, stacks of papers and rags, a cigar box, and pencils tied with dirty strings stapled to the table.

Everyone was small and brown and stared at me as if I was an alien from another world. Which I was.

Enrique did not come inside, instead he backtracked over the banana crate slats to his rusty pot-hole dodger and putt-putted away. My *Escape Option Number Three:* "Swipe a set of keys, hijack a car, and head for the airport" —departed with him.

The woman who'd opened the door motioned me to follow her to the far end of the hall. I kept my eyes on the scarred vinyl, the way I'd locked my eyes on the spot in front of Camilla's boot rather than stare uninvited on another person's misery.

I was deposited in a room the size of three walk-in closets. Along the yellow plaster wall to my right, was a long metal table piled with sheets. On the opposite wall four blue molded plastic chairs were lined up behind a low steel mesh table. Above the pile of sheets was a huge clock with giant numbers and a red hand about eight inches long that jumped with each passing second. No windows. A pair of solid swinging doors across from where I came in. The scent of a recent sour mopping tainted the antiseptic air. Everything was stark, worn, and clean. A sign on the wall identified the room as either a storm shelter in case of flood or a place to store emergency water cans.

My jailer-guide's keys jingled and clicked after she closed the door. *Oh goodie.*

I pivoted left and sat in one of the plastic chairs. I watched the red second hand skip around the white clock face. After three laps of the red arm, the sheets on the long table whimpered.

What? I stood. My knees buckled. I braced myself on the back of the blue chair until I was steady. Or at least steady enough to cross the room.

The tumbled stack of sheets on the table was alive, though far from lively. The little boy on the gurney groaned. A tumor the size of a grapefruit bulged out of his neck. *Oh, man.*

My holding cell was a surgery staging area, but not like a staging area in any hospital I knew. In the treatment centers I knew, little boys were treated before tumors grew into appendages. Unconscious children were not left unattended in dingy back rooms with strangers.

LeFave, you are out of place and, just maybe, losing your mind.

Do something! For God's sake, be useful for once.

What? I took a step toward the boy. Then stopped. How could I be expected to help this frightened little boy? I needed someone to tell me what to do. Confidence in my judgment when real people were desperate had vanished with a single early morning phone call from Tucson. *Oh, Camilla. When you wrote the letter, you thought of me the way I was before.* Whatever you trusted me to see in your letter, in Frida's painting, I cannot see because the competent Jessica you depended on is dead.

I retreated to my blue plastic safety zone and angled away from the pile of sheets. *Great, LeFave. Pretend the child is not in pain. That he's not scared. Pretend. That's what you're good at.*

My eyes dove around for something to read. A magazine. Spanish, English, Chinese—didn't matter. Something to hide behind. A brochure. A can of pest repellant with ingredients and directions. The boy moaned with every ten pops of the second hand. I stared at the wall clock. I did nothing.

Six minutes plus twenty-ticks into my clock surveillance, a masked and gloved man and woman banged through the swinging doors, one kicked a notch of wood into place to prevent the doors from closing. I could tell from what little I understood of their conversation that they were physicians. Each took a side of the gurney. They rolled the little boy out and let the doors close behind them without a glance at the awkward stranger. They were too busy for foolishness.

Soon the boy was replaced with a graying man whose shin wound bled through the two-inch thick bandage around his calf. His foot faced off to the side instead of forward, the way a foot is skewed in movie shots meant to portray someone who's fallen from a great distance and is obviously dead. He didn't moan, his breath came slow and raspy. Unlike the sound of any sleeping man I'd ever heard.

At least I had one friend in the room who understood my dilemma. The white-faced clock. I gave my new best buddy my full attention and counted the heartbeats.

I did not belong in this place, this chaos of desperate people. The clock was my friend, but the delusion that kept me safe in the real world was my friend, too, and I wanted it back. I wanted to believe I was an adventurer, a daring woman about to reunite with a tall handsome lover, the beautifully groomed gentleman from Camilla's wedding. I wanted to believe I was the sort of woman who would stop at nothing to reunite a little girl with her father.

I wanted to believe I was the kind of woman who would never come between a father and his little girl. That's what I really wanted.

Tick. Tick. Here in the real world, I was minutes away from facing the withered Diego, the gangrenous Diego. The bloated near-corpse of the infected Diego. I was ridiculous. I clenched a hand on either side of my blue plastic chair. All my noble words were just that—words. I knew that now. The entire trip was foolish and a huge mistake.

Shame crawled up my spine the way it had when I'd questioned Eileen on the day her daughter was murdered and then again when Enrique told me Diego had no family. George was right. I don't deal well with death. I go crazy. I run. I hide. And I'd done it again. Instead of staying in Austin to comfort Camilla's mother and daughter, I'd added to their worries. I'd dragged George away from his life and into who knows what sort of danger. And now here I sat in a locked room in an outlaw hospital somewhere outside Mexico City. Unavailable to people who needed me and in the way of people who knew what to do to help others.

If I accomplished my goal, I was minutes away from the brass ring of thoughtlessness. I was about to inform a dying man that the mother of his child had been murdered and that a ruthless drug cartel was poised to kidnap his little girl.

Oh, I'm good at this people stuff.

Chapter 32

I plunked the back of my head against the wall and gave up.

The police knew what they were doing. I did not. Oh, I could make up stories about rose petals and the glint in Camilla's eyes, but those were not evidence or even facts. Those weren't the sort of details that made a difference once you're standing in front of a judge.

As for my righteous commitment to Camilla's daughter? Turns out, one more time, I'm too self-centered to weather the course. Forget finding Diego. My goal now was escape. Why had the nurse, or whoever she was, locked the door? No matter. The double doors were propped open for almost a minute when patients were wheeled in and out. I'd dive through to freedom. Once I made the hall, there had to be windows and unlocked doors. Fire exits. The building was a hospital, after all.

The man on the gurney groaned in an up and down rhythm. I'm not proud to admit this, but when the poor man moaned, Sammie Davis, Jr.'s fluffy innocent body flashed. Would I have a chance to kiss his sweet face again?

Brain clash. Here I was comforting myself with thoughts of a cute dog in Texas while a stranger across the room, not twenty feet away, ached for a kind touch, a word of comfort. But I wasn't the right person. I did not know what I was doing and I needed to save myself. I needed to escape to a place where I was comfortable. Not the first time I'd made that choice. *I'm sorry, Camilla.*

The foot release on the double doors clacked. Time to make a run for it. I fumbled to standing. My feet tangled under me and I didn't untangle them fast enough.

"Excuse me!" I waved at the masked faces, but they took no notice. The injured man was gone and replaced with a new patient.

I scooted my blue plastic chair to a more strategic takeoff position and planted my feet. My back to the new human lump under sheets.

The milli-second those doors popped again, I was out of there. I'd shoot through the pass, find a door to freedom, and put miles and miles, then years and years, between me and this room. This entire ill-founded fiasco would be my secret. No one beyond George needed details of the humiliating and stupid fix I'd gotten myself into. I'd admit I'd tried to find Diego and failed. But that would be the whole story. The end of it. My full report.

The young woman across the room wept softly. She kicked against her sheeted confinement in hopeless spurts. Then a muffled shout. I checked her out over my shoulder. Her arm had fallen off the gurney. She wept louder and struggled to hoist her arm back into place as if that small success would mean she would survive whatever was ahead of her. But she wasn't strong enough.

And she was alone. I couldn't risk taking my eyes off the swinging doors to freedom. What difference did it make anyway, if her arm was at her side now or two minutes from now when she was rolled into surgery? There was nothing I could do that would make a difference.

"A quarter, even a dime makes a difference when you have nothing."

Fine. I could lift an arm without making her situation worse. I could do that much before I ran back to the world I knew. The Mexico City in the brochures.

I crossed the room and clasped my bridle-roughened fingers around her tiny wrist. When I drew the sheet back to tuck in her arm, I caught a glimpse of her chest. *Oh, God.* I cut my eyes away. Why did I have to see that damned X? I snuggled her arm alongside her ribs and tamped the sheet in place.

"Por favor. . ." she whispered. She somehow managed to jerk her rescued hand out of the tucked sheet again. She reached for me.

I patted her shoulder with the emotion of hitting 'Enter' on a keyboard then sucked back out of reach. Not quick enough. Her hand flashed and caught mine. Her grip was iron. Her eyelids fluttered.

I quick-pivoted toward my blue plastic chair. She didn't let go. I gave her hand a little squeeze and nodded toward the door as if I was late for an appointment. But, no sale.

"Quédate conmigo!" she said. (Please stay with me!)

Her words compelled focus back to her face. Too late, I cut away. What now? I was a Grand Canyon beyond my comfort zone. I smoothed my fingers over her icy doll-sized hand and auditioned another purpose-laden squeeze.

"Ayudame por favor, por favor," she whispered. *"Ayudame."* (Help me, please, please. Help me.)

Me? How? I am a frightened tourist boob who doesn't even know where I am. I have a big house. I play dress-up in English fox hunting clothes and jump horses over flower pots in cities where I stay at fancy hotels. I only landed in this place by accident, an error that I would soon correct.

A concept the young woman minutes away from breast surgery did not comprehend. She opened her eyes and nailed me to the spot. *"Ayudame, por favor."*

My usual moves weren't about to meet this woman's needs. Psychologist moves required the capacity to understand each other which we clearly did not have. Psychologist moves were all I had to offer. Thus, I had nothing.

No more hinting around. I tapped her hand crisply--a Texas good old boy 'good-to-see-you-we're-done-gotta-go,' fast pat. Then I slapped reassurance on my face and wriggled my fingers to snake my way out. I concentrated on her face and relied on a severe squint to transmit my message. *I have no way to help you. Please, let go!*

Nope. Her eyes reached inside me and teased out a bit of courage. Maybe if I said something comforting, she'd let go. Small talk in Spanish, that ought to do it. The weather, I'd talk about the weather. *"Como se . . ."*

No words came to me beyond my sketchy start. Okay, English then. It's not like the words mattered as much as the tone of my voice. Still nothing came to mind that made sense. Nothing. I'd just failed at small talk. How much further down the loser side of the 'giving person' scale could I go?

My throat closed off. Tears, denied earlier, surged over the floodgates. What a mess. What a useless mess.

Then, thank God, we were rescued by, of all things, a singer. A woman with a ballad told in unhurried, bluesy style. Her words melted out and over us.

"Te-en years ago-o . . . on a cold da-ark night . . ." I crooned. "There was some . . . one killed 'neath the town hall lights . . ."

The patient rested her eyes in mine as I poured out my shower-only version of *Long Black Veil*.

"The judge said, son, what is your al-la-bi . . . . If you were some where's else . . . then you won't have to die . . ."

No one else would have chosen a song about a man who allows himself to be hanged, rather than reveal that he was in bed with his best friend's wife, but my family is profoundly-challenged in the tune-carrying department. "Long Black Veil" and "Delta Dawn" are pretty much the entire repertoire.

"Nobod-dee knows . . . nooo bo-dee sees . . . nobody knows but me . . ."

An aide and a nurse banged through the swinging doors and rolled the frightened woman to surgery. Next a young man with a black X on the left side of his forehead was wheeled into the waiting room. I scooted my blue plastic chair to his bedside and held his hand.

"Dell-tuh Dawn, what's that flower you have on? . . . . Could it be a faded rose from days gone by-eye?"

Thirty minutes later the man facing brain surgery was replaced by a woman with her right hand missing three fingers. The digits were taped to her chest in a clear plastic bag half-full of blood and ice. She shook so violently with cold, pain, and fear that I tented my body over hers. Kicked up the volume.

"And didn't I hear you say . . . he was meetin' you here to-da-ay . . . to take you to his mansion in the sky-eye?"

Next, a woman with stretch tape holding knife wounds together on her legs and her shoulders. She had defensive wounds on her hands and arms. I clasped her foot with a tenderness that must have traveled all the way back to my Appalachian mother's touch. I was sure such tenderness and courage I did not belong to me. Not anymore.

"Dell-el-tuh Dawn . . . Every-one 'round Brownsville says she's crazy . . ."

After close to an hour, the assaulted woman was replaced with the young woman with the X on her breast, my first patient.

Oh, no. Fresh blood leaked through the gauze packs on the right side of her flattened chest. But that wasn't the worst part. Her left breast was painted hideous iodine orange and deflowered with thick black circles and lines. Such a beautiful young woman. She had all of her life--children, family, grandchildren—to live for. Or at least that's the way a girl's life is supposed to work.

She seized my hand. This time her eyelids fluttered but did not open. I scrubbed my hands together until my palms and fingers were warm, picked up her little girl hand and held it between mine.

"Del . . . tuh-a Dawn . . . all the folks 'round Brownsville say she's . . ."

Thirty minutes later, the two workers I'd recognized earlier as physicians erupted through the double doors to return my patient to surgery. Each took a side of the gurney and released the brakes. She caught my fingers and pressed them to her lips.

"Por favor no me dejes." (Please, don't leave me.)

I strung enough Spanish together to ask the male surgeon if I could come with her, hold her hand, until level two anesthesia took her to a world where she wouldn't be alone. He nodded and gently cupped his hand over the hand I had attached to my girl. I turned to say thank-you to the slit of face between his green surgery cap and mask. His eyes were shiny, almost black, and crinkled slightly at the edges.

CHAPTER 33

I guess I could trash my prissy doubt that Diego could read and write.

Four hours after the launch of my bedside singing career, Diego and I settled into the doctors' lounge-kitchen. The rooms of the hospital were too precious to have only one purpose, especially if that purpose was to rest. The steel legs of the yellow plastic chairs cut into the pocked yellow brick print linoleum. The same recently mopped pine and bleach scent mixed with the boiled coffee steam and hung in the air.

We sipped coffee with floating grounds in paper cups. Either I'd been drunker than even I had admitted on the weekend of Camilla's wedding, or I'd been such a complete emotional disaster, not one sliver of Diego's reality had made it into my brain. Take that back. One part was exactly as I remembered. The gorgeous part.

Diego studied his coffee while I told him about the murder. His face darkened with the details and the official cartel-related conclusion of the authorities. Through it all, I'd held out a faint hope that Diego would jump in to refute the notion that Camilla was involved with Los Insurgentes, but he didn't.

"Was she tortured?" he asked.

"No."

"At least that's something. I've seen--no, forgive me. You don't need more hideous images in your head."

"I think she was special to them or they made an exception for the altar."

Diego covered his eyes for a moment and slipped off the green skull cap. His full black hair dropped to his shoulders. He retrieved a rubber band, and swept the black locks into a ponytail.

"Still the long hair," I said. Still the iron Aztec cheekbones.

"Only because I can't seem to get to a barber with any regularity."

The coffee flake I'd chased around my cup finally clung to my index finger. I slipped it in my mouth. Glad to have something to do with my hands.

Diego returned his eyes to his coffee, too. "The *puta* picture of Mary Magdalene . . . that was monstrous." His wide dark eyes glistened. "To be treated like that when Camilla never judged anyone."

My quest was validated. This man would want to know the mother of his child was dead.

"Such a waste of a special woman," he said. "We see plenty of senseless death around here without Los Insurgentes filling beds we don't have. Some nights we have a dozen gunshots and stabbings. There are not enough tears for the wives without husbands, the children without fathers."

And daughters with fathers they didn't know existed.

"I'm sorry for barging in on you like I have," I said. "But, I couldn't get anyone to give me your phone number or even tell me where you were."

"Our mission requires absolute secrecy. We have to move often as it is. We take in army, police, cartel enforcers, and their victims. If word gets out that we have saved the life of an enemy, every patient is in danger, the doctors are dead men. The young ones, they'd shoot their way in just for the drugs."

Speaking of the young ones, why hadn't Diego asked about Ana Teresa?

"About Camilla," I said, "I know you haven't been a part of Ana Teresa's life . . ."

"That wedding was quite a gala, wasn't it?"

What? Where was the caring father, absentee or not, I'd risked my life to find? George was right. I'd made Diego into someone special over a seventy-two hour period, not one hour of which was I sober. Eileen was right, too. Diego's world had nothing in common with hers, mine, or the broken world of his lovely daughter.

"Camilla was so happy," Diego said. "I'll always remember her the way she was that afternoon, about to pop, bubbling over with joy."

About to pop? Bubbling over? Was he saying Camilla was too excited? That she was manic?

Stop it, LeFave. You are turning something good into something pathological. A diagnosis is a dangerous label--good news and bad news. The good news is, you don't feel so alone and medications can be more specific. The bad news is, people will see everything you do as caused by whatever label you've been assigned. Not just for years or decades, for generations.

"All I know is," Diego said, an inappropriate glint in his dangerous eyes, "the whole weekend was wild and special."

Anyway, if I'd known how to recognize a manic episode back then, I would have labeled my own behavior as manic. Followed closely with reckless and stupid.

"I enjoyed the weekend, too," was all I could manage. "But that's not why I'm here . . ."

My face burned under his gaze. I wasn't the crazy girl he knew from before. I was a woman with a life, responsibilities, and a permanently damaged heart. My only goal in Mexico City now was to help Camilla in any way I could. Even if Diego wasn't interested in his daughter's welfare.

"I only saw Camilla a few times afterward," Diego said. "Usually mornings at La Merced. From the first moment she knew, she was thrilled about the baby and so was her mother. I was grateful for Camilla's generous support and pleased to be part of her life. The work here is supported by San Luis Fernando Artes."

"Not a chance." I managed a chuckle. "Remember, Enrique brought me here in the fabulous corporate limo."

"Oh, yes, it's all coming back now." Again with the tiny, familiar grin. "Apparently, Jessica Rose, you are not naïve as you acted when we first met."

"Sadly, it wasn't an act, more like a cover for raging insanity."

"The truth?" Diego said. "My great-grandfather made a fortune when railroads came into the country. I choose to spend my share here and Enrique manages the funds."

"But your parents--"

"I said they were idealistic students who died fighting for the rights of the poor. Not that they were poor."

"Oh. In my family, 'student' translates to destitute."

"Did your life get any better, Jessica?"

"I sobered up, if that's what you mean. Went back to school, got a doctorate, now I'm a psychologist."

"Sounds like you took off."

"Like a rocket."

"Congratulations."

"Thanks. Unfortunately, my rocket was the kind that blows to smithereens when it clears the earth. I married one of my professors."

"Still great--"

I closed my eyes and shook my head. "No, not great. Not great at all. A patient with a dirty little secret murdered him to make sure the truth would stay buried."

Diego scooted his chair alongside mine and took my hand.

"There's more," I said. "David was married with two little girls when I was his student. He left his to be with me and when the younger girl was a teenager, she killed herself."

What was going on here? I'd never said those words in the same sentence to anyone. George could see through to the crossed wires in my head, but I'd never officially connected the circumstances of my marriage to David with Kelly's suicide. Not out loud.

And, why were we talking about me?

"I'm sorry," I said, quickly. "And profoundly embarrassed for answering your 'How are you doing?' with my life story. Part of it is the stark purity of the work you do here. When you congratulated me, I couldn't let your honorable presumption float past. I couldn't stand the hypocrisy."

"It's okay."

"No, it's not okay. I'm here to talk about Camilla and your daughter, not my reality television lifetime of poor choices."

"You're quite a surprise, Jessica." Again with the slight smile, the crinkled eyes.

"Quite a mess, you mean."

His attention wasn't flattering. I did not come to Mexico City to find a man who was more interested in my life than his own daughter's.

"The way I had this meeting pictured," I said, "I'd impress you with my education and the fact that, unlike before, I can both limit, and pay, for my own drinks. Then I'd tell you about Camilla, turn around, and fly back Texas."

"It took courage for you to find me way out here."

I nodded a blunted 'thanks' and launched an over-eager search of my pockets. A photo would turn the trick. "I brought a picture of Ana Teresa."

Diego sat back instead of leaning forward in anticipation. The kind man I'd trusted Diego to be would have held out his hand while I searched for the photo. He'd have bombarded me with questions about his little girl.

"Ana Teresa is smart, fun, and has a great sense of humor. She's a little quiet sometimes like her mother."

I sorted through the set of laminated photos always in my back pocket. "I didn't know how long it's been since you've seen her or if you'd ever seen what a lovely child you have. She comes over to my house a lot. The woman who lives with me is from Culiacán. Her cousins built me a little pool and one of my dogs is more porpoise than canine."

I handed him the photo. "This shot is of Ana Teresa in the pool with Miss Suzi Wong."

"One thing for sure," he said. "She's destined to be a beauty like her mother."

And her father.

A smile bloomed and his eyes lit up in that moony way that happens when parents gaze on photographs of their children.

He handed the picture back. "You're right. She is a lovely gift from God. But I'm not her father."

"I know. Not in the sense that you've been in her life--"

"Not in any sense."

"You should see her ride."

"I'm not the child's father."

What? "The wedding--"

"Camilla was a wonderful woman and I was glad to stand in, but we were never intimate."

"But-"

"I think I'd remember, Jessica."

I'd gulped down the 'friends with one night of passion' fairytale like I'd swallowed everything I was told. If I'd had a functioning brain cell, I would have recognized that Diego was doing a favor for a friend, nothing more. Had there been more to their relationship, like say--a child—he would never have left the wedding with me.

That Diego wasn't Ana Teresa's father was crushing, but along with his news came another dilemma. Camilla trusted me. We trusted each other. Her decision to keep me in the dark through the wedding was the sensible choice. Still, in the years since there had been many opportunities, many heartfelt, shared intimacies. Why had she kept the truth from me?

Diego chuckled. "Well, this is a relief. I couldn't figure out why you'd gone to all this trouble to find me. I mean, I'm glad you did, but it didn't make sense."

"My embarrassment knows no bounds. No wonder Eileen tried to talk me out of looking for you."

"No, Eileen believes I am the father, perhaps because she found me an acceptable choice, and I'm polite."

"You're cute, too." I gave him a light punch.

"I'm sure Eileen is worried sick for your safety and she was right to warn you. How is she doing?"

"Pretty much how you'd expect."

"Your heart was in the right place. Eileen knows that. It's not the first time a daughter has kept the father's identity from her mother."

"True. You don't by any chance . . ."

"I never asked."

"What about a guess?"

"For whatever reason, I picked up that the father was no longer around or that Camilla didn't want him at the wedding. Since the child would be raised principally in the U.S., not having a second parent to complicate matters seemed to suit her."

"I had my heart set that you were Teresa's father and you'd be loaded with details about the people and issues in Camilla's Mexico City life. That you would point me to friends or lovers, and those people would have stories. By the time I stepped on the plane back to Texas, I'd have a list of people who had something to gain with Camilla out of the way."

"Sorry to disappoint."

"I am not leaving Mexico City accomplishing nothing. If I can't come up with a solid reason to point the investigation away from a straight up Los Insurgentes hit, Camilla's death will go down as one more meaningless cartel hit. I can't let that happen. I need your help."

He shrugged and smiled. "I'd have to find a way in. But once we're inside her house . . ."

"*Yes.* Thank you. Thank you."

"So, you'll hang around until I can get one of the other docs to come in?"

"The odds are good. Since I have no idea where I am, and I have no means to leave."

"Whatever else happens, your trip won't have accomplished 'nothing'."

"The woman with--"

"Yes. Her priest brought her in last night. She'd never seen a doctor and was terrified. Her tumor was the size of an egg. We'd hoped we could save one breast, but the malignancy had spread to bilateral lymph nodes. She's only seventeen."

"I didn't know you could get breast cancer that young."

"Thanks for whatever you did."

"I didn't really do anything."

"Did you pray with her?"

"Something like that."

CHAPTER 34

Glorious swells of magenta bougainvillea overflowed the lofty stone walls as they had the first time I'd pulled up to Los Palomas. Again the delicate clusters of doves and flowers in the forged wrought iron gates touched my heart. The weekend of the wedding, I'd been behind the wheel of my ancient Mustang with Nancy Margaret next to me, twitchy and bossy. George in the back seat oohing and aahing in disbelief that a public school kid was friends with whoever owned this grand estate.

On the weekend of the wedding, the gatekeeper, a longtime employee of Camilla's, had stepped gaily out of the guardhouse and ushered us through as if we were long lost relatives or friends. I later suspected that his delight was rooted in his knowledge that while Eileen anxiously awaited the arrival of friends she'd invited from the Flower Mound Country Club, we were the first, and, as it played out, the only Texans who showed up.

Today's guard didn't treat us like long lost friends or relatives of any kind. This kiosk sentry, tricked out in a black uniform with gold stars on the shoulders, was from a private company and indifferent to our personal story.

"Ninguna entrada. Nadie, nadie. Desaparecen!" (No entrance. No one. Nobody. You leave now!)

The guard's hand dropped below the window for mystery reinforcement. Oh, no.

"Aye, esperar!" Diego said, big grin on his face. *"Senorita Cervantes me dio una clave a su casa."* ("Oh, wait! Miss Cervantes gave me a key.") He dangled the key between his thumb and index finger for the gatekeeper's examination.

The guard shrugged, pressed a button, and the heavy ironwork gates swung open.

Again I was stunned with what I didn't know, or even suspect, when it came to Camilla and Diego.

Diego parked the car, an Eastern European subcompact called a CliQ, inside the courtyard. I followed him to the two-story carved wooden doors, long sharp strides intended to convince the guard I knew what I was doing. Diego pulled from his pocket what looked like a three-fold ice pick. Attached to the pick was a chain decorated with a dozen or so charms in the shape of miniature arrows. Diego took me by the shoulders and repositioned my body between the guard and the door.

"I thought you have a key," I said, still all round-eyed Alice in Wonderland.

"I do. I have a key to everywhere. There are advantages to running hospitals in abandoned buildings with absentee landlords."

While I waited, I admired the lush courtyard as I had long ago. The stone fountains, banana trees, two story hibiscus plants, orchids, and palm fronds accented by yellow, blue, and green enameled Talavera pottery, had helped me understand why Camilla retreated here for school holidays and summers when we were kids.

No, that's not the truth. My fantasy that Camilla chose to vacation here because of the house's charms, like my fantasy that she'd made new friends, was merely one more Pollyanna see-what-I-wanted-to-see exercise.

Camilla stayed at her father's house because no one here knew about Major, the burned barn, and the mental hospitals.

With the third arrow and pick combination we were in the house. We crept through the living room and the enormous kitchen designed for several cooks. Next the sunroom, stoked to the high ceiling with leafy plants. I took care to step soundlessly from carpet to carpet until we reached Camilla's suite, which made no sense as we knew no one was in the house. The spacious office was organized off her bedroom in a sitting area with atrium doors onto the courtyard.

Diego positioned two small lamps on the floor. In the darkness, the twenty foot ceilings and ornate mahogany furniture made for plenty of peculiar echoes and ominous shadows. The last time I'd been in this bedroom I'd spent most of my time sitting on her giant four poster bed laughing with Camilla. She'd answered my endless questions as I combed through the scrapbooks she'd saved from all over Europe.

On the trip across town with Diego, I'd asked him straight out about Los Insurgentes and he'd agreed that Camilla couldn't have continued her work without cartel cooperation. I asked if Camilla could have been buying girls directly from El Viborito and if Adriana, George's seat mate, could have been a rescue from the Little Snake's stable.

Diego had looked up at the sky and shrugged: *What difference would that make?*

He was right. When a little girl has the opportunity to scrub hotel rooms in the U.S. over a life of slavery, sexual degradation, and pain, every day of her short life-- who cares how that happened?

He went on to say that, while he hadn't spent much time in the market area, he had the impression that, over the years, as Camilla helped families reclaim their children, she became friends with people involved in La Merced commerce of all kinds. He didn't know about Camilla's relationship with El Viborito recently, but back at the time of the wedding, she'd spoken kindly, even a little defensively about him, as if the odd little man saw personally to her protection. As for why Viborito had been after her letter, or why Camilla might have been in the hospital a few days ago, Diego had no clue.

I paused to take in the familiar walls and paintings. I pictured Camilla packing for Texas as she had so many times. How was it possible that only three days ago, she'd packed and made plans with no way to know she was leaving her father's house for the last time?

Wait. Camilla had considered the possibility she'd never return ". . . *should anything happen to me . . .*" I brushed my fingers over the leather writing pad and sat down at my friend's desk. Camilla must have sat in the chair I now occupied when she wrote her letter. My friend, what did you tell me in your careful words that I cannot see?

The answer could be right in front of me. I sat back in the brass-bradded leather chair and opened the top drawer. A personal motive meant a relationship motive and relationships are revealed in travel records, dining receipts, photographs, and notes. Camilla was exquisitely methodical and neat in her bookkeeping.

Exquisitely methodical. The sort of methodical required to make exceptional grades. Not compulsive. Not Manic. An image flashed. Kelly leaping the tango around the kitchen the August morning after she'd stayed up all night alphabetizing every CD, DVD, and book in the house. *Stop it, LeFave.* She'd cross indexed to author, artist, and titles. *Stop. It. Now.*

Camilla apparently saved everything. Somewhere in these rooms I could probably find hospital records, even childhood diaries. Maybe I could even discover the information I both wanted and dreaded--the medication, treatment, or relationship support that Camilla received that Kelly had not. But, no matter. Now was not the time for my questions.

Now was about the months and days around the weekend of Camilla's wedding and after. Border crossings and criminal records be hanged. I needed to know about the people in Camilla's life, especially any man who could be Ana Teresa's father. I dragged out a chunk of folders and plunked the stack in front of me. Diego was stationed at a four drawer wooden file cabinet along the wall.

"I'm pulling out anything and everything around the time of the wedding and since, especially anything involving a man," I said. "The fact that Camilla continued to let me believe you are Ana Teresa's father is big."

"Grab and go makes sense to me. We can sort the piles later my place."

"Perfect." George wouldn't object as long as Diego and I chose anywhere other than the Four Seasons to spend the night.

"Lucky for you," Diego said, "I possess keys to several lovely hotels with excellent security, which I'd rather occupy in case our presence in Camilla's house bothers Los Insurgentes."

Again, the easy connection of Camilla with Los Insurgentes. I shuffled through American Express and Merrill Lynch account summaries while Diego started in on a drawer crammed with pictures. Camilla's extraordinarily methodical approach did not extend to photographs.

"Maybe this wasn't such a great plan," I said, after sorting folders loaded with numbers. "Even someone as meticulous as Camilla wouldn't take up current desk space with financial records over a decade old."

"We should switch places. People do keep photographs that long and the only people I recognize in these are Eileen and Camilla. . . . Here you go, a shot from when Camilla was a bebé. She's with her father at a fiesta. Looks like she was three or four."

I joined him to take a peek. On the back of the photo, *"Mi Papi."*

"She was a daddy's girl, all right."

I didn't remember Mr. Cervantes very well from when I was a kid, but he looked exactly like I thought he would. Proud father, his overcoat a bit too large, but just right to nestle his beautiful daughter in the crook of his elbow. One of Camilla's tiny arms snuggled his neck and the other gripped doll Frida, who was almost as big as she was.

I clunked the top drawer of photos onto the floor, sat down, and composed rough stacks according to the approximate time in Camilla's and Ana Teresa's lives when the pictures were taken. Along with the expected photo chronology were two surprise characters. Alejandro Lopez-Cardenas, the Argentine polo player Camilla met when he was in the city to expand his family's banking empire and introduced at the wedding as a short term boyfriend, showed up several times. Even more of a surprise, were shots of Scott Maris in attendance at birthday parties for Ana Teresa at Las Palomas. If Scott was in the shot, Lopez-Cardenas wasn't.

The Argentine was an unknown quantity, but perhaps I shouldn't rule out the possibility that Scott Maris had told me the truth about his relationship with Camilla. Still, if the two of them were in love, why hadn't Scott bolstered his credibility by revealing his trips to Las Palomas? Both Alejandro Lopez-Cardenas and Scott Maris were excellent candidates, though the thought that either was Ana Teresa's father didn't make me feel all warm and fuzzy.

I found an empty box in Camilla's closet and piled my stack of financial records and photographs into it. Then I went back to the file cabinet for more pictures. The second drawer was equally disorderly and stuffed, with two more to go. How was it possible that two days ago I'd waited for Camilla to help me with my silly horse, and now she was gone and I was in her bedroom?

"This is weird," I said, "being in Camilla's house so soon after . . ."

"I know." Diego opened another drawer of the desk. "Most of us can picture ourselves sorting through a deceased person's things—but weeks, months, or even years after they are gone. I've seen a lot of early death. You'd think those experiences would make it easier, but it doesn't."

"No, it doesn't." *Leave the early death subject alone, LeFave.* "Diego?"

"Yes?"

"Do you believe there's any value in . . ."

"Yes?"

"Do you take flowers to your parents' graves on the Day of the Dead?"

CHAPTER 35

"Of course!" Diego said, from the chair at Camilla's desk. "Of course, I visit my family on the Day of the Dead. No one misses that opportunity. Family makes you who you are."

That part I knew all too well.

"However," he added, upbeat. "Though I celebrate at the cemetery, my parents' remains are not buried in the family plot."

"Right, right. I'm sorry." I bit my lip and reopened the cut. Diego's father and mother had been 'disappeared' by the government's secret service before the opening of the 1968 Olympics.

"You want to know something nuts?" I asked.

"I like nuts." Diego paused his search to lend me his full attention.

"The grandmother of one of my riding friends owned a horse on the Olympic Equestrian Team that summer. There are pictures from the 68 Olympics all around the riders' lounge and I've heard dozens of stories. But not a word about a protest or anyone killed by the police. When it comes to the media, priorities are all wrong."

"Oh, you mustn't worry so much about the state of the universe," Diego said, his crinkled eyes smiling right in the middle of my murdered friend's belongings.

"Nice plan."

"It's not a plan, Jessica." He dialed down his smile. "It's a way of life. In Mexico we have many troubles. People everywhere have many troubles. Only you Norte Americanos expect life to be different than it is. The whole point of the Day of the Dead is to remind us to let go of our anger about what we cannot change. I cannot change when and how my parents died and I've had little success changing how other people spend their money."

My throat caught. Let go of what we cannot change? How does a person do that?

"Oh, but I do enjoy my parents on the Day of the Dead. I have headstones for them and a special garden for each. My grandmother said chocolate was my mother's favorite sweet, and my father loved custard cups, but only the finest—which I think was her way of saying he liked the custard she cooked best. The day before the Day of the Dead, I have a great time searching LaMerced for the best dark chocolate and custard cups. Every few years I try my hand at the custard cups, but I think my father prefers those from the market. Those are certainly more appealing to the eye."

"Custard cups?" This guy was nuts.

"Yes. I tinker in the dirt and sing songs with the others."

"You *tinker*?"

"I wouldn't miss it. Because my parents are not here doesn't mean I can't enjoy the love they have for me and I have for them. Why the interest in that day? We have many Saint Days and loco fiestas here."

"The Santa Muerte at the murder scene, I guess."

Diego wasn't fooled. He knew my Day of the Dead question came from the heart and had nothing to do with the murder scene. It's a good thing I don't play poker for money.

"Along with the flowers and candies," he continued, now back to the files. "I read the newspaper for that day out loud, front to back. I leave books and articles that would interest a couple in their twenties."

"I guess I understand a little of what you mean. My mother, who was from Smokey Junction, Tennessee, had eight brothers and sisters. When we were kids, we'd go to the Jones reunion every summer. One day was spent on the mountainside family cemetery. We'd clean headstones, weed, and tend to plants. Great aunts and uncles would tell us stories about the people in the ground. I guess it was sort of the same as your celebration. After my mother died, I never saw any of her family again."

"Why not?"

"Lots happened. My father married right away into another family. My stepmother's children had lots of distracting problems. The truth is, when my mother died, the family that went to the reunions died, too."

Diego paused his riffle through Camilla's files and looked my way until he had my attention again. "Oh, dear. Jessica, you have much to accomplish. Trust me, your dead family misses you. They need you and you need them."

"You sound like Camilla. She said spirits are everywhere. We can't see them because we don't know where to look."

"She was right, you know. Camilla was born into a rich person's world in Texas—born at a country club, right?"

"Well, not exactly but close."

"And she was crazy about her mother, but down deep, I think she preferred the more earthy priorities of Mexico. Jessica?"

"Yes?"

"I am being very serious now."

"Okay . . ."

"Jessica, if you ignore your dead, you cannot experience being truly alive."

"I'd like that." Images locked in my heart and unsaid prayers choked off my brain. I wasn't ready. "I'd like to feel truly alive again."

"Then, my lady, you must have your very own, your personal, Day of the Dead party."

"You're serious?"

"Yes. You must go to where the souls of your family wait. Apologize to your people if that's what you want to do first. Apologizing seems to be your specialty. But don't stop there. After all, being dead can't be that interesting. Catch your people up on the new babies and who in the family is a good cook. We believe that you never let go of people you love. Also, the people who loved you when they were here? We believe your people don't stop loving you because they're dead."

It is time to tell the Tucson story.

At three in the morning on the Day of the Dead, my younger stepdaughter turned off the alarm she'd set for three a.m. to guarantee uninterrupted success. She collected the hose she'd earlier removed from the swimming pool pump and hooked it up to the exhaust of her sister's car. Duct tape to be sure.

She wore her glasses. Why? Her glasses had clacked to the asphalt when I dropped her urine soaked blanket into the dumpster in the parking lot of her apartment. I'd scooped the glasses up and hesitated.

I put them on. The plastic arms of her frames didn't quite hook over my ears. The world was so distorted I could barely recognize shapes. I turned and strained to read a billboard for Diet Coke a couple of blocks over. I could hear cars and trucks whiz past the sign on Interstate 10. But I couldn't make them out.

So now what? I'd ripped the glasses off my face, stripping a chunk of skin from the top of my nose. The bloody strip snagged in the nose pad dripped one scarlet blotch on my shirt. I tossed her perfect, expensive glasses on the pile of garbage. Then I clutched the slimy rim of the dumpster, and vomited.

As for choosing the Day of the Dead? I suspect Kelly was more aware of Halloween, only three hours old. I'd been careful not to push my habit of sitting in the back of churches burning candles when I needed a little light in the darkness. I was scrupulous, afraid even, to take over any more of the girls' lives than my presence, my very existence, already had. I wish I'd shared my faith in the mysterious. I wished I'd done a lot of things that wouldn't have made any difference. I wish I hadn't done some things that did.

The weekend before that last morning, Kelly had stayed with us at a resort in the Catalina foothills north of Tucson. As she and I made our way to the restaurant for breakfast, I'd remarked on the mountain beauty around us and she'd said, "That's what I've been trying to tell you, Jess. I can't see beauty anymore."

I didn't believe her.

I didn't believe such a wonderful young girl could lose touch with the very earth. I probably said as much. More great people work by the stepmother-psychologist.

What about Frida and Camilla? Had they confessed their hopelessness to someone who'd listened? Whatever the answer, Camilla and Frida found a way to see beauty again. And Kelly did not.

Everyone I knew and more than a few strangers had taken a turn at convincing me that her parents' divorce wasn't the tipping factor for Kelly. There were days when I almost believed that. What I knew for a fact, however, was that Kelly's life would have been different without me in it. There would be a difference in the way Kelly faced and dealt with her depression. If her father had stayed with her mother, I believed there existed a greater chance that she would be alive.

David was a kind and generous man. What if he'd been there with a kiss every morning when she left for school? A hug every afternoon before he settled in to hear about her classes, her teachers, and her friends? What if he'd been there to gently tuck her in every night and soothe her nightmares? What then?

Alive instead of dead is a very big difference.

I am trained to say an outsider cannot break up a good marriage. But I do not know that. I do not believe that.

"Pardon?" I asked, mentally slapping myself back to the task at hand. I'd missed Diego's question.

"I asked about Camilla's mother, what she might do with this house."

"Keep it for Ana Teresa, I'm sure. That's what Camilla would want. I honestly don't know how Eileen is going to make it through the loss of Camilla. The whole time Camilla was growing up, she devoted herself to helping her and did a great job. And now . . . when her daughter is grown and has a terrific child of her own, when Camilla is happy in her life, some son-of-a-bitch . . ."

Two beams of light swept wall to wall.

". . . Because," I said, a firm grip on denial, "a tiny percentage of Americans love co-co—caine . . ."

Headlights. Then dark. Clattering in the black nothingness outside.

I hit the floor, belly down.

Diego scooted across the rug and pulled the plugs on the floor lamps. A minute later the cone of a high-powered flashlight ducked in and around tall planters in the courtyard.

You wanted to feel truly alive? This ought to do it, kiddo.

"We were followed?" I said, once he was next to me.

"More likely the guard made a call."

Diego honed in on the source of the flashlight and determined there were two men, both out of their car and methodically surveying each room around the horseshoe. He took my hand and inched toward the glass doors.

"Diego?"

"*Que?*"

"If the guard called us in, why don't we just tell them who we are? Have them call Eileen, she'll vouch for us."

"Mrs. Cervantes is not in charge anymore. And the man I can see from here has a gun."

"But if it's a legitimate security company--"

"Legitimate?"

"Oh. Yeah."

"You're not in Texas anymore, Jessica." Diego turned and landed a wink.

Two men with guns and this guy *winks?*

"I might not know who I'm dealing with or know what I'm doing," I said, "but I will not leave this house without this box."

"Fine with me." He hoisted my box of Camilla's life story under one arm and pointed toward the pool. "Follow me, stay low, and do not stop moving."

I could do that, unless "stay low" compromised my suddenly bursting bladder.

"We have two advantages," Diego said, as we skulked along below the roving beam of light. "They haven't spotted us and no one's manning their vehicle."

Again, a surprise. This wasn't the first time Diego had slipped out of a place he'd visited without permission. I believe in Texas we called it 'breaking and entering'.

"To get out of here," he said, "we have to give up the first advantage and make reaching my car our only goal."

"Okay." I stood up and pressed my chest into his back. My knee-jerk resistance to taking orders vanished when firearms were involved.

"Stay close to me."

"Not a problem."

"Now we run," he whispered, and charged.

We were around the pool in seconds.

The flashlight nailed us. The lead gunman so close I felt his breath wheeze on the back of my neck. We made it to the car and crashed into the front seat through the driver's side. My bladder held.

"Alto! Pare. Le dispararé!" echoed off the stone. "I will shoot you also!" shouted a bilingual second-in-command, which made no sense unless our pursuers knew who I was.

Diego turned the key and the CliQ getaway rocket twanged on all four cylinders.

The frontrunner, in a tan uniform right out of *Viva Zapata!* punched the release on the passenger door I hadn't thought to lock. I slammed the sucker down.

Zapata Man banged his gun on the window. *Nothing to do with me . . . Nothing to do with me.*

Diego did a one-eighty, backed up, then aimed the CliQ at the midline of the locked gates. He reared back and stood straight up on the gas pedal.

I grabbed his arm. "No!"

"A good hit dead in the middle will pop it," he said.

"Pop it? What if it doesn't . . . pop?"

"This is Mexico. We don't play that side of the bet."

I ached to close my eyes, to hide my current situation from my brain, but I couldn't.

As for the bit where your life is supposed to flash before your eyes? What flashed before my baby blues was George Ramsdale's reflection on the gigantic high definition football broadcast at the Four Seasons Bar. His eyes growing wider and his black eyebrows arching higher as he is told the name of the Underground Metro station where he is ordered to drop the cash. Or where he must appear to buy my way out of a Mexican jail. Or a Mexican morgue.

The kiosk guard played noble and stood his ground smack in the middle of the gates until we were within ten feet. Then, a nanosecond before the CliQ morphed into a fifty mile an hour aluminum and steel wedge, he flung himself out of the way like a flea off a burning rug.

The gates whacked open and we were out. Before the first turn off the neighborhood street, the bad guys were in the rearview. The monster black SUV I'd been expecting since I dove into my certified airport taxi was now fifty yards back and closing. The bursting bladder returned.

"Outrunning them is not going to work," I said, relying on my extensive experience with Vin Diesel movies.

"Hang on!"

"Not seeing any other choice here, Diego!"

Four hard turns and we were out of the quiet Coyoacán neighborhood and fishtailing onto a wide boulevard jammed with buses with passengers hanging out the sides from loops, and hundreds of taxis with drivers who'd lost the will to live.

I checked the rear. Bad guys right on our tail. *Right on our tail.* I squeezed Diego's upper arm and moaned Sammie Davis, Jr.'s 'end of the world' pity wail.

Diego focused straight ahead and grinned. What's with this guy?

He reached under his seat and pulled out what looked like half of a red plastic football. He locked the emergency swirly light on the top of his car with his left hand and with his right he hit his horn which made the "woop, woop dat-dat-dat-dat" of a Mexican ambulance. Brakes squealed. Tiny cars, bulky trucks, and swaying buses whipped dutifully out of the way. Diego zipped ahead through a Good Samaritan hole in the solid mass of shifting steel.

Had this been the U.S., our pursuers could have taken advantage of the right-of-way cleared by our emergency vehicle. But this was Mexico City. Any driver who gave us a break snapped back into the competition so fast, we were lucky to not get clipped on the rear.

CHAPTER 36

I called George from the balcony of our room at the Camino Real Hotel. Other than being three times the size, the room had a spooky resemblance to my bedroom back in Austin with a monumental step up in taste and class.

The walls were hung with pre-Columbian reproductions and a double full length mirror inside a blue wooden frame carved with Mayan folk art painted in bright reds, greens, and yellows. Etched copper wall sconces lit the adobe with candlelight softness and warmed the marble floor made up of pink and white slabs separated by strips of gold. An antique armoire with brass-handled doors concealed the television. Not that piped in entertainment was on the agenda.

From where I stood, I could see Chapultepec Park including the zoo and the lakes and Chapultepec Castle, home of the fatally unlucky Emperor Maximilian and the gorgeous, but unhinged Carlotta. George's cell phone was cocked under my chin while the Four Seasons concierge routed my call from the hotel to where he'd sent George for the evening, the *Tres Palmas Caliente Turf Club.*

"God, I love this country!" George said. Glasses clinked in the background. People roared encouragement in Spanish. "These fellows are teaching me how to bet soccer—oh, excuse me—phu-uut-ball."

Of course, what George *meant* was, "I love the turf club near the Four Seasons at the Airport!" I didn't have the heart to mention that if I was making a list of the most dangerous places to hang out in Mexico City, a gambling hall would rank in the top three. Not that he would change his location. George suffered from selective paranoia.

Anxious for answers, I'd dumped Camilla's records on the vast coral and cream pillowed bed when we'd first arrived. Now that I knew George considered himself in good hands, I started back in on the photographs which presented quite a project. Not only were the pictures jumbled, after Ana Teresa was born, Camilla and Eileen had a habit of multiple copies.

Thirty minutes into my scrapbook exercise, Diego talked me into a break. He pushed aside the stacks.

Though I'd spent most of the time we'd had together insisting I was nothing like the girl he'd known years ago, turns out some things about me were the same. With Diego it felt right to inhabit my body. For a woman who'd flown from Austin, Texas, that morning, put in a shift at a hospital, burglarized a house, and escaped gun-wielding pursuers, I had astounding energy.

Two hours later, we sat at a white table-clothed and crystal appointed table over-looking the city. Suspended. Suspended in the Angel Sky Bar and suspended in the forward motion of our lives. It had rained every afternoon on the August weekend of Camilla's wedding and it had rained today, so that the cathedral spires and glass skyscrapers sparkled in the starlight. The tequila sours were still made with lemons so freshly squeezed my nose prickled.

Diego, always extra togs in his car, had changed into jeans with a Concho belt, a full white shirt, and re-ponytailed his hair. He'd shaved, so that now he was even more painfully handsome. Which was okay, I had a little time before I had to be back in Texas.

We lingered over steaks, more tequila sours, and shared wonderful stories of Camilla for two hours. When I shared the Dorados with him, his eyes glistened and we drifted off into how and when you lose your parents changes your life. Then we strolled the Paseo de la Reforma hanging on each other like newlyweds, the warm and edgy ambiance of Mexico City flooding my cells.

A few others walked along the quiet Paseo. Early birds on the way to morning shifts at hotels and restaurants. Hangers-on from the city's famous Polanco and Zona Rosa after-hours scenes. On the downward steps of churches we passed, old women peeked out of black shawls and held out withered palms as they have since the beginning of time.

A flower vendor, his clown face faded, sold Diego a paper cone of fresh cut red hibiscus and white calla lilies in honor of Camilla and her favorite artist. As we walked, he twisted the blooms and stems into a closed chain. Then he placed the flowers over my head and onto my shoulders.

I reached back and held his hand where he touched my neck. "I'm not the flowers type, Diego."

"I have to put them somewhere," he said. "I've already paid for them."

"Thanks." I dipped my chin to catch the hibiscus smell. Blossom dust stuck to my nose and tickled.

"Anyway, it's our tradition," he said, brushing away the fuzz. "I bought you a hibiscus and lily chain when we walked the Paseo before. Remember?"

"No, sadly, I do not."

"That is sad."

"I've wanted to talk with you about that weekend," I said. "But you're not my Father Confessor and I've already forced too many whiney stories on you."

We approached the traffic circle jeweled with the huntress Diana atop her minaret. Diego held my elbow as we crossed the street to a brass bench and sat down to be fully alive for a few minutes under the watch of the goddess.

"Now don't try to cheat me!" he said. He pulled me down to sit beside him. "I insist on one more whiney story."

I picked up his hand. "As you may have noticed, I wasn't exactly a pillar of mental health when we met. . . . I must have come across as a slut with equal parts of insanity and an alcohol problem."

"And I thought you were overwhelmed by my dashing looks and impeccable charm."

I swatted him on the shoulder and slipped in a side hug. "Sometimes I wonder how I might have been different if I'd taken you up on your invitation to stay in Mexico City a while. Maybe I'd have gotten my head straight and made better choices when I returned to Texas."

"Who knows, you could have made worse choices. We can't always know how our decisions will work out."

"You always take the high road," I said. "Camilla was the same way. In our friendship, I was the whiner for both of us which wasn't an easy job."

"It's our backward, half-Indian, half-Catholic culture."

My mind was tranquil, a rare condition.

"How much did you love the professor?" he asked.

"He's the only man I've known that I could be married to forever."

"I'll try not to take that personally. How soon did you know?"

"The moment he spoke. He didn't know I existed. I was one of three hundred students in the lecture hall. After class, I stood on the curb to cross the main university drag, barely able to wait for the light to turn green. When it did, I stepped off. By the time I reached the other side, I knew my life was changed forever."

"Then your choice was not all a mistake. Not many men ever have a woman feel that way about them."

I was revving up my "But, what if?" questions when Diego squeezed my hand.

"The 'stay a while' invitation stands."

"I don't think I could have kept up with Camilla and I'm positive I can't keep up with you. Do you ever take a day off? You could come to *Los Estados Unidos.*"

We stood and walked toward the Monument to the Revolution. The inky eastern sky now met the earth with a thin strip of rosy light.

"There is one place in the States I'd like to visit if I can ever string two or three days together," Diego said. "Have you ever heard of Chimayo, New Mexico?"

"Oh, yeah. Wow. Surprising choice. I like it. I like it very much."

The simple church in Chimayo, a tiny mountain town an hour out of Santa Fe, was one of my mystical candle burning hideouts. The church has a special room set aside to pray for children who are missing, sick, or deceased. The walls are covered with photographs and stories of lost children, discarded child-sized crutches, and limb braces of all sorts. The back room of the church has a floor of magical sand. Visitors are encouraged to take a spoonful with them. The sand can work miracles because it is a miracle. No matter how many people take away a share, the sand never runs out.

In my ear was Camilla: *Remember that death and life are not separate, and pray for me.*

Just the mention of Chimayo and I had one foot in the Land of the Living and one foot in the Land of the Dead again. Would that ever change for me?

"Out of all places in the fifty United States," I said, "you're picking tiny Chimayo?"

"I've been to the major cities."

"I'd love to take you to Chimayo, but why?"

"A man I treated told me his little boy recovered from terminal leukemia after he put Chimayo sand on the child's forehead every night for a month."

"But you are a medical doctor."

"Which is why I believed him."

We were looking up pictures of Chimayo on Diego's phone when "The Eyes of Texas Are Upon You!" burst forth in my pocket.

"George's phone." I answered.

"Call Chief Wilder."

"Why?"

"Now."

"Why?"

"Look, I have a thousand riding on Bosnia plus two goals and Spain is breathing down our necks. The phone call is on your agenda, not mine."

The Chief of Detectives picked up on the first ring.

No surprise that Don had located George through the concierge at the Four Seasons. My movements were an easy read for anyone who knew me, and George's loyalty to the finest hotels was legend. I glanced over to where Diego and a man in a black dress suit with a pre-digital instant box camera discussed an impromptu photo session.

"How's Florida?" Don asked.

"No worse than Texas this time of year."

"Not true. We have another murder."

"I should be back--"

"You need to be here now."

"Because?"

"Couple of things. Most likely the victim is an illegal from the dematerialized Flower Mound stable crew."

"How do you know?"

"Looks the part."

"Impressive piece of police work, but I've sort of got something going on here."

The Chief could give me a day. One more night.

"The body was found in an alley four blocks from the station. My guess? He was on his way here to spill to the police or to visit Concepción's brother in the jail. Either reason was enough to silence him. If you could ID the body, Doc, we'd be ahead of the game."

"There are plenty of people out at the Flower Mound, including the barn manager, who are as familiar, or more familiar, with the workers."

Diego waved for my attention and pointed to the photographer. He mimed, *"Yes or no on a souvenir picture?"*

"There is one more thing."

"Really, Don. I can locate someone, several long-time horse owners, if that would help." I nodded "Yes" to Diego.

"In his wallet," the Chief said, "the victim had a photograph of Mrs. de la Cruz with a handsome Latino on each arm. You, Miss Scarletti, and George Ramsdale are there, too. Mrs. de la Cruz is wearing a wedding dress. You have a . . . a peculiar expression and are offering the photographer a bottle of champagne."

CHAPTER 37

"His first name is Joaquin."

I spelled it out for the Lieutenant. I guess I'd expected the classic American dark-suited ex-con limo driver, a big slick driver for a big slick car. Though Diego had sent us back to Austin in a private jet, and George had, of course, slept like the snoring Suzi dog, my body was running on survival adrenaline. Clunky silver pinballs banged side to side in my brain.

The Lieutenant and I stood at a viewing window in a wide cement-floored hallway with walls painted the pond-scum green that some psychologist in the 1950's claimed made people calmer, and has been standard in every state owned mental health and medical examiner facility since. The air was cold the way cement spaces without windows are always cold.

"Last name of the deceased?" the officer asked.

"I have no idea."

Joaquin was stretched out on a steel tray, if five-foot-three qualifies as a stretch. We'd waited twenty minutes for the Chief Medical Examiner, then settled for an assistant. The assistant, a tall, thin redhead who looked like he was pushing fourteen, had a nametag that read: Tommy Ingle,

Westbank High School, Student Observer. What kind of teenager chooses dead bodies for a summer experience?

Tommy Ingle rolled the 'calming green' sheet down from Joaquin's face and patted the cotton into a neat fold on the dead man's chest. He was careful to stop above the gunshot wound I knew was on level with his heart.

"How do you know the victim?" the Lieutenant asked.

"He was the driver for Camilla Cervantes in Mexico City."

Or George was right. Joaquin was Camilla's bodyguard, and I should rip my people-reading license off the wall and comb the internet for a new profession.

I could have used George's backup on the identification. However, other than his loyalty to the Houston Astros, George was not a huge corpse fan. He waited outside behind the wheel.

Recalling George's read on Camilla's driver, I motioned for Tommy to bring Joaquin's arms on top of the sheet. Bless you, Our Lady. The serene woman on Joaquin's forearm wore a flowing blue gown inside a frame of gold stars. Most importantly, she had flesh on her face, unlike the skeletal Santa Muerte my paranoid buddy promised, with absolute certainty, he'd seen on Joaquin's arm. My license was safe for the moment.

"Anything else you can add to the paperwork?" the Lieutenant asked. "A way to locate his family maybe? Someone we should notify?"

"No. I wish I did."

I should call Diego, see if he knew anything about Joaquin's family. Considering the circumstances, that idea came way too fast.

Once back in the car, I gave George the news.

"Wide swath, Miss Rose." He shook his head. "Wide swath."

We drove to El Cristobal without conversation. The restaurant didn't technically open until four on this day of the week, but Jorge, who'd been in the back frying tortilla wedges, chopping lettuce, and making coffee, spotted us and unlocked the door. All eight televisions were mercifully dark.

The fresh fruit and vegetable fragrances rolling into the dining room sent my mind back to the endless luscious aisles of La Merced. To Joaquin circling the limo around the huge market until he found a safe place for us to disembark. How, without one remark on my hideously sotted condition, he'd offered his elbow to steady me as I stepped out.

The murder of Camilla's long time employee wasn't a death blow to my insistence that there was more to Camilla's murder than a Los Insurgentes contract, but it hadn't helped. Why was Joaquin in Texas? When had he arrived? Had Joaquin come to warn Camilla? Had he killed her to save his own life, only to discover that by doing so, he'd made a place for himself on the cartel's hit list?

The smart money would play "Yes" on the last two questions even though they contradicted each other. But then, the smart money would have spent yesterday on a fascinating scene report for the police and stayed away from Mexico City. The death of Joaquin added to the probability that the killer was from Mexico. In which case, the probability that I'd ever find justice for Camilla lost ground like a downhill Chinese bullet train.

Not that I was giving up. I'd learned something from Diego and his crazy Indian-Catholic heart-over-brain culture. If Camilla's murderer was a faceless drug trafficker already back in Mexico, I couldn't change that fact. I could, however, choose not to play that side of the bet.

George and I landed in our favorite back booth in the dark restaurant. Jorge had bested our stroll from the parking lot. Two steaming cups of coffee were in place. A bowl of sugar with a large silver spoon.

"My head's in gridlock," I said. "I'm not sure of my next move, other than I know I want to grill Scott Maris. He's the only person I'm sure knows more than I do about Camilla's life. Now, if I only had a way to find him."

George groaned as if I'd asked for a kidney and picked up his phone. "Dialing him now, boss. . . . Three rings and straight to voice mail. Wanna leave a call back number? Oh, yeah, you don't have one."

"Also, it bothers me that without family or anyone to claim him, Joaquin will end up in a nameless grave. Camilla would never have let that happen."

"But Camilla isn't here. And, 'Why,' you ask, 'is your friend not here?' Oh, yes. She isn't here because, like her body guard, Camilla was tangled up with a gang of mass-murdering psychopaths."

"Still, she'd want Joaquin to have a proper burial."

"Let it go, Miss Rose." George thunked the spoon on the table and dumped sugar into his mug directly from the Talavera bowl.

"I can't let it go. If you knew Camilla's heart the way I do, you'd understand. At only ten years old she knew that the living have a responsibility to the dead. The morgue won't keep the remains long. I should call Eileen. See if she knows anything about Joaquin's next of kin. All I need is a phone number."

George jolted to attention. "And, where--ladies and gentlemen--have I heard *that* before?"

"One call, that's it."

"And, we're off! Check your tickets my sporting friends. The horses have left the gate!"

"How a person is treated after death is important."

"You're missing something here, Miss Rose, our hope to survive this mess depends on our staying unimportant to Los Insurgentes. *Un*important. Your little adventure down south didn't go unnoticed. If you and I weren't being watched before, you can be we are now."

"What if Joaquin's family doesn't even know he left Mexico? They must be frantic."

George tapped on his phone. "This is ridiculous. Name?"

"All I have is a first name."

George closed his eyes and wagged his head, as if continuing a relationship with a social media-challenged friend was a grand sacrifice.

He set his phone on the table and glanced toward the kitchen. We both needed more coffee. Chips and queso. A tiny gun would be nice.

After a few minutes, I broke the stalemate. "I can't stop worrying about Joaquin's family."

"All I have to say, Miss Rose, is 'First Class', 'Four Seasons', and 'private jet'."

"I hate to keep bothering Eileen. But Joaquin--"

"Call or don't call, Miss Rose, pick a side."

I held out my hand and he plopped his phone in it. I called Diego first. Maybe he could save me from bothering Eileen. George kept up his end of the deal with the head wagging and moans of exasperation.

Thank God, Jorge showed up with fresh mugs of coffee and *bizcochitos* (crusty sweet biscuits), split and grilled in butter, accompanied by a honey bear and a rack of flavored syrups. George's mood was restored.

Diego only knew Joaquin as Camilla's driver, though he had the impression that Joaquin had a wife and children. Diego's impression was enough to bump me over my guilt for bothering Eileen again.

Camilla's mother hadn't been told about Joaquin. My trail of spreading misery was intact. Though Eileen was too full up with grief to be crushed by the driver's death, the news added to her pain and accelerated her fears for Ana Teresa. She wanted to help but didn't have much information on Joaquin's family other than to add that he had elderly parents. She'd look for a pay slip or tax record when she had Camilla's things shipped. Ouch. Needle stabs ticked up my spine. What if my helping myself to the contents of Camilla's office--including family pictures--before her mother had a chance to go through her things meant more grief and loss for Eileen?

I couldn't bring myself to admit that I'd broken into Las Palomas. I'd see that she had Camilla's records and photographs as soon as I'd finished whatever it was I was doing. She deserved better treatment from me. When Eileen asked about my brief trip, I answered ambiguously and assured her I was staying in Texas for a while. My recollection of how pleased Eileen was at the wedding backed up Diego's assessment that she'd bought the story of his parenthood.

I certainly wasn't going to prick any bubbles at this point.

Next, Eileen filled me in on the memorial service, with no body present, planned for tonight at the Flower Mound Country Club horse show grounds. The timing was rushed, but riders from around the country, not close friends, but more than acquaintances, given all the years showing horses together, were still in town from the aborted horse show. Flowers and photographs would be arranged in the Winner's Circle, a well-lit manicured knoll where ribbons and trophies were traditionally awarded.

The second, more intimate, service would be held in Camilla's Cayoacan neighborhood church with burial in the Cervantes' family plot. She'd be laid next to her father whose remains had been moved years earlier from his spot in Austin. Eileen perked up at least a little when I assured her George and I would attend the Mexico City ceremony. The news would not have the same effect on George.

The service at the Flower Mound would be secured and private, gatekeepers provided with a list of riders and friends of Eileen who'd known, or known of, Camilla all her life. Still, given the brutal invasion of Camilla's life and death so far, I had no doubt that media representatives including Jane Bailey would find a way in, as would Zack Harvey's army of Scientologists. The attendance of Los Insurgentes and El Viborito was a given. Too savvy to show their colors, but George was right. Our visit to Mexico City did not go unnoticed. Those loyal to Los Insurgentes would be present and watching my every move.

All it took was one club employee with dreams beyond his salary and anyone could show up in the Winner's Circle. There was Diana Sloan to worry about, too. Knowing Eileen, she wouldn't exclude her.

All in all, Eileen sounded a little better than she had when I'd called before. But then I'm the one who always wants to see people as doing better than they are. Probably not a real good quality in a psychologist. Or a parent.

CHAPTER 38

A few hours, that's all I had.

With Jorge's Mexican Bar and Grill still not officially open for business, George and I had the dark space to ourselves. When I closed my eyes for a brief escape, I could picture the factory of fifty years ago. Small women lined up at their tortilla pressers under gold circles of light from personal lamps. Each with a radio tuned to a different Tejano music or Spanish religious station.

"I need a miracle, George."

He picked up his phone and waited for instructions.

"Every person important to Camilla, anyone who'd have reason to object to her plans, whatever those plans were, will be at the memorial tonight."

"Okay . . ."

I printed "Alejandro Lopez-Cardenas" on a napkin and pushed it across the table.

"This is the polo player boyfriend?"

"Check."

"You should be paying me for this service," George said. He licked bizcochito sparkles off his fingertips and swept through screens.

"I'm not saying Los Insurgentes wasn't involved. I think they were. The instruction to give Camilla an easy death was a decision coming from the high of the organization."

I made a little stack of the Alejandro pictures to keep my hands busy while George ran screens.

"Whoa. Check out the super fox!" George handed me the phone.

Alejandro Lopez-Cardenas waved from the deck of an obscenely opulent yacht, Venice's Basilica of St. Mark in the background. His arm was around the shoulders of a striking woman in a white linen pants suit and a diamond the size of a Cheerio.

"Here's polo boy-oy . . . again," George said, and handed me the phone again. This time Alejandro and his platinum-haired wife were sharing a bottle of champagne at a beachside club somewhere in Latin America.

"Anything beyond the vacations of the rich and famous?"

I sat back, suddenly exhausted, a feeling I couldn't afford. Something about the ease of diving into a stranger's personal life depressed me. When did that happen? When did any and all of us lose the right to disappear?

"Business wise . . ." George said, "thus guy's family has Lopez-Cardenas banks in Colombia, Mexico City, and Juárez."

"Well, now that's darn handy. Alejandro was in Mexico City to open a bank when Camilla met him."

There are four tasks required to make billions in cocaine trafficking. One: Buy coca bush concentrate from starving farmers in Peru and Colombia. Two: Transport refined and diluted coca through Mexico to the addicts in the United States. Three: Get paid in American dollars. Four: Launder the profits.

Step four can pose quite a pickle. When you have rooms stacked to the ceiling with U.S. fives, tens, twenties, and hundreds, their source is rather obvious. To discourage money laundering in Mexico, citizens and businesses are only allowed to exchange a small amount of U.S. currency during any twenty-four hour period. A cooperative string of family banks in the right spots would be a big help.

"George, please tell me Alejandro only recently married Marilyn Monroe with the diamond," I said. "Please, tell me he was a bachelor when he attended the wedding?"

"Nuuu, sorry. We have loads of photos on Alejandro's yacht-slash-cruise ship with the four sons of Loopo-Cardo and Marilyn. Her name is Sheila and she's some kind of French furniture company heiress. The oldest son is a teenager and the youngest is a toddler, all polo players, if you can believe their proud papa."

"What else can you find out? I barely remember him."

George paused to bundle his fist, throw back his head, and point his thumb downward into his mouth. Gulp, gulp, gulp.

I scowled. "I don't have a lot of time, George."

"Okay, sorry. For starters, the Adriatic Sea shot with Italy in the background is from his honeymoon dated the summer before the predictable demise of your first marriage and the wedding of Camilla Cervantes and your boyfriend for the weekend."

"Which doesn't clear Allejandro as father material."

As scary as it felt to think of Lopez-Cardenas as a money launderer, the possibility that Ana Teresa's father was some random rich guy who didn't want the product of his adultery to interfere with his jet-set lifestyle made me nauseous.

I'd accepted that Camilla cooperated with El Viborito and Los Insurgentes. But with the news on Lopez-Cardenas, the notion that she participated voluntarily, perhaps even facilitated the narco-trafficking enterprise, claimed a toehold in my world. Not because of the facts stacking up against my image of Camilla as a saint, but because of her odd choices and actions at her wedding. Camilla was excited, too excited for a ring exchange that meant nothing to anyone except maybe her mother, who was pleased that her grandchild wasn't born out of wedlock.

Was it possible that Camilla's joy at her wedding was a natural high? Was she thrilled because, in spite of the awkward circumstances, the father of her baby was at her side? Ugh.

Jorge's nephew, Eduardo, visiting from La Vegas, refilled our coffee and handed George a plate with another split bizcochito. On Eduardo's walk to the kitchen he flicked on six of the eight televisions, then climbed up on a stool at the bar to catch up on international soccer scores and riots. George talked him into switching the screen over the bar to the twenty-four rumor channel. The big story was the private service for the daughter of Eileen Cervantes to be held at a "secret location," a term that made the memorial sound like a KKK meeting.

"I was hurt because Camilla never told me who the father was," I said. "But if Alejandro Lopez-Cardenas is the guy, I don't blame her. Judging from his frequent visits to Las Palomas, he'll show up tonight. Eileen has nothing against him and she knows he and Camilla were longtime friends—or whatever."

The image of the worldly Alejandro standing with Camilla's mother and eyeing Ana Teresa brought the nausea back. What if Alejandro wanted a girl to go with his four boys? I couldn't bear that and neither could Ana Teresa's grandmother.

George cut another square off his luscious biscuit and maneuvered it over to my coffee saucer.

"Okay, so let's look behind Door Number Two." I handed George the photos of Scott with the little family. "I need everything you can dig up on Scott Maris."

He swished through screens. "Oh, this is good. Criminal hit on Maris, which I can access for a mere eleven dollars . . ."

"Put it on my account."

"Here it is. Mr. Maris was sued on a ten thousand dollar credit line at the Bellagio Casino."

"Any employed man with a decent credit rating can dig himself into a ten thousand dollar hole in Las Vegas. Keep going."

"Here we go. "LinkedIn: 'Scott Maris, thirty-six years old, born in Orange County, California. Graduated with a marketing degree from Cal State Long Beach and worked for a television station in Los Angeles—same parent company as Camilla's mother--before moving to Austin. Don't see a marriage or kids, but some divorced guys leave that out."

"If Scott is Ana Teresa's father, why would he keep that a secret?"

"Because Camilla wanted him to. You women can be very persuasive. My current precarious relationship with the criminal element of Mexico City--a case in point."

"When Scott showed up at my house, he was on a cocaine buzz and terrified. That kind of fear isn't about a paternity issue. Another thing that bugs me about that boy is, how does a television producer, even on a successful show, pay for a house at the Flower Mound Country Club?"

"Why not tag the child's father the old fashioned way?"

"No time for DNA."

He frowned. "Does the little girl look like Scott Maris or Polo Boy?"

"Hard to say, they both have dark hair and Ana Teresa is a miniature Camilla."

"Why am I asking such a pedestrian question? A man in show business will have a public Facebook Page."

"I want to see Scott's face, not his Facebook," I said. "A couple of bites of lunch here and we find him. Or try to find him. If he has a brain, he's on a planet far, far away."

George's eyebrows shot up and stayed in position. "And what a fine Facebook page indeed. Hell-*luuuu,* Scott Maris!"

"What?"

"Nah . . ."

"What, George, what?"

"Mr. Maris's Friend List includes that bitch who told the world Camilla was a whore and a killer."

CHAPTER 39

"What about the queso I have on the way?" George asked.

"Queso? You just told me Diana and Scott are playmates and you are thinking about cheese?"

"That some sort of crime?"

"No a moral breach." I slid into George's side of the booth and pulled him toward the edge. He held his butter-dripping bizcochito away from me as an anchor in the booth.

"Let's hit the road, George."

Before I could sell my case, Jorge appeared and switched out our bizcochitos for flour tortillas and George's precious *queso flameado*, bubbling white cheese, jalapeños, and chorizo sausage in a skillet set in a wood frame.

George landed a firm glare. "I'm having at least one hand-rolled goodie. End of story."

"Fine. Five minutes," I conceded. "I should eat something and *fundido* is definitely rage fuel."

I positioned a flour tortilla on my plate, poured on a half-cup of fundido, and folded the tortilla into a burrito, contents still bubbling. A sizzling fundido burrito requires tightrope concentration.

"Well, my, my, Miss Rose, your prayers have been answered!" George kicked my leg and pointed to the screen above the Cristobal bar.

I could not risk looking away from the scalding dripping burrito . . ."

"Scott Maris—sweaty face and all!"

Hot sausage and hotter cheese squeezed out both ends of my power roll and down my arms. I didn't so much as squeak.

Scott blustered down the steps of the Austin Police Department Central Booking facility surrounded by reporters. If his face had been a boy's coloring project, the child would need half the Crayolas in the box. Could he be Ana Teresa's father? Could Camilla have been in love with this terror-speckled man?

"Mr. Maris!" A red-headed reporter in a matching fiery tie shouted, and poked a microphone between Scott's lawyers. "Mr. Maris, how do you intend to plead?"

"No comment."

"Mr. Maris! People in Austin are panicked about drug-trafficking violence tracking up I-35. Are you afraid the courts will make an example of your case?"

"No comment."

"How could I have let that man out of my house?" I asked George who was concentrated on rolling as many fundido tacos as he could while I was distracted.

"Mr. Maris!" Another, taller, reporter reached over the shorter of the two attorneys. "Mr. Maris, what can you tell us about the Flower Mound Country Club Murder? Is it true that Los Insurgentes is claiming responsibility?"

He checked with his lawyers who nodded permission, as if this was the question they'd been waiting for.

Scott took the microphone out of the reporter's grasp and glared into the camera. "I am an addict. I am guilty of possession, but I am not guilty of trafficking or distribution of narcotics." His words had the plastic flatness of a prepared statement. "I sincerely regret that my arrest and plea will cause more pain for my employer, Eileen Cervantes. But to protect my own freedom and my life, I can no longer cover for her daughter's criminal activities. As you have become aware, Camilla Cervantes was a deeply disturbed individual. Please consider her mental illness, and do not judge her too harshly."

I elbowed George who managed to hang on to his taco.

"Ow," he said, without commitment.

"Sorry. I can't take this horseshit. All of what he's saying is ridiculous. He's rehearsed and he's a bad actor."

Eileen and Ana Teresa could someday heal from Camilla's murder, but this?

"I'm sorry it's taken you so long to come to grips with what Camilla was into and with whom and I'm sorry it takes you so long to recognize that my paranoid view of the world has a big lead over your psychologist everyone-is-born-good philosophy."

"George, that's not the same Scott Maris who stopped by my house. Where's the man who said, 'Camilla and I were in love . . . . I'd do anything for her'?"

"Nothing says loyalty to a cartel like killing the woman you love."

If I was to be of any value to Camilla, I had to step up my game and fast.

In the understated, exacting world of horse shows, both the 'hunter' and the 'jumper' divisions are made up of horses jumping fences with one critical difference. Hunters are judged on their beauty and flawless style or 'way of going' over a series of pleasant gates, walls, and faux creeks. The winner is the horse who makes the consummate impression on the judges.

In the jumper division, the fences are jacked up and all that counts in the score is clearing fences and speed. A jumper round is scored by adding up 'faults' which are collected by knocking down a pole, crashing a fence, refusing a fence, or exceeding the time allowed for the course. If the rider ahead of you wants to win, she will cut a stride out of the gallop between fences. If you intend to beat her, you cut out the stride she did, plus one, and you convert rounded corners into wrenching U-turns. To win, you have to take chances. Not nickel bet raises. You have to go all in.

You'd think my ragged horsemanship would have steered me toward the jumper division. It would have, if I'd had the guts to gallop a horse full-tilt toward a Mayflower moving van. Which I don't.

At least, I hadn't before now. The gracious pace and elegance of the hunter division were luxuries I could no longer afford. I had to reach deeper. Up to now, I'd tried to please. My eye on the judges, I'd counted strides and apologized for bothering people.

Well, that preening crap was over.

"George? Phone."

"Yes, dear."

I used information to call the Jane Bailey studio. "Yes," I told Ms. Bailey. I'd be delighted to provide "another perspective" on Camilla Maria Cervantes. Next I called the Chief and left a message on his private line: "I need Camilla's records from Timbercreek Hospital in Dallas on. Use follow-up plans to complete the chain of treatment centers and schools, Europe, too. Send as emergency faxes. Ethical and confidentiality issues are in my court."

I was tired of being steamrolled by the aura of Los Insurgentes. Sick of stick-armed, long-haired, women behind fake newsroom desks raving about Camilla's "mental illness" and "sexual perversity" without one mention of her work helping the poorest of the poor, the most condemned of little girls. I was sick of hearing about the tens of thousands my super-rich equestrian pals were scoring for their stories, while the girls of La Merced, Camilla's girls, now without her, had less than nothing.

More than everything else, I was sick to my soul of the condescending brushoff I received every time I suggested that Camilla's association with Mexico City—her beautiful life--was about more than drug trafficking. I re-punched the number for the Chief. This time the he picked up.

"Also, find out how Scott Maris paid for a diamond Rolex, a new Lamborghini, and a mansion at the Flower Mound Country Club."

"Maris is already in the works. Which I would have told you, if you'd paused to take a breath."

"Good. You should know there's a possibility that Scott Maris is Ana Teresa's father."

"What about Mr. de la Cruz in the wedding picture?"

"I had his DNA run yesterday while I was vacationing in Florida. It's not a match."

"Right."

"So, you'll bring Scott back in?"

As much as I detested him at the moment, if Scott was Ana Teresa's father, I wanted him alive. Regardless of what else was true about a man, a father makes a difference in a daughter's life. Of that much, I was sure.

The Chief let me hang through thirty seconds of silence to make his point. To remind me who was running the investigation.

"If he's gunned down," I said, "that little girl could lose her only parent."

"Los Insurgentes is the priority."

No wonder Scott had been released immediately. "You're throwing him out there and *hoping* for a hit."

I threw the phone back at/to George.

"Wh—at?" He snatched the cell an inch above the bowl of salsa.

"Once again I'm reminded why Chief of Detectives Don Wilder and I could never make it as a couple."

I stood and headed for the door. George, the only man I trusted completely at the moment, was close behind.

The eighty thousand, give or take ten or fifty thousand, murders in Mexico are not investigated because the killings are assumed to be cartel-on-cartel, one set of criminals killing off another set of criminals. So, who cares, really?

In his press conference, Scott Maris had dumped Camilla in the "Who cares?" category. The police 'watch and wait' strategy landed Scott Maris in the same pile of corpses.

The police station closer to the Flower Mound than El Cristobal, Scott would beat us to his house. Unless he acted on the thought that flits across the mind of all Texans: *Maybe I should start my life over. Quit this foolishness, run to Mexico, and never come back.*

Or maybe that's just me.

"You're really going 'live' on the Bailey show?" George asked.

"I plan on starting the interview alive. You'll have to watch to know how the story ends."

My brain needed more time at the bunkhouse table with the pieces of Camilla's life. But first, I had to jump an obstacle who was the only person I knew who could help the process. An obstacle with a Rolex, a cocaine habit, and, just maybe, a broken heart. Before with Scott Maris, I'd been a gracious host. This conversation would be on my terms.

From here on out, I was in the jumper division. All speed and cold steel.

CHAPTER 40

The Flower Mound Country Club had added enough private security at the florally overwhelmed entrance gates to turn back an armed invasion. But not enough to hold off a nerves-of-steel jumper chick with an equestrian team card and a few life and death questions for the man who said Camilla was in love with him.

Once arrived at Scott's Mediterranean villa perched on a hill of the Flower Mound golf course, I peeked into his four car garage, no doubt showing up on his security system and in the binoculars of authorities from several levels of law enforcement. The stone and stucco house had turrets on the corners connected by arched terraces with green marble touches. In the garage, along with the yellow Lamborghini, Scott had a white Escalade and piles of packing boxes. No surprise there.

I signaled George and he climbed out of the Lincoln to join me on the narrow and unimpressive porch. Beyond the soaring palms and Italian façades, most of the stunning stone work, pools, and landscaping were reserved for the back sides of country club homes. Who needs a porch?

It's not as if a Flower Mound mom would send an unsupervised child next door to borrow a cup of sugar.

I rang the doorbell while I fought back a wicked urge to do a full three-sixty welcome wave for the Chief's stakeout team, but he'd be pissed enough.

George rang the doorbell.

"Scott's pretending we're not here," I said. "There are some ill-mannered guys after him."

George reached for his umbilical cord and out popped his phone. He tapped recall.

"Right, George," I jumped in. "That's a good plan. Leave a message. Leaving a message is the weakest and least effective way to capture the attention of a man who doesn't want to talk to you."

"We're not talking about your love life, Miss Ro--Mr. Maris! Hello!" George pointed to his ear in case I couldn't keep up with the situation. "I haven't had the pleasure of your acquaintance, Mr. Maris, but I do look forward to the opportunity. As we speak, I'm on your front porch with Dr. LeFave, and she's requested an audience. Her position is that since she allowed you into her house at your behest, she expects you to return the courtesy."

"Yeah," I sneered, "like that's going to work."

Rustling and footsteps from inside neared the doors. A man cleared his throat. Then the left half of the double doors swung inward. Scott Maris's eyes were puffy and his hand shook as he reached for George's grasp.

Dr. Intuitive is wrong again.

"Come in. Come in."

Scott scanned the empty street, then stepped aside. We followed him through the front room to a den with a glass wall that showcased a three-tiered water hazard on the golf course. The room had a vaulted plank ceiling with a chandelier made up of dozens of antlers. The deer trophies along the walls brought back George's phone shot of headless men hanging by their ankles from a bridge and the video clip of Federales lining up skulls on the flatbed of a truck. So close—the Land of the Living and the Land of the Dead. Mexico and Texas.

"I'm having a beer, what about you two?" Scott said.

He was already in position behind a bar that ran half the length of the right side of the room. Three Corona longneck empties dripped onto the slate.

George jumped at Scott's beer offer and settled into the sofa to appreciate the view. His face glowed with the enthusiasm of a desert dweller seeing the Pacific Ocean for the first time. Golf was entirely too slow for George's taste. At the moment, however, the alternative to admiration of the golf course held even less appeal. And he had his phone to play with.

Scott turned up a Corona, drained it in two long pulls, and collected another for himself and one for his guest. In case I might lose my 'jumper' steel, the diamond Rolex winked at me as Scott closed the cooler.

I took up a position opposite him. Poised at the in-gate. But Scott was more desperate than I was poised.

"I know you don't have any reason to help me, Dr. LeFave."

"No. I do not. You have not provided me with a reason."

"I loved Camilla."

"Don't even . . ." I held up a 'stop' palm. ". . . Don't. No man who loved Camilla would destroy her on national television—destroy her and her mother."

"I--"

"Your ugly lies will never go away." I chased his ducking glance until he had to look at me. "Never. You know what the Flower Mound is like. Camilla was forever the crazy little girl who burned down a barn and killed a dog. And now? After what you said? Now Ana Teresa will forever be the daughter of the crazy drug-trafficking queen of Mexico City."

"I didn't have a choice."

"You're alive. Camilla's dead. Someone's made a choice here."

"I had to say what I did about Camilla. You know I did. You're the one person who knows the truth."

"The *truth?*"

"Camilla trusted you with everything."

"No, Mr. Maris," I said, my jaws a vise. "Not everything and you know it. She wanted to, but she didn't have the chance."

He cut his eyes toward the golf course.

"You made a choice to pal up with Diana Sloan." I would not back off today. "That's one more bad decision on your side of the ledger."

Scott held his bottle to his lips, but stopped drinking. He set his Corona on the bar and watched beads slide down the label. I would have done almost anything to know the image that had shut down Scott's swallow response.

"In business, especially the media business, maintaining a public Facebook page is in your contract. Once Diana started using my site to hurt Camilla, I wanted to unfriend her, but I know what kind of time and energy she's willing to devote to her crusades."

"Did you just say '*unfriend*'?"

"Yes, I--"

"Camilla is dead! Unless the investigation turns around in a big hurry, the killer is going to get away with it, and you're using words like '*unfriend*'?"

I leaned into the slate bar so hard my chest hurt.

"Scott?"

I waited. And waited. On the tough jumper courses timing is everything. He cracked first and looked up. This was my chance to cut a stride out of the conversation. Maybe my only chance.

"Scott, are you Ana Teresa's father?"

He flinched. "Look at me." He held out a palm-down shaky hand. "I'm looking at a bullet in the head or prison as it is."

"Not an answer."

"I wish I was her father."

"Still not an answer."

Scott motioned toward the sofa where he more collapsed than sat. I joined him. Even the leather cushions trembled.

"Camilla didn't pick this house out for us. She mentioned she liked it once and I bought it, just in case."

How? *Breathe, LeFave. Do not chase. You can't jump a fence until you get to it.*

Tears welled up and over at the corners of his eyes. "Would me showing up as Ana Teresa's father do any more than make her life worse?"

"I don't know you. Tell me why having you for a father would be worse than not having a father at all."

"I love that little girl. When Camilla decided Ana Teresa would finish school here, I took that to mean she was ready to give up the Mexico City part of her life. I jumped in with both of my big clumsy feet. I had no right to ask Camilla to love me," he said. "I used the relationship at first, but I never meant to hurt her. I thought we could start over, we could settle down like a regular couple. She'd always said she didn't want to get married again, if Diego even counts. Then recently, with Ana Teresa about the age she was when she lost her father, Camilla started talking about how hard it was for her growing up without a dad. How maybe Ana Teresa should have a father figure in the house." Tears again. "But Camilla didn't want me to be that man."

"Because of the coke?"

"That was part of it."

"Did Camilla use drugs?"

He ducked his chin into his neck. "You're kidding? I can't believe you'd ask."

"I told you, I don't know what you, and everyone else, assumes I know. Did you know Camilla was taken unconscious to an emergency room last week? Drug overdose seems to be the consensus."

Scott stared at the golf course. "Camilla never used drugs."

"So, why was she in the ER? I think that experience drew some kind of line for Camilla."

"Look, Dr. LeFave, and listen. I'm trying to save your life. My house is being watched."

"If it helps," I said, "all sorts of agency cops are on surveillance here, too. And they want you alive."

"Please, you should go."

"No."

"I've said all I can say." He rubbed his hands on his knees, turned and looked in the direction of the front door.

"I believe you loved her, Scott. But, you failed her, too. This is your chance to square things for Camilla."

He shook his head.

"Okay, if you care what happens to me because of Camilla, do this much. Tell me what I'm up against. What did you two argue about at the horse show?"

"Us. The future. How I'd destroyed my chance to have a wonderful life. Maybe it didn't matter. Camilla had someone else all along. I knew that, but I also knew she'd decided to make a change, and I read that as a chance for us."

"Was this 'someone else' Ana Teresa's father?" My heart stilled. This could be it.

Scott rocked slowly, his hands clasped between his knees. "What difference does it make now?"

"The difference between justice and hopelessness."

He shook me off. I could practically see the noose his shudder was meant to loosen. Scott was not about to add another reason to kick the box from under his feet.

"Ana Teresa has no parents as it is, Scott. I don't want to accuse anyone; I don't want to mess with anyone's life. Camilla told me Ana Teresa has people in Mexico City, people who love her. Eileen's family is so small. If Ana Teresa's biological father doesn't care about her, maybe she has cousins, aunts or uncles. If her father married someone else or even if he was married and had another family when he knew Camilla, Ana Teresa could have half-brothers and sisters who might want to find her someday."

Scott finished his beer, his eyes locked on the floor, more sadness than fear on his face. Could be Ana Teresa had all sorts of extended family in Orange County, California. Scott had never given me a straight answer on Ana Teresa's father.

"Scott," I said, "A child can't have too many people to love her."

"Yes, they can." Scott raised his head and looked me squarely in the eyes. "At least that little girl can. You make it sound like these people in Mexico City would give her some kind of television sit-com family. Well, you're wrong, very wrong, Dr. LeFave. Ana Teresa has her grandmother. Eileen loves her with all her heart and soul. She is all the family Ana Teresa needs. Please listen to me." His face hardened into the expression he'd used to shut down two press conferences.

"Maybe--" I tried.

"The best thing for Ana Teresa is to believe her father was Diego de la Cruz and that he died long ago. The best thing is for her to forget she ever knew anyone or ever spent time in Mexico City."

"Maybe the identity of Ana Teresa's father has nothing to do with Camilla's murder, but I have to know that for myself." All speed and cold steel. "Take a minute to think this through. Tonight at the service is my only shot and the Chief of Detectives is on my side. I will get my answer if I have to point my finger and accuse every man there."

"You won't do that to Eileen."

"No I won't. But I will grill every man in the audience with my eyes, and I will know him."

"You will not see his eyes. He slithers in the shadows."

CHAPTER 41

Oh, God. I didn't even know the Little Snake's real name. I did not want to know his real name.

If I didn't know what I did about mania, if I hadn't treated teen girls with bipolar disorder who'd come on to relatives, celebrities, priests, and strangers, and if I didn't know firsthand that teenage girls can make dreadful choices, the notion that El Viborito could be Ana Teresa's father would be unthinkable. Camilla would be more vulnerable than most, and a much older man would have suited a girl who'd mourned her father since she was ten. If Viborito was the sperm donor, one thing would be settled—why Camilla hid the identity of Ana Teresa's father even from me.

Scott's word was all I had that El Viborito was Ana Teresa's father. He'd proved himself a capable liar, but his claim fit with everything that had happened since. Still there had to be more behind the two murders than hidden paternity. If Joaquin was dead and Scott terrified because they knew that El Viborito was Ana Teresa's father, he or his men wouldn't bother to watch my mailbox or have me followed. The Little Snake would have long ago spent the eighty cent bullet required to keep me quiet—just in case Camilla had told me.

I settled in at the bunkhouse table with my laptop. Sammie Davis, Jr. curled on my lap and Suzi Wong stretched over my bare feet, head toward the fridge. My eulogy was my weapon of choice, really my only choice I had left if I was to make a difference in the investigation, if I was ever to find justice for Camilla.

First order though, was a sketch outline for the Jane Bailey Show, an interview which had risen to bizarre, ironic importance. As much bad karma as I'd wished on the media, the one thing I could do that might help Camilla, Eileen, and Ana Teresa, was the interview on the Jane Bailey Show.

Eileen was right to not share her fears about Ana Teresa with her Flower Mound friends. "Like mother, like daughter," would echo from pool house to clubhouse. Maybe, if I did a thorough enough job on the Jane Bailey Show, the parents of Ana Teresa's school friends would give Camilla's daughter and mother more of a chance. Maybe even go out of their way to make Ana Teresa feel welcome at her new school. The thought that the mothers at the Flower Mound wouldn't let their children play with Ana Teresa made me want to cry.

I opened a fresh Word document. "Bailey Show. Goal One: Provide a down to earth understanding of bipolar disorder and clarify the nature of Camilla's emotional difficulties in a way helpful to concerned parents. Goal Two: Enlighten and soften the hearts of those who only knew my friend as *Camilla, Camilla, the Flower Mound Killa* and as the victim of the Flower Mound Country Club Murder.

My focus was all over the place. The guest list for the memorial played in a loop across my brain, one frame, one face at a time. Then I started in on those who'd be in attendance without an invitation. The guests in the shadows.

"What am I missing?" I asked Sammie, his devoted black eyes gave me notice though he was drowsy. Then he dropped his head and sputtered softly over and over like an old-timey lawnmower that couldn't start, but really didn't want to.

"Sammie, what can I do to help my friend get to Heaven?"

He stretched one leg out in front of him and cocked his head as he considered my question. Then he squinted slightly, and said, "Get the letter, dummy, the letter. And while you're at it, you might as well bring that ghastly painting."

Sammie was a wise and psychologically gifted pup. Either that, or he had an open line to channel Miss Marple when needed. I retrieved Camilla's letter from its place on top of the upside down photograph in my silverware drawer.

I read it through once without focus on individual elements. I saw nothing more than I'd taken from her words the first time.

Then I read the letter aloud to Sammie. His Miss Marple didn't kick in and still no crashing insight flashed across my brain. There were key words, "big change . . . decision." Her statement of faith, "I am confident I am making the right decision for Ana Teresa and for myself." And the words that fueled my determination, "I know that should anything happen to me, you and Concepción will watch out for Ana Teresa." I'd show Concepción Camilla's letter. She'd be pleased to know Camilla appreciated how important she was to her daughter.

I placed the letter on the right side of my screen and leaned Frida Kahlo's *My Birth* on a salt shaker next to the left edge.

Back to notes for the Jane Bailey interview.

I would start with when I met Camilla at Nancy Margaret's birthday party at the Flower Mound pool. I knew Nancy Margaret from Sunday school and was the only public school kid at the party. When Camilla found out I loved horses, she'd invited me to the Flower Mound stables every weekend until I was nine and accepted an offer to exchange stable duties for lessons, an arrangement I was sure Eileen had arranged and financially supported. I'd share how Camilla stood up for me when the other girls made fun of my jeans and athletic shoes in place of breeches and boots. I wouldn't leave out the hospitals or the rape and hideous beating. To leave out her wounds would discount her victories, including the very La Merced project the press had twisted into something ugly. Maybe, when they realized the beautiful person she was on the inside as well the outside, the Flower Mounders would even let go of Camilla's imaginary affair with Stephen Sloan.

The fax machine hummed and cranked to life. Records from Timbercreek Hospital landed on the stack of other hospital and school reports I hadn't noticed when I came in. I didn't have time to check out the reports. But oh how I wanted to.

The interview was minutes away and I had to change clothes. While Jane Bailey was not my favorite person, I wouldn't be a no-show for a live interview. Not to mention, if I didn't show, Zack Harvey would have a party with his 'psychologist in hiding' theme.

Still, if I could take just a peek at Camilla's childhood. . . . Locating a few positive facts was more important than how well I was dressed. Surely, I had a few seconds . . . . With my brain wild on exhaustion and excitement, I was averaging a rationalization a minute.

I picked up the first few pages of the Timbercreek chart.

STRICTLY CONFIDENTIAL

Camilla was admitted to Timbercreek Hospital as a high risk patient. Boxes checked for "Danger to Self" and "Danger to Others."

Reason for admission (court order, suicide attempt, runaway, school problem, etc.): "Arson. Private barn. Motive in question. A dog either died in the fire or was killed before the fire. Possible criminal complications and civil court liability."

Camilla was placed on the most restrictive floor with twenty-four hour, one-on-one supervision, and zombie drugs. She had to be so scared. Her father had just been murdered! How about putting that down as the reason for admission?

I reached for the photograph of Camilla with her father. I needed one of those reflective moments when you look at the smiling childhood picture of someone whose adult life has gone fatally sideways and ask, "How did the life of this happy little girl end in up in unthinkable tragedy?" The more I looked at the background, the less convinced I was that the photo had been taken at a fiesta. A spiral of what looked like smoke curled behind them from somewhere low and unseen. A picnic grounds?

Not that the location made any difference. Not since I knew the cockroach was tangled in Camilla's Mexico City life, one way or another, and dangerous to Ana Teresa. Could be Ana Teresa's grandfather, a man from a city laced with corruption, was hooked up with criminals and I should take Scott's advice and forget Mexico City connections myself.

I had no time for this sort of reverie. I should be on the road. *So, put the pages down.* No, two more minutes. I could run two yellow lights and make up that much time.

Camilla was in residential treatment at Timbercreek until she was twelve, a long time for a child to be hospitalized in one facility.

Though I'd chickened out of visiting her in Dallas, I did write, and she wrote more regularly, switching to email as a student in Europe. Camilla, in her usual open style, had told me all about the hospital and the other girls, which lent an odd familiarity to what I was reading. According to her chart, she'd been out on many weekend passes and holidays, all spent at horse shows, in Mexico City, or resort areas with her mother. That she kept up with her horses was encouraging. In fact, other than persistent runaway incidents and keeping to herself, Camilla's behavioral record, while not perfect, was not extreme.

The clinician in charge noted that Camilla was encouraged by staff and her mother to take holidays with other children from the hospital, but she'd refused. Camilla insisted she didn't need more friends than her two best friends in Austin.

I dropped my forehead on the keyboard.

The ice pick was back.

Chapter 42

The faxed pages blew away any remaining shred of my well-watered fantasy of Camilla's life in the years I made up excuses not to visit. I sat at the rough-hewed table and thumbed through hospital and school records, purposefully skipping the scary parts for now. I needed something positive to hold in my heart, something hopeful. I was famished for hopeful.

<u>Diagnosis</u>: Bipolar 1 Disorder, Most Recent Episode Manic, In Partial Remission.

The gears in my brain locked. Camilla's diagnosis was correct. Kelly's diagnosis was correct. Yet, now, as I had with Kelly, I wanted to fight the diagnosis. I wanted to believe that the symptoms weren't a disorder. I wanted to believe that the symptoms weren't even symptoms.

Was Camilla manic? No, no, no. When she was happy, she was "bubbling over" and who wouldn't be at her own wedding? When Camilla was fastidious with her personal and financial records, she wasn't on a high, she was extraordinarily methodical. Industrious.

Not manic. Industrious--like Kelly in high school, her eye never shifting from the prize, the number one grade point average in one of the toughest schools in the country. After all, outstanding grades require focus, right? I had done it; she could, too. We had our own secret motto: "Just because other people can't do it, doesn't mean we can't do it."

"Oh, you're taking eight classes to finish high school early? And you're drum major and editor of the school paper along with your after school job? You're an amazing kid."

I actually said those words. I actually quoted myself when I bragged to my friends how Kelly and I were so alike. So driven. Not sick. Driven. So creative. Not bizarre.

Back it up, LeFave. Sammie Davis opened his round black eyes and crept up my chest until my chin rested on his little warm head.

Why did everyone seem to think this "Five Stages of Grief" was some sort of magical formula? A list of accomplishments to check off like the Twelve Steps. Work the program and you're fixed. Well, not for me. I was stuck.

I'd researched every detail of Kelly's life. Replayed every conversation. Were we too close? Too distant? Was she afraid to disappoint me? Did she give up on me when she'd tried to confess her depression and I pointed out cactus blossoms on the trail? Did she give up on herself when she was little, curled up with her teddy bear, her mother in the next room crying? Her mother saying, "No, honey, Daddy isn't coming home after all. Not ever. He chose another life."

How had those nights changed her?

I read *The Bell Jar* again.

Did all parents whose teen daughters committed suicide go out and buy a copy of Sylvia Plath's book? Were we a secret club that kept *The Bell Jar* in print?

I wanted an answer. *Why?* What went wrong? What had I missed? I interviewed and re-interviewed everyone who knew her. I stalked old boyfriends. Grilled the clerk at the corner Walgreens. Yes, he remembered the girl with the curly brown hair, the one who bought pregnancy tests several times a month. The girl who left with bags of cookies, her hand jammed inside before the glass door closed behind her. Sometimes she threw her purchases in the trash as she left.

I attended her university class schedule. "Teachers, students, did you notice anything? Anything at all?"

I would say I was desperate, but 'desperate' doesn't even come close. I wanted to, had to, find meaning. An explanation. I wanted my "aha" moment.

I believed that if I searched hard enough, long enough, I'd discover that missing something and the world would make sense again. Now, the pieces of Camilla's life laid out before me, I was dead-locked in the same sort of breathless, relentless, bordering on hopeless, quest now. I wanted the "ah-ha" moment that would make sense of Camilla's murder.

I didn't want Camilla to be a 'cartel' statistic the way I didn't want Kelly to be a 'bipolar' statistic.

Well, that's not the way the world works, LeFave. You need to leave for the television studio. I straightened the report pages and pushed back my chair.

But, what if a phrase on the next page had a shining quote from one of Camilla's doctor's? A sweet story that would surprise the mothers of the Flower Mound and stick in their minds after the Jane Bailey Show was over? I turned the page.

After the sixth grade, Camilla left for boarding school at St. Catherine's Academy in Scottsdale, Arizona, a school with an equestrian team, where she'd stayed for two years. I'd thought the school stationery with horses and a cross was the coolest letterhead I'd ever seen. Even the Parthenon emblem on her letters from the Panthéon-Assas University in Paris a few years later came in second.

Camilla excelled in academics, though she returned three times to Timbercreek for brief hospitalizations after running away. Over the years, Camilla took off from Timbercreek a half dozen times, usually returning on her own.

She'd never mentioned running away in her letters. Knowing what I know now, I suspect that once Camilla was beyond a manic episode, she hardly, if at all, remembered the things she'd done.

After her last run-away from St. Catherine's, Camilla had convinced her mother that she would be steadier if she could finish high school and college in Mexico City and Europe. Eileen didn't like the idea of Camilla spending even more time away, but they had a comfortable routine at Las Palomas, and she admitted that the rumors at the Flower Mound, if anything, had grown more vicious the longer Camilla was away.

I grabbed a pen and wrote down the names of the schools, the honors, and the graduation dates. Finally, something I could share with Jane Bailey's audience. Facts to go up against the 'criminal and crazy' Camilla broadcast around the world.

I'd make clear that a child, a person, is not her diagnosis. Along with Camilla's school accomplishments, I wanted to convey how hard Camilla fought to overcome her emotional problems and have a normal life. Her life wasn't the typical Flower Mound story, her charity wasn't the flashy sort that landed your photo in the society pages, but she'd made it work. I wanted to add that not every girl faced with the crazy highs and gut-cutting lows of bipolar disorder could make her life work. Some girls take another way out.

But I wouldn't.

Just one more page. Jackpot. A Patient Self-Evaluation Word document completed by Camilla on one of her later Timbercreek Hospital re-admissions. Patient self-evaluations, aimed at increasing patient involvement and commitment to treatment, are frequent elements of care with multiple hospitalizations.

CONFIDENTIAL

Timbercreek Hospital Patient Self Evaluation

<u>Name:</u> My name is Camilla Maria Cervantes and I hate my life.

<u>Reason for admission:</u> My life is hell. Plus, my mom's life is pretty much wrecked because of me.

<u>What is the issue that troubles you most at this time?</u> My father was killed by a stranger for no reason. We've been left alone forever. I know a lot of time has passed and I'm supposed to be over it, but I'm not. My father told me what happens when you die and I made sure he's in Heaven, though if he was stuck in the Land of the Dead, he'd be closer to us. Also, everyone in Austin hates me, except for my two friends. One for sure. She writes me really good letters and makes me laugh.

<u>Who do you have the most difficulty with in your life?</u> Me. I'm a horrible person. My mom and the doctors try so hard to fix me (smiley face) and I just don't stay fixed (frowny face). I'll be doing oooooh so wonderful, sooooo normal-like and then, bango wango!! (Stick figure doing a cartwheel.) I get a nutso idea, like running away to Las Vegas like I just did, and off I gooooooo! When I take off, it feels like I'm shooting off the world. No one can hurt me and I don't care what happens to anybody. I tried to hitch a ride with a truck driver this time and that scared my mother, but I thought it would be cool and powerful to ride way above the other cars like that, wheeling down to Las Vegas in a BIG rig with the lights and the celebrities all below me. I promised I wouldn't, but I'll probably hitch again. It's a thrill. But no truck drivers. Why do I run away? No reason. All these feelings just bunch up inside me and I have to go-go-go! I know my mom is afraid she'll lose me, and I understand because I don't know what I'd do if anything bad happened to her.

<u>What are the behaviors you have and wish you didn't?</u> I wish I didn't care that my mother's friends know I was sent to a hospital for crazy people and I wish my friends didn't think I was crazy, too. I know, sticks and stones and all that. I don't care if they're not supposed to, words do hurt me and my mother. (Two frowny faces.)

But if I could pick just one thing and it would be fixed, I'd stop me from doing the same stupid things over and over. For me to stop doing crazy stuff, I'd have to stop seeing things that are real to me, but not real to other people.

I took off for Las Vegas because of a dream. I dreamed that I was touched by the Spirit of the Lucky Seven. Pretty cuckoo, huh? I'm saying I "dreamed" what happened because those are the right words if I ever want to get out of here, but to me it was not a dream. The Spirit of the Lucky Seven looked just like Cinderella's fairy godmother (Ha ha!). She tapped me with her golden wand and made me one of the SPECIAL PEOPLE. I know. Psycho. Looneytunes.

It sounds psycho to me now, too. But when I was on my way, I was so strong!! I believed I could win anything. I'd wear big sunglasses so no one could tell how old I am, and I'd be on television playing poker. When I won, my picture would be in all the papers, even on the front pages of those celebrity magazines in the checkout lanes of every grocery store in Austin. What would mom's snobby country club friends say then??

I'd get movie offers, but I'd only take the work if I thought the script was outstanding. (I copied that line from what a movie star said in *People* magazine.) I'd be a media darling. (Copied that too.) Everyone would love me and I'd be so famous that all the people in Austin who think I'm crazy and hopeless would try to be friends with me. I made a list of the famous people I'd allow to interview me, because I'd have such a busy, busy, happy schedule.

What a joke. Some movie star. Here I sit on the floor in a mental hospital.

Just today I've spent four hours on this stupid form. I started this thing three days ago. I keep deleting words, looking up better words, and starting over. I don't want to sound crazy and retarded, too. I've been here a week and I haven't been able to force myself to brush my teeth. I'm only on the floor in this dayroom, instead of in bed, because the rule is I have to leave my room.

A lot of the girls here blame the hospital or their parents for making them crazy, but I don't. I was crazy and sad before the first time I was locked in here, maybe even before my father was killed for no reason. The parents out at the Flower Mound Country Club (ta da!!) think I'm dangerous. They think I torture and kill animals like all the serial killers do when they're kids. (They let us watch the Discovery Channel.)

I think my friends are afraid of me, too. I would never ever hurt anyone. There must be more girls like me. When I finish school I want to help girls like me because I know what it's like to feel hopeless and different. I want to have friends. I call Jessica and Nancy Margaret my best friends even though neither one of them has ever come to see me. I know I could go to Austin and see them, but even if I could take the hateful way people look at me, I can't stand the way my mother's friends look down on her because she has such a loser daughter.

Yeah. I know. It's all me, me, me, and oh, poor Camilla. That's my real problem.

Sorry I got carried away on that last question. Okay, now for the last three parts, I'm tired of this stupid project.

What is your greatest obstacle? My biggest obstacle is my screwed up head. Since I'm a kid, I'm not supposed to know my diagnosis. But I'm not blind or dumb. In fact, I tested at a 168 IQ, but being smart doesn't help someone like me. As I also read on my chart, I am a "very bright bipolar young lady with severe impairment." That means I am hopeless. They told me to be honest, so I am.

What is your greatest strength? My mom is my greatest strength. Also, people tell me I'm pretty. I'd rather people said I was a good friend. I got my friends in trouble and I hurt them.

What is your current goal? My goal is to be the opposite of Camilla Maria Cervantes.

CHAPTER 43

I'd managed to retrieve my A-Game Ann Klein black stretch jeans from the back of my closet, locate a blue silk shirt and a Zuni concha belt, and still make it to the studio with four minutes to spare. I needed every second to decelerate the whirl in my brain and calm the turbulence in my stomach. If I didn't chill, given my predilection toward this particular talk show host, my least attractive Rose trait could take charge of the interview, and Ms. Bailey was looking at a Jerry Springer moment.

Oh, well. There are things worse than public humiliation. Missing my one chance to speak up for Camilla and ease Ana Teresa's transition into fulltime Flower Mound life would be worse than public humiliation.

Jane Bailey's producer-director, a pleasant young lady with Hollywood eyes and heels so high she tipped forward, greeted me, and had me sign a release. Then she showed me to my spot on one of two lime green sofas which made a corner on the set.

I twisted the nubby tendrils of plastic ivy on the coffee table. The ends pinched off, no doubt, by nervous guests. Like me. But not like me. It wasn't the interview that had me hyped. I was nervous because I needed more time at my bunkhouse table with the pieces of Camilla's life. Reading Camilla's Self Report had re-set my nerve endings to a higher voltage. A frequency that could enable me to see what I couldn't see before, or, if unchecked during the next thirty minutes, could spin me off in directions that weren't helpful to anyone, including Jane Bailey and the parents I hoped to reach.

Live interviews were about conflict. Jane Bailey would steer the interview in sensational directions to provoke catchy sound bites for use later. I should watch myself.

The star joined me on the other lime sofa, her attention on the cell at her ear. Jane Bailey, in a simple A-line skirt and reasonable dark heels, was smaller and less dangerous-looking than I'd anticipated. The early gray streaks in her hair and shadows under her eyes made her softer than she'd seemed on camera. I would have taken her for a high school teacher. One who'd stay after school with you if you needed extra help.

"This is why you need more than two friends, honey. Please stop crying," she said, into the phone.

"Now that's not true, lots of people like you. You're a great kid. Pammie, I have to go. Yes, it does matter what I think. Pammie, tonight we can--"

Her caller gone, Bailey sighed and turned off her phone. Hollywood Eyes in Extreme Heels caught her attention and waved. Bailey reached across the table, grabbed my hand in introduction, and apologized.

"Kid troubles," she said. "Sorry to rush you--"

The producer-director waved and pointed. "And . . . we are live in . . . Three. Two. One."

Bailey did a not-overly sensational introduction, even conceding that emotional illnesses are complicated and often difficult to identify and understand. She added that the media was guilty of making too much of sensational elements without providing audiences the full picture, which was why she'd invited me as a guest.

Other than using the word "illnesses" instead of "disorders," I was satisfied. The stage set, she turned to me.

"Dr. LeFave, thank you for making time to speak with my audience. The last few days must have been difficult for you."

"Yes."

"Given recent events, our audience is particularly interested in mental illnesses that affect children. All parents, of course, worry about their kids." She counted herself in the worried group. "Can you say something about what causes emotional diseases in children?"

"Sure. Or at least I can give parents a way to think about the dilemma. To start, the term 'disease' doesn't really fit when describing emotional disorders. Diseases are usually thought of as physical problems, such as the invasion of an enemy organism, a bacterium, or a virus. Or a default in the body such as malignant cell growth or a defect in the immune response. Most diseases can be treated, if not cured, with proper care and specific medicine. Emotional disorders are different in that the causes, physical and otherwise, are not clear cut, the methods of treatment are not well defined, and there isn't a 'cure' that works in a predictable and hundred percent way."

"Hmmm." Ms. Bailey was easy to talk to, I'd give her that.

"Of course," I continued, "when a child is having difficulty, parents want to know what caused the problem, which makes perfect sense to me. . . . I don't want to make this a lecture."

I did want to make the interview go faster, but lecturing wouldn't help. Thirty minutes is thirty minutes.

"No, please go on."

"Usually I start by explaining that a symptom in a child or an adult— say insomnia, a phobia, aggressive behavior, depression, or compulsive eating—is the result of a combination of four elements. The first is the child's physical body--genetics, overall health, brain chemistry, and current and past medical issues. The second factor is the events in the child's life, which includes how they have been parented, as well as specific past and current incidents. Third is the child's basic capacity for managing stress and change, and fourth is the adequacy and availability of their emotional system, primarily family."

I took a breath. Bailey even made a couple of quick notes. Sometimes I forget that what is everyday reasoning for me isn't familiar to most people.

"When asked why a child is in emotional distress," I continued, "all we can say with certainty is that the child's symptoms are the result of an interactive combination of these four areas."

"Dr. LeFave, my ears perked up, and suspect the same is true for other parents in our audience, when you mentioned that events can cause--"

"Influence, not cause. What happens, the events in a child's life, are only one factor contributing to a symptom."

"Right, sorry."

"It's an important distinction, because when we are anxious about a child, we are likely to oversimplify and blame."

"What about when something really bad happens to a young child, say the death of a parent?"

"You're referring to the murder of Camilla Cervantes' father? You're asking if that loss was behind her emotional problems?"

"Yes. Though I--"

"Death of a parent is certainly a powerful event, one that changes many relationships and situations in the family, but the event is still not the whole story. Even severe symptoms are rarely simple cause and effect. In Camilla Cervantes's case, for example, the loss of her father was violent and sudden. She was very young. She had no siblings to help when the tragedy occurred or later in her life when she could have benefited from a relationship with a sister or brother. Camilla had an especially strong tie to her father, a man away from his home country, which usually results in even closer ties with children. That said, I'm not saying that losing her father caused everything that came later. If that were true, every only child whose father was murdered when she was ten would end up with the same problems."

Bailey nodded encouragement to continue.

"Seeing current problems as caused by a single event, even death of a parent, is almost always a sidetrack that slows or even prevents progress. Most of us know capable adults whose lives are less than they could be because of a belief that they cannot move beyond certain trauma."

Had I really said those words? Figures. I'd somehow managed to make the interview about me. About the truth that, in spite of all my high-minded promises to Camilla, I could do nothing to make the road easier for Eileen and Ana Teresa because I couldn't find the way back myself.

"I'm sorry," I said. "I'm going off course here."

"No, no. What you're saying is helpful. You are hitting on questions we've all had since the . . . since your friend was murdered."

Ms. Bailey hadn't deserved the stereotyped dismissal I'd tagged on her in two seconds on the morning of the murder. Diana Sloan was good at what she did. Ms. Bailey actually seemed rather sane and sincere. I was going to be o-kay.

"What about divorce, Dr. LeFave? Is a child whose parents' divorce more likely to have emotional problems? I mean considering that the child's family is forever broken when she loses a parent?

Forever broken? Loses a parent? Interesting perspective. The steel claws in my chest squeezed and choked until no blood was left in my heart.

I'd been set up.

I'd been set up in the worst possible way.

CHAPTER 44

The Pollyanna Princess rides again. Brain down the rabbit hole. Sucker with a "Kick Me!" sign the size of Oklahoma on my rear.

Bailey had done her homework. This cool professional hadn't been fooled by Diana Sloan. Ms. Bailey, however, had played me big time. I was a prisoner of the release form I hadn't bothered to read. The Flower Mound Murder still the number one story, my reputation-obliterating interview would parlay Bailey into national, maybe even international recognition. And, even more fortunate for Bailey, the boost to her career came at a time when her competition, Eileen Cervantes, faced the worst moments in her life.

I'd thought my degrees and licenses would help Camilla. Now I saw that my credibility only sweetened the deal. A clip with a friend of Camilla's in a 9-1-1 on-camera meltdown wouldn't do much for syndication. But, a friend of Camilla's who is a psychologist and who happened to have a dead bipolar stepdaughter? Now that would get some play.

I'd come within a hair's breadth of trusting this sandbagging witch, this narcissistic taker. Bailey had called Camilla and me 'special friends' because she'd scavenged lingering gossip about the blood sacrificing Dorados. Bailey's career dreams had meshed perfectly with Dianna's goals. Bailey gave Diana a pulpit to destroy Camilla and Diana returned the favor by opening the gates to the Flower Mound and the powerful people who lived and played there.

And as for Zack Harvey? Where did he fit in? Was Jane Bailey a Scientologist perhaps? A Hollywood power alliance would explain how Zack located the border glamour shot so quickly. If Jane Bailey's scheme worked, Zack and his Scientologist buddies would have the story, the live video, of their dreams. "Demon psychologist reveals evil nature!" would make a nice headline. "Demon psychologist seduces own child to suicide!" would play even better.

Well, Zack and Bailey wouldn't be the first to use our family tragedy for personal gain. The routine was pulled on me a dozen times in the months after the suicide. Reporters would call and convince me they intended to do a public service article alerting teens to the signs of depression in their friends. When the stories came out, the main conclusions drawn were: Kelly killed herself because her selfish parents divorced; and, because those same selfish parents put too much pressure on her to succeed.

I should yank off this mike and run for it.

Somehow, outwardly, I managed a clear, unemotional response to Bailey's question, a general statement that the effects of a divorce depend on many variables such as the nature of the divorce, parental civility, continued calm participation of both parents, and the nature of the new families if there are remarriages. I added that geographical separation, financial stability, and the emotional maturity and availability of extended family, influenced how a child is affected by a divorce. Of course, if a child is emotionally fragile to begin with, the loss would make it more likely that . . .

At that moment, a gear slipped out of its notch in my brain. Chains yanked at closed doors. I braced for Ms. Jane Bailey's full-on frontal attack.

Then, instead of an aggressive follow-up question about divorce, Ms. Bailey asked something about early symptoms of bipolar disorder in children and adolescents. My brain, preoccupied dredging my foxhole, had missed the heart of her question. I couldn't come up with a sensible response.

Bailey repeated her question, this time in a foreign language. No, her words came out of her mouth upside down. My game face locked and loaded, I waited. She asked the question a third time.

"Dr. LeFave, since there's been so much interest in bipolar illness—disorder, could you share with our audience, what parents should look for if they are worried that a child might be bipolar?"

Nice touch, Ms. Bailey. Way to go. Now that you're off the starting blocks, you aren't wasting any time.

"Also, Dr. LeFave, could you say something about when parents should contact a professional or insist on treatment?"

Bailey had her guns in a row.

You want to know what behavior would tip off parents that their child might be suicidal? Well, how about this: *If a teenage daughter gives you back every letter you ever wrote to her in a notebook she bought especially for you, and says, "I thought you might like to have these," a lightning bolt should blaze a path of scorched destruction through your brain.*

Should have. Didn't.

"Are you all right, Dr. LeFave? Do you need a minute?"

"No. I am just fine." My cheeks flamed. I'm just peachy.

I wasn't falling for her fake concern. I knew exactly where this was going. I traveled the same road myself every night. Every night I ended up with my back against this same wall and I waited. I listened to the questions others thought I couldn't hear. The questions I couldn't stop asking myself.

The school teacher Bailey faded. Her face remolded into that of a stern judge high above me, her eyes brilliant with the excitement of knowing she had me. She leaned forward and readied to ask: *"Isn't it true that your stepdaughter committed suicide after being diagnosed as bipolar? And isn't it true that three out of four of her parents are psychologists and psychiatrists?"*

Then the finale. The question Ms. Bailey would not dare ask, but which would hang between us like a cyanide fog: *"Tell me, Dr. LeFave, if you, as a trained professional, couldn't spot a suicidal child in your own family . . . why on earth should anyone listen to what you have to say?"*

"Could I get you a glass of water, Dr. LeFave?" Ms. Bailey glanced anxiously toward Hollywood Eyes.

"Really, I'm just fine."

Miraculously, for the cameras, I maintained a normal tone and produced a decent description of the signs to watch for and situations that might benefit from professional intervention. Ms. Bailey continued the interview in a pleasant, professional manner. Actually, a quite lovely, pleasant manner. Jane Bailey was a nice person. The dangerous person was me. Ms. Bailey was doing her best to conduct an interview that would be useful to her audience with a psychologist whose brain was a bungle of silly string. But maybe that didn't show yet.

The gear that had slipped free in my brain had unlocked a dark cell in my heart. The cell I'd sealed, I thought, forever. For a reason I didn't understand, when I still had Camilla, who understood bipolar symptoms and who believed in me, I'd managed to keep the door closed. Without Camilla here to protect me, the horror show clips exploded onto the back screen of my brain.

A blonde cherub, her arms locked around the steering wheel, "Please, Daddy, don't go, Daddy!" A younger bundle, oodles of brown curls, clutching her teddy bear, her face pressed into the neck of the good woman asking what she'd done wrong. When she hadn't done anything wrong at all.

I answered another question for Ms. Bailey, but did not hear myself speaking. Did my madness show? Was this the end of my career?

Okay, fine. No more hiding. No more pretending I was the person I used to be or the person I thought I was. I confess to everything. Do your will, Ms. Bailey. I give up forever. I waited. And waited. Nothing happened.

My heart did not freeze. My lungs did not collapse. Instead, the thin candy shell that had hardened over my skin suffered a million splintering cracks, then burst into a spray of tiny flakes that caught the light. *Ten years ago, on a cold dark night . . ."*

Ms. Bailey, a smile of mild concern on her face, recapped for the audience and tagged on a cue for me. "You were saying that one event can't explain an emotional disorder, that there are multiple influences?"

"Yes. Always there are multiple influences."

"You said that for a young person to be diagnosed as bipolar, there has to be at least one manic episode?"

"Yes."

"But isn't being manic the same as being in a really good mood?"

Her question registered in my brain and filled me with an odd delight. A delight in the words separated from meaning. Still I plunged on.

"No. Bipolar is a debilitating disorder. It is not an exaggeration of the moods other people experience. The emotional swings not only affect how the person feels. The thinking of the person—particularly judgment and logic—is also compromised. The capacity to consider future results of current behavior is lost. Everything is now. Urges to run away are common. People make impulsive decisions that result in devastating consequences, sometimes physical and often humiliating. Can you imagine how a person would feel when she learned that, the day before, she'd announced to her friends that she was going on the world tennis tour, though she'd never picked up a racquet? That she had seduced her boyfriend's brother? That she'd announced to her class that she was re-writing the Bible? . . . Yes, Ms. Bailey, bipolar mania is more than the sort of 'good mood' other people experience."

She sat stunned but glad I'd rejoined the discussion.

"And the depression?" I said, and struggled to rein myself in. "Days in bed, foil on the windows. Black pain and hopelessness. Pain no medicine can touch because it's not created by injuries or nerves. It's pain that cannot be dulled or escaped because it is a raging and constant product of your own dark soul."

"I never--"

"Forgive me, for going overboard, Ms. Bailey. With all the attention on Camilla's murder, I want people to be aware of how serious and life-destroying bipolar disorder can be. Camilla would want that. Even as a teen she knew she wanted to help other young girls with problems. Camilla, like her mother, would want others to know how to recognize bipolar disorder and know that help is available. Camilla received help, was able to live beyond her symptoms, and grew into a confident and caring adult. Her death was a murder, unrelated to her childhood difficulties."

"Wow." She reached across and touched my knee. "Don't worry about the overboard. I think I speak for our listeners in saying that we appreciate your willingness to share. You've helped us better understand the human side of bipolar disorder. Thank you."

I don't remember the rest of the interview. Whatever I said seemed to please Jane Bailey.

CHAPTER 45

The show over, Jane Bailey collapsed into the green sofa. Her strained smile softened and reset her expression into faint worry lines on either side of her mouth.

As for me, I had no worries. Unless, I should be concerned about the hummingbird flitting about the set. Or concerned that I wasn't concerned. In psychology we call this sort of experience a break with reality. But how could that be? I felt completely at home in the world for the first time in a long time.

"Thank you for being so open on the show," Bailey said. "After our phone conversations, I didn't know what to expect. I know the coverage of your friend's murder has been pretty attention-grubbing."

Hollywood Eyes took our mikes off and away.

"The rumors and invasions of Camilla's privacy have been obscene," I said. I was smiling oddly, I could feel it, and I couldn't stop. "I expected this interview to be a thirty minute mammogram on a railroad track."

"I probably should have thrown in a few zinger questions, if I ever want to go anywhere in this business."

"I was thinking the same thing." I laughed as if we'd shared an inside joke.

"The program manager is the one who orders those awful on-the-spot interviews, though I can't blame him. It's his job to increase viewer numbers. As for the woman who used her influence to slip me into the Flower Mound Gold Room?"

"Diana Sloan."

"That was my fault. I should have picked up that she planned to hijack the interview."

"I don't blame you. Diana can be convincing. I don't think her life has gone particularly well."

"The thing is, Dr. LeFave, pressure to increase viewer share, to sell advertising minutes at higher and higher prices, no matter who gets hurt, is the goal of any broadcast. I'm not sure this is the right career for me. Maybe I don't even belong in the television magazine industry."

"I can certainly understand that. I'm one of those people who couldn't sell lemonade to a man dying of thirst in the desert." I leaned back and stretched my legs. A hummingbird took off across my vision and buzzed over a little girl with a lemonade stand in the Sahara. Now that was funny. The hummingbird giggled.

Jane Bailey didn't seem to notice.

"I'm a single mother with minimum child support," she said. "So I need a good job. But this place is taking too much out of me. I'm trying to decide if I should find another career, even if it doesn't pay as much. You see, all along I had a selfish reason for inviting you on the show." She closed her eyes acknowledging fatigue and embarrassment, then allowed a slight smile. *Was I offended?*

"It's okay, really. At least you didn't start with 'I have this friend . . .' and your questions are a break from my own concerns."

I could give Jane a few minutes. I owed her that and more. Then straight back to Camilla's life lined up on my kitchen table. Tick, tick.

"The main reason I'm thinking about quitting is my daughter," she said. "That was Pamela on the phone when the show started. I'm worried to death about her, and now with this whole business with Miss Cervantes— the problems she had when she was little--all the stories and fears. . . . I asked that question about divorce because my husband and I divorced two years ago. Pamela was really close to him and she blames me for him not being with her. She's as angry and hurt today as she was when we first told the kids."

"How old is your daughter?"

"Thirteen, but not one of those 'thirteen going on thirty' types. She's socially behind, I guess you'd say. She does fine in school, though she's already worried about getting into college. . . . Do you think we're pushing her too hard?"

"All I can say is, I see as many adults in my office who are angry with their parents for not pushing them in school as I see adults who are angry because their parents pushed them."

She smiled. "I guess we all want to be the perfect parent. Maybe if I just had a little re-assurance."

"I'd be glad to help in any way I can," I said, "though all I can offer without meeting your daughter are generalities that may or may not fit."

"I know. I've tried to get her to go to counseling, but she says she will not say a word and she always does what she says."

"What worries you most about Pamela?"

"She's never happy since her father left and she leans on me way too much."

"What about friends?"

"She has two really close friends, but they fight constantly and one of the three is always crying. Usually Pammie. That's why she called earlier. One friend is having a sleepover and Pammie wasn't invited."

"Does that make any sense to you?"

"Yes. The last three times Pamela's been to a sleepover, she's called begging me to come get her in the middle of the night. And in case you're thinking I'm one of those hovering mothers and that I shouldn't have rescued her, it was the parents who requested I take my hysterical daughter off their hands."

We exchanged a "been there" moment. My first out and out lie.

"No one but the parent knows what's really going on," I said. "Would she ever call her father to rescue her? I assume Pamela stays some with him."

Jane's shoulders dropped, a release that told a story. "Pamela would stay with him rather than choose a sleepover. Ted backs out a lot on plans and when he does see the kids, he brings a girlfriend. Doug, my son, does okay. He and Ted do guy things together, but Pammie—she feels like her father dumped her. I hate that word."

"I do, too. It sounds like someone gets thrown in the garbage."

"I don't want to sound like it's all Ted's fault, Dr. LeFave. I have my own new relationship, which has to add to Pammie's feeling left out. It's just, I guess my question right now is, should I quit this job since it takes so much of my time and focus?"

"As much as I'd love to know the best choice, Jane, I don't." Suddenly aware of how bizarre, and yet absolutely perfect, it was for Jane to ask me about teenage girls and what they needed, I let go of another level of caution. "Most of the time questions about work and home time are not either-or questions. Plus, assigning yourself the job of worrying about Pamela twenty-four hours a day wouldn't be a positive solution for anyone."

"If only Ted could work on his relationship with Pamela."

"You know, more often than you'd think, the father doesn't realize how important he is to his children. Infatuated with a new love, he doesn't see that the joy his new relationship gives him, feels like, and often is, a loss to his daughter."

Did I really say that out loud?

"My older stepdaughter taught me this lesson," I continued, as if Jane and I were on Sunday afternoon carriage ride in the park. "Not long after the separation, her father and I ate at a Burger King with a promotion giving out whatever kind of figurine was hot at that time. I saved mine, his daughter's favorite character, and was pleased to give it to her the next day. She smiled at first, then big tears rolled down her little face. When I asked what was wrong, she said, 'When Burger King had toys before, my daddy used to take *me.*'"

That was odd. I'd never shared that afternoon with anyone. I'd been sure if I did, I would break down sobbing and never stop.

"Pamela does feel like her father isn't interested in a special relationship with her anymore," Jane said. "Ted's not a bad guy. He just doesn't get it. I wish he could hear what you're saying from you instead of me."

"That can be arranged. I have to warn you though, I've never had much success talking people who don't want to change into changing."

She smiled. "Still, I like the honest way you say things."

"On the career question, I can say this much. It's not how many hours we work that affects kids as much as the quality of the relationship. I'm not talking about the old 'quality time' song and dance, I'm talking about working toward a close and open relationship that also encourages independence."

"The children make it all worth it, don't they?" Jane asked.

"Yes, they do."

"Do you have children, Dr. LeFave?"

"Yes. Two wonderful stepdaughters."

"Trade pictures?" Jane opened the purse on the floor next to her feet and pulled out a billfold.

"Sure." I retrieved the laminated photo always in my left back pocket, a smaller version of a professional pose the girls had taken and given us one year for Christmas. She handed me a shot of a young boy and his sister.

"Good-looking kids," I said. Which was true.

"Do your stepdaughters live here in Austin?"

"No. One's in Tucson and the younger one is in California."

"What are they doing now?"

"The older one goes to the University of Arizona. She likes the business side of life. When she was six she turned her bedroom into her office."

"And the younger one?"

"We're so alike. All about the art—words and pictures. She's at UCLA. She has a boyfriend named Cody. Kelly's a big reader like me. She's a writer, too. We write letters back and forth every week, sometimes twice a week. Oh, we email, too, like everyone else. But we don't text because I don't carry a cell phone and she's the only other person I know who doesn't. We're a two person 'society of rebels'. We've been writing since Kelly could only print and only read printing. Oh, that was fun! We always illustrate our letters though both of us are horrible artists. I have all of her letters and she saves all of mine in a special notebook."

CHAPTER 46

What had I done? Who had I become?

Concepción, her eyes threaded with scarlet and her four-foot-eight inch body a rock, met me in the kitchen in all-out panic mode. She'd tried to reach Celestino in the jail and whoever took the call told her not to call back. When she'd tried again anyway she was told an officer would be sent out to talk with her.

I held her close. Then, still afloat in the clouds of my make-believe world, I rattled off a ten minute rah-rah speech assuring her I was hard at work on a theory of Camilla's murder that would prove Celestino was innocent--an unimaginable and unforgivable exaggeration. When I saw the fear of deportation in her eyes, I spiked my promise with a hint that I could do something about that, too. Two more shakes of my magic wand and Celestino would be here for supper.

She'd stuck a mug of coffee in my right hand, the portable phone in my left, and called over her shoulder as she headed off down the hall.

"Mr. Don, very important. Call now!"

"Sure." One little cup of java, then I'd call.

To calm the "Thank God you're home! We thought you were never coming back to us!" dance, I opened a foil pack of Snausages. Suzi snapped her wiener up in a most unladylike fashion. I held one out for Sammie, but he ignored the treat and hopped into my lap instead. The boy chose me over pretend meat. Nice. He stretched out warm and sweet on my chest, his little hiney in the crook of my elbow.

"She's out at UCLA—very happy," I'd purred to my new cozy friend Jane. *"She has a boyfriend named Cody . . . We're so alike . . ."* Such sweet, sweet lies.

But still, all of it, bold-faced lies. The Rose kids do not tell lies.

In the Rose family growing up, we jumped to conclusions, rebelled against authority, and flew off the handle, but we did not lie. Ever. Not because we'd be punished if discovered, but because my Danish Lutheran father and Appalachian Baptist mother expected better of us. Sure, we'd told our share of teenage fibs about where we were going and who we'd be with. A good many of those fabrications were revealed and treated more with humor than punishment, as those were stories told in the push to enjoy life and gain independence.

Lies told as part of making our own decisions in the world were in a different class from lies told to make yourself appear better to others or to avoid taking responsibility for your actions. A lie told to appear richer, smarter, or more accomplished than you were, was to be unfaithful to yourself and to sell your family down the river.

Had I not been swimming in delusion, I would have planned what I would and wouldn't share with Jane Bailey if she asked about children. I would have managed a version of the truth. I had plenty of those. "She is no longer with us . . . A tragedy no one saw coming . . ." And my favorite show stopper . . . "We lost her."

Had I been in my right mind, I certainly would not have made up a stepdaughter, or at least made up that she was still alive. If Jane Bailey related the storybook family I'd described to someone who knew me, which would happen, my reputation would take a significant hit. Being a fraud is another undesirable quality in a psychologist.

The most amazing part of the lying experience was that I hadn't felt guilty or even awkward. I'd felt wonderful and light. I'd felt as if I was a good person again, the woman before the shroud fell, the woman who was part of a normal family. A beautiful, an atypical family, but a family held together by love and safety.

In some perverse or miraculous way, depending on your point of view, I'd linked up the Land of the Dead and the Land of the Living. Kelly was a hummingbird only I could see. I understood Camilla at this moment, more than I ever had when she was alive. *"I'm saying I dreamed what happened because those are the right words . . . but to me it was not a dream."*

What if a person could have a second chance? They can. It's called insanity.

Well, I *had* just raised the dead. That ought to count for something.

Less than two hours to go. Every word in my eulogy had to be perfect. I couldn't bring anyone back to life, but I could do my part to see that Eileen and Ana Teresa had the best chance for joy in their lives. I wanted listeners to know Camilla as I knew her, as a beautiful and caring adult and as a happy little girl before her father died, before she wrote: *"My name is Camilla Maria Cervantes and I hate my life."*

Camilla would be with me. *Remember that death and life are not separate and pray for me.*

I arranged the faxed pages, Camilla's self-report on top, and the stacks of pictures from Las Palomas with the photo of Camilla in her father's arms in the lead. Something wasn't right with Mr. Cervantes' clothes, but that didn't bug me as much as the fact that I hadn't found what she expected me to in her letter and what the heck I was supposed to see in *My Birth?*

I needed more time to re-sort the images in my head. Lost in the place where the Land of the Living overlapped with the Land of the Dead, I'd blurred Camilla's life with Kelly's like white paint and red paint stirred to make pink. Camilla deserved my full attention. Tonight was not about Kelly or me.

Next to *My Birth* I placed one of the Santa Muerte altar photos that had downloaded while I was at the television studio. Camilla, the last time I'd seen her. Still and still beautiful.

I went back to the photo of Camilla, her Frida Kahlo doll hanging from her hand. I couldn't imagine any child other than Camilla who would have liked Frida's work or any parent other than her father who would have encouraged her interest. Camilla, though, I could picture her poised on his knee or in bed, soaking up every word of what others would consider unsuitable bedtime stories. I understood why, in spite of her later studies in Italy and France, Frida Kahlo would be Camilla's favorite.

Forever.

CHAPTER 47

"Any ideas on the stabbed virgin, the sheeted mother, or the dead baby?" I asked Sam.

He crinkled his eyes, then tucked his nose under his knee. Sammie had done what he could.

Camilla loved the painting, *My Birth*, because, like Frida, when my friend was at her lowest, she found the strength to let go of what was lost and use what gifts she still had. Frida showed Camilla the way to freedom, and Camilla understood what to do. Not only did she recover physically, she used the experience to turn her life around, to give a future to girls who, without her, had no future.

Camilla had even drawn on Frida's example and overcome her crazy runaway urges. No more *Camilla, Camilla, the Flower Mound Killa*. I wanted to believe I'd helped a little in Paris. How could I have known what to say when I was thirteen and have no idea how to help Kelly when I was a full grown woman?

Camilla found a way to accept fate and move on. How? How did you do that, Camilla?

Back it up, LeFave. Why was I so irretrievably and selfishly stuck on the day my world changed instead of the day that ended Camilla's life? Only a kid when I'd landed at the Charles de Gaulle Paris Airport, goofy-eyed impressed with every detail, I hadn't had enough life experience to comprehend the fear and pain I'd seen in Eileen's face. She'd told me how no matter how many times she'd asked, the doctors couldn't promise her Camilla would live. How dare anyone ever speak to Eileen about Camilla's emotional problems after her beautiful daughter was raped, shattered, and nearly killed by a mentally ill, evil stranger? Since Tucson, I'd understood the broken look I'd seen on Eileen's face quite well.

The phone chimed somewhere under the papers and photos. *Damn.* The Chief. The message kicked in before I located the receiver. Zack Harvey, two words: "False alarm." Click.

Great, Zack. False alarm about what? Do you mean no drug overdose? Or, Camilla overdosed, but her condition was never critical? Do you mean the woman in the photos isn't Camilla? The intelligent answer was that, as soon as he'd cut off the call, Zack had propped his Godliness-equals-abundance Cole Haans on his Scientology desk, clasped his hands behind his head and was, at this moment, laughing his ass off.

I punched in the "personal cell number" Zack had circled three times and underlined in thick red ink.

"Welcome to the Church of Scientology! We care about you!" a pathologically enthusiastic young lady announced. "Please leave a message and have an abundant day!"

Next, I listened to the Chief's message: "In addition to his direct deposit salary, over the past four years, Mr. Maris made cash deposits of twenty thousand dollars in round numbers every six months. A down payment of four hundred thousand was made on the Flower Mound house, cashier's check. The last deposit was for fifty thousand, two days ago, also a cashier's check. And, Doc, do *not* contact Mr. Maris without contacting me first."

Oops. By now the Chief knew that pony had cleared that gate. As for Scott Maris, if he was cheating Los Insurgentes, he was already dead.

The blackmail possibility, that El Viborito kept the truth from Eileen with regular payments to Scott, made the most sense. Had Camilla's decision to live primarily in Texas and her talk of a "father figure in the family" turned some kind of corner for El Viborito? If he'd forbidden Camilla to take his daughter, he wasn't the sort to back down no matter the cost. He wasn't the sort to allow Scott to move in as Ana Teresa's parent.

To have his daughter with him, El Viborito knew he'd have to sequester Ana Teresa within the walls of his La Merced cartel fortress before Eileen knew he had a claim on her granddaughter. He would win a DNA challenge, but U.S. courts made parental rights exceptions when it came to child protection. In fact, with what U.S. authorities had on him, if they managed to handcuff the Little Snake, he'd go to the head of the express lane on the Texas no-kidding Death Row.

Scott Maris had deserved a bonus two days ago. How much would the crime boss pay to keep Eileen in the dark until he was ready to make his move? He'd been willing to kill Joaquin. Joaquin would risk crossing the border to warn Eileen and save Ana Teresa from the family plans of the Little Snake. As difficult as the truth about her granddaughter's biological father would be for Eileen to hear, the time had come when she had to know. Joaquin's body found near the police station likely meant he'd decided to first set up more protection for Eileen and her granddaughter.

Joaquin hadn't told Eileen the truth. I'd have been her first desperate call. If I even knew the truth. If El Viborito was Ana Teresa's father. I wasn't the most reliable judge of the truth at the moment.

Thank God Ana Teresa had her grandmother. Eileen was the strongest of all of us. My heart warmed. Ana Teresa was safe with her. Camilla—or Camilla's spirit, or however a person thought about love, life, and death—would rest with her hummingbird daughter enfolded in the wings of Eileen. The warmth in my heart had two branches. One pure and the other a jealousy I'd never admit. Eileen would not condemn my lie to Jane Bailey. Though her loss now was hideous, Eileen had enjoyed years of the feeling I'd relished for only a few moments this afternoon. She'd had the chance to plan her daughter's wedding, to see Camilla become a mother, and now Eileen was blessed to have her beloved daughter's child at her side.

The picture of Camilla with her father was most likely taken at La Merced, that was obvious now. The smoke filtering up from the grills preparing La Merced fresh fast food. Knowing where the picture was taken had seemed so important, and now the knowledge or guess meant nothing. During their vacations and summers in his Mexico City house, her father would have taken Camilla to family fun days. Festivals are big in Mexico and all about family. *Cascarones* confetti, clowns on stilts, and candy. Like the rest of the city, they would have shopped at La Merced for Day of the Dead supplies.

The hospital photos only mattered if I could be certain the woman on the gurney was Camilla. Why hadn't she mentioned a hospital stay? I studied the four photos in order. Now that was odd. The same injured painter with a rag around his bloody hand appeared in the first ER photo and in the last one. Why? I studied his features, registered a spark of hope, then one more possible lead hit the floor. The painter wasn't the only waiting ER patient to appear in more than one shot and none of them paid particular attention to Camilla.

Then I noticed a feature that was obvious, but definitely not meaningless. In fact, the obvious blew apart any theory I'd played so far without stimulating an alternative story behind Camilla's murder. I'd like to claim an 'aha' moment, a brilliant psychological breakthrough or the conclusion of an intelligent analysis. But I can't. All I could say was that when the picture was taken, Camilla and her father were not at La Merced for a fiesta.

Like those who judged and turned away from Frida's paintings, I'd fallen on stereotypes to draw conclusions. The way when you see a poor woman with bruised eyes you think domestic violence, and when you see a wealthy woman with the same purple circles, you think plastic surgery. I had a piece of the story, a meaningless tidbit from over thirty years ago that had nothing to do with Camilla's murder. Nothing I'd done had me any closer to a motive.

For the police, motive wasn't as important as evidence, and the most powerful motive meant nothing without evidence. Not for me. Find the motive, find the killer, and I hadn't come up with one reason why anyone would want Camilla dead or who would want to stop Camilla's plans. I certainly had no one to tag for the police. And I was out of time. Oh, Camilla, you made such a mistake. How could you have trusted me *"in judgment and heart"* the way my decisions had worked out? But you did.

Camilla even trusted me with her daughter. She knew there was a strong genetic factor in bipolar disorder--that Ana Teresa could well have Kelly's problems with life--and yet she trusted me? *"I know that should anything happen to me, you and Concepción will watch out for Ana Teresa."*

Camilla always spoke from her heart. Her words were my best hope. I arranged the pieces of her life in a timeline. The Patient Self Report on the left side of the laptop screen, *My Birth,* the so-called painting of "hope," propped against the screen. On the right side, her letter.

Of course, she trusted me. Like she said, I'd been there since the beginning. And Eileen was right, I hadn't given up. I would not give up now or ever. *Remember that death and life are not separate, and pray for me.*

I reread Camilla's Patient Evaluation. Then her letter. While I was the 'whiner' for both of us, she was the 'courageous' one. She'd proved that in Paris, her mother on one side, me on the other. Frida tucked in even closer. Camilla had fought death and won, then taken the strength she'd gained to change her life. I was back to where I'd started.

If Sammie could read, he would have spotted what was missing in Camilla's letter. For me it took that moment of sincere jealousy. In my strained reading and re-reading of Camilla's words, I'd paid too much attention to her words and not enough attention to the blank spaces.

For a long minute, I could not breathe. How do you see evil when what you see makes you feel beautiful inside? *The Angel of Death is so glamorous and so horrible at the same time. I can't stop looking at her.* How could truth be hideous and tender at the same time? Love can happen that way.

The afternoon David and I fell together on my Sunshine Circuit trophy blanket in the Longhorn Efficiency Apartments ignited a love I could not, no, I did not, refuse. There was beauty. There was evil, too. No matter how cleverly I rationalized my actions and inactions.

But, no one was supposed to die. For Camilla, the same was true. Beauty and love and passion can get all balled up. Then tragedy brings home the truth.

I thanked Sammie for his help and told him Camilla's story. His eyes drooped.

Dogs are wonderful friends and faithful companions, but those reasons are not what makes our bond with dogs so powerful. Dogs are precious in our hearts because of their capacity to forgive. To beat a dog is heinous because it hurts the dog, but more heinous because the dog will forgive you. A gift we all need sometimes.

The time was here to let go of the "if only" mantra that marked my days and nights. Time to live in the only world that existed. Right here in the kitchen, right now, began my personal Day of the Dead Celebration.

Because Kelly was dead didn't mean my relationship with her was over.

Time for me to accept and love Kelly with all my heart, not as I hoped she'd be, not as I needed her to be, but as the girl she was. To love her, I had to accept her choice. Death was her choice. To love her, I had to respect her decision.

I shuffled the picture, the reports, and Frida's *My Birth* from the center of the kitchen table. Then I reached into the silverware drawer, slid my hand under the plastic tray, and retrieved the facedown eight-by-ten photograph.

I found a clear molded frame, slid the photo into the slot, and welcomed Kelly Julia LeFave back into our odd little family.

CHAPTER 48

No one was supposed to die.

The drama had played out in neon in front of me and I'd hadn't known where to look. Worse still, I was the ringmaster, the one who'd sold the fiction of Camilla's life to the world. My see-no-evil blindness made everything possible.

I knew who killed Camilla Maria Cervantes. I also knew who murdered Joaquin, though they weren't killed by the same person.

George drove with his eyes crossed, Suzi flopped over the console next to him, her flat chin on his thigh. Concepción was a sad bundle in the corner of the backseat, her gaze locked straight ahead. I rode shotgun with Sammie, his nose pressed on the window. George had expected Concepción's company, but not the dogs, who would require the car's air conditioner throughout the ceremony. I wasn't at liberty to explain the plan, but George knew my silence was to protect Concepción. Which meant something big, and probably dangerous, was up.

My insistence on a detour downtown to speak with the Chief hadn't helped George's mood. Once his Lincoln was calibrated to the run every yellow light on Congress Avenue, we were in front of police headquarters without a hitch.

Another difference between jumper and hunter horse show competitions is the requirement of a personal strategy for the rider. The charming walls, brush boxes, and gates for hunter courses are set up with a guide, with carefully measured strides between obstacles and plenty of deep corners to fine tune your horse's balance and speed. With jumper courses, fences must be taken in an order, but the strategy of turns and strides are up to the rider. Thus, before each class, jumper riders walk the course on foot to compose a plan. Camilla's memorial would be my Day of the Dead Grand Prix. The competition would be more brutal than any I'd faced before. I had one chance.

George swung the car into the fat space next to the entrance marked "Chief of Police." He kept the motor running.

Concepción and George, neither comfortable this close to the police station, stared straight ahead as I clamored out. Sammie trampolined off Suzi's back and perched on the top of the driver's seat behind George's head. The boy dog wailed high, then low, then high again, the sound of an approaching ambulance when you can't quite tell where it's coming from.

"Who knows, Miss Rose?" George said, his eyes still crossed. "Maybe one day, far into the future, a genius will invent an instrument which allows people to communicate with each other without having to show up in person. Heck, we might be able to carry this newfangled miracle in our pockets."

The Chief wasn't in. Back in five minutes. Too long. His lieutenant stepped in to 'protect and serve' while I left Don two notes. First, my strategy. A diagram of the jumper course--which fence I would take and in what order. Next, the 'order of go', the order riders would enter the show ring. The Chief would be furious that I was calling the shots and angrier still that, as he would see it, my stubborn quest for immediate answers and my passionate confrontations put me at risk. Still, he knew the difference between my hot-head meltdowns and a well substantiated showdown. He knew I had a reason behind the rush.

On our way through the building to the parking lot, I went over the plan with the lieutenant. Once again fate had intervened. If I'd told the Chief my plan in person, I'd still be in his office, arguing. And the strides into my first obstacle would be off.

When riding a pleasant hunter course, slight errors, a little too fast here, too slanted there, can all be fixed by tidying up on approach to the next set of fences. The thing about riding a jumper course of enormous fences at top speed is that any mistake is a big mistake. Once the rhythm is off between you and your horse, a winning round can quickly convert to a demolition derby.

The people of the Flower Mound Country Club had shown up to honor Camilla Maria Cervantes at last. In the rows behind Eileen and Ana Teresa were dozens of Eileen's friends, including Diana Sloan, and the daughters of Eileen's friends who had known Camilla all their lives and pretty much from afar. The turnout for the memorial was so impressive, I wondered if Camilla's ignored wedding invitations had reached the right people. I was pleased for Eileen. Camilla would be happy for her, too.

Beyond family and longtime friends, the horse people had arranged a special way to honor Camilla. A perfect fit in the Winner's Circle.

The fanciest of hunter classes is called an 'Appointments' Class, offered in only the grander shows. In an Appointments Class, the course over fences is judged by smoothness and style, as well as the overall presentation of horse and rider. Manes and tails are braided. Leathers are shiny clean and stainless steel bits gleam. The rider wears a red or black topcoat with tails, usually with a tuxedo stripe, a white tuxedo shirt with a canary wool vest with brass buttons, black patent leather trimmed high top boots, an old-fashioned puffy stock tie with a gold tie pin, and a satin Abraham Lincoln top hat. Even a leather sandwich pouch with an actual sandwich, appropriate for British royalty, is required. Judges often taste and comment on the integrity of the sandwich before awarding ribbons and trophies.

The riders who filled the rows behind the reserved section were decked out in their finest appointments riding habits. The effect was magical. Stardust over Camilla, long overdue.

No Alejandro Lopez-Cardenas. No Scott Maris. At least not under the spotlights of the Winner's Circle.

Eileen addressed the group first, her words steady, her face gentle, her strength amazing through unashamed tears. She lingered over her final words. I understood that. As horrible as the embryonic mourning is, when it's past, you crave the early pain when you could still feel her around you. Pain beats forgetting all to hell.

Camilla's mother shared stories of the happy girl before Mr. Cervantes was murdered. Ever so lightly, she spoke of the hospitals, the emotional highs and lows that left her and her daughter permanently scarred. She shared the daughter who was the world to her, how she could not imagine going on if not for her granddaughter. Eileen could not replace Camilla in Ana Teresa's life. But neither she nor Ana Teresa would forget for a moment what a wonderful mother and daughter they had lost.

"Joseph and I loved Camilla so much, maybe too much," Eileen said, then closed with the adage that parents aren't supposed to bury their children.

Next and last was my turn, my chance to share the story of the little girl who taught her young friends that when someone you love dies, your responsibility to that person is not over. The little girl who taught me that without the kind words and prayers of those who love you, the doors of Heaven may not open. I bit my lower lip, the taste metallic, but sweet.

So here goes, Camilla.

I opened with step one of my strategy--the announcement that I intended to write a book on Camilla's life to honor my friend and help others see the world through the eyes of a child with a serious emotional disorder. I invited anyone who had a Camilla story to meet me in the riders' lounge in the main barn after the memorial.

Then I spoke of my friend's generous heart and her sense of what was important in life.

I paused to skim the shadows beyond the Winner's Circle. A disconnected chain of gold and rubies flittered low to the ground where the Little Snake slivered along the eaves of the main barn. Blood in my veins, searing before I began to speak went to cold blue ice. *"He slithers,"* Scott said.

The Chief's army was foxholed all around us by now. El Viborito was a monster wanted in two countries and, unfortunately for the Little Snake, Don Wilder was the last of the Boy Scouts. He couldn't be paid off and he would take the slimy creature down. But for me to win, the Chief had to let me ride in first. Once I was in the ring, I had to make use of every inch allowed, every twist in direction. Each stride had to be a heartbeat perfectly throbbed.

Cut the distraction, LeFave. Concentrate. One unfocused moment on a jumper course and you're done.

"My friend's favorite artist was Frida Kahlo, a painter from Mexico City," I said, and retrained my eyes on the faces under the lights. "She chose Frida partly because Frida, like her, was the child of an Anglo and a Mexican Indian. Her favorite is titled *My Birth*. I didn't bring the print because Frida's raw images can disturb those not familiar with her story, and some who are. *My Birth* shows a dead woman giving birth to a dead infant with the head of an adult. The painting was her favorite because Frida had painted the story of her birth."

I paused. I squinted and the floodlights blurred the crowd but I could better pick out movement or non-movement in the shadows across from the Winner's Circle. He was there. In the same place and dead still. Unafraid. And why should he be afraid? When had words ever mattered to a man who got everything he wanted?

"Because Camilla and Frida Kahlo both suffered a great deal and died young, I'd like to close with a statement from a 1954 newspaper article, a statement that may sound like an odd choice for a memorial. At least one person, Camilla, will appreciate the sentiment."

I read: "'On July 13th, seriously ill with pneumonia, Frida died in the Blue House. Cause of death is officially reported as pulmonary embolism, but never confirmed. The final entry in her diary was, *I hope the exit is joyful--and I hope never to return – Frida*. Suicide is suspected.'"

Of course, Kelly would appreciate the sentiment too.

What did Camilla have that Kelly didn't have?

Absolutely nothing.

CHAPTER 49

When a person leaves you through hard, cold choice, you cannot get her back.

You cannot get back the person you were before she made that decision.

You will have to live with what has happened for the rest of your life though every cell in your body screams that you cannot. You have lost that argument. I do not care how good you are at debate.

You cannot go back and reverse the choices you made, either. You cannot reverse time to the day, to the moment, when you made a decision that changed lives in ways you never imagined. Nor can you go up against Lady Fate and win. But that's okay, because Lady Fate messes with all of us. We all have to accept Fate's meddling and move on.

I made my way to the riders' lounge, clicked on the Tiffany shaded floor lamp, and took my place in the oversized leather chair next to the light. What did I think? A therapy session was about to take place? Hardly. I was about to tear into the biggest obstacle I'd ever faced with as much speed and courage as I could spur.

At last I could accomplish the task my new friend had set for me, a task even more important now that Ana Teresa had lost both her parents. Later, in La Merced, I would locate the aunts and uncles and cousins, the Mexico City people who loved her. Maybe she had a big family that had to set up card tables in the dining room for family holidays. I'd find Joaquin's family, too. Ana Teresa will have lots of people to watch out for her.

I didn't hate Camilla's killer. I loved her with all my heart.

For the other victims, the killer had to pay. I didn't hate their killer, either. I couldn't. How far would I have gone if I thought there was a way to have a second chance? One afternoon, months after the suicide, David found me curled up sobbing in the garage. After trying every method he knew to comfort me, he said, "You can get past this, Jessie. It's not as if you were attacked, beaten, and raped." I just stared. How could he make such an absurd statement? A person can recover from a beating. Didn't he know I would have gladly volunteered, if that would have brought Kelly back?

When Camilla wrote in her letter "I am confiding in you because you've been with me since the beginning . . . when you came to France . . ." she spoke about when she was born as Camilla Cervantes. She'd tried to tell me again with *My Birth*, an infant with the head of an adult.

I hadn't seen Eileen step out of the darkness. No more posturing as if Eileen and I would have a nice chat, after which she'd let George drive her downtown to be booked. Eileen braced herself against the doorframe and steadied the delicate silver pistol in her hands. Turns out the Virgin of Sorrows had wept at Eileen's birth, too.

"No one is taking my little girl again."

"She wanted her freedom, didn't she? She wanted to raise her family with Joaquin and her family in Mexico City."

"I shouldn't have let her marry him. He came to my house when he heard. He came to steal my granddaughter. What did he have to offer her? Ana Teresa is mine. Her mother belonged to me. Ana Teresa has always been mine."

Eileen had done a bang-up job messing with Lady Fate while the Virgin of Sorrows looked on. "Camilla" was the newborn in *My Birth* entering the world as an adult.

Eileen had bought herself a second chance--a half-Anglo child from the streets of LaMerced. With so many to choose from, it wasn't hard for El Viborito to find a girl who closely matched Camilla. The chosen child's willingness, even joy, wasn't hard to imagine. Diego's shrug had told the story: When a little girl has the opportunity to scrub hotel rooms in the U.S. over a life of slavery, sexual degradation, and pain of all kinds, over and over every day of her young life, who cares how that happened?

No one was supposed to die.

Eileen, the fairy god mother, transformed a child prostitute into the talented and beautiful woman Camilla would have become. No rush. She had years to perfect her work, clothes, handwriting, languages, riding lessons from the best. Years to educate her on the exclusive way wealthy people relate to the world and people. Eileen schooled her on Camilla's relationships, particularly with me. Camilla was shuttered away at ten and Eileen's Flower Mound friends had understood Eileen's hesitance to share details of her daughter's life. After all, Camilla was a loner and crazy. Maybe a killer. During the years in Europe, she had only one visitor from Austin.

Not sure plastic surgery, new teeth, and reconstructions would be enough for the new Camilla to pass for the original, Eileen invited me to Paris to drink in the story of the assault. I'd buy into the new Camilla and pass along what I believed had happened to the other riders. If anyone later noticed a small touch out of place, they'd blame the devastating assault. Her occasional off-beat accent was assumed to be the result of the crushed larynx.

The girl Eileen purchased brought her Frida Kahlo doll, the one her father gave her, with her to Paris.

As for the little girl who led the Dorados? The child who wanted to be with her father in Heaven, the little girl who believed and prayed that this life on earth was only a dream? I had no idea if she'd ever even heard of Frida Kahlo.

I'd even fallen victim to the assumptions I regularly warned patients against. I'd seen bipolar features in the new Camilla because the little girl Camilla had symptoms. I'd assumed a troubled little girl grows into a troubled young woman. I'd paid more attention to features that fit the diagnosis I'd already settled on rather than notice features that did not fit.

As for her letter? 'Camilla' was making the biggest move of her life, a move that could cost her life. She worried about Ana Teresa. *I know that should anything happen to me, you and Concepción will watch out for Ana Teresa.* Concepción and me, she'd said. Not one word about Eileen.

"Eileen," I said, "if anyone understands what you did, it's me."

I wanted to keep Eileen free and talking as long as I could. I was fortunate because she wanted to talk to me. Not in the icky artificial way the killer in a bad movie conveniently stands around and ties up every loose end before he's shot or arrested. Eileen wanted to talk to me because she loved me. She didn't want to kill me, she really didn't. But she would.

"I didn't mean for anyone to die."

"I know that."

"A mother needs a child to be who she is."

"I know."

"How did you find out?"

"I couldn't stop asking myself, 'How had she done it? How had Camilla, not only moved past her bipolar symptoms, but grown into a wonderful, stable adult? How, was that possible when Kelly, with such similar symptoms, killed herself? What had made the difference for Camilla? What if I could have provided that for Kelly? How had I failed Kelly?'"

We were quiet together for a long minute.

"Camilla left me in Paris, Jessica."

"I know. I found a photograph of a toddler who was supposed to be Camilla in her father's arms. It didn't make sense that your husband, a wealthy man, would be in a public market in ill-fitting clothes and worn down shoes. The father holding his princess was a workingman in La Merced, not a shopper. I was too young to remember your husband, but his picture is still on the wall at the station."

Eileen leaned her back into the frame, her shoulders slumped, and tears pooled at the edges of her eyes. "She gave up the struggle, Jessica. Camilla wanted to be with her father. I couldn't go on without my little girl. I couldn't come back from Paris as the pitiful woman whose crazy, hopeless, only daughter committed suicide. I couldn't."

"Eileen, believe me, I do not judge you. I don't know what I would have done if I'd thought there was a way to buy a second chance."

Her attention after Kelly's suicide, a least some of her attention, was to observe. She needed to know if I'd matched up anything in Camilla's childhood with Kelly. To make sure I hadn't noticed anything about the little girl Camilla that would predict suicide. Scott Maris ended up as part of the cover, too. He'd found out the truth and blackmailed Eileen to keep her secret. "I used the relationship at first," he'd said.

"Felicia Martinez González wanted Camilla's life, you know. She wanted to be Camilla."

"I believe you. I've seen the girls in La Merced. So many pretty young girls with nothing."

"I gave her everything, anything she wanted, even Las Palomas. Even you. All she had to do was be my daughter. Was that so hard?" Anguish filled her eyes, her voice—her entire body.

"We were friends," I said.

"Just to be my daughter, nothing else. Was that so bad?"

"No, it wasn't and I know that after all this time, you loved Felicia, too. After the Little Snake and his friends were finished, you scattered rose petals."

"I never wanted to hurt anyone."

"I know that, too. You had El Viborito take care that Felicia did not suffer."

"I couldn't believe it. Felicia wanted out. She was going to take Ana Teresa with her."

"She was pregnant."

"She didn't want to be my daughter anymore, Jessica. She'd been in the hospital twice. I told her the new baby would be just as welcome and cared for as Ana Teresa. But she wouldn't listen. She was leaving Las Palomas to live in that slum."

Eileen's green eyes glistened with tears. Those eyes. El Viborito outdid himself finding a girl in La Merced with those eyes.

"Eileen, I'll stand by you through this, I will."

"Why couldn't you leave things as they were, Jessica? I tried to warn you."

We'd been right about the flat tire. The killer hadn't wanted me dead. At least not back when the tire was slashed.

"Why," she said, "why did you insist on going to Mexico?"

Eileen crumpled in the door frame, exhaustion and pain beyond any level I'd ever seen. Her eyes shifted from pain to regret, then to determination. Only her hand was steady. She lifted the gun for a clear shot to my face.

"I killed my daughter," she said.

"No. You didn't."

"Yes, I did. I killed her when I let them take her. I let her go too far away. She used a hoof trimmer. She sat against the back of her horse's stall, like . . ."

"I know. I see that now."

"She was still alive when they called, but I had let my baby go too far away. I failed her."

"You didn't kill Camilla and I didn't kill Kelly."

"Why did Camilla leave me, Jessica? Why?"

"I don't know. I've searched and studied and struggled in every way I know how to find an answer to that question and I've failed. There are plenty of experts and books out there to answer the question and there's no help there either."

"I know. I searched, too."

"What I do know is that, as much as we love someone, we cannot know another's pain. If a girl wants to end her life, no matter how much you love her, there's nothing you can do to stop her. Your love is not enough. I'm not saying there aren't times when people are pulled back from the brink of death and go on to live happy lives. What I am saying that those people were not as intent as Camilla and Kelly were to escape the pain this world was for them. Both of them tried and tried to get better, to see something beyond sadness, beyond hopelessness. But they couldn't."

"Why?"

"I don't know. I can't know and neither can you. It's just what happened."

I reached out my palm for her gun. She pulled back and held it steady. Aimed at my face.

"Ana Teresa is staying with me," she said, her eyes hot and strong. "She belongs with me. Ana Teresa never belonged to Felicia."

Quiet figures in dark clothes closed in behind Eileen.

The gun trembled in her hands. Her eyes stared at a spot somewhere over my head, somewhere in another time, when the Dorados were little girls full of hope. Eileen didn't have any hate for me to help her pull the trigger.

"Frida's last words, Jessica. When you quoted Frida, I knew it was over unless I stopped you."

"I loved Camilla, too."

Eileen sensed the officers closing in. She dropped the gun and waited as the circle closed around her.

I crossed the tile between us and pulled her into me with all my might. The Chief let us have our moment. We stayed together our arms locked, weeping and swaying as one grieving woman.

"I couldn't lose another little girl, Jessica."

"I know. I know."

The lieutenant stepped up with handcuffs. I waved them back. He checked with Don and returned the manacles to his belt.

Voices of the officers arresting El Viborito wafted into the barn. I may have called the shots, but the police walked away with the Championship Cup. An arrest that would lead to dozens more convicted and many young girls with a chance for a better life.

Eileen, her head bowed, walked ahead of the police out into the night. She wept softly, the saddest sound I have ever heard. "All I ever wanted was another chance. I never wanted to hurt anyone. One more chance. That's all. She was my baby. My baby."

I caught up with her and held her hand until she was settled in the backseat of the police car. As I turned Zack Harvey popped up in front of me with a camera and a reflector screen.

"Thanks for the photos, Zack. They helped."

"You're welcome."

Zack smiled and walked away. He did not take a picture.

Tonight was a marker night for both of for Eileen and me. *My Birth*, Frida's odd parable about a new beginning, was Eileen's now, though an odder new beginning I couldn't imagine. The lesson of *My Birth* belonged to me as well. The time had come for me to accept that I'd done my best, and my best wasn't that bad. I wouldn't let Kelly's memory fade, but her suicide would no longer be the veil that keeps me from the world.

There was a bonus. I would never judge anyone else's crazy behavior because I knew we all go crazy when the hurt is too much.

After a few minutes with the Chief of Detectives, I joined George, Concepción, the babes, and Ana Teresa in the Town Car. We drove to the Mt. Laurel house where later that night Concepción put her arms around Ana Teresa and explained that her 'grandmother' would not be available for a while. Ana Teresa would stay with us. She could decorate the unused room across from Concepción's however she wanted. Concepción was calm for the first time since her brother's arrest. The Chief had promised that, since Celestino only came to the attention of authorities in his effort to help the police, he would not be deported.

There was time enough to tell Ana Teresa the sad story of a mother's love gone wrong. There was time enough to find out if she had other grandmothers in La Merced. Time enough to sort out the legal details.

Maybe the kind working man holding her mother with her Frida Kahlo doll, maybe he was still alive. Who knows? Ana Teresa had relatives in La Merced. She already knew them, Felicia had seen to that. The only news would be her true relationship to the people in her mother and father's families.

Suzi Wong and Sammie Davis, Jr. slept with me. I would never again be the person I thought I was before Kelly's suicide, but that's okay. I was wrong-headed about a lot of things back then. All of us have made decisions we regret yet must live with the rest of our lives. Now I knew why I'd never forgotten the expression in the eyes of the girl with the yellow double hibiscus behind her ear.

What I'd seen in her dark and desperate eyes was the reflection of a terrified nineteen-year-old girl from Texas. A prime target for a crime of the heart.

THE END.

www.ingramcontent.com/pod-product-compliance
Lightning Source LLC
Chambersburg PA
CBHW071246170626
46809CB00001B/84